CALL YOUR
DAUGHTER HOME

This Large Print Book carries the
Seal of Approval of N.A.V.H.

CALL YOUR DAUGHTER HOME

DEB SPERA

THORNDIKE PRESS
A part of Gale, a Cengage Company

Farmington Hills, Mich • San Francisco • New York • Waterville, Maine
Meriden, Conn • Mason, Ohio • Chicago

LIBRARY OF CONGRESS CIP DATA ON FILE.
CATALOGUING IN PUBLICATION FOR THIS BOOK
IS AVAILABLE FROM THE LIBRARY OF CONGRESS

ISBN-13: 978-1-4328-6704-1 (hardcover alk. paper)

Published in 2019 by arrangement with Harlequin Books S.A.

Printed in Mexico
1 2 3 4 5 6 7 23 22 21 20 19

For Mamaw

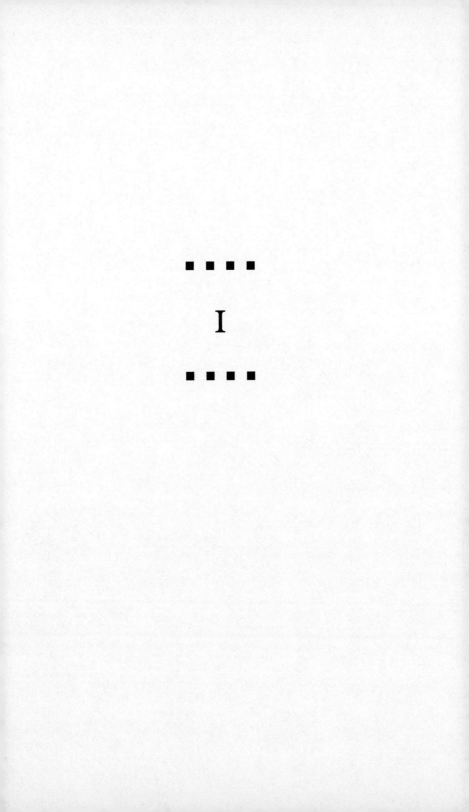

I

1

MRS. GERTRUDE PARDEE

It's easier to kill a man than a gator, but it takes the same kind of wait. You got to watch for the weakness, and take your shot to the back of the head. This gator I'm watching is watching me, too. She smells the last of my menstrual blood so she's half in, half out of the water, laid up on the ridge of dry land that is our footpath through the swamp and out to the main road. I'm propped against an old cypress. We're a pair. I'm sick with pain. The hours of wait have made me stiff, but it don't matter. None of that matters. All that counts is this ridge laid out like a rope between us. This big ole thing's got her back to the nest my girl Alma spotted earlier today. She's a ten-foot mama, big enough to feed us through fall. Got two shells in this gun, but only one chance for a kill.

When we come to Reevesville, I was hoping to get Alvin straight, but it looks like he's going to run me crazy. Ever since the boll weevils took our crop he ain't done nothing but drink for nigh on a year. We left everything we had in Branchville, including two of our four daughters, and come over here to his daddy's sawmill for work. I hoped steady work and some food in our bellies might set him right, but he ain't right. Maybe he never will be. First, he closed the mill at one o'clock yesterday and didn't come home 'til late last light. Then he found the letter from my brother, Berns, telling me of a job over in Branchville. He hates Berns for taking care of what he can't. He whaled on me, and warned me to stay put. He's still mad from the last time I went to see my brother for help. Now my eye is swoll shut, I can't see out of it and the only letter I've had for a month giving me the news about my two oldest children is burned and gone.

Alvin laid in the bed all morning until his daddy come over here and raised hell. Now he's gone off to work, sick with drink, and we're left with nothing but the sound of our own bellies. I've about worked myself to death here, and it ain't done any good. I'm the woman of a house that don't exist.

10

Alvin's daddy blames me. He don't say it, but I can tell. He won't so much as look at me when Alvin's drinking, which is all the time. My body is the battleground for my husband's affliction. I heard Alvin's daddy say to him on more than one occasion that he ought to have a boy so he has somebody to help him. Looking at Alvin, I can't make sense of what his daddy tells him. Now Alvin's saying out loud if we had a boy we could have saved what little we had in Branchville. Says it's my fault he's got cause to prowl.

We got four girls; two are reaching their courting years. That could be a good thing, but I don't know who will have them — they got no dowry. I worry for the trouble that's sure to come sniffing. My first baby, Edna, she's fifteen, won't think nothing of talking to anybody who'll look her in the eye. She'll come to the devil's own end. My second child, Lily, is thirteen and thinks she's got grit, but she don't. She'll follow you the whole way home hitting you as you go, then beg to be let in the back door for fear of the night. My two youngest, Alma and Mary, are ten and six.

By the time I was Lily's age, my mama was addled, talking out of her head regular by then, but every once in a while a fit

11

would pass, and she would remember to mother me.

"Gertie," she told me once, "when you are married and with child, I hope all the happiness in the world for you, but I hope you know and understand the duties of a wife, because a woman can make or ruin a man. It takes both working together, but the woman is the main one when it comes to making a happy home."

Alvin rode up on a horse to take me away before I ever laid eyes on him. My daddy arranged for him to marry me. Alvin's a big man, rough from the start, but he was churchgoing, and Daddy said he worked hard. The day I left home, just two weeks before my fourteenth birthday, Mama was sitting at the table wringing her hands muttering about a hurricane. There weren't nothing but rain clouds that day, but she wouldn't let it go. A girl wants her mother when she leaves home, but mine couldn't see me no more. I took a satchel of what I could carry, one nightgown and another dress, two aprons and some undergarments. Once that was full, I took a quilt that me and Mama done together — it was mostly mine because of the cottonseeds in the squares, Mama's blankets had nary a seed in them — and laid a cast-iron skillet and some pots and linens I'd been saving for my wedding day down in the middle. I tied the blanket up around my neck and laid the satchel over my shoulder. I took my old rag doll off the peg on the wall of the room me and Berns slept in and laid it in Mama's arms.

"Take care of the baby," I told her. It was the only thing that could get her to stop going on about the storm. She kissed and rocked that doll. I wished the whole time it was me instead.

The cicadas are screaming this morning like a warning, but I don't need them to tell me how hot it is. August don't ever let up. It ain't even seven yet, and I got sweat coming through my dress. This thing's so old and stretched out, it don't stick to nothing but wet. I got the last of the clean rags pushed up in what's left of my underdrawers for my menstrual cycle. I got to get Alma and Mary to Branchville if they mean to survive. Mary, the littlest, is sick. Her skin's so pale I can see the veins running underneath like tiny creeks. The child's had no food for two days and now I fear what the day will bring. I give them a bit of snuff to ward off the hunger, and wipe them down best I can from the pump outside. They are both bone thin, I know. We're all weak from hunger, and I don't see how the tide will change before I lose one, or both, of them.

I aim to see my brother about the contents of his letter, and maybe he and his wife can take Mary and Alma for a bit while I sort things out. I've got to try. Mary can sew some, and clean. She don't take much from a plate, and Alma can shoot a gun and gut a hog. She knows her times tables, too. I taught her, though arithmetic ain't handy these days when there ain't nothing to count. Zero is zero, no way around that — still, that's a real good thing for a little child of ten to know.

I fetch the shotgun for our travel but leave the vomit and waste Alvin made in the night. Flying creatures slip through the torn screen door covering the mess. Outside is no better. Polk Swamp has no mercy. I've pulled leeches as big as baby garter snakes off my girls, and their feet got ulcers on them from the constant wet. The swamp is a beastly place. It's ripe with things nobody wants to know.

This shotgun was my mama's, a Fox Sterlingworth, side by side, double barrel. Her daddy gave it to her, and when my daddy died, Berns walked it to me when Alvin wouldn't let me out of the house for the funeral. Berns saw to it the funeral wagon was pulled down the dirt road in front of the house where we used to live so I could pay my respects from inside the screen door. After the burying, he come back, and Alvin let him in when he saw he had that gun. Berns laid it on the table and told me it come from Mama's side of the family, so it was only right it go to the daughter. Alvin took possession of it and wanted to sell it, but I told him it was good for hunting. This gun has put food in our bellies. I intend to carry it on our walk today. Times is desperate hard, any fool will kill you on the road for a nickel. That much is fact.

We set out before the half hour and cut through swamp, where trees give us shelter from the hot. I know the way through to Branchville. Takes longer than going along the train track, but we need protection from the heat of the day. Blackflies feed on us like it's suppertime. Oh, what it would be to feed like that! Alma keeps her eyes to the edge, looking for snakes or something to catch.

"Mama, look," she calls out to me from the path ahead. I follow her finger point, and spy the biggest gator nest I ever seen. I look quick for the mama, but she ain't in sight. She's got to be big if I was to judge from the size of her nest.

"Lord, Alma, that's a bigun, ain't it?"

She smiles, proud she's seen it. Mary tugs at her sister and asks, "What is it? I want to see."

Alma pulls Mary close and points 'til the child spies what her sister found, then Mary turns to me in a fright, but I keep walking.

"Gators don't hunt 'til night — we're safe," I tell her, and together we move past the ridge and through the vines.

Alma scampers on ahead to show she knows the way. She's fast. I seen her catch a squirrel by the tail, then snap its neck before it could turn and bite. She's always been spry, but her quickness is fading from need. She's run from the grasp of her daddy's mean-spirited hands more times than I can say. One day I fear he will pick up the shotgun and be done with her. If he does kill us, it will be on my soul. These two children will rest in hell for the sins of their mother, because I've yet to baptize them.

My daddy taught me to hunt. It's mostly about the wait. So I am hunkered down, waiting. This gator's eye ain't left mine. Daddy hunted gator regular and taught me how they nest. Gators lay their eggs on shore and cover them with sticks, leaves and whatnot. After a gator lays her eggs, she stays close by to hunt and eat, waiting for the call of her young. Daddy once told me when the young is ready inside the eggs, they cry out until the mama comes and breaks them free. Then she carries the babies one by one to the water and stays with them for nigh on six months. No other reptile does that. After that time, if the babies don't leave for other water, she'll kill them so's not to compete for food. I seen big nests in my life, but this one looks to have upward of seventy-five, maybe a hundred eggs. I'm not partial to gator. It grows in the mouth before you can get it chewed enough to swallow. We ate it many a night, but gator ain't no easy prey.

Coming into town I see faces older than what the truth is. Some carry cardboard suitcases on their way by foot to the train station. Likely they think things are better up north — maybe that's right. If I had me money and no mouths to feed, I'd try. You always got to try. I hope to see nobody I know, so we stay to the edge of town and cut around the woods to my brother's place. This curse on my face is best left unseen. Branchville likes to talk, and my older girls who live here with my brother don't need any more dirt slung upon them by the sharp tongues of those who think they've been deemed by God to lay judgment.

Mary is wilting from fever, but we press on. I carry her while Alma holds the gun and sing to them the song my mama used to sing to me: *"Go tell Aunt Rhody, go tell Aunt Rhody, go tell Aunt Rhody the old gray goose is dead."*

Mary's a little bit. Don't weigh more than a four-year-old. She lays her head on my shoulder and sleeps while I sing, *"The one she's been saving, the one she's been saving, the one she's been saving to make a feather bed."*

Alma holds on to my dress while we walk along through tall weeds.

"The goslings are mourning, the goslings are mourning, the goslings are mourning because their mother's dead."

The pain in my eye bounces to the beat of my heart and shoots through my head and shoulders like some kind of wild fire. I fear he broke a bone — I can't see out of this eye. I can read Alvin pretty good after all these years, but he had his back to me so I didn't see his fist when he swung around and knocked me backward. He stood over me swaying before he took a match to my letter, vomited all over the floor, then fell to the bed.

He wasn't always so mean. Alvin never was no stranger to hardship, none of us is, but once the boll weevils come in 1921, it broke him. They took everything in sight. All around us the world disappeared in the haze of black on everything. I went to bed every night and woke up every morning to the sound of boll weevils chewing through all we had. They come like a wave in the ocean, laid their eggs and come back to kill off the next planting season. Got to be so bad, they took root in the flour and we had to eat them in our biscuits for fear of having nothing.

In the early days Alvin made enough money to see to it we was fed, but that changed when he started to drink regular. At first it was only a bottle here or there, but quicker than I knew, if I didn't steal from his pocket, every last cent was spent on drink. Alcohol made my husband feel bigger, but he couldn't see that all it did was make him jagged. For a time I exchanged goods with my neighbors: a jar of tomatoes, a dish towel or apron I sewed from old rags, what I could put together that might have some value to somebody. But then some old boy at church said, "Poor Alvin, he is given a hard row to hoe with a woman who don't know her place. He is an unlucky dog."

That's when he started in on me. Got so bad nobody would trade with me no more, like I was some kind of leper. We stayed away from church, and I learned to keep my eyes to the ground. Finally I did what had to be done. I walked all the way to Alvin's daddy's place in St. George and told him his boy was sick with drink, that he had four children that were hungry. I told him how it was. Now Alvin's daddy won't look me in the eye because he had to be made to see by a woman. No man likes that.

When I come through the woods I see my brother and my girls picking what cotton is left to harvest for the season. There's dots of white fluff surrounded by black thorns across a wide field scorched by sun. They got burlap sacks slung 'round their shoulders, and I see the hunch in their backs and the blood on their hands well before they raise their eyes to see me.

Berns stoops over his work. Berns Caison the Third was what we always called him. He wasn't ever no third of nothin', but we called him that 'cause he liked school and was good with words. My oldest girl, Edna, stretches her arms in the air just like she does when she wakes up in the morning.

That's when she sees me. She brightens and I see the girl in her. "Mama!" she yells and runs to me from across the field. My Lily watches from where she stands, hands on both her hips like she's looking for a fight. Berns lays his hand across his brow and squints just like Daddy used to. For a minute I think I've seen a ghost. He's a stringy man but he's got grit, even if he ain't much bigger than a woman. He gives me a hard look, sees I'm alone with my young'uns and his shoulders stiffen. He knows why I come.

There's only one good way to kill a gator with a shotgun. If it's to be quick it's got to be to the back of the head, a round spot upward where the broad of the back and head meet. You got to get up behind without it knowing. That ain't no easy task. Daddy says he once saw a gator eat a deer he was tracking along the banks of the Edisto River. Said the gator jumped out of the water, grabbed that deer by the throat, and took it into a death roll. Now I know that's a lie — Daddy always did like tall tales. He taught me well enough to know that no gator'd waste energy on food as skittish as deer. No, it'll go for a pig, or a coon, maybe even a bobcat, but deer are too nervous, too prancy. If a gator gets you it's 'cause you're lazy or stupid. I'm neither.

Berns gives the girls some bread and butter, and sends them out to sit under the willow tree in the yard so's we can talk, then pours me a cup of coffee left from the morning. He sets the percolator back on the stove and joins me at the kitchen table, then slides the sugar bowl toward me, but I shake my head. I can't stomach the sweet.

"Did you get my letter?" he asks.

"Alvin burned it 'fore I finished, but I saw about the job at the Sewing Circle."

"Mrs. Walker died, so the job is open and her house is for let. Ten dollars a month."

"I ain't got ten dollars, Berns."

"You would if you had that job."

"I got Alvin to worry about."

Berns looks at his hands, the knuckles practically worn to the bone.

"I don't see Alvin worrying none about you and yours."

I can't speak to that, so I don't. I drink my coffee and look out the window to my girls in the yard. Mary, poor sick baby, lies with her head in Alma's lap. Edna's going on about something — that girl talks so much she could make paint dry quicker.

Lily sits off to the side. She's got her daddy in her.

"Why'd he do it this time?"

Berns is on me now.

"He was drunk."

"Drinking a lot, is he?"

"Like he's going to prison for life. He wants Lily to go live with his daddy. Be his slave for when his new baby comes. Says he can't say no, so I did."

Berns gets up and washes his cup in the sink. He is a good husband. He and his wife, Marie, have a good marriage. She suffered from swamp sickness two years ago, and lived to tell it, but now she's lame and needs a cane to walk. Yet she gets up before the sun, and walks five miles every day to the Sewing Circle outside town where they sew burlap bags for seed. They've got no babies but Berns don't care. Having a baby would likely kill her. He's a different kind of man and gets no sympathy for it.

"Marie says Mrs. Coles might hold the job for you if 'n you ask."

I stare at my brother. "I can't go over to the Coles family house looking like this."

He comes to sit across from me and sets his elbows on the table before saying, "Gert, we barely got enough to eat as it is, and we can't raise these girls. I don't know nothing about girls, and Marie don't have the energy for them. Lily's hanging with that Barker boy. He's no good, but if I tell her so, she says I ain't her daddy and she don't need to listen to me."

"I'll talk to her."

"That ain't it, Gertrude. She's right, I ain't her daddy, and Marie ain't her mama. These girls need you."

I sink my head to my arms just for a minute's peace. Berns exhales loud before he scrapes back his chair and stands.

"I'll take Alma. That's all I can do. I can't take care of a sick child, Gert. I can barely see after the healthy ones. You got to sort this out with Alvin."

Before he leaves to finish the day's work he tells me to get Mary to a doctor and then closes the door. The room is quiet. Mama used to hold my head in her lap on the sofa and stroke my hair until I'd close my eyes to sleep. I was always afraid of what the night might bring. If I shut my eyes and stay still, I hear her voice inside my head singing in her wobbly way the same song I sing to my girls, *"The old gander's weeping, the old gander's weeping, the old gander's weeping because his wife is dead."*

When I lift my aching head there sits two

dollars Berns has left on the table before me.

Under the willow tree by the road I tell my girls the news. Mary cries for her sisters until I separate them and tell Alma and Edna to go on back to the field. They each give me a kiss and do what they're told. Lily goes to follow, but I yank her backward by the hair and tell her if she sasses anybody in this house she won't have a hide left to sit on. I slap her to make her look at me and say, "Lily Louise, if I hear word about that Harlan Barker, I'll let your daddy deal with it. You know what that'll mean?"

"Yes, ma'am."

She's stone-faced.

"You know what your daddy will do to that boy and likely you, too?"

"Yes, ma'am."

"Say it."

I want to know she understands me.

"Mama, please, I won't see him no more."

"He comes 'round, what will you tell him?"

"My daddy will kill him."

"He comes around, you tell him your daddy will cut his throat. You tell him that." She's crying now and I'm glad.

"Mind your aunt and uncle. Go on now."

I shove her to the field where Alma has

25

nearly cleared a row of cotton, perked by the bread and butter she's eaten.

I carry Mary in one arm and the gun under the crook of the other. We are a sight for anyone on Main Street who cares to look, but my head is down so as not to invite stares. The Coles family owns the Sewing Circle and most of the land in Branchville. Maybe they own the whole town. Can't say for sure. My daddy worked for them and his daddy before him. We worked leased land from the Coles, but that was before the boll weevils cleaned us out. After, the Coles took to making the tenants raise chickens. Daddy worked that land all his days, and early on when times was good, the Coles family give us a store-bought fruitcake soaked in rum every Christmas, all wrapped up in red cellophane. That was a time of plenty.

Once, when President Taft come to town to speak at the railroad depot, everybody got off work for the day. We got to go and hear him, whites and coloreds alike. Folks come from miles around. I was eight years old, and Mama and Daddy walked Berns and me by the hand to town. When the train come it looked like a live animal, squirting water and belching columns of black smoke. One colored girl, in from somewhere far off, had never seen a train. She cried out, "It's the devil, I see the fire and brimstone! May God save us all!" and then she passed out, sure hell was upon us. I asked Daddy if that was true, but he laughed and said, "No, that's just nigger talk," and put me on his shoulders so I could hear the president.

The only thing I know about hell is what's writ in the good book. Mama thought if you talked about hell it could be visited upon you, so she kept a spirit tree in the front yard to keep the demons from the house. For many years the only trouble I knew was what a young girl's mind could conjure, ghosts and monsters, nothing like real life.

The Coles family house is pure white and grand as the entrance to heaven. Old oak trees grow up on both sides of the walkway all the way to the front porch, where rocking chairs sit waiting for a body to rest in the cool of the day. Walking through those trees and up those grand steps makes you feel like you're on the path to glory. The columns hold up two stories of house fit for a king, and the wide door is a blue I've only ever seen on a robin's egg. I put Mary behind an oak tree and tell her to stay while I tend to business. The brass knocker on the door is so heavy I fear to lift it, but the sun is high in the sky, and I don't have time to waste. I've got to get home before Alvin does. I knock twice, then step away so as to be polite.

Old Black Retta comes to the door in her maid outfit, crisp and white. She's as old as I know and been working for the Coleses since she was a girl. Her own mother was owned by the family, so she's got no cause to put on airs, but she takes one look at me and hisses, "You need something, go 'round back. This door's for proper folk."

I look her in the face and say real strong, "I'm here to see the Missus."

"You got business, go to the back."

She's about to close the door in my face when I hear Mrs. Coles ask from the grand hallway, "Retta, who is it?"

I holler out so she can hear, "It's me, Gertrude Caison, Missus. I'm here to see about some business."

"Step off this porch, you're not fit to stand on it," Retta whispers. She only uses her sugar voice around the Mister and Missus.

I do as she says and scramble back from the porch and onto the stone path. I lay my gun to the ground and smooth the hair from my face. Retta holds the door open so Mrs. Coles can come out on the porch to get a look at me. She's a fine old lady. Her hair is done up, and she wears a green dress with white pearl buttons at the neck. I know some about her. I know she's got electricity in this house. She's registered to vote and raised five kids, but one hung himself in the barn when he was still a boy. I know her daddy was from New York and that she owns the Sewing Circle. There's no grand-kids, and I hear tell the Mister and Missus have supper on china every day with cloth napkins in their laps even though it's just the two of them.

Mrs. Coles steps out, looks down at me and asks, "Gertrude Caison?"

"Yes'm. It's Pardee now, but it was Caison 'fore I got married."

"You're Lillian Caison's daughter?"

"Yes, ma'am."

"She was a good woman."

"Yes, ma'am, she was."

"What happened to your face, Gertrude?"

"I fell, Missus."

She gives me a hard look then says, "State your business."

"I come to see about a job at the Sewing Circle and the let on Mrs. Walker's house."

"Can you sew?"

"Oh, yes, Missus. I'm good with sewing. My mama taught me."

"Your mother could sew anything."

She clasps her hands under her bosom

29

when she talks, just like Mama used to do. Retta steps out on the porch and stands behind the Missus.

"Yes, ma'am. I have two dollars as deposit for the house, and if you can give me that job at the Sewing Circle, I will see to it I'm here by the middle of next week."

"Why, what if we needed you to start tomorrow, Gertrude?"

"Ma'am, I can't start tomorrow. I've got to sort things out with my husband and get my four girls moved. But I can start work come Wednesday."

I walk up a step and hold the two dollars up to her. She looks at that money and asks me again, "What happened to your face, Gertrude?"

"I got hit, Missus."

"That your girl?" she asks me.

I turn to see Mary scoot back behind the tree.

"One of them," I tell her. "That one there is Mary."

"Come out here, Mary, and let me see you."

But Mary does as I told her and stays put behind the tree.

"I'm sorry, Missus. She's shy with folks."

Mrs. Coles drops her hands to her sides and looks up into the oak trees.

"Redbirds in the yard all day today," she says. "Retta doesn't like that, do you, Retta?"

Retta shakes her head. "No, ma'am, I don't."

"Don't expect nobody likes to see that," I say.

Everybody knows redbirds in the yard mean a death will be visited on you.

"I don't know," the Missus says, and I know she's meant that for me.

"I'll work hard, Missus. You won't ever have cause to complain."

"There's no running water at the Walker place. How will you wash your children?"

"I'll wash them on Saturdays in the kitchen. We'll boil the water on the stove. They'll be kept clean."

The Missus seems satisfied for she finally takes my money and tells me she'll hold the job and Mrs. Walker's place, but the first month's rent will come out of my pay, which is fine with me. The job pays twelve dollars a week. We can make a go of it on that kind of money. When she gets to the door she turns back and says to me, "You come to my front door again looking like that and I will put you on the street, you hear me?"

I say yes, ma'am, and wait 'til she goes before I pick up my gun and pull Mary 'round to the side of the house where no one respectable can see us. I hold the child in my arms and give her a squeeze before we start the walk home, but then a screen door slams and there's a loud "Pshhhh. Pshhhh."

When I turn around there's Retta coming at me with her purse thrown over her arm and a parcel tied up in a dish towel.

"Gertrude Pardee."

She's mad at me for not listening, but I don't care and aim to tell her so when she shoves that parcel at me.

"There's some dried beans and biscuits in there. Some meat, too."

This is a woman who don't give something for nothing, but my need's outgrown my sense. I take what's given.

"Come here, child," she orders Mary.

Mary does for Retta what she wouldn't do for the Missus. She obeys. Holding on to my skirt she steps in front of me.

The old woman looks down at her and says, "Let me see your tongue."

Mary does as she is told and Retta peers down at it. She looks in Mary's ears and turns her around, inspecting her arms and legs and feet. Mary buries her head in my side and trembles.

"This child's riddled with worms and

burning up with fever."

She talks like I'm a fool. I feel the fire in me.

"She needs a doctor," she tells me, like I don't know.

"No money for that."

Retta looks off toward the Coles family's house, and I turn to go before she can go back and talk the Missus out of what she's already decided.

"If your mama could see you, Gertrude, it would break her heart. You meant the whole world to her."

"I know that," I tell her.

"You'd never know to look at you."

I fear for what I'm about to say, but I mean to say it anyway. I know the consequence of what I aim to do — the talk it will stir. The sun is already on the west side of the sky. There is nothing for my child but the certainty of death in that swamp.

"Keep Mary for me. I'll be back in four days," I say.

Retta opens her mouth and lets it hang there.

"No, Mama, no!" Mary cries, and grips me 'round the legs. "I'll be good."

"Shut up, girl. Shut your mouth before I shut it for you." I give her a shake. She stops wailing, but don't let go. "She's a good child, and she don't eat much."

"Why me?" Retta asks, staring at me through squinted eyes, like I'm going to steal what she already gave me.

"Mama used to say if you don't ask for help, nobody will know to give it," is what comes out of my mouth. I don't know for a fact Mama ever said that to me, but there it is all the same.

Retta puts one hand on her hip and looks from Mary to me. She didn't expect that.

"It's the Christian thing to do," I say.

She makes up her mind, and she steps forward, putting out her hand. I pry Mary off me while she whispers, "I'll be good, Mama, I promise. I'll be good."

Once Retta sees Mary ain't letting up, she yanks the child free of me and marches down the road that goes through the center of town where everybody will see her leading a white child home with the Lord as her reason. Not even Retta's husband will speak against that. I set my sight on the sun, though it warbles through the water of my good eye, and head for home.

The sun casts long shadows on the land. Won't be long now. All the night creatures have started their call like it's a contest, so loud I can't make one noise out from the other. It's a wonder any mother can hear her babies crying in this rumpus. Even if her young was ready for the world, this gator won't turn her back to me.

The nest sits sprawled to the south of the footpath. Every kind of plant sits atop it, like a grave covered in haste. The dying day is upon us. Before he rounds the bend, I hear Alvin coming up the trail. I know the stomp of his feet when he's drunk, the sound of his long belch.

My mama's voice calms my nerves. *"The goslings are crying, the goslings are crying, the goslings are crying because their mama's dead."*

I scoot up slow alongside the tree, and the gator moves at me. I lift my gun. Alvin is upon her before one takes notice of the other. Too late, the gator swings her head to Alvin and away from me. He hollers and jumps back. I step out from under the tree to the clearing on the ridge and take aim with my good eye. When I pull the trigger, there's a splash and her tail disappears into green moss. Alvin weaves, like he's stood up too fast from a heavy bar stool, then falls forward into the murky dark of the water.

"She died in the mill pond, she died in the mill pond, she died in the mill pond, standing

on her head."
His body floats in the reeds. Easy prey.

2

MRS. ANNIE COLES

Every time the telephone bells ring, I am amazed. For the first few weeks, hello seemed too insignificant a word to say, though I hated the formality of stating the name of residence, then self. "This is the Coleses' residence, Ann Coles speaking," sounds ridiculous. I'm me announcing me. A simple hello in the quiet of my own home should suffice. My husband pulled more strings than I can imagine, and gave me not just one telephone, but two — one for the house and one for the Sewing Circle. All of Branchville has benefited from my husband's foresight, and now here we are, the first rural town for miles to be connected to the modern world.

"The bells" is what Edwin calls the ring, and now that phrase has stuck. To pick up the telephone and hear in your ear the voice of another person, it could be any person,

37

speaking to you from where they are, in some other house or place of business where a completely different life is going on, is remarkable. Life has all at once grown exponentially larger than I could have ever dreamed. Electricity, the automobile and now the telephone have made it clear that possibility is endless for an enterprising mind. I can only imagine what it must have felt like to navigate a flat earth only to discover its roundness. But the astonishing part, for me, is what comes after any great discovery. The "aha" of wonder fades, and the "why not" takes up its rightful place in the world. By then one thinks, of course. After only one month, it's as if the bells have always been a part of our lives. July is, all at once, ancient. The new has swept in and made itself a presence. Now instead of walking through the house and outside to the automobile, I must stop to pick up a telephone call.

Two long bells designate the call is meant for our residence, so my pivot from the dining room to the parlor is as natural as breath. I've made the mistake and answered only once when the call wasn't meant for us, long enough to hear Mr. Laing, the proprietor at the mercantile, learn of his father's death. That fixed me. I've exercised caution since. Though I am not a superstitious person, the contraption has brought only good news to this house. I find myself always hurrying to answer as if I am a child running after St. Nicholas for fear of missing a gift, so I'm a bit out of breath by the time I arrive to pick up the receiver.

"M-Mother, I have n-news," Lonnie says. It is a challenge for my son to speak. The fact that he has made a telephone call is testament alone to the marvelous invention. This is the boy who refused to turn five on his birthday for fear of school. His will is there, but his courage is still in its infancy, but better late than never, even at forty-eight. I've said that phrase long enough that perhaps he is beginning to believe.

"Tell me," I say.

"A c-call c-came." He sighs heavily, already frustrated by his affliction. "B-Berlin's of Charleston is interested in the m-menswear line."

"I'm not surprised."

"Yes, b-but, they want a m-meeting to see the shirts in person, on M-Monday."

Lonnie's earned this moment if for no other reason than for having done this without me. He's the one who had the notion for expansion, did all the research on the newest electric sewing machines and calculated how quickly productivity would pay them off. He designed the shirts, chose the fabric and sent the inquiries. For months he's had a string of rejections, losing hope after so many no's. I told him his defeatist attitude was foolish; good is good and right is right. He is the future. He says that's what a mother is supposed to say, but I disagree. Lonnie has a creative mind and a flair for business. I'm not blinded by this simple fact because he is my son. I know the talent my children possess just as well as I know their weaknesses.

"Relax and enjoy your victory," I tell him. "I'll be there straightaway. We'll solve it."

My first thought is, here is your reason to go to Charleston. It's been too long, and now I have cause. The second is, Lonnie needs a proper celebration. He's always been in the shadow of his older brother, particularly when it comes to his father, but he's come into his own and his efforts now exhibit reward. There must be a keepsake for such a momentous day. Papa always said, "If we don't celebrate the small movements forward, we forget they existed at all."

The attic is fifteen degrees hotter than the rest of the house. The heat is stifling even for me, a woman rarely bothered by temperature. The smell of the room is odious. Something must have crawled up here and died, though I don't see droppings. I try to lift the attic window to clear out the stink but it's stuck from age, so I give it a bang on both sides and it budges somewhat. Creaking it open a few inches, I make a mental note to return to close it later. We've had more than one animal that's crawled up and died in this old space. This attic has so many things compartmentalized and hidden away it's a wonder our past doesn't collapse in on us. In one section there's a tin bathtub that Edwin himself was bathed in, his parents' bedroom furniture, stuffy old things, and all of his late brothers' effects, two boys who died of disease before he came along. In another section is the rocking horse our daughters used to fight over. Sarah carried the facial scar from Molly's scratch into adulthood. It sits among many things that brought us pain. After my boy Buck died, I boxed his things and made Edwin put everything here, in the attic. And then again after our daughters left so abruptly, and in such anger, I removed their things from the rooms they occupied and placed them here. I don't know what I was thinking. Perhaps by extracting the remnants of their presence I was excising the pain of their absence? I must remember to clear this room before next summer. I'd hate to have the boys inherit our ghosts.

The past is finished, and there are new seeds of possibility sprouting in every direction. I aim to continue toward the new crop. To have a revelation of sorts, a second wind at my age is what our maid, Retta, would call a blessing. Though, to me, God is no more real than the Easter Bunny. I'd rather place my faith in science. Still, I'm willing to concede she has a point and a new wind blows.

At the back of the attic I find the old cherry chest my father gave me when I was a young girl. This is all that exists of me before I met my husband. My father filled this chest with things he felt I'd need for marriage. He was a pragmatic man, unsure of what to give a motherless child, a girl no less, on the most special day of her life, so he filled it with my mother's things — jewelry, crystal, china, beautiful and delicate laces and silks from around the world — so that I might have my old home within the new, a piece of my past for the future. He knew instinctively what would settle my restless spirit. I didn't understand my father then, but I do now.

This old chest contains what little I have

left of the man. The wooden box is no longer stylish but I haven't the heart to throw it out. To do so would be akin to discarding my own father. I've not grown that callous. I heft it open and peer within. Tucked away in the corner beneath my christening gown is a small square red box, loose with age and lined with black velvet. My father's pocket watch lies inside like a prize, gold with an inscription from my mother to him on their wedding day. He carried it wherever he went. On every continent in the world, at every moment of the day, he said my mother reminded him of time and how quickly it passed. The woman made sense, that's all I can say, and I wish I'd known her. To hear Papa talk of her, she must have been a queen, but now that I am old, I only wonder what the sound of her voice was like. It would be enough to know that.

I open the back of the watch and, with the small key from the box, wind the thing 'til it jolts to life just as it did some forty-five years ago when I last wound it in my father's hand on his deathbed. Time continued to lurch forward long after he stopped breathing. This will be just the thing Lonnie will appreciate. If nothing else, perhaps it will remind him of the time he wastes being afraid of the world.

Before I take my leave I stand and listen. I enjoy the house to myself on occasion. Retta fought leaving work early, but I told her she does no one a service by working herself to death, particularly me. There's such a difference in the quiet when everyone is gone. Sound travels well in this old place, even from up here, the clock in the entry hall, distant shouts of men across the property, the creaking and settling of the floorboards beneath my feet. This place has an identity all its own. It's a rare moment when I get to stop and listen to its voice.

The drive to the Sewing Circle is pleasant enough; cotton is being harvested on the other farms this week, so workers stop and shade their eyes from the sun as I pass. None of them are yet accustomed to a woman driver, though they've seen me behind the wheel countless times. I raise my gloved hand outside the window and give a wave to the Negroes in the fields and they wave back. Their presence reminds me this is the week of our old harvest. Our first year of tobacco as main crop has thrown us all off-kilter. It requires a different care, to which I am unaccustomed. There are three stages to a harvest now instead of two: the

44

picking, the curing and then the selling. Cotton was so much simpler.

The workers, with their bags slung to one side, are stark against the dotted white fields and high sun. They sway in unison as they move from plant to plant and row to row. They are singing old songs from their ancestry. I lean my ear to the open window to catch the music, but the rush of wind and the roar of the engine make it impossible.

The cotton is starting to come back, but the remnants of the blight are still sore on the eye. Tobacco will be our much-needed savior. There are no tobacco fields south of our farm. All eyes are on Branchville and Orangeburg. If we do well at market, next year come this time there will be a diversification. Every field south in Orangeburg will yield a different crop.

Edwin and our eldest son, Eddie, have fretted in the barn over that tobacco for weeks now. I'm grateful a small corn harvest has consumed them for the better part of this week. They're going to worry themselves sick about that tobacco, and there's no reason for it. Worry is something I've never understood. What good does it do, except drain possibility from the day? Like father, like sons, I suppose. They certainly didn't get that from me. My daughters, however, had pragmatism. They left us without ever looking back.

The women at the Sewing Circle are steady at work over their machines. I see Lonnie through the glass window that separates our office from the women, sitting in my chair with his head bent forward. He has a circular spot as big as a silver dollar at the top of his scalp just like his father's. I give the ladies a hello as I wind my way through the machines to my son. They smile or call to me; their hands never leave the cloth they are sewing. I love the sound of the machines at work in unison. If I close my eyes the sound could easily be a train starting its engines and coming to life. This factory may as well be a train for the places it will take us. I've no doubt that in one year's time, if all goes according to plan, we will double in size, and put to work twice the number of women we have now. For a business that started with six seamstresses in the back room of a church, we've done quite nicely for ourselves.

Lonnie doesn't raise his head as I come through the door. Three sample shirts in blue, brown and yellow are laid before him, inside out, as he examines the stitching. He picks up the scissors next to him, poised to make the first cut.

"Don't even think about it," I tell him.

He lifts his head and looks at me, his face contorted with despair. He labored over those shirts, and has done them three times over, insisting they aren't right.

"They are perfect. Don't do another thing."

"No, the stitching is weak at the p-pockets. They won't last a m-month."

"Don't be ridiculous, they will last years if cared for properly."

He looks from the shirts to me, drops the scissors on the desk and hangs his head. I lay the package I brought in front of him. He looks up inquisitively and I nod for him to open it. He does so with great care, just as he did when he was small. He personified everything then, his mittens, the Christmas tree, wrapping paper, treating every inanimate object as if it had a soul that could be hurt. He even went so far as to speak in comforting tones to the objects of his attention. I turn the shirts to their proper side and fold and stack them as he opens the tissue paper inside the box. Lonnie turns the watch over in his hands, examining it, and I'm once again amazed at how alike he and Papa's hands are.

"That was your grandfather's and now

yours. He was the most entrepreneurial man I know, and you are very much like him."

"He started sooner than m-me."

"Late starts in life have no less relevance than early ones. In fact, I would argue they have more relevance. Experience in life can only be judged by the obstacles one has to overcome to get it."

I strip my hat from my head and he stands, offering me the chair. He pulls another alongside me.

"I think you should do the m-meeting," he says.

"Absolutely not," I say. "This place will be yours within a year. You must learn how to converse with the outside world sooner or later. Besides, you're the person who best understands the product."

"I c-can c-coach you."

I stare at him for a moment, then lift my pen from the inkwell and a sheet of paper from the top drawer.

"What would you have me say?"

I write everything he tells me, how much each shirt costs to make, the time it takes to make them, pattern and color choices. He's near perfect in his elocution. I hand him the sheet of paper, covered front to back with all he's said, and tell him to memorize it. He sits and stares at his own words.

"We'll practice on the train."

He lifts his head with hope.

"I'll make the trip with you, but the meeting is yours alone."

He closes his eyes and shakes his head no.

"Stop," I say, and he pinches his nose and folds the paper into fours. I take it from him and place the paper and watch into the pocket of the shirt he wears, the one he made for himself. "Now that is a sturdy pocket."

He nods his head and straightens his spine before going to do his afternoon work on the floor. I open the books to look over our accounts while he sets the chair against the wall. The telephone rings on the desk before Lonnie is out the door. He tenses and waits, while my hand hovers above the receiver, one long and one short bell, not for us. He smiles from relief and walks out to the table of fabric, lifts a bolt of colorful burlap cloth with an array of large flowers displayed and unspools the material. Laying it across the counter he cuts the material with a long straight blade into clean rectangles, measured to size, and stacks them neatly so each woman can retrieve as needed.

It was Lonnie's idea to use colorful prints to make seed bags. He noticed how women in town used the old ones for aprons, dresses and bedcovers, and brought it to my attention; strange how I never noticed. Now it's all I see. Half the women in the Circle are dressed in discarded sacks. The room is awash in red, blue, yellow and green, flower and geometric patterns, each dress styled and adorned differently. Some have ribbons at the waist and buttons at the collar, some are no more than the original sacks with holes for arms and head. You can spot dress designs from the same family as easily as you can spot the poorest in the crowd. Mothers and daughters sit shoulder to shoulder dressed in matching outfits not unlike how I used to dress my own daughters. Once I made my girls matching dresses with wings and watched them sail around the house for weeks claiming to be fairies. Those were the days when magic was very real; fireflies were fairy horses and lilac fields were summerhouses of the kingdom.

Whole generations have come and gone in the Circle, and for a moment I'm nostalgic for all that my workers have that I no longer do. Each other. When I am finished here in this place, on this earth, will I miss them? Is missing something that hasn't yet happened as potent as missing that which already has?

I reach for the telephone directory Lonnie ordered at the beginning of the summer.

He's marked and circled clothing shops in the yellow pages of the manual of every store in Charleston. I, too, have done my own study of two separate pages of the book, though no one would ever know to look: Mr. and Mrs. Morgan Abbott, my daughter Sarah's telephone number, and Mr. and Mrs. Fitzgerald Osteen, Molly's residence. I was both thrilled and terrified when I found my daughters in these pages. All the early memories of them came back to life when we installed the telephone, and then when I saw them registered, another cascade of recollections, good and bad, appeared, just like magic. Fifteen years it's been since I've seen my girls. I know they are older, but in the wake of this invention, memories of their youth have flooded my mind — another aha. I've memorized their telephone numbers from staring at them so regularly. Surely if my son can overcome his fears, I can overcome mine and call his sisters. Do I have anything to lose? Hasn't the time come to mend fences?

It is still early when I return home, and I'm relieved to find Edwin absent, once again claiming the peace of the house for myself. Stripping my driving gloves off, I lay them across the dining room table and walk straight to the parlor. I perch on the sofa and pick up the telephone. When I last spoke with our daughters, we fought over respect and their unwillingness to give it. By the time the fight erupted, Sarah and Molly had been living in Charleston for well over a year, visiting with us sporadically, and even then only a few hours at a time, when it suited them, usually around dinnertime. I found it rude and said as much. Sarah cried, but Molly got her back up and said she held Edwin and me both responsible for Buck's death and the demise of our family. It was a blow in light of how Buck died, and I withered under the accusation. Edwin was furious and threw them out of the house. I knew then as well as I do now she didn't mean what she said. She was angry. She lashed out. Sides were chosen. The boys picked us.

After lifting the receiver, I dial Sarah's number — she was always more malleable than Molly — but there is no sound on the other end. I've done something wrong but don't know what. The instruction manual lay in the drawer of the coffee table. I turn to the table of contents and find the chapter that explains how to place a call. I was supposed to wait for the tone before dialing the number — simple enough.

"Mother," my husband calls out from the dining room, causing me to jump. Edwin's come through the back door and kitchen without me noticing. The man is stealthy, that's all I can say. Early in our marriage he took great delight in sneaking up on me. He stopped when I took equal pleasure in pouring cold water on his head in the early mornings while he slept. I tuck the number between the pages of the book just as he enters the room to find me, receiver in hand. He has a layer of dirt over his whole being. Tassels from cornstalks cling to his shirt and pants.

"What are you doing?" he asks.

"Learning to place a call," I say. "I'm practicing with Lonnie. Good gracious, Edwin, you're filthy. Go up and bathe while I get supper on the table."

"Teach me later," he says.

"Who are you going to call?" I ask.

"You, while I'm at market."

Before he leaves the room I remember. "Edwin, would you go and look in the attic? Something has died up there, and I've forgotten to shut the window."

He murmurs his consent and climbs the stairs, his footsteps fading in the distance.

3

MRS. ORETTA BOOTLES

I am an old Negro woman, too old to carry a crying white child across town and through the thicket of cypress that leads into Shake Rag where we live. I ran best I could the whole way. This child's eat up with worms worse than I ever seen in a body that still has a soul. She is up against the day.

There was redbirds in the yard all this morning before I come to work and then in the Coleses' oak trees, too — like trouble following me. One lighted on the porch rail and looked right at me while I did the breakfast dishes. I fretted all day over what they mean to tell us. Right after Miss Annie left the kitchen I got down to dealing with the good Lord for fear of what must be coming.

"Father," I told him, and pointed so He knew I meant business, "you know I rub rough, but I'm tenderhearted and I ain't ready to lose my husband. Even if You want to call him, I won't step aside. You got to go through me if You want Odell. Keep him safe and I will do whatever You command."

Not two weeks ago I spied a tremor in Odell's right hand. He said it was nothing, but I know how seeds shoot into the sun to get full grown. Something has took root in my husband, and I won't have it. Preacher says it's wrong to bargain with God, but Jesus is the one started the bargaining. John 3:3 says, "Jesus answered and said unto him, verily, verily I say unto thee, Except a man be born again, he cannot see the Kingdom of God." That's what the Bible says clear as bells on Sunday morning. *You believe in Me and you get eternal life.* He don't give eternal life first. He makes you a deal. Up to you whether to take it or not. Access the Savior, then be saved. No matter what the price, the promise will keep. Everybody wins if the promise is big enough. That's what the Bible says, and that's what I always believed — until now. Now I fear my promise and the child in my arms will be the death of us both.

I had my first presentiment right after Mama got sick, and I became Miss Annie's full-time maid. I can't speak as to why I never had one before — only know I've had them regular ever since. I was working for Miss Annie by myself when I was seventeen and she was twenty-eight years of age. She had four little ones then. Molly hadn't come along yet. She had her hands full with them children. Mama had taken to the bed for almost two months. Mr. Coles told her she missed too much work and she needed to move on out. He said I'd do fine in the main house, that the room off the kitchen would suit me, but Mama didn't like that notion and she had Miss Annie's ear.

Miss Annie said no to Mr. Coles, that it weren't right to move Mama after all them years of service to the family. So Mr. Coles backed down and let her have her way. Still, he charged Mama ten dollars a month to live on the property she served as a slave on. Times change but people don't. Black folk is fine to do the work long as they don't have an opinion.

Mama taught me everything she knew. I can cook and clean and iron. I know my way around a garden. I can pickle and can anything you can eat. I know where to dig for dandelion greens, and how to cook 'em so they lose the bitter. I can name the healing power in every plant, and I know everything there is to know about babies. I been changing diapers since I knew how to walk. Me and Mama helped birth half the colored children in the county, and then Miss Annie's children, too. I mopped Miss Annie's brow when she screamed. I was so scared the first time. Never seen a white woman give birth. Took me by surprise to find we got all the same parts. By the time Miss Molly come along, I was delivering babies to half the town, white and colored alike.

After I took over running the house for Miss Annie, I'd go home every night to help with the feeding and cleaning of Mama. We had ourselves a system. My brother, Willie, worked the cotton fields all day and then come home to help me. I'd clean out the chamber pot and clean Mama off best I could while Willie'd start the woodstove and I'd cook what we had. Sometimes we had us a nice rabbit Willie caught in the fields, or fish he caught over on the Edisto.

Mama was sick as could be. Her legs and feet got to be so big she couldn't stand on them for the pain. She thought she could cure it, said it was gout, but it didn't never get better. No matter, every day and night we'd talk. She wanted to know the happenings of the day, news of the boys and their schooling. I was skittish running that house without Mama. Even from her sick bed she helped me, but no matter what she said my soul was burdened and my sleep was troubled. Mama would sing or rub my head. She'd talk about the seasons and how life fit into them perfect. Everything passes is what she was saying. I know that now. She'd talk 'til I could get myself calm enough to rest 'fore sunup. It's a frightful thing not to sleep for worry but she could always soothe me.

"You know what you're doin'," she told me, and though I knew she wouldn't lie, I couldn't help but doubt myself.

One night Mama talked me to sleep, and deep in the night I felt myself sinking into the bed like a heavy weight was sitting atop me — so heavy I couldn't breathe. When I was able to push the feeling away, smoke filled my nostrils. I saw our house on fire with flames rising up the walls all around us. I reached for Mama, but she weren't next to me. I could hear Willie crying my name above the noise and fumbled to him 'til I found his hand in the black. We stretched out across the room 'til we found Mama and caught her around the waist. We had to pull on her to get out. She kept yelling, "Save the mirror! Save the painting!" We got her to the yard, then Willie turned, and before I could stop him, he run back in

— straight into hell. I thought he was lost forever.

I woke in the dark that night with such a start and such a cry that Mama put her rough hand on my brow to calm me. I spoke of the dream and she said, "Child, don't say that! The Lord brought us up to this point. I got a full cupboard, a few dollars in my pocketbook and we don't owe nobody nothing. Anything happens, we're fine."

Next day I was dressing Buck, when I heard the fire bell ringing and the call for help. I ran to the window and yelled down to the yard boy, "Whose house is it?"

He hollered back, "It's your house, Miss Retta, it's yours!"

I tore out of that house and ran through the field quick as my feet could move. I saw smoke rising and black folk yelling — passing buckets of water down the line from the well. When I got to the woods, I was out of my mind, screaming, "Where's Willie? Where's my brother?"

I found him sitting a far piece behind the house, on the edge of the wood. Sitting on the ground covered with soot. He was a mess of snot and tears, rocking back and forth like a baby in need of comfort. In his arms was Mama's mirror and her painting of a boat out to sea. He got them both, but

Mama was gone. I wasn't there to help save her.

I don't know what the redbirds mean to say, but if this child is a clue, I've got work to do. She's curled up like a bug under a stone in the sling harnessed between the fig and peach tree just to the side of my house. Odell put that up for me in need of ways to be useful when my mourning got bad. There's times I rest in it, but not near as much as I want. I give her a shove so she rocks while I carve off the bark of a pomegranate bush out by the woodpile with my old butcher knife. I got to make worm tea, and pomegranate bark works best in the first step of healing.

The second step is to stir the bowels. Not much fruit around for that. Apples are wormy in these parts. After three years' time, those trees still ain't back to normal since the infestation. But the figs will do. This child is starving, her body eating itself. If I feed her wrong she could turn for worse. Then I got a dead white child on my hands. Jesus, I know it's a sin to worry about a dead child when I got a live one, but the trouble I bring on my house is enough to kill a body.

After I finish my gatherings I come 'round

60

the front of the house and see Mabel marching down the lane in the dust. I know she wants to see if the talk she heard on her walk home from work is true. Lightning bugs bounce around her in the dusk. She is a Christian woman who knows her verse, but she's got no sense. I try not to judge but it ain't easy. I put my hand up to Mabel before she reaches the corner and hold it there 'til she lifts her head, then I holler out, "I can't visit right now, Mabel, you go on home."

She hears the child crying. I can see by the turn of her head. She's weighing what she ought to say with what she wants to say, but I don't have time for her foolishness. She don't know what it is to be inside my skin.

"Retta?"

"Go on home, Mabel, I can't talk right now."

I expect more will come knocking, but I can't think about that right now. Odell's gonna be home soon, and what I have to do needs more than the two hands I got.

There's a hymn that lifts me when the burden gets too great. I sing it as I cart the wood through the screen door, past the sitting area and into the kitchen. I sing it while I the light the kindling and stoke the fire.

"Oh, my Lord, oh, my good Lord, keep me from sinkin' down." I sing it low like a lullaby when I step outside and scoop the child from the sling to carry her inside. She clings to me like a spider newly born. *"I mean to go to heaven, too, keep me from sinkin' down."* I sing it as I steep the bark in the boiling kettle, me swayin' with the child in my arms. *"I look up yonder and what do I see? Keep me from sinking down."*

The child whimpers.

"Shhhh, shhhh," I say. "Look up, look up at the angels."

She lifts her face to the roof of my house like she's seen some distant memory. *"I see the angels beckoning me. Keep me from sinking down."* I hear the bells of Odell's wagon before he comes through the yard half past the hour — those old mares breathin' like they climbed a mountain. And, oh, Lord I sing. I sing for Odell and his crippled leg, I sing for myself, an old woman with a child dead and gone, and I sing for this little one who ain't got nothing. Nothing at all.

I was the first of my kin to move away from the plantation and take up property here on Hunter Lane. After Mama died, none of us belonged on that place no more. That time was gone, and we needed to move along with it. Pretty soon everybody got to moving over near us and quick as we could turn around there was nine decent houses nestled back in the woods with twenty-two children runnin' 'round — everybody raising a family 'cept me and Odell. Each year that went along with no child weighed on us. But we kept on. Odell would be up before dawn, and I'd have his saucer of coffee and biscuits waiting before he headed to the railroad station. He'd spend the day shoveling coal as a fireman for the trains that run from Branchville to Columbia and back. He was a big, strong man. Worked physical labor sixteen hours a day, longer right before he was hurt. After he'd leave, I joined the womenfolk along the lane heading out to do the white lady's cleaning and wash. Every colored woman on the street had a job washing and cleaning for white folk. "Shakin rags," was what we called it. Got so everybody in town started calling our neighborhood "Shake Rag." It stuck.

Odell and me married after Mama died. We was writing letters the whole fall before she passed while he worked at the railroad over in Williston. That summer his mama come over and asked me and Mama to write Odell. Said he was down in the mouth and homesick as could be. So I wrote and he wrote me back. We told each other a little something about every day, just news around town, nothing more. One letter he wrote said, "Dear Oretta, O, O, O, how I love the letter O. Your friend, Odell."

Then one day shortly thereafter, he surprised us all and come home for a family dinner on a Sunday afternoon. It was a pretty day. The leaves was just dippin' into the candy colors they change to before they let go of their branch. It was a party with everybody bringing something to add to the table. After we ate he stood up and said to Mama, "Miss Sally, I aim to marry Retta. I took off work for two days, so we could get it done tomorrow."

Mama turned and looked at me, and my blood ran so hot I jumped out of my chair and said, "No, you ain't marrying me tomorrow, Odell Bootles. That ain't how it's done!"

"How's it done then?" he asked.

"You got to ask me first."

"You know I love you."

"No, I do not know that."

"Well, I write you every day, don't I?"

That's when it come on me that I loved him, too. But I couldn't say so with all them eyes on us, even though now I suppose they all saw it in me even before I did. I said yes finally, but I told him he needed to put in for work on the Branchville line. I wasn't raising my babies away from family. Said when he got that done, we'd marry.

Afterward, Mama said to me, "Child, you might have missed your boat." But I knew Odell in the heart and he knew me the same way. He wanted what I did.

By the time Odell's put up the horses and fed them in their stalls, I got two cups of worm tea in the child. She minds good, but when she sees my husband coming through the door, she starts fresh with her crying.

She screams, "I'll be good," so loud Odell backs out the screen door and waits on the porch.

"Hush now!" I say and she does. When I go out to Odell, he's leaning sideways on his wood crutch.

"What's happenin' here, beautiful woman?" he asks.

What's happening? How can I answer that question? Even if I open my mouth to try, I can't.

"Fill the washtub. I've got to get this child in it. She's got fever."

Few things make a man feel like a man after he's stopped being able to find respectable work. It don't matter that Odell is afflicted — he helps me. Whenever I got a need, he stands up. He's the strongest man I know. He helps me pull the washtub through the front door and onto the rug I braided myself. Together we haul it across the floor and into the kitchen, where I pour the boiled water in to mix with the cold. The child scoots up against the corner of the sofa like we're about to boil her alive. Can't be too hot or too cold. Too hot and it will drive her fever up, too cold and it could shock her heart enough to stop it. Odell fetches the soap.

"I'll get you supper after I get her clean," I tell him.

"Don't you worry 'bout me," he says, and goes for more wood.

When I undress the child, I see how bad off she is. Her ribs and bones jut out so far they look like they could pop straight through the skin. She is covered in bruises and ringworms.

"Mercy," I hear Odell whisper as he steps through the door, one arm full of wood. We look at each other across the room, and I fear that one word will take all I got left in me. He stokes the fire with birch wood and goes back outside, where I hear him settle on the porch swing, close enough to come should I need him. I lift and carry the child to the washtub and lay her in the water. She's so weak and tired she can't lift her head — just lies there looking up at the angels. Night is upon us, and the promise of death will not break until the day is done.

"Nothing's going to happen to you while Miss Oretta's here. You understand me, child?"

She nods her little head and whispers, "Mary. I'm Mary," then closes her eyes while I scrub her clean.

I scrub her head and under her arms, between the toes and where she was attached to her mama. I hold her steady while she stands and squats so I can clean along her bottom. She holds on to my shoulder to keep from falling over. I scrub all that is in and behind her ears and when I'm through the water is so thick with dirt and tiny creatures, you can't see to the bottom of the tub. If she survives the night, I know I got to do the same tomorrow.

I put her in a cotton nightgown; I keep extra in a suitcase under the bed. She sets on a chair while I tie up the bottom so she can see her feet when she walks. I put her on my lap to comb the knots, as big as fists, out of her hair. She lets me comb without a whimper. The slop jar sets on the floor at my feet. We'll need it. When Odell comes back through the door she pushes up against me like she could climb straight through my old bones.

"That's Mr. Bootles," I tell her. "He's all right."

Odell nods. "Ma'am."

She gets to trembling so bad it's like she's seen the Holy Ghost himself. Then the retching begins. That's the tea doing its job. I reach to the floor, pick up the slop jar and set it on her lap. She leans her head over it and throws up all she took in. Odell stands still as a tree in the middle of the room while I rub her back. Somewhere far off, the sky rumbles.

"Child needs a doctor, Retta."

"No doctor is going to come out here at night, Odell."

"Then we got to take her to him. He'll take her in."

"No time for that."

"I'll fetch Roy to help me with the horses."

"I ain't leaving the child with no doctor."

I mean to keep my promise to the Lord. This child is my burden. If I save her life, I save His. The air between us is heavy.

"Old man, you got nothing to say that I want to hear."

He turns and goes out the screen door. Ain't nothin' I can say that will make him understand. I rub her back and hold her hair away from the mess.

"Get it out child, get it all out."

When she's done, she falls against me. I lay her on the couch and rub her head 'til her breathing calms. When she finally closes her eyes, I peer into the slop jar to see what's come up — maggots twist and float in the waste.

After I get the child to sleep and feed Odell and me, we retire to our bedroom. I rub Vaseline on Odell's stump. His leg is one big scar from the burn of his accident. After all the years that have passed since he was so hurt, he still feels the pain like it was yesterday. He lays back on the bed while I do for him like he does for me. It don't matter to me none he is without a leg. He is still a man. Took me a while to convince him of that, but I rub his tired body every night. He says I brought him back to life, but I'm the one that was saved by his living.

"You got to have faith, O. There's things we can't see. We can only see what's in front of us, what our eyes make out. We don't have God's view. Could be this is a blessing. Maybe something good can come of it."

"Woman, you are something else."

Odell don't understand what I know, what

I seen, and I'm careful not to trouble him. Husbands don't need to know everything. He's got to keep his mind straight, focus on his own health. He pushes too hard as it is. He's asleep before I can put my head on the pillow. I lie quiet so as not to trouble him, but inside my thoughts run like they're being chased. The child's being eaten up from the inside, and them worms need something other than human flesh to feed on. Tomorrow I got to get something of substance in her stomach that can pass through.

I am glad to be with Odell when the rain comes. It's a summer storm, powerful but quick. He sleeps up next to me like he always does. Says it soothes his soul. But it's my restlessness that gets calmed with his big old body next to mine. Nothing can hurt me with Odell by my side. I done what I promised I would do, but I know that promise is more than one day's work. The child's got no spirit left. It's a terrible sight to behold in one so young. She'll need some fight, and I aim to give her some while she's in my keep. I rest my eyes for a minute. A good storm helps. The storm outside calms the storm within. I wake to a hand on my arm and the girl standing by the bed shaking like tomorrow ain't coming. I lift the bedsheet, and she crawls in next to me, hot as coal. I sing soft 'til she calms.

"I looked out to Jordan and what did I see, coming for to carry me home? A band of angels comin' after me, comin' for to carry me home . . ."

You got to settle yourself with death. I been able to do that with everybody but Odell. Losing him would kill me. I've said to him more than once, "If you die first, just wait for me there, I won't be but a minute behind."

I wonder, though I would never say it, if I done a service or disservice to Odell by prayin' for his life to be spared when he got hurt all them years ago. It was my need that couldn't let him go. Mine. Not his. It's a woeful thing to have such powerful need. You can feed on need, but you'll always want for more. To love is not God's hope, but Satan's will.

Odell wakes next to me and I press against him for comfort. What a sight we must be, the three of us lyin' in the bed. He reaches over my shoulder and finds the child's head, and rests his hand for just a moment. Nobody died under my roof today, but somewhere a creature died. For something to live, something had to die. The redbirds promise that.

"Gonna be all right," I tell Odell.

He lets go a powerful sigh.

Somebody in this town will have something to say before this is said and done. Nothing's happened yet, but something will.

4

GERTRUDE

Alligators feed once a week, and sometimes, if the prey is big enough, they don't need to eat for almost a year. But I don't know how long it takes a gator to eat big prey. Daddy never said nothing 'bout that and I never asked.

I smell the storm coming from the north before it hits. Mama could always smell a storm before it come, sometimes days ahead. She passed her nose right on down to me. I smell it in the wind, a heavy sweetness, full, like something's about to bust. Same way I felt before my time come to give birth to each of my babies. Ripe — that's what a storm is. I got just enough time before it breaks to shed my clothes, and use what's left of the kindling to make a fire. If I had one more dress, I'd burn the one on my back, too. It does me more harm than good as thin as it is, you can see clear

73

through it. The sun is gone, but I got firelight to see by. I squat naked by the pump while the thunder rolls in, scrubbing away the day's deed. I wash every part. I don't feel the cold, though it's cold enough to hurt. I'm past that. I will be ready when they come for me. I will be respectable and clean. I pour a bowl of cold water over my head to rinse the soap from my hair. I know what I must look like. I am an animal in the woods, not fit for proper society. No matter — even an animal has its virtue. I got a nose like a fox. And I smell what's coming.

Mama always made us pull the mattresses to the floor before a storm hit. She was scared lightning would get us in our bed. Before she got sick, storms were the only thing I ever saw Mama throw a fit over. If it was real bad weather, she'd scream and cry every time thunder would roll across the sky. Nobody could reach her. No matter what we said or did, she couldn't be calmed until it passed. Sometimes it was two, three days before her thoughts come back to us. Her mind wandered around back then even before it left her altogether. Daddy said it's 'cause Papaw got hit by lightning, and she saw it happen. Stepped out on the porch to smoke his pipe and boom — like God himself reached down with His bony fingers just for her daddy. Got to wonder what sort of sin welcomes that kind of haste. It knocked Mama backward clear to the center of the house. That whole episode got caught in her head. No matter how she tried, she never could get it out. Anybody finds out what I done, they'll say I weren't in my right mind, but I ain't like Mama. I know every minute of every day and where each thought is inside that time. Sometimes the years go by so fast it's like flipping pages in a book, but a day can take so long a whole life's gone by before the sun sets down.

Tomorrow is Saturday. Alvin's due at the sawmill by six, and when he don't show, his daddy will show up to raise hell. Morning will come quick. I got to get up and work instead of listening to the no-good company of my own thoughts. I got to be ready. With a candle for light, I clean what I can see of Alvin's waste and vomit dried up on the floor. Flies and insects cover the spots in a mighty swarm of tiny creatures. Likely they'd do the task of cleaning for me, but then they'll lay eggs and multiply. They crawl up my hands and arms, and onto my dress, biting and stinging the whole time, but I don't feel it. I swat at them. I can kill ten, maybe twenty, in one swipe, but they always come back.

The notion of food makes me sick, but I know I need the strength, so I eat a mite of corn bread Retta give me before I pull the mattress to the floor. It takes me three good heaves. Alvin used to do this for us. The story of Papaw shook him. Got to be he'd pull the beds down without me asking when storms come up. He didn't see no eccentricity in the need to stay low. I lay my head in the middle of the bed and stretch clear across both sides before I close my eyes. I'm sick as I ever been, sick with pain and what I done. But I'm tired, too, tired for the ages. There's sweet temptation in lying down and never getting up. Instead of prayers I speak out loud. "Mama, bless me." I listen for her voice, what kind words she might give, for she was a kind woman. But she is gone. I've lost her in the wind.

My sin against Alvin is a terrible thing, I know. The Bible tells us so. But what sin is worse, the sin of living in squalor with no hope as a prisoner in the place that's supposed to be your haven or the sin of murdering your husband? You got to be responsible for your house. That's your job as the woman. That's what Mama said. If Alvin weren't happy with us, with me, then I must not have seen a clear way as to how to make him happy, but I tried even if it didn't work.

I guess I wasn't smart enough. And if what Mama said is true, about the woman being the main one to make a happy home, then the sin of killing Alvin is no worse than the life I built for my children. I will carry it on my shoulders. I will take it and swallow it and bear it if it means a chance for them girls to live with food in their bellies. I will go to hell or jail, whichever comes first, but if they have a chance, I mean to give it to them, even if killing casts a shadow on their name.

Sometime in the night, before first light, I wake to the storm. I've lost sense of its direction, like the sky just gathered above and spilled all it was holding on top of me. Lightning and thunder so mixed together I can't tell one from the other — just one big roar. Rain pounds the ground, and wind rattles the tin roof. The old house sways on its stilts. This place will be an island before long if it ain't already. Then the swamp will bring up everything that sits inside it: gators, moccasins, bullfrogs, ticks and leeches — all of hell's creatures.

With a lit candle I peer into the mirror to look at my face. I fear I am blind in my left eye. Even when I pry it open all I can see is the blackness of the blood inside. In the dark I fix a poultice of wet snuff and lay back down. The cool mixture soothes the throb. Alvin's daddy will come soon. He will know what I done. He will want his revenge. I know the fierceness of the need to protect your own. I close my eyes while the heavens curse around me.

When I come to, the clock reads 5:30 p.m., and Saturday is nearly gone. My heart jumps to my throat for the time wasted. Good for nothing to waste a day lying on the bed. I step out to the front porch to listen for something human. What is left of my fire outside lies black and dead in the weeds. The footpath to the swamp is washed over with a wide pool of water. There's no sign of Alvin's daddy. I've been given another day. Maybe she heard me. Maybe Mama heard.

5

RETTA

Since Mrs. Walker died two weeks ago, I sometimes catch sight of her out on the lane, usually in the early morning just as dawn comes up. I can't say if it's me wishing her there or something else. Sadness can play powerful tricks on the mind. I am a foolish old woman who loves a crippled man more than she should, a woman with no business having a white friend nor caring for a white child. In the days that followed my friend's death, I saw her figure rise from the ground and take form out of the heat of a summer day. I always see straight through her, but that don't make her any less there. She lived on that corner for thirty-five years, one block from where Shake Rag begins. I watched every day in Mrs. Walker's life, and since her death, the women of the Sewing Circle coming along slow in a little pack working toward the miles ahead and the day ahead of that, and the specter of my friend tugging alongside them just like she used to in the living world.

But not today, today she is standing in the pouring rain looking tired and bedraggled. I notice her there when Odell and me load the wagon along the side of the house and settle the child in the back. I can see her from the yard standing in the center of the road — mud gathered about her hemline. Today she ignores the passel of women walking to work. Today she is watching me.

I prayed for Mrs. Walker before and after she died. I can't reconcile with a God that don't help you know you're gone. Where is the promise of life everlasting? I can't make sense of what's happening, but I mean to have answers to my questions when it comes my time to go. Oh, the questions I have. I wish I could bury them in the side yard with my baby girl, but they plague me. I swear if I don't get the answers I want after I get to heaven, I will turn around and go.

Mrs. Walker gave me all her chickens 'fore she died. Every one. She even signed a paper saying it was her wish I have them so nobody would accuse me of stealing. She brought me them chickens one by one, six in all. She loved them, even gave them names.

"This here's Georgia," she said handing over one of the laying hens. "She's nervous and likes to be talked to. If you don't wish her a good morning, she won't give you eggs, so you talk to her, you hear?"

She brought five fat chickens and a rooster: Georgia and Kentucky, Florida and Mississippi, Alabama and a scrawny old banty rooster named Sugar.

I asked once at her kitchen table, "Why you name that rooster Sugar?"

"I believed if I named him sweet and treat him sweet, he would respond as such."

"Lord have mercy," I told her, "you can't change the nature of a beast any more than you can change the nature of a man."

"Can't say that 'til you try."

"Did it work?"

"Not yet."

"That's what I thought."

"Can't always stand to the side, Oretta. Sometimes you got to try to change what you don't like."

She saved Sugar after some old boys left him for dead at a Saturday night cockfight. Found him in the field off the side of the road on her walk home from church and nursed him back to life. It didn't matter what she called him or how she cared for him, he stayed mean. And don't you know she loved that old rooster all the more for his bad temper. Got a mess of chickens from him, too. He was up on those hens every chance he got.

I knew it was serious when she brought me Sugar. Put my heart right up in my throat. I told her I'd be happy to care for them chickens if she needed. I said she could say what she would but I wasn't keeping them. I'd just hold them for her 'til she wanted them back.

"No," she told me, "I can't be no burden to you, Oretta. You got enough on your shoulders. They're yours now. You do as you see fit."

She didn't want to be no burden. No burden — nothing extra to carry. A white woman didn't want to be no burden to me. I never heard the likes of that. A week later she was dead, and I wondered what she carried in her that she knew about and never said aloud.

The street this morning is littered with workers scattering to get to wherever they're going in the rain, under newspapers, jackets and umbrellas to keep from getting wet. Firemen and porters off to the train station, the good women of Shake Rag with their heads tied up in scarves off to clean, the white women of the Sewing Circle stepping through mud and leaping over puddles as they walk the miles beneath their feet. It's Saturday. Every one I see will put in a full day of work before we rest on the Sabbath.

The child lay on a quilt in the back of the wagon, under a canvas Odell rigged to keep her dry. She's too sick to walk. She come through the night, but her fever's strong and she's still not eaten. I hold the umbrella high to cover Odell's head while he worries with the reins. He cannot get them settled in his hands. The rain calms to a drizzle by the time we are out of the yard and onto the road. I finally put my hand over his so he'll know to stop fussing, and I feel his tremor. He pulls away and holds the reins like he always does in his right hand, but his fingers are white about the knuckles from clinching so hard. By the time I get my mind cleared enough to remember, I look up to where Mrs. Walker stood, but the horses are upon, then through her. She disappears in the summer rain.

Heads turn to watch us as Odell and me ride down the lane and through town. I am glad to have the rain as excuse not to speak. By the time Odell hauls the wagon around the back of the Coleses' house by the kitchen door the rain's stopped. The child stands in the wagon when I call her. I hold

Odell steady while he lifts her up and over the side. She squeezes her eyes shut until he puts her in my arms. She lays her head on my breast. I could be carrying an armload of cotton if I didn't know better, for she's no weight at all. Odell uses his crutch to steady and push himself back up onto the wagon and takes the reins once again in his hands.

"Where you headin'?" I ask.

"I'm going to drop a line in the Edisto. Fish ought to bite today."

"You up to it?" I ask.

"Up to fishin?" He shakes his head like I've gone crazy, turns the straps of leather over in his hand and stares straight out to the fields alongside the house. Six weeks ago these fields was full of tobacco and men, women and children sweating in the hot sun to get it harvested.

"Get inside 'fore somebody sees," Odell tells me.

"We done nothing wrong, Odell."

"That child don't belong in this house."

He looks at me and I stare back.

"You wanna take her with you?"

He lets go of a breath and snaps the reins against the old mare's backs 'til they go steady out the yard and down the road.

I lay the child in the room off the kitchen

where I sleep when Miss Annie needs me to work late on occasion. The same one I lived in after Mama died. Miss Annie put a lock on the door for me all those years ago, then handed me the key.

"This is your room now," she said. "Do with it as you see fit."

It's small but has a window looking out to the backyard where the barns and outbuildings sit off in the distance, and you can see the old slave cabins through the trees. I swear sometimes I still see smoke comin' up from those chimneys though it's been more than thirty years since anybody lived in them.

I rub the child dry and strip her down to her underpants 'til her dress can dry. Her teeth's chattering, and she's shaking from fever so bad I got to lay her under a pile of blankets and hope for the best. I fetch a glass of water and promise to check on her.

"You got to rest while I work. Don't make no noise, you hear? I don't want to cause no trouble for Miss Annie."

"Yes'm," she whispers.

Odell is right about the child not belonging in this house, but what was I to do? We got Homecoming over at Indian Fields Camp the first week of October. Every farmer in the territory will put down their work and gather for worship and communion for a whole seven days. That's less than six weeks away. Camp takes time to get ready for, and I still got to get the canning done, beans dried, pudding made, kitchen and bedding packed. There's much to do.

I just finish putting on the coffee when Miss Annie comes through the swinging door, surprising me so that I jump high enough to scare the both of us.

"Lordy be!" I say and clutch my heart.

"I'm sorry, Retta," she says and sits at the table with a list before her.

"You're up early."

"I've made a list of things we'll need for Camp," she says. "I want to do something special for Saturday jubilee. I get so sick of all that fried chicken."

I talk as I pour the coffee and mix it white with milk and a teaspoon of sugar just the way she likes it.

"What about Frogmore stew for Saturday supper?" I say, "The boys can bring shrimp and crab in from Edisto, and we got enough smoked alligator and sausage left from last winter."

I set the coffee in front of Miss Annie, and she says, "That's just the thing."

I pour myself a cup and lay it on the counter where I do my work. Miss Annie gets quiet and scribbles more to do on her list.

I got one ear in this room and one in the next as I pour flour in the bowl and make a hole in the center with my fist. I fill the hole with lard and milk and mash it together until it's good and thick, then snake it up and choke it off at the top to set on the cooking sheet. Mr. Coles likes my biscuits, so I make them fresh every morning. There's a creak from the bed in my room, but Miss Annie don't notice. I gather eggs from the icebox but my hands shake when I crack them open. Eggshells fall in the bowl and I got to dig them out with my fingernails.

I break the quiet. "What you thinkin' so hard on, Miss Annie?"

She waves her hand like she's swatting away a bothersome fly, so I shut my mouth. She takes up her coffee and blows before taking a sip while I fry bacon in the skillet.

"I guess I'm just thinking about the girls," she finally says. "Wondering if I invite them, whether or not they'd come out to Camp. They could bring their husbands. They had such a good time when they were small. Remember?"

"Sure do."

I reach 'cross the bowl to take a sip of coffee. Miss Annie's girls, they're women now, ain't come 'round to see their mama for over fifteen years. Last words Miss Molly said was she was never coming back and she ain't been. The older Miss Molly got, the more fiery she burned, just like her mama. Miss Sarah wrote some in the beginning, but that tapered off. Last letter she told Miss Annie that Molly's working a proper job for a woman named Clelia McGowan. She's causing a ruckus in Charleston with her fight for women's rights. When Miss Annie heard about the job she went down and registered herself for the vote. She wrote and told Sarah knowing that news would get to Molly. But Miss Molly still ain't wrote back, and after a while, Sarah quit, too.

"Why don't you call them on the telephone and ask?" I say.

"I've considered it."

"Time has a way of softening folks."

"I wish I understood how it came to this. I've tried. I've gone over and over it in my mind. It hurt me worse than when Buck died."

"What hurt you worse than when Buck died?"

Mr. Coles steps into the kitchen and comes to the counter to pour his own coffee like he does every morning. I see the

88

surprise on Miss Annie's face. She's spoken her mind, and now she's got to answer for it.

"I just miss the girls."

He loads two teaspoons of sugar into his cup and stirs.

"Our daughters aren't girls anymore, Mother. They turned their backs on you, the woman who birthed and gave them life, a good life! I have no use for such ingrates. The sooner you put them from your mind, the better off you will be — we'll all be."

"Oh, Edwin, you don't need to defend me," she says.

"Just stating facts, Mother." He picks the morning paper off the counter and points it at her. "Impudent behavior doesn't deserve attention. Of any kind." Then he kisses her forehead and leaves the room.

Miss Annie sighs before pushing back her chair and standing.

"He's worried about the tobacco crop. He's counting on that tobacco."

"Yes, ma'am."

"Maybe you're right about the girls, Retta. I don't know."

"Can't hurt. Breakfast will be ready in just a few minutes."

I pour the eggs into the skillet and scramble them in bacon grease.

"Take your time. I am moving at a snail's pace today."

She leaves me with my own thoughts. The day is young. I used to be calmed by the promise of a quiet room. I set aside a small plate of eggs and a biscuit for the girl. I will feed the child and she will eat. All will be well.

After Mr. Coles leaves to survey the tobacco hanging in the barns and Miss Annie has gone to the Circle, I unlock the door and pull the chair up to the child asleep on the bed. I touch her to wake but she don't rouse, and I am heartsick for a moment thinking the worst. When she finally opens her eyes and looks at me, they are glassy with fever.

"I want my mama," she whispers.

"Your mama has business to care for. She'll be back in three days' time. Come on now, sit up and eat."

"What if she don't come back?"

Lord, this child, asking questions that don't need to be asked.

"Your mama knew you 'fore you knew yourself. Mothers don't leave. She'll be back."

I take a spoonful of eggs and hold it to her lips. She takes them in her mouth, then gags and spits them on the bed. She starts crying again. Mourn so strong it gives rise to my own.

"Stop that crying, stop it."

She quiets but her body heaves. She's lost inside herself. I crawl on the bed and hold her 'til she gets it out. Finally she eats a bit of biscuit with honey, but not enough to sustain. After, I get her wrapped in a blanket, set her in the chair by the window and pull away the curtain just a little ways so she can see the garden and beyond to the barn. The horses are in the paddock. I tell her to give them names while I get the bread kneaded and pull the door closed. I am at the sink when I hear boots stomp. The screen door opens at the same time the door to my room does. Mary stands there just as Mr. Coles steps across the threshold and into the kitchen. He's come back early from the fields but for what I cannot say.

"What's this?" he asks when he sees her.

I am caught. The child scurries away from the open door backward toward the window, and I hurry to her side talking as I go.

"This here is Mary. I'm taking care of her while her mama is away."

I lay my hand atop the child's head to steady her tremble.

"Are you being paid to care for this child, Retta? Earning a dollar off my back?"

"No, sir. The mother needed help for a few days is all, and I thought it the Christian thing to do. I'm real sorry not to check with you first but it happened yesterday after I finished my work. I had no way to ask."

"A white woman asking a favor of you?"

"Yessir, I believe I was last in line for the asking."

He stares at Mary, who clutches my skirt.

"Does Mother know she's here?"

"No, sir, I didn't want to trouble nobody. She's a quiet child, shy with people, but no bother at all."

"How long are you tasked with keeping the child?"

"Three more days, sir."

He stands there, looking at her, fiddling with the change in his pocket.

"I don't want you worrying Mother with this. Understand? You keep her hidden away."

"Yes, sir."

"Mary's your name?" he asks the girl.

She nods, watching him.

Mr. Coles pulls out a hand full of change, sifts through and finds what he wants. He holds out a nickel.

"You ever had a nickel of your very own, Mary?"

She shakes her head no.

"This one has your name on it. Come over here and see."

She pulls away and walks to the door, where he stands holding out the shiny coin. When she gets to him, he places it in the palm of her hand and points to the lettering.

"Right there is your name, do you see?"

She shakes her head no, and that gives him a good laugh.

"What do I get for that?" he asks.

She shrugs her shoulders.

"I think I ought to get a hug for big money like that, don't you?"

He puts out his arms. She is a good girl and does as she's told. Mr. Coles swoops her up. The child hangs limp in his embrace like a lamb in the mouth of a lion.

6

GERTRUDE

I rise early on the day the Lord has made before the sun takes its rightful place in the sky. I put a pot on the stove and soak the beans Retta gave me. In them, hidden like a Christmas surprise, is a bit of pork back. I ain't had a good butter bean in many years and a bite of pork in twice that time. I think of my girls, safe with Berns and Marie getting what I can't give. They'll have something in them by now, a bit of toast and butter, some coffee maybe. They'll be wiping sleep from their eyes. I think of Mary and all the times I said I'd give her to the ragman if she weren't good, then I hand her over to the ragman's wife like she was yesterday's garbage. Oh, my head, my head. I wish I could slice it off and store it on a shelf 'til it's healed. But I cannot. There is work to be done.

I scrub the whole place clean, even the

walls, then gather and take stock of all we got and lay it on the springs of the bed. It's paltry, not enough of a dowry for any one of my girls, but if they can find their way together there's enough to start a home. There's some kitchen tools, dishes, my cast-iron skillet, a big pot, two pieces of brown crockery with lids, some silverware and a knife with a wooden handle big enough to cut watermelon. There's my Bible, frayed and half ruined from water damage, and a meager amount of quilts and linens, but the girls will be kept warm enough to live. I find a metal toolbox underneath the house in a corner next to the pilings. I'm surprised since I never did see Alvin use the tools. Inside are a hammer, some nails, a screw-driver, wrench and pliers. In the middle of the box is a clear glass bottle laid flat against the bottom — more than half full. He must have been drunk when he hid it and forgot it was here. The liquid inside is pure gold. I hold it to the sun. It tints the trees amber, making them seem like something out of a dream, but that's deceiving. I know the treachery it holds.

I do all the washing, including the dress on my back, and then, naked, pin it all out on the clothesline. The storm has helped some with the heat, but August is August no matter which way you turn. All we got hangs on the line. It's dusk when I sit down to the supper table. The heat's tolerable naked, so I stay that way. No sense in worrying about my body and who sees it. No one comes here that don't have to. I hated my body and what was demanded of it for the longest time. It just seemed to me like something I didn't fit inside. But then I gave birth to Edna, and I remember thinking how sorry I was to have thought so poorly of it. My body did everything it was supposed to. It built the child in my arms. I never gave a thought to what it could do until a baby latched on and fed from me.

I got a feast of beans and corn bread — enough to last three, maybe four days for one person. Wouldn't last but one with the girls home. I taste what I got like they're sitting at the table with me. The butter beans are the best I ever ate, and the corn bread is so sweet I don't miss the butter. I allow one bowl and place the rest in the crockery to store in the cupboard for tomorrow, then wash my dishes under the clear night sky. Tomorrow I will give myself to what comes. But tonight, I fill a glass of what Alvin left behind. The gold swirls as it reaches the top. The smell burns the inside of my nose. I sit on the bottom step under the night sky and let the bugs feast on skin I ain't never willingly shown the outside world, and take up the glass and drink. The fire slides down my throat and warms my belly. It takes hold and loosens the pain. There is the virtue. I lift the glass again, drinking into the night, drinking 'til it's gone, swallowing all of what swallowed my husband.

Come Monday I am dressed and matching the corners of the bed blankets when I hear the creatures in the swamp yell to one another like they do when danger is upon them, and I know Alvin's daddy is coming through the woods even before I hear his stomp and bad temper.

"Alvin! Alvin!" he hollers. "Goddamn it, Alvin, get your lazy ass up."

I lay the shotgun along the inside of the screen door and step out to the top of the steps and wait. A bull coming through a herd of chickens would be quieter than this man. I know I ought to be scared, but I ain't. We're on Alvin's daddy's land. He's got plenty of it and uses the trees for timber. That built him a nice house with indoor plumbing over in St. George. It's a pity Alvin's mama didn't get to see the high living. She caught the swamp sickness in this very house and died when Alvin was a boy.

Alvin said her death changed his daddy, and I do believe it took its toll on Alvin, too. There was another marriage so Alvin could have a mother, but she run off after a year and nobody's heard from her since. Now there's question of the legal state of his marriage to the third wife, being no divorce was ever had with the second. It makes me wonder what Alvin's daddy knows that we don't.

Wife number three is no more than sixteen and pregnant with her first child. Can't imagine the likes of being married to such an old man, but she acts like he's the king of St. George. I know he likes that, so he's lookin' to give her everything she wants, including one of my girls to order around.

When Alvin's daddy catches sight of me, he turns his head away and hollers over his shoulder, "Go fetch your good-for-nothing husband."

He stands at the edge of the yard, his back to me, looking over the property like he's a plantation owner surveying his slave's house.

He jumps when I say, "He ain't here."

He didn't expect me to talk back, but he still won't turn to face me, and I realize this man ain't never looked me in the face, ain't never called me by my given name. Not once in all the time I've known him, like I was less than a dog in the yard. If he looked now, he'd know. If he stepped inside my screen door he'd see I've scrubbed his son from this place. Even so, I cannot hide what I done. My rage is such that I don't want to anymore.

Alvin's daddy turns toward the house and looks around like he can't make sense of what I said. "Where is he at then?"

"Don't reckon to know. Never came home from work on Friday."

The quiet causes him to still. He cocks his head to one side like he's just come to his senses and looks around like maybe somebody is playing a joke and will pop out from behind a tree. There ain't no joke here.

"Where's your brats?"

"With my brother. I took them on Friday. We got nothin' to eat here, Otto. Nothin'."

Otto is his name, but I never before called him by it. I was always too scared. He knew my daddy. Heard him tell a man down at the sawmill once about how he knew Mama was sick — that he and Alvin did the Christian thing and took me off my daddy's hands. I've come to hope maybe Daddy was thinking he was the one doing Otto the favor by helping a wayward son with a daughter not afraid of hard work. Why else would Daddy give me in matrimony to such a man? Unless he thought that was my worth. Then why teach me what he did? I learned. I wasn't stupid. It must be something I don't see, don't know, won't ever know. A man's thoughts are a stranger to me.

There are crows flying in lazy circles above us — first two, then three more join. Five crows' cries cut through all the sounds in the swamp. *Caw-caw-caw.* Otto grunts like he's made up his mind and walks across the yard toward the steps. I guess he's aiming to prove me a liar and see for himself. I put both feet on the next step down to meet him should he come.

"He ain't been home, Otto. Last I seen him was with you."

He's upon the steps, but he don't come up. Instead he works himself into a fit, kicks over my washtub and tries to rip the wood rail from the stair.

"Goddammit, goddammit."

Above, the crows call so loud and fast it sounds like laughter. Otto stamps and yells 'til he runs out of steam — a red-faced fool. He puts one hand on his hip and another on his big belly and tries to calm his breath. The truth of his boy is standing right here in front of him, only he don't want to see, even if it's to accuse. He don't want to see the mark his son left on me — the old and the new. I want to tell him, *I put your boy down, Otto,* but I don't. I see the man for what he is. No worse, no better than his son. He is the root of the tree he grew.

"You see Alvin, you tell him he done shit in his dinner bucket for the last time. I'm done."

He spits on the ground like he means me harm, but his words go through me.

"I'll do that."

Otto walks out the yard, into the swamp and across the ridge where he come from, passing his own boy's grave with nothing but hate in his heart. I walk to the bottom of the steps and sit. Beside the pump are all the little things the girls found in the swamp since we come here: bones, fossils, glass-colored rocks. Each treasure holds a memory of the girl who found it. Among the bounty is a sand dollar. Alma dug it from the swamp; up along the edge of the yard, the edges burrowed in the clay. She come runnin' from the vines holding it to the heavens asking what it was. It was gray from age, but whole. I told her that it came from the ocean miles away from us.

"How'd it get here, Mama?" she asked.

"Can't say, a bird maybe? Your mamaw's

people were sea island people."

Mama used to talk about the sea and the food that came from it. Said it was a wild and beautiful thing, but not to be trusted. It could pull a man under and drag him out to the heart of it in a matter of minutes. Daddy promised someday to take us, but he never did.

I got to walk through the swamp to see what's become of Alvin. What I hope for and what is might be two different things. I place my hands on my knees and haul my body up. When I am inside the door I pull my dress over my head and retrieve the shotgun from the jamb of the door, stepping outside again where the sun warms my bosom. I will go naked in the heat — I'm Eve in the garden, with a gun.

Most of the ridge is still sunk below water, and a cypress has fallen across the path like a footbridge. On one side water, black as tar, is still. Only mosquitoes break the surface. On the other, where the tree has fallen, vines and moss lie so thick on the water, it looks as if you could step upon it and find solid ground. The ridge can be seen but only barely. Water from either side laps over and settles in the mud of Otto's heavy footsteps. Light plays tricks in the swamp; bits come through the trees like sliced ribbons. The storm's moved every-thing around, but I spy what's left of the nest, half sunk in the risen water, riled from the storm. All that work the mama gator did is gone. I'm not fool enough to think she ain't hiding. She's here somewhere; I just can't see where, not yet.

I hold my hand over my bad eye so the right can get clear of the blur and look over each parcel of swamp one piece at a time. What I am expecting to find, her or Alvin, I can't say. I go slow. Halfway across, caught in the roots of a tree is a piece of red-checkered cloth. Alvin's shirt. Big enough to see if you are heading home from the ridge, easy enough to see if you are looking. I scoot 'round to the top of the ridge and step one foot into the water. It sinks in the mud clear up to my ankle. I grab ahold of a branch above me for balance, then lean out and over the water to fetch the cloth with the barrel of my gun, but I can't reach, so I climb up onto the tree that's fallen. Hold-ing one hand tight around the gun and the other to the bark, I crawl on my belly along the trunk and over the water. The wood scrapes my skin. The trunk gives way some, settling more from my weight, but stays sturdy. I reach out with the barrel of the gun, careful not to drop it in the muck, slide it up under the cloth, then give it a yank and lift. Ripples run over silvery darkness. The water breaks into tiny bubbles across the pool, like it's teeming with fish, only it ain't fish, it's gators. Babies. Nigh on a hundred of them, snapping and swirling like red ants in their nest. Just beyond I spy the mama in the corner of the swamp opposite the ridge. She's sunk low beneath the fallen nest. Her eyes are open and she's lookin' straight at me.

7

RETTA

On Sunday I sent Odell to church alone. I couldn't take that child sick as she was. I knew they'd send someone to speak with me before the day was done. They've all been talking about me taking this child. Worried for my soul, worried for what will become of me and likely worried I've lost my mind. Maybe they're right. I figured they'd send somebody by now, but when Odell got home from church he came alone and all the day went by without a soul at our door. Come dinnertime, after I bathed the child for the third time in as many days, this time cutting her nails and cleaning beneath them, there was a knock at the door. Odell didn't even look up from his chair. That's when I knew he was responsible for whoever was standing on my porch.

When I opened the door I found Preacher there, smiling. He always knows when dinnertime is. We womenfolk laugh about it. He comes 'round each house rotating every evening 'til the month is through and starts in again 'til he's had a visit with all his parishioners. Says he's minding his flock, and I can see how that's true. Everybody gets fed when Preacher's around. He feeds our souls and we feed his belly. He's never come to my door on a Sunday evening 'cause he knows Odell and me look forward to our time alone. I'm his Wednesday. He says I am enough to see him through 'til the end of the week. I do have my questions, and he does know his Bible, so he sees me through, as well.

Preacher's a young man, no more than thirty, and ain't never been married. I can't understand it. He's a good man, handsome, strong and able, a God-loving man. He needs a woman, but he claims the right one ain't come along. He's on God's time, he says, not man's. He come here five years ago from Chattahoochee, Georgia, and works for Mr. Coles during planting and harvest. He minds the church year-round and gets by on what he earns and what we can give.

"Preacher," I said, when I opened the door, "it ain't Wednesday."

He smiled wide. "Sister, we missed you in

church today. Odell said you were otherwise engaged, so I came to pray with you myself before the sun sets down."

"Come on in, Preacher," Odell hollered from his chair. "Retta's fried up a mess of catfish and hush puppies that would shame your mama."

"I can't argue none with that." Preacher laughed. "Everybody knows Sister Retta is the best cook in the county."

Odell laughed, too, and I opened the screen door to let him pass.

Preacher is a friend to Odell. Mama used to tell me, keep your friends young so they won't die off when you get old. Preacher didn't look down on Odell for being the rag-man. To the contrary, he climbed up in the wagon with him and spent whole days riding around counties meeting the folks who work and live there. Preacher said it was because of Odell that folks took to him so easy. But those two did for each other. Odell's become the messenger for Preacher, and Preacher's caused folks to see Odell as a man blessed with the spirit. My husband carries prayer requests from far and wide, and when it ain't harvest or planting time he carries Preacher himself to the people who got nobody else to pray for them. Odell's been to more funerals and weddings than anybody I know, and everybody sends him home with something they want to share. Yessir, Preacher changed Odell's life like only a good friend can.

The child was laid up on the sofa when he come through the door. She finally took food Saturday night. The worms have attached to the excreta. That's a good sign they are moving through her body. I spread a mixture of mashed garlic and Vaseline along her bottom to kill off any eggs. Her fever broke during Odell's time at church. She burst forth a sweat, and when it was through, she had color in her face and could eat some corn bread and cabbage. Even ate a half a peach off the tree outside, but she's a wisp of a thing, so I was on guard for any sign of change for the worse.

All she talked about since she got that nickel was how she couldn't wait to show her mama. I tied it up in a handkerchief so she wouldn't lose it, and she's kept it in her fist ever since. I needed to focus her mind elsewhere, so I found a good stick in the yard, took some old blue yarn Odell was given and showed the child how to crochet. She took to it easy, pulling the thread through loops in an even, straight line while I cleaned catfish for dinner. She has a good head for counting and I told her so. She was on to rows before ten minutes was done. Her crochet and that coin give her more comfort than I ever could.

"Hello, little Miss," Preacher said to the child. She looked up from her crochet and gave him a little wave.

"Let's go in yonder to my bed so you can get your work done," I told her. I laid her against the pillow and put another under her back so she could sit up and work.

Preacher took up our hands after we filled our plates. We bowed our heads together and he prayed, "Thy will be done, on earth as it is in heaven. Amen and let's eat!"

Odell smiled and we passed the food. Wasn't 'til I served myself that Preacher said, "You're burdened this evening, Sister."

"My burden ain't your worry," I said.

"As a Christian your worry is my worry."

"Is getting up in somebody's business without them asking you the Christian thing to do?"

Odell sat up straight and said, "Retta."

"No, no," Preacher said to Odell, "that's fine."

He put his fork down and laid his hand upon the table before he turned to me and said, "Jesus witnessed to anyone He had the chance to because He knew His time was limited. His love was such that He was called to do so."

"That's right," Odell said.

"Being a meddlesome Christian ain't Christian, it's hypocrisy."

"No now, Retta, stop. That ain't right," Odell said.

Preacher took up my hand and I allowed him.

"Sister," he said, "I try not to break the laws of Christianity, but I am a mortal man. I have broken the laws more than I want to confess, even when it wasn't my intent. If I have offended, I hope you will forgive me. I am here as friend and pastor."

I understood what I didn't before. Preacher didn't come to admonish, he come in support. Nobody will go against Preacher.

What could I say except, "I guess there ain't no hypocrisy in truth."

Odell let out a breath. There was a sudden ease in the room, like the sweetest of summer breezes, the old air washed clean.

"I've taken on too much worry," I confessed.

"The Lord gives us strength."

I looked to Odell with the pain of all the years and told him, "I don't have it. Not for what I fear is coming."

Preacher asked, "Ephesians 6:11 says

what? It says, put on the whole, what? Huh?"

"Put on the whole armor of God," I said.

"That's right, so that ye may stand against the wiles of the devil. For we wrestle not with the flesh and blood, but against principalities, against the rulers of the darkness in this world, against spiritual wickedness in high places."

"I try," I said.

"You do more than try. You do. And you keep on doing. That is your promise to the Lord. And what is His promise to you, Retta, huh?"

I could not speak. I was afraid if I did that the world would swallow me. I could only shake my head for fear of being eaten. Odell reached across and took my other hand, but I couldn't open my mouth, so he said it for me. "He promises to carry our burden for us when it gets too great."

Preacher smiled. "That's right. Ain't that right?"

I pack two balls of blue yarn in a small bag and give it to the child to carry for our morning walk. She says she's making a blanket for her mama. That will be her task for the day while I get my work done. We step out to the porch and down the steps

111

into the morning. Mrs. Walker stands in the lane like she always does, waiting for the day to come. She turns her head and sees me with the child and smiles. Mabel is on the corner, too, waiting in the dim light, for me, for a story, but I don't look her way. She's always got something to say even when there's nothing worth saying.

The child wants to walk some today, and I'm in no mood for socializing, so we cut through the woods by Shake Rag so I can bypass the lane. I forgot how the energy of a child on the mend is like an animal coming out of hibernation. She moves slow but with new eyes. We walk through a patch of milkweed so thick we both get a fit of sneezes. I carry a stick to knock the spiderwebs from the path that have grown mightily overnight. The sun is peeking over the top of the land, so the stick finds what the brightening sky don't reveal.

"We got us a jungle today," I say.

The child looks around scared like something's going to jump out from behind a tree. She raises her arms to be carried, and I lift her. I talk as we walk to get her mind ready for the day ahead, telling her she's got to work hard if she plans on getting the blanket done. I remind her that tomorrow is only one more sleep at my house and then her mama will be here to fetch her so she's got to keep her mind on her work. She gives a little jump in my arms.

"If Mr. Coles wants to show you the barn where the animals live, what you gonna say?" I ask. But she pays me no mind. There's a nickel in her pocket and the dream of a blue blanket finished and wrapped around her mother. She's so full of them two things she can't hear no more. She's lost in the promise of tomorrow, and though I should, I cannot take that from her.

Once inside my room at the Coleses' house, our room now, I settle the child on the bed and draw the curtains. Harvest for tobacco is finished and done, but there's still men working about the place. I got no time to worry for this child. She has to care for herself, and I tell her so.

Before I go, she says, "Miss Retta, do you think if I make my mama this blanket she'll see how good I am?"

"Your mama knows you're good, child. She told me that herself."

She nods her head but don't say nothin' back. This time I take no chance and lock the door behind me. Mr. Coles is first to the kitchen. He pours his coffee and tells me Miss Annie wants grits. Mr. Coles hates grits. Says they're nigger food, but Miss Annie likes the way I do them with butter and bits of bacon. I set the pot of water to boil, and he don't say nothin' more. I don't know I'm holding my breath 'til he's gone.

Nelly shows up at the back door shortly after. Nelly is an Indian girl who comes every year at harvest and helps me Monday through Friday with kitchen work. She stays with me all the way through Camp and has for the better part of eight years. I'm too old to do it all alone. When she showed up in July of this year, she was heavy with child.

"When?" I asked.

"Two months, maybe more."

"Is this good by you?"

She smiled and covered her mouth — she don't like that she's missing teeth — and said, "Yes'm. It's good by me."

Nelly and her people are Catawba and live way back in the woods, where they keep to themselves except at harvest time when they all come out to work. Nobody knows the footpath through the trees except her people. They got a whole tribe back there and don't like strangers coming up on them without being asked. I've been there many times. I delivered Nelly when she was born and all her brothers and sisters, ten in all. Nelly's mama, Adoette, I call her Ado, has learned from me how to help with births. Now that I am old, she's taken up delivering babies in my place. After Camp in October, I don't see hide nor hair of Nelly for over nine months, but I never have to send for her; she always knows exactly when to come.

When she comes through the door this morning Nelly sets to work like only a twenty-two-year-old can. She's wrung the necks of five chickens, dipped them in boiling water and has all the feathers plucked before I can say my full Christian name three times. By eleven o'clock I got three cast-iron skillets filled with fried chicken. Nelly's shucked the corn and peeled and sliced all the cucumbers and tomatoes by the time I finish rolling out the dough and putting the cobblers together, two blackberry and two peach. We got to feed a dozen men at noon. Nelly never learned to read nor write, but she is a hard worker, and I am glad for her company. Before Camp begins, Nelly and me will have canned and jarred every vegetable in the fields, made jelly and preserves from all the fruit we can find — peach, grape, blackberry, apple and fig — and put up enough walnuts and pecans to last through winter. She knows where my hands are going before I do.

Nelly is wiping up the flour from the counters, and I'm draining the chicken, when we hear a bang from my room. She looks like a ghost has crawled up behind her.

"It's nothing," I tell her, and slip the key from my apron pocket while she goes to set the table.

Inside the room, the slop jar is toppled. Urine and excreta have spilled along the floor and rug aside the bed. The child's skirt is up. She yanks it down and scoots to the corner, staring at the open window. The curtains are parted. She cries out, "I'll be good, I'll be good."

"Stop that cryin, ain't nothin' a mop and bucket can't fix."

She does as I say but trembles all over. I walk to the windows to close the curtains and see Mr. Coles walking away from us toward the men who are coming in from the fields. They surround the pump, taking turns washing, three at a time, and part for Mr. Coles as he approaches.

"Put on the whole of God's armor," is what Preacher said.

After Mr. Coles bends down to wash his face and hands with the soap I laid out this morning for just such cause, his oldest son, Eddie, hands him a towel. He stands, puts his face to the sky and wipes it dry.

So that ye may stand against the wiles of the devil . . .

When he finishes with the towel, he lays it around the top of the pump and steps aside, making room for the others.

For we wrestle not with the flesh and blood . . .

They clamor about to finish so they can get to their meal. The one I have made. These are hungry men.

. . . but against principalities, against the rulers of darkness in this world.

Mr. Coles looks toward the window where I stand. His eyes fix to mine, and I pull the curtains shut. On the windowsill sits a brand-new shiny nickel.

II

8

ANNIE

A tire on the automobile went flat on my way to the train station this morning. I must have run something over, but I've no idea what. Stranded on the roadside I found myself up against time without a soul in sight. I had a choice: go forward and meet my son or go back for help. I left the automobile tilted sideways on the grass by the roadway and set off on foot. The train station isn't far, but I am not as quick-footed as I used to be, and the month of August is not to be toyed with. More than one person has suffered from heat stroke in these parts this time of year. So many trees have been excavated for the road the sunshine has become more than just a menace; it's become a danger. I likely would have missed the train altogether had Dr. Southard not come along in his carriage.

"Is there a reason you are out walking in

the hottest part of the day?" he stopped to ask, looking at me as if I'd grown another head. I was so flustered that my manners escaped me, and I climbed into his carriage and directed him to the train station without so much as a please or thank you. He reached back and pulled the bonnet of the carriage up for shade and put his horses to a trot. The wind resuscitated me, and we made it with time to spare.

Lonnie was pacing on the platform. Even from afar I could read his anxiety. He insisted on being absurdly early. I told Edwin I was taking the train up to Columbia to visit a friend. It was a harmless lie. Two hours up and back, we'll be home in no time and surprise him if and when we have success. Victory will change how he sees his son. Edwin is embarrassed to have Lonnie working in a sewing factory and is determined, still, after all these years, to make a man of him. What my husband doesn't yet know is the Sewing Circle is on track to become a real influence in the county. I may not live to see it flourish in the way I believe it can, but Lonnie will. He will solidify the Circle's foundation for success. Expand or die, that's what the politicians say. I posted that exact phrase above the desk in the office so Lonnie can see it every time he enters, and I do believe it's helped. In the end Edwin will see what I see. Our son is a force who's been hiding in plain sight for years.

The train station sits empty, save Lonnie and me. No one comes and goes to the city in off hours this time of year. It's harvest season, and there's too much work to be done. Retta's prepared pralines for the journey, Sarah's favorite. I hope Sarah will be accepting of my showing up unannounced. I never should have let our resentment grow. Positions are taken, lines are drawn, and before you can think again, time is gone. I've withheld myself from who and what I love, my daughters and Charleston. We shall make up for the loss. That is my hope.

Otis McEntyre takes my money at the window without looking to see who is purchasing the tickets. The only time that man lights up is when supply trains make their run through the station. Then he jumps from his seat and races outside to count each boxcar, proclaiming in the end, to no one but himself, the exact number of cars the engine pulls. "Imagine that," he says every time. No matter the number, he is astonished as if it's the first time he's seen it. Give him a machine over a person any day of the week.

Lonnie excuses himself to the men's room while I purchase box lunches and two bottles of Coca-Cola at the counter for the train ride. His stomach is upset. He claims it's something he ate, but I know better. He's mopping sweat from his brow and sighing heavily. He'll be fine once he gets to the other side of his mission. It's the shift into the unfamiliar that is always the hardest. I'm forced to knock on the bathroom door when the train pulls into the station. Lonnie comes out wiping his mouth with his handkerchief.

"Really, Lonnie," I say, "you're just making it worse for yourself."

He ignores my comment and gives me his arm. Despite his discomfort, he cuts a handsome figure. He's dressed impeccably in a green-and-white-striped seersucker suit he designed and made. Seersucker was originally only used and worn by the poor people of the region, but Lonnie liked the fabric, and in an act of what he calls reverse snobbery, he designed an elegant men's summer suit. "Let the poor lead the way for a change," he said. The tightly fitted jacket with a high pinched waist and narrow shoulders fits beautifully. He's wisely chosen suspenders and a bow tie that were purchased at Berlin's when he was a younger man, proving that the right accessories never go out of style. He looks like his father, and I can't understand why he doesn't have women fawning over him. His speech affliction has held him back in every way, but afflictions mustn't be death sentences.

The car is virtually empty of passengers, save two men and a woman traveling, it seems, together. Lonnie sits in the bench seat across the aisle from me to practice his script. He doesn't want to rehearse aloud; it makes him more self-conscious. Once we're settled I undo myself. It's such a relief to take off the hat and gloves. Appearances are so bothersome. There was a time I didn't have to work so hard to maintain them; youth has its own simple value that we never fully appreciate until it's gone. I had many proposals when I was young, but said yes only to Edwin. Now I am Dear or Madam, the words of people who look through instead of at.

"Drink the soda," I say to Lonnie from across the aisle. "It will help."

I sip the cold liquid to calm the butterflies in my own stomach and focus on the pictures of the outside world as they pass by my open window. I always loved trains, their roar, their might and speed. I never grow weary of it. We will be in the city in two hours' time, and I shall relish every moment.

My very first train ride was at the onset of the Civil War, when Papa came to retrieve my brothers and me. He was traveling back and forth from Charleston to Manhattan for his textile trade while we, his children, stayed in the city of our birth, cared for by our mother's spinster sister. His plan was to spirit all of us away at night, but Auntie refused to go north out of principle and was so heartsick over me going that she hid me in the laundry hamper so Papa couldn't find me. I'll never forget the anger on his face when he finally discovered my hiding place. He carried me, running, with my brothers at his side, through the crowded station. We arrived in the last few minutes before the train left. I was six years old. Most of the time we lived in New York, that loud and wretched city, but we spent some years away on ocean liners, traveling with Papa for business throughout Europe and Asia. Seasickness plagued me, but even that I would have endured if it meant going home. Finally, six years later, when I was twelve, Papa permitted me to return to Charleston. My brothers chose to stay and seek their fortunes alongside Papa, but not me. All that time we lived in New York and on ships I longed for space. I longed for the Carolinas.

By the time the train rolls into the Charleston station Lonnie is pale, and neither of us has touched our food. He's gotten himself so worked up it takes him a good thirty minutes to hire a carriage.

"Do you need a shot of whiskey to steel yourself?" I ask.

"No," he says, "I just w-wish I w-was a different kind of m-man."

"Well, you're not. You are your own man. Let the work speak for itself, and for God's sakes, breathe. They are just people. The Berlin boy's father came here with $1.83 in his pocket and began this very store until eventually his sons took up the business. They are no different than us."

He nods his head and goes back to his script. I leave him to his thoughts so I can gather my own, and as the carriage turns down King Street, I gaze out the window to see if there is anything left of what I remember from my youth.

Oh, Charleston. If the South has grown weary of discontent, you would never know once you set foot in this city. In spite of the ever-growing population and increasing automobiles zipping along the streets, I still recognize every landmark, every tree and every tombstone. There is Kerrison's, where Auntie bought my first pair of heels, and Colton's, the old pharmacy with the sign shaped like a thermometer. I've stayed away too long. Spite has stolen years from me. The church bells strike two as the carriage arrives in front of Berlin's on the corner of King and Broad. It's a lovely store, with all the latest men's fashions in the window. Lonnie's eyes light at the sight of the colorful summer suits that adorn the mannequins. We make plans to meet back at the train station at five o clock.

"Promise to have a good story to tell me," I say.

I watch my son straighten his shoulders and stride into the store carrying the shirts he's designed. He doesn't look back.

At my behest the driver takes me down Broad Street and around the Battery so I may take in the sights. The beauty is undeniable. When I returned to Charleston as a girl, the city lay in ruins, but even the crumbling rubble couldn't hide its treasures. Back then, the scars along Broad and Meeting Streets were powerful reminders of what we human beings are capable of doing to one another. Buildings were in shambles, and wounded soldiers in ragged uniforms loitered on corners, hungry or seeking money for the long journey home. No one would believe me now if I attempted to describe how badly the city was torn asunder, although there are a few photographs that exist as testament to my memories. Only the homes in the center of the Battery neighborhood lay intact, as if a secret pact had been made by both the Union and Confederacy to protect them.

The driver stops in front of the house where I grew up, and I pay him for his services. I'll walk from here. My childhood home was within the Battery and, so, survived. It was used late in the war as Union headquarters for officers. After returning I recall remnants of their presence throughout, small things, spectacles, a button from a uniform. I ran from room to room, lying in the middle of each with my arms and legs outstretched. In the drawing room Auntie placed Papa's pipe on the end table, just as it was before we left, and in the drawer the tobacco he allowed me to pack it with. Noise from one side of the house to the next was virtually undetectable. I couldn't hear Auntie in the kitchen talking to the help. I couldn't hear the boys in the street playing baseball. I could only hear what was present in the room I was in: my breath, the ticking clock and my footsteps on the wooden floors. I was so happy. I always longed for quiet, even as a child.

I peer from the street through the wrought-iron gates and into the windows, but no one looks to be home.

"Can I help you?"

An old Negro man in overalls steps out from behind the hedges. In his hands is a large pair of shears. I'm startled, and he apologizes for frightening me.

"I used to live here as a child," I tell the man. "The Anderson family?"

He shakes his head. "No, ma'am, can't say I know them. The Maybank family lives here now, but there ain't nobody home. They go over to the Blue Ridge Mountains this time of year on account of the heat."

What else is there to say? I am forgotten here. Walking the streets, I resist the urge to grab a stranger, tell her my name and ask if she knows who I am. Surely someone will remember me. *Move on,* I tell myself. *Gird your loins, buck up, do what you came to do.*

Sarah and Molly live a block from one another, and only two from where I grew up. It comforts me they have each other. Being the only girl in my family I always envied my friends who had sisters. Sisters share secrets. My girls were always close, sometimes to a fault. When three are together there is always an odd man out, and I seemed to serve that purpose as the only other female in the home, predominantly in their teenage years. My goodness, there were months coming home from the Circle where I steeled myself against what I knew was coming. I always assumed Molly would outgrow her contentious phase, but time seemed only to exacerbate. Sarah was much more malleable but only when her sister wasn't around.

Sarah's house is on East Battery, and Molly's is around the corner on East Bay. Each home faces the Charleston Harbor.

Sarah was so sweet when I finally worked up the nerve to call on Saturday. I was both terrified and delighted when she answered.

"Mother?" she asked upon recognizing my voice. "Is everything all right?"

Hearing her stirred me. It's a strange thing to hear your daughter's voice for the first time after so many years. When Edwin threw them out of the house in the heat of that terrible argument so many years ago, all Sarah said, as her sister and father raged, was, "Mother, please," over and over again, "Mother, please," as if I could stop what was already in motion. Looking back I wonder if I could have. Buck's death hurt us all in ways I still can't understand.

"No one is dead," I said, "if that's what you're asking."

I wanted to tell her the fairy kingdom is thriving, that the lavender is back in the south field and you can smell it as you come around the bend for a good half mile before you arrive, how some things even boll weevils cannot destroy. I meant to say how this summer the fairies were out in droves looking for her and Molly, that the fireflies were so thick in the forest behind the slave quarters the woods practically glowed in the dark of the new moon, but my tongue grew thick and I didn't know if she would remember the whimsy of her youth. Instead I asked after her health and that of her sister's.

She asked about the fruit trees. When each child was born I planted a fruit tree; Sarah was my plum. Before I could ask about Camp, Edwin came in from the fields unexpectedly. I asked if we could speak again. She hesitated, but I promised to call the following day and hung up before she could say no. I never told Edwin. He's as hardened against them as they are to us. It will take time to heal the hurt. But we can heal. We can be a family again. I'm convinced.

We spoke once more. I haven't brought up old wounds nor has she. I've learned a bit more of Sarah's and Molly's lives. Molly is still employed and earning a decent salary, though her husband is wealthy and they don't need the money. Her husband doesn't mind and is even encouraging, but that is all Sarah has told me. Though she never said it outright, I could read between the lines. Molly has no interest in speaking. Perhaps seeing me will diminish her resolve, as I know how the mere thought of seeing Molly diminishes mine. I am her mother, after all.

Sarah is married to a prominent man and sees to a large home. She has a full staff, though she says none can cook like Retta. Retta gave Sarah all of her favorite recipes when she first moved to Charleston, but Sarah says none of her cooks can prepare them properly. She wrote how to make each dish word for word, but it wouldn't have mattered for all she understood of them. She still tells the cobbler story.

"Get yourself some peaches," Retta told her.

Sarah asked, "How many peaches?"

Retta said, "Depends on how much cobbler you want."

Sarah wrote it all down anyway, trying at

least to capture the ingredients if not their quantities, but lost all hope when they got to the crust.

"Pour your flour in a bowl," Retta said.

"How much flour?"

"Depends on how much cobbler you got."

Oh, how I loved hearing Sarah tell that story again. Her imitation of Retta is gold.

"I must see you soon, sweetheart. Let's make a plan," I said.

"Let's wait and see, Mother. Let's go slow."

"Yes, yes of course. We'll go slow."

Go slow. Impossible. I've wasted so much time already. Going slow could mean a death sentence before this is rectified, and I'm not prepared to die without my girls. No. Slow is no longer an option. Not with the days ticking by as they do. Yesterday it was Christmas. Tomorrow it will be summer again. We cannot afford patience. I may be seventy, but I still have the mantle of age and perspective to offer my children. She needs to listen to her mother. I finally take myself in hand and do the thing I've avoided for hours. I knock on my daughter's door and pray she will not reject me.

A Negro girl, no more than twenty, answers. She is dressed in a black maid's uniform and white apron, and is surprised to see me.

"Yes, ma'am?"

"I'm looking for Sarah Abbott. Is she in? I am her mother."

The girl's eyes grow wide. "She's not here, ma'am. She walked over to Miss Molly's house. You know where that is?"

A cargo ship coming into harbor blasts its horn, and I jump for the unexpected noise.

"I'm sorry. I've traveled a long way and would love a glass of water. May I come in and sit down?"

"Ma'am, I can get you that water, but I can't let you in. I would if Miss Sarah was here, but I can't without her permission."

"That's fine, just water then."

I sit on the porch step and look out at the sea where Fort Sumter lies empty in the distance. Black cannons along the Battery face the fort. The briny smell of the ocean remains the same and I am transported back to days where I would sit on the balcony outside my bedroom, listening to the waves lap the shore. There is comfort in the constant coming and going of the tide. The front door opens and I turn for my water. Instead a child stands barefoot on the porch. She's no more than eight. Her blond hair is loose about her shoulders and her countenance is that of a serious child, one who observes. She is a miniature replica of Sarah at that age.

"Hello," I say. "And who are you?"

"Emily."

"What a beautiful name. Emily was my mother's name. Is Sarah your mother?"

The child nods her head, my daughter's daughter.

"I brought pralines for your mother. They are her favorite. Would you like some?"

"No, thank you," she says.

"I'm Annie, your mother's mother. Do you know what that means?"

She doesn't.

"That means I am your grandmother."

"No, my grandmother's dead," she tells me. "Mother said."

The maid returns to the porch with water in a beautiful crystal glass.

"Emily Ann," the maid tells her, "you know you ain't supposed to be out here with no shoes on."

The child scurries back inside. I stand, take the glass from the girl and drink every drop of water. I was so thirsty. I hadn't realized until now just how much. Sarah's maid offers to telephone Molly, but I decline. I thank her for the drink and steady myself on the rail.

On the street, I hire a carriage to take me

to the train station. The smell of gasoline from automobiles coupled with the stench of horse manure sours my stomach. I arrive to the station early. Dropping the pralines in the rubbish bin, I sit on the bench to wait for Lonnie and watch the trains as they come and go. An hour or so later, he comes running down the platform empty-handed and flushed with excitement.

"One hundred shirts, M-Mother," he says. "Berlin's wants one hundred shirts f-for their stores in Charleston and Chicago!"

He throws his arms around my shoulders; so happy he doesn't notice my gloom.

The conductor cries, "All aboard."

Lonnie helps me up the steps and down the aisle to a seat by the window, then hands the tickets to the conductor. He sits alongside me and stammers through his victory while I pretend to listen. It's the end of a workday, so the car is full of people returning home to their families, they will all be home in time for supper. The train gathers momentum and pulls out of the station. Oh, I've left my hat in the carriage. But never mind, who cares about an old woman's naked head? Pretense, at this age, is long gone.

9

GERTRUDE

There's no shade to shield me from the sun as I walk the short cut to Branchville along the railroad tracks, but no matter, the true heat of the day is almost gone. The sun is low in the west while the moon has already risen in the east, like one is chasing the other around the sky. Soon it will be dark, but I know the way. I got my gun and as much as I can carry folded up in a sheet slung over my shoulder. A cast-iron skillet beats against my hipbone with every step. There'll be a bruise there by morning.

I want my brother. Get to Berns is all I could ever think of when I was hurt or needed something. I always knew if I was with him he would help me best he could. I want him now. I can confess to Berns, and he will help me like he always has. When I was little he let me run along after him. He'd be in the fields working, and I'd be alongside him asking so many questions that he finally said he needed quiet to think. One time, not long after Mama took sick, I asked what he was thinking on, and he told me what was on his mind.

"Everything has the pull of gravity," he said. "The bigger the mass, the bigger the pull. That's why the sun is so strong and why it pulls all the planets around in its orbit. And the earth has a gravitational pull that causes the moon to orbit around it, and the moon's gravitational pull is so strong it moves the tides."

I asked him what that had to do with what he was thinking about, and he said, "It makes me wonder about people and if we pull things around and into us, into our orbit."

"Like a magnet?" I asked.

"Yes," he said, "like a magnet."

"Maybe that's how prayer works," I said. "Like a magnet that pulls good to bad."

He looked at me then like I was somebody new to him. Not just his little sister, but somebody with thought and wonder just like him. After that he took to telling me things he thought I should know. Berns never lied to me or I to him, even for a joke.

The sun is long down when I come up through the woods, but the waning moon lights my path. Dishes clank in the distance, and with my good eye, I see Edna and Lily by the pump cleaning the supper dishes. Once past the outbuildings I can make out Alma through the window wiping down the kitchen table. Even from here I can tell the weary has left. All she needed was food. I come upon Berns standing outside the barn looking into the sky. He looks so tired. He don't sleep like he should.

"Everything where it should be up there?" I ask.

He jumps, surprised to be caught.

He looks me over and asks, "Where's Mary?"

"Left her with Old Black Retta on Friday," I tell him.

"Mary's in Shake Rag?"

"I'll get her back tomorrow."

"Gertie."

"Berns don't, not now."

He looks to the sky and lets go a heavy sigh. If Mary troubles him, what I've got to say will keep him from a lifetime of sleep. I got to dole this out in pieces. At the kitchen table I tell my girls to gather 'round. We sit in a somber circle. The lantern at the center of the table casts yellow light and shadow over the room and all their faces. Berns and Marie stand side by side leaning backward against the kitchen counter. He's got his hand covering hers and both their legs are crossed at the ankle in the same direction. Outside, the whip-poor-wills call. Autumn is coming. In a few weeks' time it will be nesting season.

"Your daddy is gone," I tell my girls. "He's left and ain't coming back."

"Good," Lily says.

"Where'd he go, Mama?" Edna asks.

"Don't know but we're on our own now, and we got to make good. I got a decent job and a place for us to live right here in Branchville."

Alma busts into tears.

"Don't cry at the supper table," Lily tells her sister.

Alma wipes her face with the back of her hand, but she can't stop crying, so I pull her to my lap.

"Everybody's got to work if we mean to eat. Berns, Marie, I thank you for what you done for us. I hope we can do for you one day."

Marie sits and joins our circle, but Berns hangs back, watching. I look up and meet his eye 'til he looks away and out the back door. Marie reaches across the table to hold Edna's and Lily's hands and smiles like there's something she's just remembered to

141

say. Marie would've been a good mother. Better than me.

She says, "Hearsay in town that the rains this past Saturday got so bad they flooded all the old slave cabins over at the Magnolia plantation. Hearsay folks had fish swimming in their parlor."

Berns claps his hands and says, "Noooo."

Marie shakes her head with conviction. "Yes. That's what they said down at the railroad station. Old boys in town say they overheard the passengers talking about it while they were coming up from Charleston. Said the river left its borders."

"Fish swimming in the parlor! Imagine that!" Edna says and starts a fit of laughter so hard that everybody can't help but join in. Her mirth is contagious. Lily makes a fish face and that starts everybody up again. Even Berns laughs.

"You girls run outside and catch lightning bugs while I talk to your mama," Marie says.

That's where she don't know children, only Alma and Mary still chase the light because they're young. The older girls got no interest, but they go anyhow, happy to be on their own. Berns walks to the hearth and pulls down his rifle from where it hangs above the mantel. I want to tell him not to worry, but I don't.

Before he gets out the door I say, "I got to take Edna to the swamp with me tomorrow to round up what's left."

"How much you got left to carry?"

"Two loads of kitchenware and linens."

"Leave Edna. I'll come with you."

"We can do it without you, Berns. Ain't no need to leave your work."

He looks at me and says, "Alvin comes home and finds you two leaving he'll kill you both. We'll leave at dawn."

Before I can say anything more he's out the door. Marie fixes me a cup of coffee like I'm company, and I welcome the bitter.

"How's your eye?"

"I can't see out of it yet, but I expect it'll be all right."

"You going to be able to see to sew?"

"I can see to walk. I guess I can see to sew."

"You sure he's gone?"

"Time will tell, I reckon, but I believe we've seen the last of him."

Berns's weakness for me is a worry for Marie, though she ain't ever said so. Back in the day he used to talk more, but the older he's got the more he's gone quiet. Why that is I can't say, but I can guess. Marie knows how to draw him out and give comfort. She will tell Berns what I said. He'll sleep.

Me and the girls lie on a pallet in my old bedroom. Alma lays up next to me long into the night. Neither of us can sleep with all that's happened.

"Mama," she whispers after Edna and Lily have fallen off to sleep. "I ain't crying 'cause Daddy's left. I'm crying 'cause I'm glad he's gone. That's a sin. Will I go to hell?"

"No. One sin ain't bad."

I wrap my arms around her until finally we sleep.

Berns ain't never seen the place where we live. It's the backside of nowhere, and I am ashamed to show it. When we moved to the swamp, Alvin forbade my brother to come visit, so I told Berns to stay away for fear of what Alvin might do. Berns heeded the warning, but he wrote me regular and made me write back, so he wouldn't worry. At Christmas they sent along a little package with candy and soaps Marie made for the girls. No matter how many of them letters Alvin got to first, I never stopped looking for them, and they never stopped coming. I do believe they were intended for Alvin, too, as a reminder somebody was watching. Somebody cared.

Berns and me don't talk the whole way to the swamp. I wish he would say something, so I can say my piece, but he don't, so we walk in silence. We come through the swamp barefoot and quiet so the wildlife don't know to hide. It teems all around. The ridge is clear today, a big difference even from yesterday. I walk ahead of my brother through the vines and across the path. Two baby gators sit atop the same tree I crawled up not two days ago, sunning in a strip of bright light. It ain't 'til we are upon them that they turn and leap into the water. I point, though I know Berns likely already spied them. He was taught to see the land, same as me. Daddy's blood runs through both of us. When we come to the clearing, he looks at the house and says, "This it?"

"This is it."

He walks to the pump, pulls a long drink, then soaks his head in the cold stream of water, and I do the same. Berns climbs the stairs behind me and comes through the screen door. I got what's left of what we own tied up in two quilts ready for the journey.

He stops at the door and looks around. I see my mistake. I've scrubbed us of this place. Alvin's nowhere to be seen. Berns knows, same as me, sometimes what ain't there is as telling as what is.

"How many times in all these years you reckon he hit you?" he asks.

"One too many," I say. I take hold of a quilt, throw it over my shoulder through the loop and heft it up with my right hip, but Berns don't move, just stands there popping his knuckles on both hands.

"You know where he went?" he asks.

My brother is asking a question. He'll ask once, but not again. What I thought would be easy, ain't.

"Don't know. Don't care."

He nods his head a slow yes before crossing the room and bending to pick up his load. When he straightens, his eyes are filled with unshed tears, and I'm sorry, sorry my soul is added to his fret, but before I can say so, he says, "Let's go," and leads me from this place.

We go back along the footpath, over the ridge and through the swamp like we just done, like I done days before, like my husband done every day since we first moved here. There was some kind of promise then, of steady work, if nothing more. That's all gone now.

The cicadas and bullfrogs holler their chorus. Once we get to the other side of the swamp to the main road where the railroad

146

tracks begin, I lay my burden down to catch my breath. I can't help but look back. I can't say what I'm looking for. I can't say what I'm thinking. I'm just looking, caught in a river of thoughts so deep I can't pull out 'til I hear Berns say, "Leave it be, Gertie. That's dead and gone."

Dead and gone, dead and gone. I heft up my load and follow my brother on home.

10

RETTA

Mrs. Walker's in the lane this morning and I'll be damned if Sugar ain't by her side. The dead and the living right next to each other like it was an ordinary day. Sugar pecks around her feet like she is a tree for shade. It's a powerful thing to need a friend when you can't have her. There's things that can only be shared among women, things menfolk want to fix but can't, things too late for fixing. Mrs. Walker might say different, but she wouldn't offer no suggestions as to the how of the fixing. She'd just lend her ear to the problem at hand.

Mrs. Walker come to town just two years after my Esther died, some nineteen years ago. Word followed that her husband killed a man in a fishing camp over a plate of food. Knifed him with the blade he used to clean fish. She told me after he got home she caught him around the side of the house washing the blood from the knife. He handed her the string of fish and walked past her like nothing happened. After he got sent away to prison, she was alone in the world and not of her own volition. Nobody talked to her and nobody helped her, so she had to leave that life. When a woman marries and takes her husband's name she is forever bound by his action and not her own. It ain't right, but that's the way it is. When Mrs. Walker got here, every white woman in town stuck their nose up at her. I said "how do" first time she moved into that house across from Shake Rag, and she always spoke back.

One evening she was sitting up on the porch and hollered out, "What's your name?"

"I'm Oretta Bootles."

"Oretta, why don't you come and sit a spell? Have some sweet tea?"

I told her no, thank you, I had to get home to my husband. I was thinking I can't be seen sittin' on no porch with a white woman sipping tea, what would people say? There was a time I worried about that, but no more. She asked regular and one spring day I said, "Don't mind if I do."

There was no harm in the woman. She welcomed me to her porch and then to her kitchen for sweet tea and coffee. I never been to Charleston but when she talked, it came alive in my head. She said the bells from the churches on Sunday morning called to one another like mockingbirds for a full thirty minutes before services. As soon as I started living with the expectation of having a friend by my side through old age, I found her dead on the kitchen floor. Now the whole world is upside down in thought and action, and my days are filled with worry about what I can't see that's waitin' around the corner.

By the time I get Odell out the door and clean the dishes, Mary still hasn't stirred. I forgot how hard it is to rouse a tired child. She sucks her two middle fingers when she sleeps. I hate to wake her, but the day presses. I found a nightgown and some underthings of my daughter's that I kept stored, and dressed Mary in them after her bath before bed. I never thought they'd see use again, but I'm glad they have.

Yesterday scared the child. After I drew the curtains shut, she ran to the window and snatched up the nickel before I could gather my thoughts. She clutched it in the same fist that held the other coin and said, "I'm sorry. I'm sorry. I'm sorry," over and over again. The shame in her runs deep. I sat her on my knee, patted her back and looked at the crochet she had done.

"Look at what a fine blanket this is gonna be," I said. She quivered at my touch.

I stilled myself and said, "Mary," and she listened. "Only the finest child could make a blanket like this. This ain't no easy task. You got the gift of crochet."

She listened as I talked. I got her calm, then we both went back to our work. The rest of the day a piece of my mind stayed with her in that room. I've refused to call this child by name since she came into my care, like that would protect me from feeling somethin'. Senseless. Mary is her name and I aim to call her by it.

Mary asks to be carried this morning so I lift her up and set her on my hip. Reminds me of a time long ago. I don't scoot around Mabel today. Got to deal with her sooner or later. Mabel and Mrs. Walker are laid out on either side of a straight line like they're something to choose between. Mrs. Walker's attention is on Mabel, who's digging in her pocketbook for something that must be awful small for the time she takes to find it. Mrs. Walker laughs with her head back like she did when she'd get tickled. She always could help me see Mabel different than I do.

"Gonna be a hot one today," Mabel hollers out. "You'd think now that September is upon us we might have some notion of autumn."

The sun ain't even broke from the horizon, but Mabel fans herself with one of the cardboard fans from the funeral parlor like it's noon. She's got a drawer full of fans from all the kin she's buried these past five years. I reckon I ought to feel sorry for the woman — she's lost two sisters, a brother and a husband — but I can't see how any of them deaths have changed her. I don't know how a soul ain't altered by all that death; Lord knows I am changed by my losses. But not Mabel, she goes on seeing what she wants to see and ignoring what she don't, like me carrying a white child in my arms. Just pretends what's really happening ain't. I never saw anything like it. We take up our walk together side by side toward Mrs. Walker.

"Where is her mama?" Mabel finally asks.

I give Mabel a taste of her own medicine and ignore her. I stop in the lane beside Mrs. Walker, hoping Mabel will move on, but she stops and waits alongside us. Mrs. Walker and I turn toward her house, which sits quiet and dark under tall pecan trees. I stand by my friend and she by me. We got our toes in the yard when the first crack of sun rises from the fields.

"Lookie here, Mary," I say. "This is the house you're gonna be living in after today."

"Another white woman on the corner of Shake Rag? It ought to go to a colored family," Mabel says.

I hold my tongue for the sake of Mary who wiggles with joy, plants both hands on my face and kisses me on the nose like I just gave her the biggest present in the world. Sugar pecks at my ankles breaking the spell, and Mrs. Walker fades into the morning light. I feel her go right through the center of me. Takes my breath away. I shove Sugar in the behind with my foot to get him to move toward home.

"Looks like that rooster don't like your house no more," Mabel tells me.

"Never did."

"Preacher come by Sunday evening?"

"Mmm-hmm."

No sense in lying, she's got eyes in her head. She don't say nothing, just waitin' for me to confess, like she's my sister.

Finally I ask, "What is it you want, Mabel?"

She thinks about it and says, "You got an

open spot down at Camp this year? My niece needs her a job. She's got two young'uns and a husband who ain't got work."

"I don't know yet." That's the truth.

"All right, but if you got needs, you think about her."

I got to think about her niece now, too, a woman with an able-bodied husband? Never mind Mrs. Walker, Mabel is the empty vessel here. No matter how much you do, nothing is ever enough. She is a hungry ghost.

I don't lock Mary in our room today. I remind her of the need for quiet, which is silly given the quiet that already lives in her, but I repeat it anyway 'cause that's what we do with children. Nelly comes to the door an hour early like I told her, and I bring her by her hand into the room. I take up Mary's hand, too.

"Mary, this here is Nelly. Nelly, this is Mary. Nelly's been a friend of mine for all her life. Nelly, Mary has been a good friend to me for three days now. She can crochet better than a grown woman."

Mary holds out the blanket she's worked on so Nelly can see, and Nelly steps forward to look at it, hiding her smile behind her hand. Mary smiles, too, the quickest I've seen her do with anybody yet. We stand in a cluster. I give Nelly's hand a squeeze and she squeezes back. One of us will be by Mary's side until the day is done.

After breakfast, Miss Annie retires to her sitting room upstairs to write out invitations for Camp. She's got a sick headache that even coffee won't cure, so she's stayed home from work. Says she's fine, but she's not. I've known her long enough to read the signs. She's holding her jaw how she does when she's mad, so tight it's no wonder her head hurts like it does.

Eddie tumbles through the door like he's still a boy. He's slight like his brother. They both got full heads of red hair, only where Lonnie is pale and soft, Eddie is muscled and brown from working outside with his daddy. He teases me same as he did when he was a boy and lifts every pot lid to peer under, then snaps at my behind with a dishcloth. You'd think now he's grown he'd quit, but he still dances around me in circles singing the song he made up as a child. *"Butter beans, butter beans, How I love those butter beans, fresh and green, what reigns supreme, is Retta's pork and butter beans."*

Miss Annie delights in his spirit. Around his daddy, though, he's all business, just like Mr. Coles. It's a wonder how a grown man can be one thing one minute and another the next, but he can. Neither he nor Lonnie have brought home a woman they will have, or one that will have them, even with all their money, but Eddie don't seem to mind. I think both boys might be happier with a kind woman by their side, but it ain't my business to say. They seem content living together, just the two of them. I shoo him out to go see his mama. She'll feel better when she sees him.

There's a ham in the oven for supper, and from my room off the kitchen, Nelly peels potatoes to boil for potato salad. She sits with her back against the wall and her feet up on the chair by the bed. Her legs got some swelling in them, and I can see the tired in the girl. Nelly ain't used to hauling around extra weight, and I know the broken veins on her legs got to hurt, but she don't complain. It's good to sit for even part of the day when you're carrying heavy like she is. Mary sits alongside with the yarn between them. When I go to check on them, I pause at the door and listen to Nelly telling Mary a story.

"The bad ones came upon a village with a plan to kill the women. The women knew they must take action so they changed themselves. One woman became a snake, another a gator, and the others changed to

156

birds. They hid and waited. The bad ones got tired of looking and went on their way, leaving the village in peace. The next day all the women came back, and the village had a feast to rejoice in their return."

Mary wonders at the notion of turning into something other than what she is. Children can't see that for every day they are on this earth, they are changing. I suppose God designed it that way to spare us the fear of what change means.

The men have had their heads together in the dining room since supper. Eddie sits next to his daddy at the head of the table. They've been sittin' for near on two hours looking over maps and wagon routes to Florence. No way around the hazards of the journey. They talk about how long it'll take to get through two different swamps — nobody wants to be in those waters after dark — versus the time they lose to skirt them.

"Give me a best- and worst-case time line," Mr. Coles asks two of the men. Four others do arithmetic on paper to see how many wagons they'll need to cart the tobacco to market. The tobacco fella from PeeDee has been here a week to oversee the preparation and trip. Pete from PeeDee, that's what he calls himself. He ain't nothin' more than an old country boy done good. Flue Tobacco's been growing up in Peedee for over five years now, since before the blight. Mr. Coles has been watching them up in the northern part of the state for two of those years. Miss Annie said he walked the house at all hours when the boll weevils come, worried all the time about the next planting season. When Pete from PeeDee wrote and told him bugs don't like tobacco, that sealed the deal. I think he figured — well I know 'cause Mr. Coles and Eddie discussed it regular — that if the state grew enough tobacco it could be rid of the boll weevil population altogether. Chase it on elsewhere like it did when they come up to us from Texas.

Pete used to work at R.J. Reynolds Tobacco, and now leases himself out to help new farmers get into the tobacco market. He's promised a good price if the crop is as good as what they had last year. Said last year's crop was an all-time high; practically double what it was the year before, up from twenty to forty cents a pound. This year, he claims, will be more. If I hear that man say "All-time high," one more time, well . . . He got here a week ago and is staying over at the boardinghouse until it's time to go to market and runs his mouth like nothing I ever seen, asking foolhardy questions no outsider needs to know the answer to. People in town, white and Negro alike, cross the street when they see him coming for fear of having to hear his life story or tell theirs.

When I bring the hummingbird cake and coffee into the dining room, Mr. Coles watches me place them on the sideboard and put out the plates and forks so they can help themselves when they're ready. The table goes silent while I work. I keep my hands steady. Mr. Pete ain't used to that kind of silence.

"Miss Retta," Pete says, "I've eaten the best meals of my life since I got here. Where'd you learn to cook so good?"

I get so flustered I nearly drop the handful of silver I'm holding. Ain't no white man ever called me *Miss* Retta. When I turn to answer, all them men are looking at Pete from PeeDee like he's from a foreign land. The man that don't have enough sense to know not to talk to the Negro help when he is a guest for dinner at a table such as Mr. Coles's. Eddie is about to bust a gut trying not to laugh. Mr. Coles stares for a long hard while before Pete swallows, finally understanding what he didn't before.

Mr. Coles says to me without looking,

"That'll be all, Retta."

I am happy to return to the confines of the kitchen, but the telephone rings in the parlor and Mr. Coles tells me to answer.

"This here's the Coles residence," I say into the speaker.

"Retta, it's Sarah. Is Daddy in the house?"

Oh, I ain't heard her voice in the longest of times. She sounds so proper, I can't believe it's the same child I helped raise.

"He's in the dining room, sweetheart."

"I need to speak with Mother."

"I'll get her for you."

"Who is it?" Mr. Coles hollers from the next room.

Miss Sarah hears and says, "Please, Retta, don't tell him it's me."

"Business for Miss Annie," I holler back.

"Oh, thank you, Retta," she whispers. "I miss you so."

"You just wait right there," I tell her softly. "I'll go and get your mother."

"Yes, all right. Please hurry."

Miss Sarah. I remember that little blond head and those bright blue eyes. She was a sweet little girl, but her loving, kind nature gave way to fear of her own shadow. Miss Molly, though younger, was her big sister's protector. Molly learned from her sister what not to do just as much as she learned

160

what to do. That child wasn't afraid of nothing but her daddy, and she'd even fight him if it were to stand up for Sarah. When I get to Miss Annie's room I find her sitting at the desk staring out the window.

"Miss Annie, Sarah's on the telephone."

She jumps in her chair and turns.

"She's there now?"

"Yes, ma'am."

She sets her mouth in a straight line and rises to her feet. When we get to the parlor she marches to the telephone, picks it up and says, "I have nothing to say to you," and without a single pause, lays the receiver back in the cradle.

"Miss Annie?" I say. "That was your girl, Sarah."

"I'm aware, Retta," she says. "I'm such a fool."

She grabs her head with both hands and sways. I hurry to her side.

"Should I fetch Mr. Coles?" I ask.

"No," she says. "Not a word to him."

I help her back up the steps and get her to the bed. Her color is the same as the white spread she lies against. I place a hand on her head to feel for fever, but she's cool as can be. Cool in this heat. I never felt such a thing.

"Draw the curtains and sit with me, Retta.

Just for a moment. I'll be fine. I just need to rest my eyes."

I set one hip alongside the bed, and she puts her hand in mine and holds it tight, like she needs to be pulled up the mountainside. I rub my thumb slow over the back of it 'til she settles herself and sing the hymn she likes best.

"There is a balm in Gilead, To make the wounded whole, There's power enough in heaven, To cure the sin sick soul."

11

GERTRUDE

When we get to the house I tell Berns to leave our things on the porch so I can sort them. He drops the load he's carried and takes his leave. He will send the girls to me when he gets home. I told those girls there better not be a single chore left for him to do by the time he gets home.

Marie told me Mrs. Walker died on a Monday and that Retta found her, but nobody can say why she was in the house of a white woman she didn't work for. Nobody knows how old Mrs. Walker was when she died, just that she kept to herself at the Sewing Circle. Never put up a fuss, just did her work and went home. Didn't have no living family and paid for her own funeral two weeks before she died, like she knew it was coming. Marie said her death took the wind out of everybody she worked alongside. Reminded them of what's coming.

Mrs. Walker's house is made of gray-and-white clapboard. It's small but sturdy, and sits far enough back from the road that nobody knows your business, but close enough to run for help if you need it. A bright red pump sits outside on the back porch, just steps away from the kitchen door. Water that close can't help but make life easier. Pecan trees are filled with nuts, ripe and close to ready. We got some shucking to do, but there's more than enough. A vegetable patch sits out near the clothesline, but it has been picked clean of beans, tomatoes, peppers and squash. Two ripe watermelons sit in the empty vines. I pick them before the raccoons get them and lay them up by the screen door on the back porch. There may be time enough yet for a small fall crop of potatoes, but only if we get the seed in quick enough. In the middle of the yard sits a green outhouse with a red roof. The inside is clean and without snakes. It's a good yard, well kept and with plenty of possibility.

I carry one watermelon and roll the other with my foot through the back door and into the kitchen. There's a pot of burnt oats on the stove that must be what Mrs. Walker was making when she died. It's a wonder the house didn't burn down. It's a good pan, and I can use it if I can get the burn out. She's got everything here that's needed to start a house. There's flour, lard, cornmeal, dried beans and white rice in jars lined up on the counter. A whole cabinet is filled with canned vegetables, likely what she picked from the garden. There's a full sack of grits and another half sack tied shut with a rubber band. There are three jars each of scuppernong and fig jelly, most likely a trade or gift since they're so few. Mrs. Walker could have survived off what she has here for six months or more, but for us there's enough for a few months. We'll have to add to it to make it through winter but this is more than I seen since I was first married and more than the girls have ever known.

Through the kitchen is a parlor with a wood furnace set against the wall furthest from where I stand. On the end table by an orange sofa sits a package wrapped in brown paper with a note on top that says, "Oretta, I made you this dress. You'll need to take out the hem, but the color will be nice for you."

I undo the string and open the paper. Inside is a navy blue dress made with good quality material. It's got a white collar and pockets. Why wouldn't Retta take the dress after she found Mrs. Walker? Sitting right out in the open, a brand-new dress? That's a curiosity. If she didn't take it, she must not have wanted it.

Beyond the parlor are two small but good bedrooms side by side facing out toward the road. Mrs. Walker's bedroom has a four-poster bed made of oak and a matching dresser with a round mirror. The other bedroom is empty, like it's been waiting for somebody to come along to use. I got the ticking for two more mattresses. We just need the corn shucks to fill them. Lucky for us there will be plenty of those lying in the fields this time of year.

Two more dresses hang in Mrs. Walker's closet, one for work and one for Sundays. They're old-timey, and too big for any one of us, but I could get two, maybe three dresses out of them if I count one for Mary. Mrs. Walker's bed ain't made — like she's just stepped away for her morning chores. There's time and sun enough left for me to wash and dry the sheets if I do it quick before the girls get here. Mrs. Walker slept with a bottom and top sheet so thin they'll dry fast in the late afternoon sun. When I yank them free, there is a wobble in the board beneath my feet. No nails hold down the board, like it's loose on purpose. I lift it, careful of what lies beneath. Snakes, like most evil things, like the cool of under. Below the board is an old wood box with carvings on the sides. There is no lock. When I open the lid I find it empty and wonder for its purpose. I leave it where it was found and place the board back in its home. There's no time to ponder such things. I pull the sheets from the bed and cart them outside to be washed. A cold wash will have to do, though they should be boiled since we don't know what killed her. I lay the wet sheets in the wringer by the tub and turn the handle to squeeze them dry, then pin the sheets to the clothesline. They snap in the breeze.

There is work to be done, but this house will keep us warm and dry in the coming months. The quiet here is like a heavy blanket draped over a mighty object. Even the dark whisperings of my mind are still. This house feels like a reward.

Somewhere nearby, a screen door slams and a child laughs. A whistled tune is carried through the air to my ear as clear as a songbird, though I don't know the melody. I have neighbors near enough for me to hear them and them to hear me. I am all at once reminded of other lives beyond the one I have lived.

12

Annie

I should have kept the girls with us during the summers when they were growing up. If I had put them to work the same as the boys, maybe things would have turned out differently. Hindsight is tricky business. I was naive to think my friend Mirabelle would benefit Sarah and Molly, perhaps add to their education. When she volunteered to have the girls summer in Charleston, I knew she would expose them to the finest music, literature and parties, all the social gatherings I missed as a young girl. Mirabelle was always at the top of our class in school, even beating out the boys. She read every book imaginable — Austen, Twain, Shelley, Brontë, Tolstoy, Dostoyevsky — and read one every two days. Her circle of friends, the ones I inherited through her when I came home, was vast. My daughters loved summers there, but they were altered in

168

those years. The circle of refined and privileged women I grew up with never understood real work. Mirabelle was no different. She grew up kept and remained so even after a late-in-life marriage. She never had children of her own and doted on mine. In truth, I felt sorry for the woman.

"If a man ever marries me, it will be because I win him with my mind," she said often with a sly smile. "We all know what I am not."

She finally married a widower when she was in her late thirties. He was a rich, fat oaf, overindulgent and prone to grandiosity. His vitriolic hatred of "Yankees," as he was wont to say, never fully spilled onto me because of Mirabelle's and my friendship. But she knew what my father was, and still never put a stop to her husband's talk. That should have been the first warning. My mother's Southern heritage saved me from the man's spew, and he treated my girls with courtesy, but touted his opinions with regularity, and I found it troublesome. It was Mirabelle I trusted. It was because of her I allowed the visits to continue for all the summers of their teenage years. They came home with so much, "Mirabelle said this, and Mirabelle did that," that I finally told them over dinner one night, "You do know Mirabelle isn't your mother?"

In the end it wasn't her husband that fanned the flames of rancor, but Mirabelle herself. She knowingly usurped my position. She didn't think I should be working outside the home and said as much.

"A woman's mind should remain purely focused on bettering herself and the lives of her children," she told me with that fake and sticky kindness. "Especially given the circumstances." The circumstances of death she meant. She didn't approve of me working after the death of my son, but what good would I be to anyone sitting around drowning in grief. I like working and am proud of what I have accomplished.

"I'm only thinking of the children," she said, as if she were their mother. When I heard of her death I was glad.

"You've gone quiet," Edwin says as he pushes his plate away. "What's on your mind?" All that remains of the meal he's eaten is the bone from the steak. The man is always hungry at the end of the day. Retta removes the dinner plates to the kitchen. There is a violet haze across the sky that deepens as the sun sinks low. The billowed clouds turn to dark purple bruises across streaks of pink and gold. What's on my mind? Deception and its many faces. My

170

husband is right. I've raised selfish girls.

"This headache has fatigued me, that's all," I respond, though my headache has dissipated. Sustenance has pushed it from the front to the back of my head, and what's left has settled at the nape of my neck.

"Shall we call for the doctor?" he asks.

"No, no," I tell him. "I'll be fine."

It's a moderate night, the mildest we've had in ages. September is always a relief. There is no breeze, but the honeysuckle is still sweet in the air, and the cattle call to one another in the distance. I refer to these late meals as our European dinners. I prefer late suppers in the summertime. They are a peaceful and elegant transition from a day of hard work. But tonight, nothing helps. My mind is fixed in a trap I cannot escape.

"Do you ever wonder why he did what he did?" I ask Edwin.

"Who are you talking of?" he asks.

"Buck."

His face darkens. Retta refills the sweet tea and lays a small plate of lemons by my glass before disappearing back to the kitchen.

"What good can come from this kind of rumination, Mother?"

"Don't you ever wonder?"

"Of course I wonder, but what good does

171

it do? He took that explanation with him, didn't he."

The telephone rings in the parlor, two long bells, but I'm not running to answer as I normally do, and Edwin asks, "Don't you want to get that?"

I can't tell him I have listened to the telephone ring for the better part of the day. I can't say I've avoided answering, that I know who it is and I'm in no mood to hear the story I know has already been manufactured for me.

"It's rung several times this afternoon, but every time I answer, there's no one there," I lie. "I've run myself silly answering the thing and for naught."

He scrapes back his chair and walks to the telephone himself, picks up the receiver and says hello three times before finally hanging up. When he returns to the table, he shrugs his shoulders and I mimic him. Retta cuts a fresh lemon meringue pie and serves the both of us. I tell her to go home, that I'll see to the dessert dishes. She reluctantly acquiesces. Edwin watches me while I eat. The sugar turns my stomach.

"Stop looking at me as if I'm going to implode," I tell him. "It's just the headache talking."

The telephone rings again, and this time

it is me who is up and out of my chair, and across the room. My heart is in my throat when I answer, but it is not Sarah or Molly on the other end of the line; it's the tobacco man, Pete, asking for Edwin. I call for my husband and hand him the receiver. I know from Edwin's countenance the news isn't good.

"Will leaving sooner make a difference?" Edwin asks, turning away from me. I retreat to give him privacy. When the call is complete, he comes back to the table, takes his seat and fishes a cigarette out of his shirt pocket.

"The commodities market is shifting, which could impact the price of tobacco," he finally says. "We have to leave a week sooner than anticipated if we are to be first to market."

We spent a small fortune changing the crop from cotton to tobacco. Just getting the barn ready so the tobacco could cure properly was expensive, let alone the cost of labor to oversee the finicky crop.

"Can you do without Lonnie?" I ask. "We're under deadline."

"For what?" he asks and then listens without expression while I tell him of our son's accomplishments.

When I am finished he exhales a trail of

smoke and says, "So you lied about going to Columbia?"

"I didn't lie per se. We wanted to surprise you."

"A lie is a lie, Mother. Is there anything else you mean to tell me, or is that it?"

"Oh, honestly, Edwin, I thought you would be pleased. It's a financial boost for us. You know how we need the money."

"Good for you then," he says without meeting my eye.

"It wasn't me. Lonnie did this, every bit of it."

"Please, Mother, I know good and well you helped him."

"Only to encourage, Edwin. That's all."

"All right. Good for him," he says, "but he can't stay behind. I need him."

"It's in both our interest to have him stay, Edwin. Surely you can find someone to replace the boy."

"No, Annie," he says, stubbornly. "Have you heard a word I said?"

"Edwin, I'm leaving the Circle to Lonnie. You've got Eddie to help you with the plantation. He'll be running this place when it comes time. Lonnie needs something, too."

He opens his mouth to speak, but I stop him, "Before you fight me on this, you should know I've made up my mind."

He sits back in the chair and takes a long draw from the cigarette before saying, "What about the girls?"

For a moment I'm afraid he knows my secret.

"What about the girls?" I ask.

"You once wanted to leave them the business."

"That's a cruel thing to say."

"I don't know, Mother. One day you miss them, the next you are cutting them out of the Circle. What am I to think?"

"I want Lonnie to have the Circle," I say when I trust myself to speak.

"Our son is a goddamn thumb sucker. You've run that business for thirty years. If you need help, put one of the other women in charge. The boy goes with me."

He stamps his cigarette out in the leftover meringue and gets up from the table. The Circle has long been an unspoken source of conflict for Edwin and me but not because of any outlandish jealousy for my time and attention. Papa provided me a substantial trust and prevented Edwin from touching it, Papa's parting shot to my husband for not following proper channels and asking his consent for my hand in marriage — at least that's what Edwin believes. The trust stipulates I can never leave the money to my husband, only to my children. The slight was surprising, for not once in all of our marriage did Papa show any underlying tension. But it was there all along. Edwin saw what I could not.

The plantation is in the red. With the loss of three straight years of cotton, we've nearly milked our bank account dry. It pained Edwin's pride to ask me for the tobacco money, and, of course, I was happy to contribute. I've never viewed it as my money; it's always been ours. I did what I could without hurting the Circle, and the bank helped with the rest. No one, not even the boys, knows the truth of our financial predicament.

He comes out of the kitchen wearing his hat, the automobile keys in hand. "I'll need every available man I can get if we're to leave within the week. I've got to get the word out tonight."

Loud chirps and the beating of frantic wings interrupt my husband's departure. Two cardinals fly down the steps and through the parlor. They are confused, flying toward and into dusk-lit windows. I hasten to open the front door in hopes they will find their way to the light. Edwin folds a newspaper and stalks them while I try to shoo them to safety. One makes it free to the trees in the front yard, but the other flies back and forth from the dining room to the parlor, and perches on the end table. Edwin corners the animal and in one swift move strikes the creature. He scoops it from the floor in the folds of the paper.

"Is it dead?" I ask, and he opens the paper for me to see. A female cardinal lies between the pages on its side, stunned, one eye blinking.

Edwin carries her to the front porch, and I follow. I always thought of female cardinals, not unlike seagulls, as the unfortunate gender of their species. The males sport such stunning plumage while the females are a dull shade of brown with few sharp features. Seems unfair. Edwin flings her to the yard and returns inside, but I stay and watch as the other bird flies down from a low branch to land beside her friend as if in vigil. Inside the telephone bells ring twice. I listen as Edwin answers. After three escalating hellos he shouts, "Goddammit, stop calling here," and slams down the telephone.

13

RETTA

When Mary and I approach the lane we see that every window of Mrs. Walker's house is open. The chattering of girls reaches our ears long before our feet touch the yard. Mary walks faster, but she don't let go of my hand. A dance of sounds catches my ear, cabinets and doors opening and closing, a tribal beat to an old song I used to know. Gertrude's got them girls working. Every rug's been pulled outside and hung over the porch rail to beat. Every dish from Mrs. Walker's cupboard sits in a basin by the pump ready for wash. The smell of fresh corn bread in the oven comes up through the yard and out to the road. Mrs. Walker's dresses, my friend's clothes and underclothes, her towels and sheets, washcloths and aprons hang out on the clothesline like it's any ordinary day.

Mary hears her kin and hollers out,

"Alma!" And wham, out the kitchen door and off the porch flies a girl twice as tall as Mary, but not much bigger 'round. Mary runs to her sister laughing and tries to knock her down, but the girl just grabs Mary and twirls her around in circles. The rest of the family follows with the screen door swaying between each arm that pushes it open, two more girls, followed by their mother. Her eye still bears the mark of her husband's fist, but the swelling's come down some. There are no fresh marks that I can see. He does not follow nor do I hear his footfall in the house. Maybe he ain't here. Maybe that's why they're so happy? He was a rotten egg from the start, always itching for a fight. Always found something to occupy myself with when I saw him in the street. Most everybody I know did the same. Some meanness you got to steer clear of, otherwise it finds its way to you.

The girls cluster 'round Mary, pulling and tugging, and I watch the bunch of them together. They all got the same straw-colored hair; you'd know they're family if you was to see them in town, together or separate. They're all bone thin, and not a one of them has shoes. They'll have a time of it come winter. I'm meddling now, looking on too long, at what no longer concerns me.

Gertrude calls to me from the center of the yard, "Thank ya!"

I wave at her so she knows I heard, and Mary runs back and hugs me around the knees. I pat her on the head and watch as she runs back to her mother and sisters. They are a sight for these old eyes. Before I turn back to the road, before I free myself of this promise I made four long days ago, I am flushed with a blinding heat, so hot I fear my knees will give way. My vision is disrupted. The yard and all the air around is filled with black dots that blink wherever I turn my eyes. But they ain't dots, they're bugs. Black bugs, swarming and clouding all I see. They come in a frenzy, sounds and all, and leave just as quick when I shake my head to get them loose of me and come back to my senses. What was beautiful and simple only a moment before, this reunion of family, is tainted by what I could not see then but do now. He's here, on the porch, watching. Alvin. I see him. I know that lanky slouch. Yes, I can see him. And I got to wonder if he was the redbird's promise.

At home I've chopped tomatoes and pepper to add to the rice, and by the time I hear

180

the horse bells coming up the lane, the red beans are near finished. Odell is late tonight. I got three plates pulled out when I remember it's just the two of us. *Left again,* I think to myself. The thought comes so fast it feels like I've been struck. Having Mary reminded me of a time when there was always three of us around the table. And now that she's gone, there is another kind of reminder. I thought I got used to the empty of the house, but now that it's quiet again, the hole feels twice the size.

I was two months pregnant the first time I met my baby girl. Odell and me waited ten long years for a child, and when I finally blossomed all of Shake Rag rejoiced alongside us. It was spring, and I was working in the garden at the end of a long workday trying to get my seedlings in the ground after a spring frost. I was digging down on my knees when she come to me clear as the day is long, a baby in the garden, fat and black as could be, sitting up strong and raising her arms to the sky in sheer wonder. Some of my spirit left me then. Like a picture in a book, I watched my own face lean down next to my child. I lay my own cheek next to my baby's cheek and felt skin so soft and new.

"Hello, my daughter," I heard myself say,

as if I had said it out loud, only I didn't. It was a voice inside me, loud and clear.

When the pieces of me came back together I stood to get my bearings. I was a middle-aged woman then, though still young enough for childbearing. The day was clear, but the sky was full of hawks hunting. Birds of every kind swooped and squawked to fight them off. I didn't stop to make sense of what that meant, I just rushed to meet Odell at the station after he got off work.

"We're having a girl," I told him when he stepped down off the train.

"How you know?" he asked.

"I met her."

"Woman," he said, "you are something else."

He was used to my ways by then. We was so happy. I was too young to know there is no such thing as any one thing. Everything, even great happiness, has another side. Turn over a leaf and see how the front and back differ.

It ain't 'til Odell sits down to eat, I notice he's started without prayer. I suppose what's bothering me is bothering him, too, though he would never say so for fear of hurting me. Getting a man to talk about what troubles him is like digging in winter soil. So I ask, "What is it, O?"

He lays the fork aside and folds his hands together. "I saw Mr. Coles on my way home from Bamberg this evening. He was leaning up against his automobile out by Mortgage Hill like he was waiting on somebody."

"Uh-huh." I don't trust myself to say anything more.

"When I come through he put out his hand to stop me. Said they were short a man and a wagon to cart tobacco to market."

"What's that got to do with you?"

Odell drops his head from the weight of my question. He gets weary of me.

"I ain't saying nothing against you, Odell, but you got no business hauling that crop to market. I heard the men talkin', it ain't safe. There's at least three, maybe four days' ride to Florence through swampland, likely more, and the same home. It'll be too hard on you."

"I drive a wagon all day, every day, Retta. This ain't no different."

"There's a big difference come the end of the day when you're camped in a swamp, old man."

"Preacher's hired, too. We'll look out for each another."

"Preacher's young and you're afflicted."

"So what? I got the energy. I ain't dead.

183

It's useful work. I'm pent-up going from corner to corner looking for any piece of dirt I can find for a scrap of money, depending on my wife to provide."

There it is. I asked and there it is. That's it then. He's going. It don't matter what I want. He's gone past that and found his reason. We stare each other down.

"What's he gonna pay?"

"Twelve dollars a day, same as all the men driving the wagons. Equal wage."

"What about your hands?"

He holds both out in front of him across the table, strong and sure with nary a shake in either.

"What about them?"

I can't eat no more. I can't talk no more. I can't think no more. I leave the dishes for tomorrow and go to bed. I know when I wake the kitchen will be clean.

When our child died Odell was gone to work. He didn't sleep the night before, but he made me sleep, made me go to bed 'cause he saw how crazy out of my mind I was with my poor girl. She was drowning in sickness and neither one of us could do a thing about it, though we all tried everything we knew, including the doctor. Odell had to work that next day. There wasn't nothing to be done about it. I don't feel like it was my fault that I slept, and I don't feel like it was Odell's fault that he didn't. We did what was put in front of us. We did what good parents do. What happened there was God's fault. Our girl died at three o'clock that afternoon. Esther Marie Bootles. She was eight years old.

On the rail line, that very same day, Odell caught fire near Columbia shoveling coal for the engine. He was dead on his feet, not in control of his faculties; otherwise he would've known the boiler was stressed. He don't remember it blowing, only remembers waking up with his legs on fire. Railroad lost two good men that day; Odell's friend, Vernon, lost his life and Odell, his leg. He went over and over what happened for years, the way I still go over and over Esther dying, but no matter how much we look at what happened, no matter how many times we think back to what might have been if we could've done one thing different, no matter what, we always come up the same. We live over and over in the happening only to be left with what's already done. That's the day I stopped asking God for help. Took me a long time to understand that I had to give to get. I don't dispute God's existence. I never did stop believing, but He ain't who

He's made out to be. I don't much trust Him and I reckon He don't much trust me, but we got ourselves an understanding. And that's the best I can do.

14

GERTRUDE

I always loved to sew. Mama had a sewing machine in the house when I was small, and for as long as I can remember I wanted to use it, but Daddy said no. Said a six-year-old child had no place around a machine. But as soon as he left for the fields, Mama let me stand along the backside of that machine and work the pedal. I pumped and pumped while she sewed and sewed. She said I wore her out. When I was seven she sat me at the machine, and by the end of the day I made my first apron out of a flour bag.

I told my girls that story over dinner last night. I said Mama's words, "Between us we got all the talent in the world, but we got to use every bit to pull ourselves up. We been down," I told them, "but we ain't down no more. We got to look at this chance like we're being born all over again."

We only had four chairs around the table, so Mary sat in my lap. We all were having watermelon from the yard for dessert and the girls spit black seeds in a bowl that was sitting in the center of the table. They had themselves a contest, and none of them wanted to pay attention to what I had to say.

Alma spit two seeds at once, and they landed in the bowl. She put her arms up and hollered, "Winner!"

I couldn't help but laugh. We all did.

After they settled down I said, "While I work at the Circle, Edna and Lily, it'll be your job to mind the house and get Alma and Mary off to school."

"School?" Mary asked.

"How else you going to learn to read and write?" I said. She laughed and clapped her hands with happiness at the thought.

"Once chores and school is done, ya'll go house to house and business to business 'til you scrounge up work. Alma, you keep Mary with you. Ya'll understand me?"

All of them nodded like they heard. I placed the nickels Mary received from Mr. Coles to the center of the table. "Every nickel is bread in our mouths. I don't care if you scrub a porch or take the needles out of a porcupine. If it pays you do it. Mary, you bought our bread for this week and next. We are much obliged."

She was solemn as could be. "You're welcome, Mama."

"Edna and Lily, get supper started at night 'til I can get home to help. We have to portion out what we got to eat if we mean to make it last. There won't be much, but it will be enough. Alma and Mary, ya'll set the table and help clean and put away the dishes. I'll try to get us a head start best I can with money and what we need, but we got to keep a clean house and steer clear of trouble. We're weak alone but mighty together."

I looked double hard at Edna and Lily. They're the ones that got to hear what I'm saying. I put my hand in the center of the wooden table, our table now. They laid their hands in mine and for the first time in a long time, I felt like we were home.

The Sewing Circle is a wide and airy room drenched in sunlight, like a golden palace. Forty sewing machines sit side by side in rows of five and two large presses rest on each end of the north wall. All of the sewing machines are manual Singer machines out of Chicago, just like Mama used to have. They face a wall covered in floor-to-ceiling windows so you can see out to the natural world while you work. The windows are all opened. It's the beginning of September and some breeze blows through the room, which helps fight the heat inside. The smell of Carolina pine is everywhere. Marie tells me it's good the trees are there 'cause the morning sun never blinds. Sitting along the side wall are rows and rows of all sorts of brightly colored burlap for seed bags, and up in the corner by the presses is a dumb-waiter and shaft that carries fabric from an upstairs room.

Mrs. Coles steps up on a wooden box and claps her hands. Her son Lonnie stands beside her. She's taller than him standing on that box, and she lays her hand on his shoulder, to keep her balance or to calm him, can't say which. I never saw so many women in one room together without more men around. They all take their spots and stand waiting for the Missus to speak. I keep along the back wall, unsure where to go since I ain't been assigned. Marie says I got to talk to Lonnie first.

"Good morning, ladies," the Missus says.

And everybody says right back, "Good morning."

"Let's take a moment to welcome the newest addition to our Circle. Gertrude

Pardee, welcome," she says.

Everybody turns, looks and claps. I study the shoes on my feet — Mrs. Walker's shoes. They're too big, but they cover my toes. My eye still ain't right, so I keep my head toward the left shoe 'til they turn back around and the Missus continues.

"Today is a special day, and Lonnie and I have brought you all a present." She looks to a side door that Marie opens. Four men are on the other side waiting like it's all been planned out. They haul in, two at a time, six new sewing machines. The women in the back stand on tiptoes to see over each other.

"These are industrial electric sewing machines, ladies, the most modern on the market. This machine is fast and efficient, and there is a small bulb behind the rear cover that glows while you work."

Everybody likes that, you can tell. Lonnie stands on his tiptoes and whispers in his mother's ear. She nods in agreement for whatever he's said.

"Today we are announcing our expansion from seed bags into menswear. We will start with shirts, one design in three different colors. With the advent of electricity, these six machines will take us into the future. In a few years' time, we will have replaced all these old relics with newer and faster models. Lonnie and I intend to expand our line to include not just men's shirts, but women's wear, too."

The women talk among themselves with excitement, and I can see how that pleases Mrs. Coles and Lonnie.

"Ladies," she says again to get everybody's attention, "this is a new era. It is our hope that you will continue to work and grow our little company. We are quite proud of what we have built here together, and we hope you are, as well."

Everybody claps. Miss Annie points to the men in the back, near where I am standing, and they begin unwrapping the brown paper from the machines like it's a ceremony. Six sturdy machines set atop gleaming wood. They're black and trim, like a cat with gold markings. So fine you want to run your hand along the top just to feel the curve.

"These fine gentlemen will explain the working procedures of the machine to the women who will be operating them. We will begin making shirts as soon as patterns are cut and machines are learned. We already have our first order. Tell the ladies what it's for, Lonnie."

He turns red from embarrassment.

"One h-hundred shirts for B-Berlin's of Charleston," he replies.

"One hundred shirts," Mrs. Coles repeats. "Isn't that something?"

A hoot goes up and everybody laughs. These are satisfied women. They got good jobs, they got strong purpose, and now I am among them. It don't seem real.

"Lonnie, will you read the names of the women who will be handling the shirt line, please?"

Her son helps her down, and she walks to the side door to sign papers. Lonnie steps up on the box to read who's been chosen, calling off six names. Marie is among them. She turns and smiles at me and I smile back, proud to know her. One lady squeals, she's so happy, and everybody laughs. I'm put on a machine to sew seed bags, but I don't mind. I like to work alone. All I got to do is sew three sides of burlap all day. There's two fifteen-minute breaks before lunch, and two more before the day's end. I use that time to take apart Mrs. Walker's dresses so I can see how much fabric I got to work with. If I go fast, I can put together one new dress a day for each of the girls and do the finishes by hand at night. Come lunchtime I eat the bit of food I brought, corn bread and fig jam. Marie is swallowed up and pulled outside by a crowd of women. She tries to include me, but I don't want to talk. I welcome the quiet. Though none of them asks, I see how they look at my face. All of them know, or know somebody, who's been marked by a man's fist.

The old dresses come apart easy. The threads have loosened over the years, but you can tell where they've been mended because of how much tighter the stitch is. I save the blue dress for our last fifteen-minute break. It is a dress for a fine lady and looks store-bought, but I recognize the hand stiches around the collar and pockets, so I know it's not. Once the dress is turned inside out, I study the seams. The stitching is from a machine. This dress is well made and lined with silk so soft I can't believe worms made it. It will take time and care to undo this dress, more than the few minutes I got, but I can get a start. I will mar the cloth with my scissors unless I go slowly. *Let out the hem,* Mrs. Walker wrote, so that's where I begin. Along the bottom, into the hemline, I make a small cut and ease the threads apart, one by one, so I can cut them, careful not to tear the delicacy.

Mama used to sew newspapers onto the backs of her quilts to keep them stiff so she could sew on the batting without a wrinkle, and that's what Mrs. Walker's done along this hemline. There's a stiffness that holds the bottom of the dress in a straight line, like something bought out of a catalogue. When I get an opening big enough to fit my hand through, I reach in to pull out the paper, only it ain't newspapers I pull out. It's dollar bills, eleven in all. Eleven one-dollar bills and a letter that reads, "I know you wouldn't take this if offered, Oretta. It's all I got of value, so it's only right it go to the one person of value to me. Go to Charleston and remember me when you do. Your friend, Dorothy Walker."

Edna tells me Lily's sick in the bed and has been most of the day, so she and Alma have cooked some of the canned tomatoes and grits. A pan of corn bread will last us through breakfast. I go and set my hand on Lily's forehead, but there ain't no fever, which gives me relief. She turns away from me when I ask her where she feels bad, and I don't have time to worry after her if she can't be bothered to talk to me. I can't quit thinking about that money. Eleven dollars is enough to cover the let on this house for a month.

After dinner, Alma and Mary do the dishes while Edna helps me draw out dress patterns on the newspapers and brown bags I got pinned together on the parlor floor.

Eleven dollars.

Edna slides her dress over her head and lays it out straight on the paper and pins it down so I can draw around it. I can't be charitable in the pattern I draw for Edna. She's not like her sisters, who haven't finished growing. She is a full-grown woman now. We got to make this to fit, with nothing to spare.

"Am I to have the blue cloth, Mama?" she asks.

Eleven dollars could buy a whole bolt of fabric. More than any blue dress can provide.

"Mama?"

"I don't know, Edna. Can't say as yet."

"Who's going to get the blue? I think it should be me since I'm oldest."

"I said I don't know. Go get Lily. I need her dress."

Eleven dollars could buy a good-sized piece of a butchered hog. That would give us enough meat for winter. Edna goes to get her sister, and I hear Alma and Mary outside laughing while they clean the dishes.

"She says she don't want to come."

"Lily," I shout from the parlor. "Get in here."

Eleven dollars could buy shoes for all four girls.

Lily don't come, so I get up off my knees and go to her. She's got her face turned to the wall.

"Lily, take off your dress so I can make your pattern."

"No," she tells me.

"What is wrong with you, girl? Don't you want a new dress?"

"I don't care about no dress."

I pull the covers from her, and she curls into a ball and screams at me.

"Stop it! I don't want to."

"Get up and let me have that dress."

I yank her up by the arm and off the bed so she is standing, but she fights me when I try to lift the dress up.

I shake her and yell, "Stop it!"

There is a great rip under the arm seam when I try to pull it over her head that I will have to spend the better part of the night to repair. When I finally get the dress off, she runs from me to the parlor. From where I stand, I see what she's hidden from me, what I should have seen for myself but didn't. I see what I don't want to see and now must, why she's mad and why she fought me. The rise of her belly and swell of her breast ain't natural for a thirteen-year-old girl. This is what she and that Harlan boy have wrought. After all I have done for her. A great blackness swallows me. No amount of money can fix what this is.

15

RETTA

I hear the screams before I hear Mary yelling my name to come help. I'm out to the porch, and Odell ain't far behind as she comes running up and into the yard. She's crying so hard I can't make out what she's saying.

"Mary," I shout, "you got to breathe so I can understand what you're telling me."

"Mama's going to kill Lily," she lets out between sobs.

I hand the dish towel I'm holding to Odell, who tells me to wait for him, but I'm already off the porch and out to the road before he can finish his sentence. He calls my name twice more, but Mary is pulling me to the house of my old friend where the yelling and screaming is so fierce it's a wonder nobody's dead yet. The noise is enough to bring all of Shake Rag out to their yards. In the parlor, the girls are tear-ing at Gertrude, trying to rip her from their sister, who lies half naked on the floor underneath her mama. Gertrude's got her hands wrapped around her own daughter's neck. She's possessed and mad with rage. Alvin is everywhere, above her, below her, beside her and in her, as she tries to take the life she gave as if it is her God-given right. In three strides I am on the floor in front of her.

I slap her hard across the face and shout, "Turn her loose! Turn that girl loose."

She lets go, but Alvin lingers in the room like a bad smell. The child scrambles up, coughing and sputtering, and runs past her sisters to the bedroom. She squats in the corner and watches her mother. Gertrude is on her hands and knees, panting like a woman in labor.

"Get out of my house," she screams.

I first think she means me, but her eyes ain't focused. She's looking for the girl.

"Get her out of my house!" she tells her daughters.

"Mama, please," the oldest cries.

"Get her out!"

All three girls weep.

"Stop it right now!" I shout.

I lower my voice so only who's in the room can hear.

"All of Shake Rag is outside listening to your crazy. You want Miss Annie to turn you out?"

Gertrude stands and leaves the room, putting herself in the kitchen as far away from her daughters as the house allows.

I turn to the girls and say, "Go get your sister dressed. Stay in the bedroom while I talk to your mama."

They go and shut the door behind them. I gather myself and step to the kitchen where Gertrude is. Every comfort a body could have from a friend used to be in this kitchen. It never held anything but laughter and confidences kept. Until I found my friend dead on the floor I knew no sorrow in this room. This is where we talked each other through the change of life, talked about our work, about God. This is the room that kept our wits. But I can't feel my friend here no more. It's like she's been overtook by what's come to roost, like her spirit's been erased. I ought to be glad for that. It's what I prayed for. But I ain't. I'm sorry for myself and sorry for this house.

Odell's come to the kitchen door and stands on the other side of the screen. How long he's been there I can't say. He knows I see him.

"You got a bigger problem than that girl

in there," I tell Gertrude. She needs to be made to see.

She's breathing like an angry bull.

"I got a bigger problem?"

"Where's your husband at, girl?"

She's surprised at that question.

"That ain't your business."

"You're yelling loud enough for everybody to hear, that makes you everybody's business."

"He left us. Ain't coming back."

"And you reckon since he ain't coming back everything should work out fine? That why you're so mad?"

"I don't reckon nothing. You don't know nothing about me."

"Retta, come on," Odell says from the door.

"Oh, you reckon all right. You got a reckoning happening all around you that you can't see, but I do. What'd that man do to you, girl?"

"Get out of my house."

This time she means me.

"You need to listen to what I tell you."

She turns away from me and grips the counter to hold herself upright.

"He's still got a hold of you."

"Leave me be!" she yells over her shoulder.

"Oretta, honey, let's go home," Odell calls

from the door.

"I'm coming," I say to him.

But before I go, I step in toward Gertrude and say to her, "You lay another hand on that child, Gertrude Pardee, and I'll see to it Miss Annie puts you and your girls on the street. We clear?"

I wait for her to acknowledge what I'm saying, and when she finally does, I leave her there leaning against the cabinets, spent.

Out in the lane a group of men from Shake Rag has gathered. Mabel is the only woman among them. She's come running to the street with her hair half combed out, standing in the middle of all them men like she's one of them. Beyond her on front porches, wives stand in nightdresses surrounded by children, listening, trying to see in the dark. Shake Rag ain't used to trouble.

"Everything all right, Retta?" Mabel asks.

"Everything's fine."

"Ya'll go on home, ain't nothing here to see," Odell tells them and they do.

Odell and me lean on one another. A half-moon lights enough of the world around us to see our way home, enough so the stars seem less bright in the sky. Night promises to pass quiet, now that everybody's gone back inside. No more noise comes from Mrs. Walker's house, but now I'm restless as can be. Things are shifting. I can feel them. At home I lie next to Odell, my head on his chest. I like the strong beat of his heart. I never grow weary of the sound.

"Retta?"

"Uh-huh?"

"You got to promise me while I'm gone to go easy."

"You the one that needs to go easy."

"I'm serious. Don't get messed up with that white family. No good can come of it. I'll know if something happens to you, Retta. I'll feel it in my bones."

I look up at him. "I can't have you worrying, now can I?"

"No, Sister, you cannot. It won't be good for me."

He grabs me around the waist and squeezes me like we're forty years younger.

"Odell, promise me you'll come back."

"I'll be back quick as you know. Now you promise me."

"I promise."

He kisses me and I give myself to him.

After he's asleep, I go out of doors to sit in the still of the night on the porch swing. Mrs. Walker's house lies quiet in the dark. I look for my friend, but she ain't there. It's too late to be out in the lane, I tell myself.

But I know different. Now I'm just telling myself stories.

16

ANNIE

Every day the telephone bells have rung between the one and two o'clock hour. And each day I've stood by waiting for them to stop. I've had countless imaginary conversations with Sarah. She either begs my forgiveness, professing love and sorrow for her betrayals, or with cold assertion tells me there is no child, there never was, it was just my mind playing tricks on itself. That is the talk that wounds me most deeply. These torturous imaginings have robbed me of valuable time. An unseen force has me in its grip. These endless conversations I've had in my head with Sarah these past few days are what finally prompt me to answer the damn telephone with a simple, "Yes?"

Both Lonnie and Eddie are in the field with their father, checking and rechecking everything before day's end. They will all sleep here this weekend in preparation to leave on Monday. I've organized their child-hood bedrooms so they'll be comfortable, and Retta has prepared a picnic for me to bring to the barn for dinner. They won't stop to eat unless food is brought. Edwin is relentless before he leaves town. Always anxious about leaving, he sees to every repair before he goes. Only now his time is limited, so he is on edge more than usual. We all are.

"Hello, Mother, you finally answered the telephone," my daughter says. Only it's not Sarah on the other end, it is Molly and she's already got her dukes up.

"What is it, Molly?" I ask.

"Straight to the point," she says.

It's no use responding to Molly. She loves a fight, always has. The child would get so angry when she was small, she would hold her breath until she passed out.

"This isn't your business, Molly. Sarah is the one to reconcile her lies."

"Sarah and I wanted to tell you," she says, ignoring me. "We debated over and over what to do, but in the end decided against it."

Molly takes a breath. Someone in the room says something, but it's muffled and I can't make out the words. Nonetheless, I know the voice. Sarah is there. Molly tells her sister, "She deserves to know."

"What is it I deserve to know, Molly?"

"You have three grandchildren, Mother. Sarah has Emily and James, and I have Willa. James and Willa are fourteen and thirteen and Emily is eight."

She pauses, waiting for my response, but I fix my eyes to the grandfather clock opposite me, and watch the pendulum swing for two full minutes before she speaks again. Only this time she's crying.

"They are wonderful children, Mother. Willa is very much like you, strong-willed and determined."

"You thought it best for my grandchildren to think me dead?"

There is a click on the line. A man's voice interrupts.

"Hello," he says.

"This line is taken," I say.

"Sorry," he responds and hangs up.

"We didn't want to tell them that," Sarah says into the telephone. I imagine them sitting or standing with their heads together in some room of the house. I strain to hear past them, but there is nothing else to give a clue as to where they might be. "We'd like for you to meet them, Mother."

"But not Father," Molly says, "just you."

"And why not your father?"

"We feel it best," Molly says.

"Sarah, is this coming from you as well, or have you been swayed by your sister?"

"From me, as well," she says.

"Why? You both know good and well that your father worked hard to provide you with enormous opportunity. He doted on you."

There is another click on the line, and I shout, "This line is taken!"

"Mother, please," Sarah says. "Let's not do this over the telephone."

"And this is how you repay him? You're spoiled, and I'm ashamed of you both. If you think I am going to deprive your father of the knowledge of his own grandchildren, you are wrong."

"Then we can't have you see the children," Molly responds.

"Suppose I do what you stipulate, Molly, who will I be? Some long-lost forgotten auntie? Am I to engage in these lies upon lies to children? What sort of mother are you?"

The line clicks again interrupting us. Before Molly or Sarah can say another word, I slam the telephone down. It rings once more before I am out the back door.

There was a time I remember thinking how big and fine our house was, how we would raise our children here, and once grown, they would bring their wives and husbands to our dinner table, and later bring their own children for visits. But that dream changed when Buck died. His death brought forth the worst in everyone. I thought that might change with time, but it hasn't. Misery, like illness, is insidious, and my daughters have the virus. Some people need to blame others for their unhappiness. Parents are always easy targets.

Edwin, the boys and I eat ham sandwiches standing in the long shadow of the barn alongside one of the horse wagons, one of six loaded and ready to go. Men, women and children stand wherever there is shade, hastily eating sandwiches brought up on platters by the yard boys. Twenty wagons in total sit one in back of the other as far as the eye can see in various stages of readiness. Eighteen wagons will carry five hundred pounds of tobacco and two wagons, supplies for the trip. There is so much left to do it seems impossible they will be finished in time. What should've taken a week must be finished in days, but it must get done. The tobacco must be brought down from the rafters, tied together, loaded, lashed down and covered with tarp. Each man will be tasked with providing their own bedding and medicines, but two meals a day will be on us to provide. We need satiated men. Come Monday everyone will be gone.

I've brought each of my men a bottle of cold soda pop, and Edwin drinks in long gulps. Both boys do the same. Eddie and Lonnie reflect their father in stature, though neither boy has the strength of him. They stand the same when they drink, legs apart, head tilted in the same manner, a postural echo. Edwin finishes his meal first and moves down to inspect an already loaded wagon, double-checking each knot in endless strands of rope that tie down brown tarp sitting atop a mountain of yellowed tobacco. They've got to keep it dry. The least bit of moisture could cause rot or mold.

"How long will you be this evening?" I ask.

"After dark," Edwin replies.

"Shall I ask Retta to run hot baths?"

"I'm n-not staying," Lonnie says.

"Why not?" Edwin asks.

Lonnie looks at me as if expecting me to answer for him.

"Don't look at me," I say as they all turn to me for explanation. "I'm sure I don't know."

"I've w-work to do y-yet for the C-C-Circle," Lonnie says. His face turns red from the effort.

"What work?" I ask.

"The s-stitching on the c-collars isn't r-right."

Edwin shakes his head and sighs.

"Oh, for God's sake," I respond. "The stitching is fine. Your father needs you here. Do you expect everyone else to carry your load?"

"I don't mind handling things," Eddie says.

Eddie relishes being the older brother. He spoke on behalf of each sibling long before they developed language skills. He never stops to think of himself. His hands are raw from work, and red and open from incessant washing. He most certainly needs the help, but to ask for it seems some sort of weakness. My sons are men in the prime of their lives, with the whole world at their doorstep, but they are like two crippled old bachelors. If one blinks, the other is blind.

"I think I can handle whatever work needs to be done for the Circle," I tell him. "Believe it or not I know a little something about running my own business. You'll go where you're needed."

Eddie looks at his brother, but Lonnie has trained his eyes to the ground. Edwin wraps his arm around my shoulder, kisses my

212

cheek and says, "Relax, Mother. He'll stay and help, won't you, boy?"

Lonnie looks down the long line of wagons and nods his head yes.

17

RETTA

I see Odell in the distance before I come up from the backyard. I made six pitchers of fresh squeezed lemonade for the afternoon and aim to take it up to the barn myself instead of sending Nelly. Nelly's swelling has worsened. I can't feel the baby under all that flesh, so I put her in the bed by the kitchen to keep her off her feet. She fought me to get up and work, but I told her if she did she wouldn't have a job come Monday, so she listened. I gave her a passel of green beans to pop for supper. That satisfied her. I know the signs for trouble and she is carrying them.

All the workers in the fields, Odell, too, started before sunup and won't likely quit 'til after sundown. They're in a hurry. I don't take favor in hurry. Never have. That's how folks get hurt. The yard boys help me haul the lemonade. They're like puppies hoping for leftovers. Odell is working in a hot September sun, sweating alongside every man, woman and child. That old cuss has taken his place in a long line and figured out a way to lean on his crutch and use one arm to help load tobacco crossways on the wagon. I told him just last night to stay in the wagon while they loaded that tobacco. Don't nobody expect him to do manual labor. They're lucky to get him at all is the way I see it, being as how Mr. Coles was in need and Odell helped him out. But he don't listen.

On Thursday Mr. Coles had two fresh horses brung over from the neighboring county for O's wagon, and when Odell ain't been up here sweating his sorry ass off, he's been working the horses in the lane. He's not driven a fresh horse in twenty years, but he sits in that wagon holding himself as upright as I've seen him in a long time, reins in hand ready for the spirit that is not yet known in those creatures. A young horse spooked is a dangerous thing, but Odell is a steady man and they calm under his sure hand. As much as I worry for him, I see him with fresh eyes and want him the same way I did when we was just married. My worry and desire is a back and forth that bothers my day.

Eddie hollers across three wagons loud enough for everybody to hear, "Odell, we need you to come to market every year so Retta will make us fresh lemonade in the afternoons. She doesn't take good care of us when you're not around."

"Mind your manners," I say and smack Eddie's rear end with my hand harder than I rightly should. He laughs longest of everybody, crazy man. I save enough for Odell who waits at the end of the line. He thanks me when it comes his turn. His hand trembles against the wet glass so hard he needs both hands to hold on. I don't look him in the eye. I can't get ahold of myself.

After the long Saturday, I'm grateful to finally hear the horses coming down the lane, their bells clanging before them. After Odell eats the grits and crawfish I cooked, I run a hot bath in the kitchen while he rests. I gather the soap and washrag in my hands to help scrub and rub the dirt-tired out of his body, but he takes it from me and washes himself. I can't reach him no matter what I do or don't do, say or don't say. Truth is, since being asked, he's been good as gone in his mind, itching for the road and ready for what lies beyond the next bend.

"You got a young man's notion in your

mind, Odell, and you best come back to the facts."

"I know what I can and can't do, Retta," he tells me, "as much as you know your own mind. You got to let me be."

"I ain't doubtin' you, Odell," I say back.

"Yes, you is doubting me. You act like I'm a crippled up old man who can't wipe his own rear end. I can do, Retta. It's you that got me better, I know that, but I got real work left in me and I aim to do it."

"What about me, Odell, you think about that? What will become of me if you lose your sense?"

"I ain't going to lose my sense. I got sense. I always had sense. More than you, Retta. Have some faith in me. Lord have mercy."

Odell takes care of his own leg before bed, says he needs to get practiced at it, while I finish my nightly chores. When I am done I sit out on the swing and stay long after Odell has snuffed the lantern in the bedroom. The rest of the night yields nothing but my own fear of what has not yet come.

There is light glowing in Mrs. Walker's house, the only light on the street. Mrs. Walker and me said, as we got older, the night might as well be day for as much sleep as we got. Neither of us was good sleepers. I told her we should meet up in the middle of the night for a talk. We never did, but some nights I looked.

She'd have to get up and walk to work every day. It weren't good for such a big-framed woman. No amount of coffee can keep a body going day in and day out with no sleep. The tired in her grew, but I didn't think it nothing but a lack of sleep and age. I was wrong. There was something else in her I didn't see, but she did and never said. After I found her dead on the floor, after I run from that room for help, after I sat in the back of the funeral parlor with all them white women talking about Mrs. Walker like they knew her best, after all that, I wondered if there were things in my own self that lay hidden, and if they are there, these unseen things, who can see them? Not Mrs. Walker now that she is gone. And now Odell is leaving, too. There won't be nobody left to pull me from the edge but me. But I can't see what is to come. I cannot see. I fear I will stumble over the edge without knowing, and tumble to the sharp rocks below, too late to save my own soul.

When I finally retire for the night, I keep to my side of the bed. Though I want him to, Odell does not reach for me.

18

GERTRUDE

It was after Circle this afternoon when I finally had time to walk to the Barker house. Lily came behind me at my heels. We ain't spoke once in the three days since I found her secret. She mended her own dress, but it hung crooked on her body. She don't know nothin' about the world or how to live in it. I reckon I got some blame in that, but she made her choice and it ain't us. She's turned womanly in a little girl's body with a little girl's mind and no idea what's about to happen. Ain't nothing or nobody can stop it. Her life is laid out in front of her like a dark sky, only she's too dumb and headstrong to know what hand her actions have dealt.

Lily always was a troubled child. She didn't learn good. Couldn't hold her thoughts together and had nightmares so bad she'd wake up screaming. I'd take her into bed with us some nights when she was small just to keep her quiet. But one night when she was only six years old Alvin hit her so hard I thought he killed her. After that she got headaches. Some days they'd be so bad I'd have to cover her eyes with a cold wet cloth to ease the pain and block out the light. Not long after that she turned on me.

"Dirty cow," Alvin called me.

He'd knock me to the ground and say to our girls, "Your mama is nothing but a dirty cow."

"Say it," he'd tell them. "Say what she is."

The others wouldn't, but Lily did whatever he wanted, to escape his wrath. He stopped letting me touch her until she stopped reaching for me.

Berns and Marie wouldn't know the signs of Lily's trouble, what with all the work they got on their plate and no child of their own to learn from. But Edna knows better. When I asked Edna if she knew her sister was with child she lied and said no. I know her lies. She bites at the bottom of her mouth like she's punishing the words that come from it. She'd lie even if the truth would suit her better. I won't ever tell her that I know. She'll try to hide from me. Better for her that I know the lies. I can help what I can see.

Lily and me trudged through a field of sweet grass to get to the Barker house. They're sharecroppers, like Berns is and Daddy was. They got a field to the right of the house, but the cotton looked worse than Berns's crop. There was a good-sized garden in the back. Had some tomatoes hanging low and heavy that needed picking. The house itself was covered in vine and looked like it might collapse under its own weight. I couldn't tell if that was from age or neglect. The roof sagged, and I didn't need to see the inside to know that on a rainy day there's pails everywhere to catch the leaks.

Harlan's mother answered the door, and I wondered if she already knew what I was about to tell her. Either way she didn't let on. That's a woman who's grown used to hiding. I know that kind of woman. She was plain-faced, nothing to look at, and bone skinny like most folks these days. Older than me, but I can't say how much. Hard times age a body. Her dress looked like it had had little flowers on it at one time when it was new, blue flax maybe, but they faded away. She invited us inside, but I wanted no part of her house. This business could be seen to

221

on the porch.

"My daughter's with child," I told her, "and it's on account of your boy."

She took a hard look at Lily, and her face fell, then she called backward through the door to her son. He came to the door pulling a shirt over his head, and mother and son stepped outside together.

"Is it true?" she asked Harlan.

He shrugged.

"It's true," I said. "She's got the belly to prove it."

"Then he'll make it right," his mother replied, but she didn't look at me, only him.

Two heads taller, he looked down at his mother and said, "She's the one who bewitched me."

"She's thirteen and you're nineteen," I said. "She don't know nothin' about such things."

"She knows enough. Maybe she learned it from her mama?"

Harlan's mother slapped him hard across the face. His face turned red with her palm, and he dug his hands so deep into his pockets I could see the boy in him.

"Go fetch the Reverend," she told him. "Do it now before your daddy comes home. He'll be easier on you if it's already done."

The reminder of his daddy and what his

daddy could or would do was enough to get him off the porch and on a fast run to town. His mama turned and went back inside, leaving us alone. Lily sat on the steps with her back to me. She's got spite in her wider than a river. Alvin lives on in Lily, maybe in all of us.

When the Reverend came from his dinner table, napkin still around his neck, I signed my daughter as wife over to a boy who is likely no better than the husband I killed. I left her on the porch steps by his side. Neither of us said goodbye.

It's too late for me, too late. I was a fool to think it wasn't. I sit on top of Mrs. Walker's bed working late into the night on my girls' dresses. I am in Mrs. Walker's house, surrounded by Mrs. Walker's things, but all the good she was won't rub off on me. Goodness don't matter no how. I can't see how it ever did. My mama was good, and it didn't matter. We all live and we all die, that's it. Good don't feed nobody or clothe nobody. Good don't change facts. Good ain't no good when you got babies to feed. It's all a big lie. Lily has stepped beyond my reach. Maybe I should have let Otto have her. Can't say which is worse. What's done is done, there's nothing left to save. Lily's sisters cry in the bedroom next to mine.

"Stop your wailin'," I holler through the wall.

I can't take all that noise. It riles the bone under my eye. They stop, but I still hear their whimpers. Now the young ones are afraid of me, too. Good. They should be. Fear's somethin' useful.

Mary calls out from the other side of my bedroom door, but I don't answer. She creaks open the door and sticks her head through.

"Leave me be, Mary," I tell her.

"Mama, I'm making you a present," she says. "You want to see?"

"No, I don't want to see, I want you to leave me be." She minds and closes the door behind her.

Retta said there was a reckoning happening all around me, that's what she said. Is Alvin the reckoning? She said I got to turn him loose. I got to turn him loose? I thought I did that when I pulled the trigger. It's him that needs to turn us loose. He needs to go on to the fires of hell where he belongs. Maybe it would have been better for him to kill me, I don't know anymore. I'm lost. How do you fight evil? Mama would help me if she was alive. She would have been a light for my girls. She would've loved them the way she did me. They could have had something beautiful to remember like I do.

"I wish you was here," I whisper to my mama in the sky, though I know the foolishness of the wish. She's gone. Thinking otherwise is just the mind playing tricks on itself.

19

RETTA

Our wagon is piled so high with tobacco a good wind could tip it over, so Odell asked Roy and his wife, Sue Ann, to stop by and give us a ride to church. They're a good family, with four children, three boys and the youngest a girl, named Comfort. Them children mind so good that I never once heard or saw Sue Ann raise voice or hand to them, though their daddy's had to take them out to the woodshed a time or two. Can't see how that ain't necessary with boys. That's what they understand. Roy's a railroad man like Odell was, and Odell loves Roy like a son. Sue Ann's good people, but she's got no time for friends and small talk. That will come when she's gets the children raised, but for now, she's got them working and reading and writing. They all go over to the colored school during winter. It's a long walk, but they don't mind. This family ain't

226

had one bit of bad luck, and I hope they never do.

Roy puts a wooden box on the ground so Sue Ann and me can climb up in the back of the wagon. Sue Ann's had the children stack hay and put tablecloths over it so we can rest easy. We sit up close to where the men are to join in conversation. Sue Ann and Roy have so many questions for Odell about the two new mares in our corral and his trip to market, they don't notice the distance between us. Odell's happy to answer, acting like he's carrying the Ten Commandments to market instead of a wagon full of tobacco that will be used to make cigarettes.

Odell tells Roy how smart the horses are, how they listen to his hands through the reins like he's touching skin. All I know is they got wild in them. Roy had to come over and take our old mares to stay on their land. He took them 'til Odell comes home, so I won't have to bother with them. I feared for those old horses when the new ones showed up in the yard. All that brayin' and snortin' and stampin', they could smell the female in each other.

Roy and Sue Ann's boys sit at the end of the wagon with their sister between. All eight legs dangle over the back. It's a little party for them to be riding in the lane to church with us, like we're a one-wagon parade. All of Shake Rag smiles and waves as we pass, but I cannot share their joy. It's been empty of Mrs. Walker for days. Empty as can be without my friend. This lane's become a hollow tree.

The heat's broke, and you can smell the first of autumn if you try. It rides in the breeze like gardenias. Everybody, colored folk and white, is out today. Gertrude and her three girls is walking to church, too, all of them in clean new clothes and braided hair. They don't speak to nobody and nobody speaks to them. Mabel told me what's become of Lily, and I can't help but wonder if she ain't better off for it; though between Gertrude and Harlan it's a close call. Gertrude's got bottles hanging off the oak trees by the kitchen door, and the front of the house. Likely she thinks that spirit tree is gonna catch what ails her, but no glass bottles can stop what you carry past them. I know sure as I'm sitting here her husband's dead, but she ain't saying. Anybody holding on to that kind of lie's got trouble.

I put a smile on my face when I see Mary and raise my hand off the sideboard as we roll past. She gives me a little wave, too, but stops when her mama gives her a poke in the back. Mary takes a few more peeks. She's little and can't help herself, but her mama and sisters ignore me. I'm fine with that. Long as Gertrude does what's right, we won't have a problem.

Old Canaan Baptist church holds fifty-seven Negro congregants most Sundays, and more during holidays and summertime. It sits in the middle of a wide field surrounded by oaks older than what anybody remembers. Behind the church is the cemetery where Mama, Daddy, Willie and all of Odell's people is buried. Wooden headstones with our people's names written in paint mark every grave, and each family plot is circled with white pebbles and shells. Mama wanted shells around her grave 'cause she said the sea brought us to these shores and the sea will take us home. "The seashell holds the immortal soul," she said. That is what our people believed on the shores of Africa from whence we came. Our own sweet baby girl, Esther, will rest here one day alongside me and Odell when our time comes. When our girl died I couldn't bear the thought of her laying up here without me or her daddy, so Odell buried her in the side yard by the house so she could be close to us, and he built me that sling so I could lay beside her. I got a shoebox of seashells sitting in the closet, waiting for the day we can all go home together.

Our old clapboard church ain't got nothing but a dirt floor, but the benches are sturdy and made of good, strong Carolina pine that my own daddy fashioned long ago. There's no bell to pull when it's time to worship, but we all come on time just the same, filing in one after another, the young and the old, the weak and the strong.

Me and Odell, along with Mabel, Bobo and Myrtis, are the oldest living members. There was a time before the boll weevil blight we had a good number of old folk, but hunger and disease favor the old as well as the young. Just three months ago we lost Mr. Baker to the swamp fever. I still miss seeing his skinny little behind sitting on the side, jumping up to do whatever anybody needed. He was a stooped old man, but he had more energy than a sixty-year-old body, let alone an eighty-five-year-old one. It was a blow to us all when he went, even though we had sense enough to know he was likely to go first. The oldest of us sit together in the front pew, a reminder to everyone in that church that one of us will likely be next to travel on the sea back to the Promised Land.

Since Mr. Baker died, Odell has taken up his work, standing to the back of the church greeting folks and giving out hugs; only today he takes Mr. Baker's seat by the wall in the front of the church. He's mad. There ain't no reason he can't help from where we sit, but he needs distance from me. He wants to act the child, let him.

Sue Ann stands up and sings "His Eye Is on the Sparrow" to start the service. It's an old song, one I was born knowing. Her voice is as sweet and clear as the bird itself. Her girl, Comfort, dances alongside her mama, and soon folks is swept up with the same abandon as the child. One by one they stand and sway, Odell, too, but I got no use for dancing. When the song's done, Preacher steps to the pulpit to deliver the word.

GERTRUDE

Mama and Daddy sang in the choir when Berns and me were small, so we sat alone during service. I bothered Berns to no end with my wiggling, so Mama asked Miss Thompson to sit in the pew alongside us to make me mind. She sat on one side of me with Berns on the other so they could corral me. Miss Thompson had no husband or children of her own and she was kind to me. She'd bring a pencil and paper for me

231

to draw and write on during that long hour. I never listened to the sermons but I did understand I was in God's house, so I figured whatever my prayers might be, if I wrote them down and left them somewhere in His house, He would know where to find them. I wrote down many prayers and hid them throughout the church, trusting God would read each one.

One Sunday the Reverend spoke of Matthew 9:22, " 'Jesus turned, and seeing her he said, Take heart, daughter, for your faith has made you well.' "

I was drawing at the time but I remember him saying, "I want to talk today about the prayers of a child."

Then he pulled from an envelope all the prayers I wrote, and he read them one by one for everyone to hear and showed each for them to see. Then he asked me to stand, making public what I thought private. Though my parents looked at me with pride, I was ashamed and never did it again.

Though I haven't been back to this church since I married Alvin, some of the people here today are old enough to remember me from that long ago time. Old enough to remember how Mama and Daddy helped with the church, old enough to remember me and Berns getting confirmed at twelve years old. But I find no memory of them in my mind. These people don't care about me, and I don't care about them. I'm just here to make right what ain't. After today, my youngest, like their sisters, will have their place in heaven.

Near the end of worship service, I stand and say to the same Reverend who married off Lily, "My two youngest daughters, Alma and Mary, have yet to be baptized." My family stands alongside me like how we practiced. Everybody likes baptisms, even at the end of a long sermon. Baptisms send people into the rest of their day like they've renewed a vow they're happy to keep. The Reverend calls us forward, and Berns leads us out of the pew to the front of the church.

We face the Reverend with our backs to the people. Edna stands to my right, Marie and Berns to the left. I hold Mary and Alma by the shoulder in front of me. They listen to what the Reverend says, holding hands in their matching blue dresses with little white collars. Edna is in the brown of Mrs. Walker's everyday dress, and I'm in the black of the other. It took me two days to sew the dresses, and all of yesterday to finish them. Though the girls are shoeless, we are clean and presentable enough to stand before God.

"It's an honorable thing when we dedicate our children back to God," Reverend says. "And an honorable thing when parents are willing to promise the child, or in our case here today, children, these two little girls, to their Maker."

He looks at me and says like he's God's own personal messenger, "When you surrender your children back to God, you are promising to raise them up in the way of God so one day they will be a servant to Him. That's what baptizing is all about."

RETTA

"Brothers and Sisters, walk with me to the Bible."

Bobo calls out, "We're here, Lord."

The Preacher looks up and says, "When Jesus sought out Thomas eight days after He was resurrected, it was because Thomas doubted Jesus. Doubted what his brothers had told him was true. Thomas doubted."

"Amen," is whispered as folks settle into the spirit.

The heat in the room is almost intolerable. Mabel's passed her cardboard fans down the row. I'm grateful for the relief.

Preacher says, "Jonah himself doubted when he ran from God. We all know how that turned out."

"Yessir, we sure do."

"What does the Bible tell us about Jonah," he asks us, "huh? What's it say? The Lord's word came down upon Jonah and the Lord told Jonah, to go, where?"

"Ninevah," we tell him. We know our Bible.

"That's right. Why'd he need Jonah to go to Ninevah?"

Sister Myrtis calls out, "To put a stop to their wickedness."

Myrtis's whole head turned gray by the time she was thirty years old. Said it was her children that did it. Since her husband, Bobo, wouldn't raise a hand to them, it was she who ran after them every time they made trouble. Finally she made them children cut their own switch off the tree. The long march to the apple tree and back is what set them straight, and I told her so.

"To put a stop to their wickedness," Preacher says. "God saw a problem and sent His servant to fix it. But Jonah didn't want to go, did he?"

"No, sir, he didn't."

"He ran," a child shouts.

"That's right, child! He ran away from God. He took a ship out to sea in the opposite direction of where God told him to go. So God sent a terrible, powerful storm.

The ship was tossed on the waves and looked to be lost, but Jonah knew what the others on the ship did not."

I wonder if Odell remembers that tomorrow he takes leave of me, if that has crossed his thoughts. Maybe he's eager for it.

"Jonah knew it was because of him God sent the storm. He could not bear to have all of his brothers on the ship lose their life because of him, for they were on the sea a good while, and he had come to know these men as men do who travel long distances together. Ain't that right, Brother Bootles?"

"That's right, Preacher," Odell says back.

"Jonah told the men to toss him into the sea so their lives could be spared. They were afraid but did as he asked, and what happened?"

"The sea was calmed," we say.

"The sea was calmed. A giant fish came to Jonah and what did that fish do, children?"

"Swallowed him," they cry out.

He laughs, pleased with our young. "Swallowed him up whole. That's what happened. The Bible tells us so. Ain't that right?"

"That's right."

"Jonah made a promise to God that if he lived, he would do as God asked and go to Ninevah. He would tell the people there that

God was displeased with their wickedness. God heard him. And what did that fish do? Children?"

"Spit him out," they holler.

And all the parents holler back, "That's right, that's right."

"Even though he was afraid, Jonah went to Ninevah, he followed what God wanted him to do, he reached for God in his fear and doubt. A lot of times when we go through our problems or circumstance, that's when the devil has us. You hear what I'm saying?"

"Yes, sir," we answer.

"I seen and I heard people say they locked Jesus out of their lives when He did not come when they wanted Him. He saw my hurt and my pain and my loss, but He did not come like Preacher said, or like the Bible said, so I gave up on Jesus. I'm within now. My doors are shut and He is on the out. But just 'cause you give up on Him, don't mean He's given up on you!"

"Oh, I'm glad He has not!" Odell cries from across the room. Big ole tears stream down his face, and just as quick I am crying, too, for Odell, for my husband, for this man who is a man among men and for my own sorrow for I see now my terrible error. I am rooted to my seat in shame. I have doubted the man who has never doubted me.

GERTRUDE

"Where is the father of these girls?" Reverend asks.

"He ain't with us no more, but my brother, Berns, and his wife, Marie, stand by our side."

There's no cause to question what I say, and the Reverend don't.

"I need to ask you a litany of questions and you need to answer yes or no, and I hope you will say yes."

He says the last part like a joke and the people laugh. This Reverend is new enough to still be happy about his work.

"Do you believe in our Lord and Savior, Jesus Christ?"

"Yessir."

"Do you believe Alma and Mary are gifts from God?"

"Yessir, I do."

"That's two yeses." He laughs. "Hallelujah!"

"Hallelujah," the people answer.

"Do you promise to teach and train your daughters in admiration of our Lord and Savior, Jesus Christ?"

"Yes."

238

"And to the aunt and uncle of these girls, if by chance their mother falters on this promise, which she has made before God, do you promise to take these children up and train and teach them in the way of admiration of our Lord God?"

Berns and Marie agree.

He cups each of his hands in a bowl of water a deacon has brought forth and lays the water on the girls' heads. They jump from the cold of it.

"By the power vested in me by our Lord, Jesus Christ, I baptize thee in the name of the Father, and of the Son, and of the Holy Ghost. Amen."

"Amen," everyone says.

We turn to face the people who smile at us for all the hopes of good fortune to come. In the back pew sits Mrs. Barker. Her husband ain't here, but she's got both her boys alongside her. Next to Harlan, at the end of the row staring straight ahead at her sisters, is Lily. She looks at me, her eyes round and scared, but I look away. She's cast her lot.

RETTA

"Sometimes," Preacher says, "Jesus will seek you out, because He has a purpose for your life. You know what I'm saying?"

239

Folks laugh through their tears, Preacher laughs, too.

"Awwww, He's coming after ya. You'll be tired of hiding. You can sit high, or you can sit low, if He wants to find ya, He knows where to go. Huh?"

"That's right," we call back.

Preacher whispers, "Ya'll listen, this is for the believer now. All of us are reaching, but we are not reaching with expectation. We stretch out to God, but we are not looking for nothin' in return. When God came to Thomas the doubter, He said to him, I want you to put your finger in My hand, your hand in My side, and feel the power of the resurrection. The power of what you are called to believe. 'Cause I can't use you if you aren't a believer. If you don't believe what I tell you, you can't be My preacher."

"Amen!"

"If you don't believe I have a plan for you, you can't be My witness or My songstress or My healer."

"No, sir!"

"You can't reach out if your arms are folded, you got to extend out of your circumstance, extend out of your hurt and pain. God can use you."

Feet stomp and hands clap. Dust rises from the floorboards and floats in the air

240

like tiny stars in the bright sun. Any notion of heat has left us. We're clay in God's hands now, standing in unison, like a wave looking for shore. We know the power of God.

"And when they walked my Savior to a hill called Calvary, they hung Him on a cross. They stretched out His hands, huh?"

"Yes, thank You, Lord."

Everybody knows what Preacher is telling us. Everybody knows what God had to do to His son, His only begotten son, such a terrible thing to give up a child. Odell and me know how terrible. We know.

Lost in the rapture, Preacher's tears mix with the sweat that pours down his face. He tells us, "God showed everybody on the hill that terrible day who asked the question how much does He love us. He stretched his arms out wide to show us how much."

"Yes, Jesus, yes."

"He stretched. He reached. In full capacity 'til He couldn't reach no more, and that's when they put the nails in His hands."

I cannot stay still no more. I leave my bench and reach for my husband. He sees me coming and stretches his arms out for me. The room is filled with the Holy Spirit.

"I believe in you, Odell, I believe in you," I whisper to him.

Odell brings his arm around me and kisses

the top of my head. "I know, I know."

I've come home to my husband, and he has forgiven me. We stand side by side, me to his left, his crutch on the right, but he is the one holding me up.

Preacher mops his brow, then asks all of us, "You wanna know how much He loves you? Stretch out your arms."

And we do, Odell and me, all of us. We do as we're told.

20

ANNIE

I am wide-awake. Well past the midnight hour I lie in my bed clutching the blankets despite the heat. I need them to hold me down, otherwise I might float out the window and into the night sky. I know what I am bound to do before I rise, though my actions will do no good, offer no comfort. I've had a full weekend of so little rest, every waking moment feels like a dream. Reason has left me.

No matter how I try to resist, in my darkest days the barn always beckons, and I am compelled to face again and again the thing I hate. I've lost count of how often I've wandered alone to that dreaded building in hopes of a single clue, a morsel of understanding. For the first month after Buck died, I slept there every night despite Edwin's protests. I asked Edwin to add electricity to the barn when we put it in the house, but he refused, worried my request might reignite my ritual. In one small hour of one insignificant day, everything I held dear was destroyed. I wasn't a good mother, that much is fact, but I was the only kind I knew how to be.

This morning the men took leave and the relief I felt has been replaced by deep discontent. Over and over, back and forth my brain plays Buck's death and the incessant fights with my daughters; over and over I look for a scrap of knowledge to understand what went wrong. Nothing good can come of my imaginings of what might have been. I wrap a blanket around my shoulders and walk like a nomad through the desert of my own home.

I visit the boys' bedrooms and sit on the bed where Lonnie, just last night, slept. His scent lingers on the pillow. My memory of him and Eddie as boys has faded so significantly I doubt I was ever witness. There is a time and place for memories, and old age is where they often come to reside. I used to gather them one after another, thinking, *I won't forget, I won't forget.* But it is the details that leave first and in their wake is only the one big moment. Maybe it's a year or five years, maybe a day, some terrible day, but beyond that all the details fade. What's left is a wave so big it smothers. Children are such a wave, the birthing and caring and rearing. When you're in the throes it all seems interminable. Then, whoosh, it's over. I don't know why I was surprised when the children grew up, but I was. I thought, in their youth, it would last forever. Now I see that it was my youth, not theirs that was speaking. The past is now and now and now.

In bare feet I wander down the stairs, the cool wood beneath my feet, and retrieve in the kitchen, above the stove, a box of matches from the shelf. The kitchen door creaks when I open it. I leave it ajar for I won't be long; besides there's nothing here to protect. The moon weaves in and out of black clouds against a dark blue sky. Nighthawks float silently amid them. Light and moving shadow make every inanimate object appear frozen in time: the old well now boarded up, no longer in use, the root cellar and its wooden door carved into the hill like an army bunker, the plow with its glistening blades, another relic, under the old cherry tree. I move through space like a figment of my own imagination, but even that's not true. There is no imagining here. I've taken this walk many times, always alone, always the same whether day or night, wishing, praying, for back then I did pray, for a different outcome. Though the ritual has changed, this walk, this barn, is my penance.

Though older, the building is markedly different on the outside. It had to be reconfigured to cure the tobacco. I remarked to Edwin that the missing slats gave the impression of disassembly when he first began reconstruction. "Are we coming or going?" I asked. Initially, I was glad to see a differing appearance as if somehow that would change what I remember, but to no avail. The barn still looms large on our land, perhaps never more profoundly than now. Or maybe this profundity is simply a reminder of what's always been here growing like the dandelion, impenetrable grief. Hack at it, dig it up, burn it even, it always comes back.

Edwin's hunting dog comes running from his kennel up by the barn, barking the entire way. He halts when I hold out my hand in command and sits while I turn to see if anyone has stirred in the house, forgetting no one is there, then heels as I continue. Before I slide the barn door open, I snap my fingers and he lies next to me. Despite the emptiness, the smell of ripe tobacco permeates as if the scent has seeped into the wood. This building holds many memories: mine, Edwin's, the children's. For Edwin, memories of his childhood, for me, in the early years of marriage it served as haven from the eyes of watchful parents, and for my children? I can't know their memories, but their brokenness and absences speak volumes.

I extract a match and strike it against the emery alongside the box. It catches flame with a whoosh, and I hold it in front of me to illuminate the spot I seek. The excuse I gave myself for years after Buck's death was I was young and inexperienced with children. I had no mother of my own to learn from. As if that forgave the transgression of not seeing clearly my own child's pain. When he stopped sleeping I thought it a phase, something that would shift back to normalcy. Under the illusion my notion was right, I believed Buck would comply, as children ultimately do. Children are supposed to grow up, get married, have babies of their own and share their lives with us. Buck changed that. Buck was the catalyst for everything.

I lay the matches along the dirt where I found my son and with one lit match, ignite the whole box. "Here, Bucky," I whisper. "Here is your light in the dark."

It catches like a miniature bonfire. An owl

streaks across the rafters, settling in the far corner, gold eyes staring at me. I kneel in the dirt beside the flames. This is where I found him, lifeless at the end of a rope. He was too small to stand atop anything to jump from, so he tied a rope to the inside door in a clumsy noose, then knelt and leaned into his last breath. Such a deliberate act; at any point he could have changed his mind, stood and walked away — twelve years old and already weary of the life he had with us.

It's a terrible thing to lose a child. Many women endure it and many more will long after I am gone. Some become weak and frail from such a blow, but not me. I became hard, as if a layer of armor grew over my skin — some impenetrable ancient alligator.

The flames that ignited with such fierceness falter in the absence of kindling until finally I am left in the dark. I place my hands in the dirt where I found my small sensitive boy, my meadowlark who sang and danced when he was young, before he turned silent, and rub them until small pebbles are caught and lodged in my palms. I am bleeding when I come to recognize the futility of my examination. By the time I walk back toward home, the clouds have swept over the moon and the sky has shifted into total blackness. Our house, clear and vivid only moments before, stands in muted shadow. There will be rain tonight. The dog leaves me at the door. I stand at the kitchen sink washing my hands, watching him trot back from whence he came. He disappears from view like he was never there.

In the top drawer by the sink are scissors Retta uses to cut the chicken for frying. She keeps it sharpened. I remember how I taught the children to carry sharp objects all those many years ago.

"Hold them away from your body, children. Never run, they are dangerous."

The parlor is dark but my eyes adjust. I have lived in this place for fifty-four years, I could be blindfolded and still know every nook and cranny. The telephone wire is easy enough to find in the dark. I pull it taut in one hand then make the cut that connects us to the outside world. Such a tiny thread, it's much easier to snip than I imagined. I return the scissors to their home, pour myself a glass of water and climb the steps. Back in my own bedroom, I mix sleeping powders with the water and swallow — just enough for one night. I will sleep until the thoughts quiet. Until daybreak.

III

III

21

RETTA

Dear Odell,
There's been a long two weeks of quiet and we've heard no word from you or Mr. Coles. If it took five, maybe six days to get to Florence and another three for the selling of tobacco, then you've got to be on the road home by now. I put you coming up the lane by late September. That's my arithmetic and that's my prayer.

The sound and smell of you is absent from the yard, the kitchen, our bed. In your place is a loud quiet. Ain't that an odd thing? Whoever heard of a loud quiet? Not me, not 'til now. It ain't just your voice that's gone, Odell, there's a whole choir full of voices missing. Since you been gone, feels like everybody's left me all at once. No matter how much I sit by her grave, I forget what our Esther's voice sounded like when she called my name, the high pitch of Mrs. Walker's laugh over something she thought funny, Mama fussin' over my worry. Nor can I see the signs that were once present to me. Mockingbirds cry all day above the din of other birds, into the fall of darkness and again before the sun awakens. The wind comes and goes in gusts with no pattern or reason. Only the smell of autumn riding its coattails promises something, but what I cannot say. The scent of pine is so strong, it's as if my memory leapfrogged over autumn and landed on Christmas. But no matter how I try, I can't see the Christmas that's coming. Instead, I watch your face in my mind's eye as you read my letters. With every word I write, the memory of you grows stronger, so I write this letter and more so I can hang on to that picture of you, and imagine your voice in reply. Come back soon, O.

Love,
Oretta

The spot where Odell sleeps is cool, such a relief from the heat of my body in the sheets. Strong winds have come. Long past the midnight hour I am awake again, in our bed listening to the rustling of trees. I always forget how when a season gives way to the next there's always a fight. Now the winds have come to blow the last of summer away.

What's that? There it is, steady and getting stronger. Horses' hooves, two or more coming toward Shake Rag. They turn up through the lane and into our yard. They've come for me. I sit in fear to rise, for they are in a terrible hurry to tell me something. The raps on the door are strong, each in rounds of three: *boom, boom, boom,* the fist of a man, no, of two men.

I rush to open the door, but this news has brought me something altogether different than I expected, though I should have known what was coming. Nelly's daddy stands in his overalls breathing with the heaviness of a man who's hurried from a great distance. A young white man I ain't never seen before steps off the porch and into the wind. He is wiry and trembling, with a cleft mouth. The ridge from his nose down through the bottom of his lip is so wide I can see his teeth. He wants to speak, but nothing comes out when he opens his mouth. Maybe he can't talk, I don't know. Nelly's mama is supposed to deliver her baby. There ain't no cause for them to be here unless there's trouble. Nelly's daddy is a man who speaks mostly Catawba but he knows some English.

"How fast is the pain coming?" I ask.

"Ain't stopped."

The white man is frantic in the yard, turning in circles.

"What do you mean it ain't stopped?"

"It's come and taken hold."

I worried for this. I tell him to stay put and I'll be out directly. The white man makes a loud noise, but no words attach to it. Look how upset he is with me, upset I ain't coming now, this minute, with only my nightdress on.

"Who is this?"

"Nituna's betrothed."

The man comes and stands by Nelly's daddy. I had forgotten Nelly's Indian name, Nituna. Been many years since I heard it. I gave her the name Nelly when she told me her real name. She was fourteen. I knew Mr. Coles wouldn't have no savage in the house, so I told her she needed to answer to Nelly and she has, but Nituna, that's her real name. It means daughter.

Though the need for hurry is clear, we can go no further 'til a truth is said to this white man.

"Son, if you are to be of any help to Nelly,

you got to simmer down."

I hold his eye and don't let go until he calms himself. Only then do I go inside and go about my business. We got to hurry, but I also got to think. The book Mama and me made that's got notes from all the births we oversaw is laid on the top shelf of the closet. I can just reach it from my tiptoes. Ain't no scarf that can hold down this old gray hair, but I tie one on anyway. The wind will have its way no matter.

Nelly's two weeks out from where she's supposed to be. That's good. The baby will be formed proper. But there were signs I worried for. She needed to be off her feet more than she was. Just this week I tried to get her to stay the night at Miss Annie's house in my room off the kitchen so I could see to her, but she said no, and there weren't no amount of threats that could change her mind. What's done is done, no use thinking about that now. I got to stay with the task at hand. When I step out and close the door behind me, Roy is in his pants and suspenders out on the lane doing what he promised Odell. He's learned of Nelly's trouble.

"Go on back inside, Roy," I tell him. "Nothing you can do here."

"Now, Retta," he shouts over the wind, "I

told Odell I'd look after you. You got to let me get the wagon."

"Ain't no wagon can get through where we need to go."

The white man is back in his saddle. He moves easy while Roy talks. He guides his animal alongside to where I stand on the porch.

"Roy, come get me in this saddle."

Oh, his face. If I weren't so worried, I'd laugh. Roy will tell Odell what a sight I am, this white man pulling me onto the horse and Roy pushin' me up from behind. I must look a sight. They get me up in three hefts with what used to take only one. I don't have a breath in me before the boy turns the reins to go back from where he came.

"Don't trot, son. Take her to a gallop. I can't bounce like I used to."

He and Nelly's daddy go past the path off Battle Creek and up straight through the woods beyond. Their ancestors are buried here. I feel them before my eye can see. They lay along this hillside. Though the graves ain't marked, the weight of the lives that once was cling to me. These people was laid to rest the same way my own slave kin was, in unmarked graves covered in periwinkle, their bold blossoms clear even in the night like they're being fed from the bodies beneath — a sacred plant for a sacred place.

There's the rush of a creek nearby. I can't see in the dark, but it's here. Even with the wind I hear the gurgle of a stream I do not know. We come through the trees to an opening in the woods marked by a magnolia, old and twisted. In the middle of the open meadow sits a big vegetable patch, past its time but well tended. Up along the far side by one section of woods sits the cabin, a neat little place made of logs. Even in the dark I can see the prize that is here. It don't have a porch, and that's a shame with such a view out the front. But they are young and got time to build.

Nelly's cries from inside the house pierce me. Why does birth feel impossible when it is upon you? You forget in the throes of all that pain the reward that's coming. There is a long night ahead of us. The men lead the horses to the stable to wait.

Inside, I take off my shoes and take stock of the room. Her mother, Ado, is here beside Nelly. Her Indian name, Adoette means big tree, which is strange 'cause she ain't nothing but a little bitty thing, but she is strong. I taught her everything I know about birthing babies, and she's done good for herself. In the hearth is an iron kettle of boiling water they prepared for the night ahead. Ado knows how this goes. Nelly's house is just one room but it's clean and orderly, though the floor is dirt. Two glass windows sit on either side of the front door to let in daylight and see the beauty of the land beyond. The bed's wooden headboard is handmade and polished. A husband's gift to a wife? It's pushed to the far side wall that leaves just enough room for a table, two old chairs and a sofa. Nelly keeps her kitchen the same way I keep mine. Flour and sugar canisters sit on the counter, and the percolator sits on a small cookstove. Everything is ready before it's needed.

"I'm here, child. Retta's here."

She is so swollen. In this dim and yellow light, I cannot see her eyes. She thrashes on the bed. Ado is by her head, singing a song I do not recognize in a tongue I do not know, that sounds like a lullaby. Ado looks up, and though her voice don't let on, I see the worry in her eyes. I speak with force to pierce through the pain while I lay my hands on her body to see what is happening.

"Nelly, this is a mighty nice house you got here. Look how clean and neat this place is."

She's cold to the touch but wet from strain. Her belly is a ball of stiff.

"You listening to me, Nelly?"

She nods her head yes, panting.

"You got your canning done and laid up nice on that shelf. Where'd you learn how to do all that, huh?"

She tries to answer, but another pain tears through her. She bends backward trying to get away from it.

"We're going to get this baby out of you so it can meet its mama. I know you're ready for that, ain't ya, girl?"

"Yes'm." She can barely say the words without shrieking them.

I lift back the sheet and hold her knees apart so I can see what's happening. Now I understand the hurry. I understand the power of Nelly's pain. In the dim light of the lantern a small foot dangles from Nelly, and it ain't moving.

The first birth I ever did by myself with Mama looking on was when Buck slid out of Miss Annie so fast I had to catch him. Oh, I thought Mama was going to die of fright. But I caught him. I wasn't going to let nothing bad happen. When I placed him at Miss Annie's breast, Mama said, look at what a hurry he's in, ready for the world! Miss Annie thanked me, and before I knew my mouth ought not to run free in a white man's house, I said, "Next child will come so fast you best be ready to reach down and catch it yourself."

I was thirteen.

The next birth was harder than I ever saw, and Mama had to take over. I watched her lay Miss Annie up on her left side. She stuck one arm all the way up to her elbow to turn the baby, but it was too late. The baby was born blue.

"Nelly, the baby is breech."

I got to holler for her to hear. She's mad with pain. If the child and mother is to survive, this baby's got to come out now. If Mama said that once, she said it a hundred times.

"I got to reach inside and feel what is happening. Help me best you can by staying still."

She understands though she is desperate.

I slip my fingers inside and find the other foot. I am able to get it out, but the skin is cold and blue. Dear Lord, dear Lord.

My own Esther come after eighteen hours of labor. I did it myself, with just Odell for help. All my people were dead and gone by then, and I knew more than anybody about what to do. I didn't want nobody but my husband, but Odell was afraid. I told him how it would be and he helped me. Mama used to say to all the womenfolk, "Call out to your child, what is his name?" and the woman would call his name.

"Call to your daughter now," she would say, and the mother would call her daughter.

Mama believed whichever soul was at the gate would come through as it was called. I called out to my girl.

"Esther Marie Bootles!" I remember how I called and called filled with so much pain, laying all bunched up in the washtub, ready to push her out into the warm water Odell made for me.

I yelled, "Come to us, come here, come now," so loud it sounded like I was punishing my girl instead of loving her. Esther finally came, like every child does, easy or not. Like this baby will come tonight.

"Ado, I need you to get up on her belly. You got to push when Nelly does. We got to get this done right now."

She helps me pull Nelly down to the end of the bed so I can prop her legs up. Nelly bucks and screams. Ado climbs up on the bed behind her daughter's head. She knows if she means to save her girl, this baby has to come out.

"Open your eyes, Nelly, and look at me!"
She does.

"Women give birth every day, and so will you!"

On the next push, Ado bears down easy on her daughter's belly and I'm able to guide the baby out almost to the waist.

"A girl," I tell them.

I reach in and up the baby's back, but I can't get ahold of the cord before she slips back inside her mother.

"What is her name? What is her name, Nelly?"

I see their confusion and remember. These people believe it's bad luck to name the child before it's born. They want to see who they are naming.

"Call out to your daughter. Call her home."

"Gygeyu'i," Nelly cries in her native tongue. I love you.

"No! Command her home. Make her mind! You are the mother!"

Nelly yells over and over between breaths, "Daughter, home."

Ado strokes Nelly's head and whispers, "Gygeyu'i, gygeyu'i."

I love you. I love you.

In the next push, the baby slips further out, and I am able to cut the cord to loosen the stranglehold.

"You're doing real good, Nelly. Real good!"

I slide my hand and arm into our girl, up her daughter's belly and stretch my fingers to her neck where I feel the cord fat around her neck, twice tied there. It will not loosen. I come back to the child's waist and guide her right shoulder out. When the left shoulder follows, Nelly screams. I reach back inside and lift the first strand of cord off with my fingers. It slides over her face, mouth, nose and head. The cord gives and I'm able to do it again. I look at Ado and nod. She is relieved.

"One more push, Nelly. One more and we will see her face."

In the next spasm, Ado pushes down so I can release the head. When I do blood gushes from Nelly, and she falls faint against the bed.

"Daughter," I say to the limp child who has no life.

She has a full head of black hair. I ain't never seen a baby with this much hair that weren't Negro. I am surprised by my own emotion. It comes upon me with a force I cannot control. I push words from my mouth for there is no time to give in to what has come to consume me.

"Your mother is here for you, Daughter,"

I say to the child as I rub her. "Your grand-mother has made bread for your arrival. Come home to us. Come home, girl."

I hear my own mother's voice like she is in the room alongside me. "Retta, put your mouth over the baby's nose and mouth, and suck out what is there."

I do this three times before handing the child to Ado. I mean to turn her belly onto my arm and push her back, I want to do this, but there is no time. Nelly is bleeding.

"Take care of the mother, the child will follow," Mama told me.

Ado gathers her granddaughter into a blanket they likely made for this very moment. She goes near the fire to warm and rub her to life. I put my fist inside Nelly's womb and press her stomach so the after-birth will come. Nelly has gone quiet, exhausted from her work. The body does for her what she cannot do, and the after-birth is born into the bowl that sits upon my lap.

I must stop the bleeding. Nelly sits up, as if awakened from a bad dream. She is confused, looking for her child.

"Lay down," I say. I reach to push her back on the bed but my hand, bloodied from the womb, goes through her to the other side where there is only air. It is not the physical body that rises, but the spirit.

"Nelly," I call. "Stay with me, stay here with me."

She don't listen. Her spirit is looking for her girl.

I command her again and again, "Nelly, Nituna, stay here with me. Stay with Retta," but Nelly goes to her mother and baby while I stay with her body to stop the life from draining out.

"Ado," I holler, but she does not listen. She is working on the baby, rubbing her back, then turning to push her belly. The child lies lifeless over her grandmother's arm. Nelly sidles up beside her mother and daughter and knits herself between them. Ado stops what she is doing and takes a sharp breath in. Then she looks at me and closes her eyes, her hope gone. She is caught between the spirit of her daughter and granddaughter. She cannot be reached.

"Adoette!" I shout. "Come away from the fire. Bring the child to her mother's breast."

Ado opens her eyes and finds me in the light.

"Bring the child, Ado," I shout. "Your daughter wants her baby."

Ado places the girl, naked against her mother's breast. Nelly comes, too, and settles herself into the body she left. I reach

267

for more cloth and hold it firm against our girl, my Nelly, until the blood lessens and finally stops.

The child lies limp across her mother's breast. Ado squeezes Nelly's breast for milk and places it on the baby's eyes and lips, then opens her mouth to force her to the breast.

"Sing to her, Ado, sing to your daughter and granddaughter."

With the wind howling around us, Ado keens a song, the same song she sang when I came through the door.

Nelly's breast rises and falls.

I slap the baby along the back, and her color begins to change.

"Here is your daughter, Nelly, she is here. Open your eyes and see your girl."

Nelly's breast rises and falls.

Ado gathers strength in her song. She sings with such sweet heart that I am moved to join, only I don't know her words. The baby's hand rests on Nelly's breast. A finger moves, then two. The baby takes a breath, and her whole hand reaches out, grasping as if to stop from falling. She finds only air and then the hand of her grandmother, the big tree who has come to guide her.

"Name the child, Ado."

"Una," she says. "It means remember."

Daughter, remember. "Nituna, Una," we call.

Nelly's breast rises and falls.

"Remember your daughter, Nelly, she needs her mother."

Una's eyes open.

"She is looking for you, Nelly. Una has opened her eyes to find you."

Nelly's breast rises and falls.

It does not rise again.

Una opens her mouth and wails.

22

GERTRUDE

Berns has been sick for three days now, and even after a doctor and medicine he ain't no better. Marie took Friday and today off work to tend to him. She won't let me come near for fear I'll get whatever he's got and give it to my girls. I walked the mile out to their place to give her three dollars for medicine since they used what money they had to feed my girls. She took it but wouldn't let me see my brother. Said it ain't safe. She's tired, that much I could see. My problems took their toll on Berns. Now Marie is suffering, too. There ain't no good reason for Berns to catch sick living so far out and away from the swamp, but now he has and I fear for him. I hung some bottles in their trees two days ago and left some food on the porch, but nothing's changed. Whatever's got ahold a Berns ain't letting go.

On Monday we was down six women at the Circle. One woman on the shirt line was out missing so Marie went to the office and told the Missus that I knew the new machines and could do shirt collars. Mrs. Coles gave Marie the okay, so I moved next to the sick woman's twin sister who was so worried her hands shook while she worked. She spent the better part of the day ripping out seams and starting over.

By Thursday we was down four more and today we got word from the woman who sits next to me her sister is dead. She's so busted up the Missus sends her home. Soon as the sister goes, Mrs. Coles comes out of her office to shut down the line. I set aside the collar I am finishing and go to her.

She's folding starched shirts to send to Charleston. Our aim was one hundred shirts in three weeks' time, but we're behind. I stand in the doorway until she notices me. She's got a mouthful of straight pins she's using to hold the shirts in place after they're folded.

"I'm sorry to bother you, Missus," I tell her, "but I can do collars and yokes both if you want to keep that line going."

She takes the pins out of her mouth and says, "You know yokes, Gertrude?"

"Yes, ma'am, I do. I can sew anything,

and I know the machine."

"Your face is healing quite nicely."

"Yes, ma'am," I say, 'cause I don't know what else to say.

"Your mother was a very good seamstress, one of my first, you know."

"I did know that."

"Did your father care for you while she worked?"

I ain't sure I heard right, so I ask, "Ma'am?"

"Your father. Did he help care for you?"

"Yes, ma'am, he did, but he couldn't sew none."

"I don't expect he could. Thank you for your offer, Gertrude. By all means, keep the line moving. Thank you."

It's Friday now, and I've done upward of nine shirts today, which still puts us shy of one hundred. I likely could do more, but the women in front of the line got fear deep down in their bones and it's slowed them. I'm the opposite. I run in front of my fear. All that needs to be done gets done, and then some. Everybody's walking around like they ain't slept, and likely that's true. If one woman coughs, they all lean away. All of today the friends of the sick and perished have cried at their machines while they worked. Many a seed bag's been dusted with tears and that's a fact. On toward the end of the day the doctor comes through with his black bag and walks to the back office where the Missus is waiting for him. She shuts the door behind them. He ain't there but a few minutes when Mrs. Coles comes to the front and stands by the windows. She looks over the lot of us before she speaks.

"After speaking with Dr. Southard, I've decided to close the Circle until what has taken hold loosens its grip. The doctor feels, and I agree, that's what is best to stop the contagion, which appears to be diphtheria."

A moan goes across the room, like everybody here just got the wind knocked from them.

"There is hope," she says. "The government is distributing vaccines."

The Missus turns to look at the doctor, who steps up beside her and says, "I'll begin vaccinating tomorrow, free to the public, at the elementary school and every day thereafter from ten to one."

"With any luck we'll be back to work by next Wednesday," says the Missus. "We will pay half wages until then. Better to live to work than work to death. I will see you all again next week. Stay well."

The doctor tips his hat and leaves us with

our worry. I got more than a body can carry. Before all this there was whispers from the Reevesville women at the Circle who say there's talk about Alvin and why he's gone missing. They say Otto is on the warpath. Up until the past few days they all been looking at me side-eyed and whispering behind closed hands. Marie said it's just gossip, but I know better. When Otto wants something, he don't let go, even if it means finding the son he hates to get it. He's promised his wife a servant and aims to give her one that won't cost.

There is a dread in and around me all the time now. In the leisure part of the day, after supper while the girls tend to their evening chores, is when Alvin comes to me in all his force. I smell him — hear him. I still see his last moments before I pull the trigger over and over. I should have waited 'til he saw me there, saw his fate, every human needs to reconcile their life, but I shot him in the back of the head like an animal and now I cannot shake him. The girls feel it, too, for they are like cats in the house. I've changed the rules since Lily's been gone and the illness took hold. Until danger is past, they must stay where I can see them. Mary and Alma sleep with me now while Edna hangs out her bedroom window looking for something or somebody to see or talk to. She's calls out to every person that's passes in the lane.

"You know me?" she asks anybody who will listen. "I lived in this town when I was little?"

She's only fifteen and already wants to be remembered. Still wants the outside world though there is no solace to be gained. It's a terrible thing to have your children afraid, but they must be if they mean to survive. Unseen things are all around us, best for them to know that now.

I got to get to Marie and Berns. I've heard no news since yesterday and they likely need my help. Edna knows to take care of her sisters. They got the gun if they need. Though it's only got one shell, the sight of it alone will be enough to stop a person with wrong intentions. I wrap up two jars of green beans and some grits and corn bread in a parcel, and go to my bedroom closet to fetch a bag to put them in when there is a knock at the kitchen door. Ain't nobody got cause to come up in here. Mary runs from one end of the house to the other and flings open the kitchen door before I can stop her.

"Mama," she hollers.

I hear her and Retta whispering before I come through the parlor, and I have to bite back my own rage. This woman needs to step back and learn her place.

"What is it?" I ask Retta.

Alma and Edna are at my heels. They don't care who is at the door or what they're bringing with them. They want a story.

"I got need for a kitchen girl starting Monday. Can your eldest cook and clean?"

Edna speaks first, though it ain't her place to do so.

"Yes'm, I can. Mama taught me." She looks at me and knows she done wrong.

"What you want her for?" I ask.

"I just told you why."

Edna is bouncing up and down like she's a child instead of a grown woman.

"You want your girl to make money?" she asks.

"What kind of money?"

"Dollar a day plus meals."

Before I can say anything, before any of us can, an automobile drives right off the lane and pulls up on the grass in the front yard. A sheriff steps out from behind the wheel and puts on his hat. He's all I see until Otto comes around from the other side and slams his car door shut. Both men look around before walking toward us women. All of us go quiet. We got trouble. I step out on the porch past Retta to greet them. I

276

can't know what she'll say, but she best stay behind me if she knows what's good. The girls come out and line up at my back. They got no love for their grandfather, nor he for them. Like their father, he never once gave them a kind word.

After the sheriff shows me his badge, he asks after Alvin and when was the last time I seen him.

I tell him and he asks, "Why didn't you report him missing?"

" 'Cause I don't care if he's missing."

"Where'd you get that mark on your face?" he asks.

"My husband."

"Do you own a weapon, Mrs. Pardee?"

This is it. This is Alvin bearing down on me. I grit my teeth so hard I could break my own jaw. I never took out that second shotgun shell. He'll see one missing if he looks.

"I do."

"Do you know where your husband is?"

"No, sir, I don't. But I bet he does," and I point to Alvin's daddy. "Do you know where my husband is, Otto? You's the last that seen him."

Otto looks like he bit down on a pickle. He didn't count on me talking back.

"Last I seen he left to go home to his wife

and kids," he says to the sheriff.

"That what you told this officer?" I ask Otto. "That he comes home to his wife and kids like a decent man?"

He spits at the ground, and for the first time since I known him he looks me in the eye and says, "That's what he did every day after work, went home to his wife and kids."

That sheriff says to me, "Can you tell us where you were on Friday, August fifteenth?"

" 'Scuse me, sir, she was here in Branchville," Retta says. "She had a meeting with Mrs. Annie Coles about a job."

"He didn't ask you, nigger," Otto says.

Retta don't look at him, just the sheriff. "No, sir, I'm sorry, sir, but Mrs. Coles will tell you if 'n you ask her. I know. I was there when Gertrude came calling."

"That's right," I say, "and I was at my brother's house 'fore that."

Alma shouts from behind me, "We all was."

The sheriff stands up straight, and I can see he's mad. Now he's got to deal with the Coles family. Don't nobody like that.

"I'll see that I speak to Mrs. Coles this evening," the sheriff says.

He turns to go and gives Otto a look as he walks back from where he came, but

Otto don't move. He calls to the sheriff, "That's it? My son is gone and that's all you're gonna do? This woman knows where he is."

That sheriff turns around and looks at me, but I only got eyes for the father of my husband. I'm off the porch and they all come up behind me. Otto jumps when he sees me coming, but holds his ground.

"What did you do to your boy, huh, Otto?"

"Shut your mouth, girl."

The sheriff stands by the open door of the automobile waiting on Otto; he whistles for him to come, but Otto don't move.

"He was your son and you never showed him nothing but scorn. You never did a kind thing toward him."

"I give him a job."

"You give him that job so you'd look good. So nobody would talk about how you let your son and his family starve to death. He drank that money and you knew it."

"I take care of my own," he yells.

"Ain't nothing you ever give Alvin but hate. He was your burden. I didn't see one bit of love between you. Where was you on August fifteenth, Otto? Where was you after the mill closed? Was you home with your child bride who's carrying that bastard baby or was you with the son you wish you never had?"

Otto turns purple and steps up to me, and when he does, I rise to meet him. He's got the same itchy hands as his boy. I see the slap before it comes, and I turn my face into it. I feel Alvin in his father, but he don't have the same force. Otto is an old man looking for his youth, and I am a woman finished with mine.

"Goddammit," the sheriff says as he comes back up the yard.

"Shut your mouth, you good for nothin' trash," Otto says and raises his hand to hit me again.

"Stop it," Alma cries and runs at him with her fists raised. "Leave our mama alone!"

Otto flings her to the ground and then I am up and on him. I kick and scratch and pull like the animal I am. If Otto was dinner he would be torn apart, but Edna grabs hold of me and pulls me back, crying and yelling, "Stop, Mama, stop."

The sheriff pulls Otto backward toward the car, and Otto yells the whole way, "You see that? You see what kind of mother this woman is? Not fit! And she's got daughters!"

I yell as they go, loud enough for the sheriff to hear, "Where is your second wife, huh, Otto? How come you got two missing people in your life now? Sheriff, how come nobody ever looked for her?"

The men get in their automobile and slam the door, each glad to be away from me for their own reason, this screaming woman, this creature. They drive away quick as they came and don't look back. The girls clamor around, crying. They're in a state. Retta leaves us and walks back to the lane.

"I'm all right," I tell them.

I stand in the yard long after they are gone. He'll be back. This ain't never going to be over.

My eye is pounding as I walk the last light of the wooded path to Berns's house. Otto has opened a closed wound, so now there is only the blur of the natural world, but I know the way. Bullfrogs bellow in fervor and multitude. Around the bend and before the meadow, a dogwood tree stands in full bloom, though it ain't dogwood season. I got to touch the blossoms to make sure what I see is real. A dogwood blooming in September makes no sense. Something is in the wind. I catch the scent in patches of dead air around me. Sickly sweet, the kind you don't smell in September.

There is a stinging on my ankles and up

my legs that feels like I've walked through a patch of briars. When I pull my skirts up to see what ails me, I find an army of fire ants marching up my legs stinging and biting as they go. I push them off with my skirt and look to see where they come from. All around me are rust colored mounds of dirt and sand. Ant houses bigger than I ever seen that reach tall as my calf. There must be upward of fifty. They weren't here two days ago. I take a half circle around the path to avoid stepping on the mounds that cover the way. My feet crunch against the pine needles thick on the ground and the bone beneath my eye pulses so hard my face feels like it will explode right off my head. There's pressure in the air. Like these animals, I feel it, too. I'll see to my brother and get back home. Whatever is coming, we got to get ready.

There is no light in Marie and Berns's kitchen so I knock before I open the door and call out. My ear catches what my eyes cannot see in the fading light. The rattle in Berns's chest is down low in his cough.

"I'm here, I got food," I holler.

"Leave it on the table and go, Gert," Marie calls out and then coughs the same deep cough as Berns.

She's got it, too.

23

ANNIE

When Monday morning comes it casts a deep red-and-orange glow with its arrival, like a sunset in the morning. We're upside down. I've slept and slept well. I stretch like a young woman from the sheer luxury of it, but the pops and shifts in this old body remind me I am not. All the noises of the house leap to my ears so quickly I wonder if I'm not hearing things. There's the chatter in the kitchen, the *tick, tick, tick* of my clock on the chest of drawers, and a new sound, two impatient raps against the front door. I tie my dressing gown at the waist and step into the hallway to listen for the clip of Retta's shoes across the downstairs floor. The doors between the kitchen and dining room swing and creak in her wake. She turns the front doorknob, and I settle in to listen for who or what has come.

"Telegram for Mrs. Coles."

283

My first thought is my daughters. They are determined to reach me. That notion is quickly followed by the dread that something terrible has happened. I'm not sure why I even differentiate the two. They are, after all, inextricably tied together. The hallway sways, and I hold the door frame to right myself before descending the stairs. There is a mere boy at the door. No more than fourteen if I am to judge by the lack of facial hair. I relax but Retta is frightened. She doesn't realize they would have sent a man if the news was dire. I give the boy a tip, and Retta closes the door before he has turned to go and waits for me to read the news inside.

"Retta, you should have offered that boy a drink of water."

"Miss Annie, please tell me if anything has happened to my Odell."

I open the telegram and read.

"Edwin is letting me know he and the men are delayed in coming home by another week."

It's already been two weeks, and I can only imagine Edwin's bad temper at being unable to reach me.

"That's all it says?" she asks.

"See for yourself."

She scans the letter and looks into my eyes

for what it means.

"No news is good news, Retta. If anything happened to any one of Edwin's wagons, he would tell me. Whatever has delayed them is just business, no more."

I can feel the fear in her.

"If there was trouble, he'd say."

How can I tell her that I am relieved at the delay? We are removed from expectation of men and I'm glad for it.

"Let's make good use of our husbands' absences and ready for Camp. Imagine what we will accomplish without them being underfoot."

Fruit sits ripe in baskets all along the kitchen counter, each separated by identity: grapes, apples, peaches, figs and plums. The hues are rich and deep: red, purple, orange; it's as if I've walked into a Cézanne painting. The new kitchen girl stands beside Retta coring and slicing red and green apples. She is the source of the chatter I heard from my bedroom this morning. The girl is quick with her knife. For every apple sliced a bite finds its way to her mouth. Retta introduces the girl, and I recognize features in her face — she's Gertrude's daughter, only without her mother's manner. This girl is a spinning top of energy. In an odd non sequitur, she compliments the electricity in the house as if I were the inventor, then with utmost delight, leans and flips the light switch up and down for good measure.

"Stop that, child," Retta scolds.

Poor Retta likes a quiet kitchen. While I don my driving gloves I tell her we can't afford to wait for Edwin to do the hog butchering if we mean to have the pudding finished in time for Camp.

"Send word to the Norris brothers that I want to hire them this week to butcher two hogs."

Pudding is Edwin's favorite breakfast dish, a delicacy earned after a full year of hard work. We always make it fresh for Camp. Edwin's mother made it before me, and her mother before her. I never learned the recipe, but Retta knows. I was appalled when I first learned what it was made of. The innards of a hog as delicacy was something I never imagined seeing, let alone grow accustomed to eating. After the pig's lungs are ground into a paste, Retta makes a large batch of white rice and mixes it with some garden herbs, rosemary and such, then cooks it in a steel kettle drum over an open hearth in the backyard. The intestinal sack is thoroughly cleaned and soaked in vinegar, then stuffed with the pudding and tied off. She uses the length of her hands for measure, and hangs it in the smokehouse for days. Despite the ingredients, it's delicious.

Edna sneaks another bite of apple. Anyone with eyes can see what she is doing. "Edna," I tell the girl, "have the entire apple, there's more than enough."

Retta is reprimanding her before I'm through the back door.

Being alone at the Circle is an oddity. Though I miss the whir of machines and chatter of women, I am able to box stacks of seed bags for shipping and seventy-five shirts all before noon. I run my fingers along one of the collars and admire the contrast of the black stitching against blue cloth. Every shirt bears the individualistic expression of different-color thread, as if each was made uniquely for a gentleman instead of on a factory line for the masses. To think we started with ten local women from Branchville and now have three neighboring counties represented for each coveted position. It's remarkable what one can grow on the heels of tragedy. This became my focus when Buck died, what I could see to do when I couldn't do anything else. The fed plant always grows.

It's 12:30 p.m. when Jackie, our mailman, arrives to take what I've readied. We were ahead of schedule before the illness spread. Shipping what we have to Berlin's before the deadline will buy goodwill for the rest. Jackie is a squat man, shorter than me, and has tufts of silver-gray hair poking out from his cap. He's strong as can be. Strength like his is wasted on a mail route, and I've told him as much, but he claims farming aggravates his sinuses so badly his eyes swell shut every spring.

I hold one of the yellow shirts up and say, "What do you think, Jack? Would you wear this?"

"Too snazzy for a country boy like me," he says. "Those are big-city duds."

He hefts the first box up, his head barely glancing the top, and pushes the door open with one foot, but a gust of wind blows the door shut, knocking him backward onto his behind. He curses, apologizes and jumps to his feet to try again, this time backing his way out the door.

The wind picks up on the way home. At a stop sign on Main Street, Dr. Southard crosses by foot, his black bag by his side. I lightly press the horn, and he walks over to my window and leans in when he sees I mean to speak with him.

"Am I free to reopen Wednesday?" I ask.

"Could be a few days longer. I'm sorry, Ann," he tells me. "More likely by the end of the week, but I'm optimistic."

He looks utterly exhausted, poor man. I've not considered the toll this has taken on him.

"You look like you could use a good meal. Won't you come for supper tonight?"

He hesitates.

"Do you already have plans?"

"I don't," he says. "I am at the beck and call of the afflicted."

"Say yes, then. Edwin has still not returned from market, and I am starved for intellectual stimulation." He agrees.

By the time I am home and through the kitchen door, I am drenched in sweat. The afternoon has grown thick with humidity. Retta and Edna have cleared some counter space, and two large pots of apple pie filling bubble on the stove that will be canned and used throughout the year. The brew has made the kitchen a wall of heat.

"Norris boys will be by this afternoon," Retta tells me, wiping her face with a dish towel.

"Excellent," I say. "I'll go to the slaughterhouse and give them a head start."

"Miss Annie, let them boys do everything,

that's what you pay them for."

"Nonsense, the work will do me good. I'll just unlock the boxes and lay out the knives. They can handle the rest."

I tell her we'll have a guest for supper, and she says the yard boys caught a mess of trout this morning. Said every time they cast a line they got a bite, like that in itself was a small miracle.

"Who are the Norris boys?" Edna asks as I am leaving the kitchen.

"Only the very handsomest brothers in the county," I say. "There are seven of them."

"Seven brothers, imagine that," she says. "Their poor, poor mama."

Upstairs I change into my work dress, fasten the buttons up the front, then scoot next door to Edwin's room to retrieve the keys to the slaughterhouse. In the night-stand next to his watches are the keys to the many locks around the plantation. I slide the fat ring of them neatly over my wrist, where it dangles like an odd charm bracelet.

The air outside has turned thick and orange. So thick the stench of animals welcomes me long before I've gone around the slaughterhouse to the pigpens. We have three pens and each holds ten hogs. Pigs are intelligent creatures. Years ago there was a farmer from Greenville who used a pig to find his missing child, but it is common knowledge that pigs are pack animals and can turn vicious if their numbers become too large.

I am astonished to find our pigs lying individually in deep holes. I've never seen anything like it, and for a moment I think the farmhands have played a trick. But piles of dirt lie beside each hole, and it becomes clear on closer observation the animals created the holes themselves — as if they have dug their own graves. Thirty fat pigs lie like soldiers in trenches ready for war.

Though they are reluctant to move I push and poke them up from their holes until I find two fat sows that satisfy. They are big pigs, upward of four hundred pounds, and will feed family and guests enough pudding, ribs, roast and bacon for the entire week of Camp. The rest of the drift will get a reprieve but only until our return. All of October will be bloody work.

Separating the sows is not easy. The braying from the lot of them is deafening. The other eight crowd, attempting to dissuade me of my actions, but I slap the two sows forward and into the holding pen so the boys will know which I have chosen to kill. By the time I have entered the slaughterhouse, the pigs have retreated to their holes, and the two I've separated have begun to dig.

When I was ten years old and living in New York City, I came upon a street urchin charging all the children in the neighborhood a penny to see a human hand. Everyone paid, I did as well, but when he opened the box to show his prize, I immediately recognized the ruse and called him out.

"That's not a hand, that's a pig's foot."

Perhaps he thought because I was rich and well-dressed I wouldn't recognize the animal. Perhaps he assumed I was an easy mark or maybe my accent gave me away as the enemy, but I'll never forget the look on the boy's face. I called him on his lie, and for a moment I relished his discomfort until he struck me across the face and broke my nose. God, I hated that city, so much barbarity. I think of that story every year come pudding time.

Along the south wall of the butcher shop Edwin has fashioned a long row of a dozen wooden boxes, all under lock and key, that contain all that is needed for slaughter. Though most everyone you meet in this county live with their houses and barns open to whoever may visit, Edwin, as was his family before him, is a stickler for locks.

He feels it prudent to dissuade even the best of men from temptation. We have abundance, and there are those who believe what is ours should be theirs.

Edwin is the one who always prepares for butcher. This is his domain. He gets the stations ready before the men come, so they'll go right to work. During slaughter, they talk like henhouse chickens, laughing and kidding one another, telling stories about this one or that one's daddy. The young ones boast of their adventures with girls and brag about how they handle a knife or gun until the older men grow weary of the game and turn their tongues on the boys' youth and naiveté. It's all in good fun, and the young demonstrate patience at the teasing, though it's sometimes tinged with cruelty.

The keys to the boxes are clumped together on Edwin's key ring by size. Even so, it takes me many tries to find which key unlocks which box. I finally fling them open one by one. On top of the first box lies Edwin's checklist naming what each subsequent chest contains. Aprons, gloves and canvas tarps are neatly folded beneath. In the second box are the blades and knives. Some date as far back as Edwin's great-grandfather. Only Edwin handles these; it is a patriarchal duty, a generational tradition.

The knives and blades are locked in a box within the box under another lock and key, reminiscent of one of those Russian doll sets. The key to the second box is separate from the others on the ring. Why not keep them together? The knives and saws are each housed in rich soft leather weathered from age. I like the sharp contrast of the smell of the leather and the steel that lies within. The box is far too heavy for me to move, so I drag it to the front of the chest, so the open lid will not slam shut, and reach in to extract the holsters one by one. The saws lie on top next to the other like puzzle pieces. Edwin has tamed the things. I remove and lay them alongside one another on the table. The knives are stacked along the bottom in neat lines like dominoes. When I lift the first butcher knife from the box, the eighteen-inch blade slips from its sheath and I make the stupid mistake of trying to catch it with my right hand. It slices through my palm, and I jump from its trajectory to save my feet. My skin is like paper these days, and the cut is deep. I clutch my apron to stanch the flow. It doesn't hurt. Not at first. The deeper the wound, the less pain, initially anyway. By tonight the throb will have set up house.

I can't see how I was so careless. I pick up

the knife by its wooden handle and return it to the sheath, but the knife doesn't go all the way in; something is blocking the way. With my good hand I reach in and find at the bottom a soft pink rag with little crescent moons. What I didn't see before, I see clearly now. Every knife protrudes from its pouch. I lift the next knife from the box and slide it from the leather, laying it on the floor next to me, then reach in and find something hardened and bunched tight along the bottom — a stick? I give a yank to loosen, and it comes up in one awkward bundle, clumped and brown with age. Not its, they, them, there are four things here. Each is separate, but each is the same. I pull them apart to see what they are, and am incredulous with my find. They are underpants, four pair of children's underpants.

24

RETTA

I am the last living member of my family — the very last. Born the day freedom came. Soon after, Daddy and my older brothers took leave of me, Mama and Willie, and set out to make their own way in the world. Daddy hoped to find a job up north so he could send for us. But they took on debt, and white people don't like to be owed nothing — especially by Negroes. They rounded up my brothers and daddy, put them in a chained pen with hundreds of others and set them to work hard labor to pay off that debt. But no amount of lifting and digging and hauling made what they owed less. It was there they all caught sick and died.

We didn't know nothin' of it 'til years later when Willie went hunting. He found a record, and on that record was our family name. Next to our name was the money owed, the words *3 males* and the dates they each deceased — no first names was recorded. They died within days of one another, so we don't know who went first, in between or last. There was some comfort in knowing they was together, though it is my hope Daddy died first so as not to bear the loss of his children.

It was Mama who showed me and Willie the work they done and how the town was better for them being in it. Mama said, "All your people built this town. Slave folk built the stores and churches, and the shelves and pews within. They built the funeral parlor and the coffins for the dead."

She'd say, "We all born the same, we all die the same, ain't no difference in that truth. But when you a Negro, you got to watch your mouth. What's said can't be unsaid, what's done can't be undone and what white folk do, don't concern you. We're put here on this earth to work, that's all. If your daddy and brothers would have been happy enough with that fact, they'd still be here today."

Every thing and body has its place is what she meant. What I remember has always been the same. The railroad has always come through and taken folks to and from other places, just like it took my daddy and brothers. The Coleses' houses and outbuildings have always been here. Cotton's always been grown — least 'til now. The town's still got the same stores owned by the same families. Truth is I know every bit of Branchville from the time I can remember. Only Shake Rag is new, and even that's already forty years old. When we found this patch of land, we finally found our own place.

This girl Edna don't understand her place, don't none of her sisters know either. Since Edna come for work this morning she ain't stopped runnin' off at the mouth. She talks like the whole town agrees. It's a wonder she thinks at all. There's a lot to learn if you know how to keep your jaw clenched; otherwise the world is full of blind fools. Maybe she can be taught, but at fifteen you're a fully formed person, and the likelihood of any real learning is finished. She's been here for half a day and already she's fed me a line of bull about her daddy.

"He's got a good job up north in Detroit making automobiles. When he gets enough money we're gonna go live with him in a big house with a yard. Daddy says Detroit is big so we'll have to get used to city livin', but I think I was meant to be in a city. I'm a city person."

She's told herself this story so many times she believes it. But I know the darkness that hangs around her mother's neck, and likely hers, too, with a man like that for a father, so I hold my tongue.

"In the big city every house has indoor plumbing, every single one. Can you imagine?"

"No, I can't."

"Imagine a whole room just for your toilet needs. I never seen a real bathtub. Hearsay they got one right here in this house."

"They got two," I tell her.

"Oh, please, can I go see? I think I could spend a whole day just walking around this house looking at all the things they got."

"No, you can't, and when Mr. Coles gets back, don't let him hear you talk like that. It'll be your last day if you do."

She pulls grapes from the stem and sighs.

"I never seen so much food in my whole life. Do you eat what they eat? We gonna eat dinner soon? What are we gonna eat?"

She don't even take a breath between sentences.

She pops a grape in her mouth and says, "I never tasted anything so sweet. Try it," she says and pushes it to my lips. I'm so surprised I let her.

"You listen to what I'm saying, girl?"

"Yes, you said not to walk around," she says. "Someday I'm going to have a big house just like this and a whole passel of kids. Me and my husband will go to balls and such. I'm going to wear bright-colored dresses, not ugly old brown. We'll have darkies working for us just like how Miss Annie's got you. Maybe you can come and help me with my own children. Would you like that?"

This child's got no sense of what's real.

"Stop asking so many questions. Use your ears and not your tongue."

"I can't help it."

"Can't help it? You can help it. Just keep your mouth closed."

I've no sooner got the words out of my mouth than Edna claps her hand around hers and points out the window to what's beyond. Miss Annie is coming across the backyard with her hand in the air, wrapped and dripping with blood.

Edna flies out the back door untying her apron, flinging it behind her as she goes, and I follow, trying to keep up. Miss Annie stumbles and falls to her knees. Edna comes along the other side, but Miss Annie waves her off.

"I got her," I tell Edna. "You go fetch the doctor."

"No," Miss Annie cries. "That's who's coming for dinner."

She looks at Edna and says, "Go tell the Norris boys never mind."

Edna looks at me confused.

"I don't know where they live," she says.

"Oh, for God's sake," Miss Annie says. "Tell the yard boys."

Edna stands looking at me unsure of herself, but before I can tell her what to do, Miss Annie screams, "Do as I say."

"They're in the barn," I tell Edna.

She turns and runs for the barn.

"What is wrong with that girl?" Miss Annie asks.

I help her up, but before she comes through the kitchen door, she puts a hand against the house and leans over to vomit in the bushes. I hold her from behind and pat her back while everything comes up.

When she gets her breath she says, "I'm all right."

But she ain't. There's a tremor in her whole body. She shakes like she's freezing. "Let's sit you down so you can show me where you're hurt."

"Show you where I'm hurt?" She laughs like I said the funniest thing she ever heard, laughs all the way across the kitchen. By the time I get her to a chair at the table, I can't tell whether she's laughing or crying. I wet a clean rag and unwrap the cloth that she's used to press the wound. There is a deep gash on her right hand.

"Miss Annie, it's a bad cut, but nothing a few stitches won't fix."

She mumbles under her breath like she's arguing with somebody.

"Dirty liar," she says.

I hurry to fetch the brandy, and she knocks the glass from my hands when I try to get her to drink. It shatters and splinters on the floor.

"I didn't ask for that."

"Miss Annie, are you sick?"

She looks at me and her eyes fill with tears.

"Am I the last to know?" she asks.

"Last to know what?"

"All these years. I am an old woman whose whole life has been nothing but a lie."

With her good hand she reaches for the bloody rag she came with but it's beyond her grasp. "There, Retta. Take that and see. Tell me I am wrong."

I unfold the rag and understand right away what's upset her. I see the little crescent-moon designs on the cloth beneath the blood. These belong to a child. Miss Annie goes quiet. When I finally get the courage to look at her, she says what I been dreading for more years than I know.

"They were hidden away, Retta. Locked and hidden away. There are more. So many more." She puts her hand to her mouth, like she's trying to catch the words that come out.

"Sweet Jesus," is all I can say.

"Tell me what I'm thinking is wrong. Tell me I'm wrong."

I take a deep breath and say it. "You ain't wrong."

Miss Annie sits in fret until the fret gathers into me.

"Go to the slaughterhouse, Retta. Take Edwin's keys. Lock up what I found before someone sees. Hurry, Retta! Go!"

I am shaking when I take the keys to do as I am told.

Black clouds gather in the east and lightning flashes within them. Animals cry in their paddocks. Sheep, cows and chickens all bleat in loud choir. I open the chicken coop, and do the same with the paddocks. The creatures fly and run to the woods. They'll come back after the storm. They always do. Edna runs to me from the tobacco barn.

"I done like she said."

"Good girl," I say.

She jumps when thunder rolls across the sky.

"I got to get home. Mama ain't there."

"She still ain't come home? It's been three days."

Eyeing the storm clouds, she says, "I got to go. She'll be mad if I don't see to my sisters."

"Go get them. They can stay quiet in my room until you finish helping with supper."

Inside the slaughterhouse, my eyes take a moment to adjust in the darkness. When they do I spy a pile of silver blades lying one atop the other. Each blade is separated from the container that held it. Between them sits two stacks of children's underpants, girls separated from boys, twenty-two pair in all.

"Keep your mouth shut, Retta," Mama said when I told her what I suspected. "You don't know nothin' for a fact."

I listened to her, but Lord, Lord it plagued me. Now I wonder if trouble won't find you again and again if you don't speak the truth. I wonder if you got to call what you see by its proper name, to cast out the sin within. I leave the knives on the floor of the slaughterhouse and gather up the children's underthings. Holding them I feel what was dead come to life. I lay them inside the box, close the heavy lid and fasten the lock, but Miss Annie's wishes don't matter any more than mine do. The truth is in the open.

25

ANNIE

"I'm afraid I cannot stay for supper," the doctor says when I come up to the door behind Retta to greet him. "A storm is blowing in and I shouldn't be caught out."

He's covered in Spanish moss that has been tossed from the trees by the wind. He picks it from his shirt and hat as he addresses me.

"Retta, please bring a glass of wine for the doctor."

She disappears to do as I asked.

"I'm sorry, Ann, I really musn't. I know it's late notice, but I've been so busy I haven't stopped to heed the barometer."

"Come in, Doctor. I'm afraid you must stay even if for a moment." I raise my bandaged hand. "I've had an accident."

Edwin was on the hiring committee for the doctor. John Southard was a young man then, and while totally competent, he was viewed with suspicion by Branchville, as Northerners often are. I expect they looked at me the same way when I arrived, but the Coles family is a powerful one, so I never felt the object of their judgment. I only noticed it after the doctor arrived. The rest of the committee wanted to hire a Southern doctor, someone from the region, but Edwin convinced everyone that we needed an outsider's perspective, someone who knew of things we didn't. He felt it the best way to protect the town. Of course the committee submitted and hired the man. No one says no to Edwin. It took several years for the town to forget the doctor's Yankee roots. It was his wife who won everyone over. So fat and gregarious, no one could resist her charms. They were an odd pair. Fat Lady and Stick, Eddie nicknamed them. Men and women liked her. She volunteered for every church function, raised funds for the needy and made quilts for the sick. In time everyone softened. Even Edwin liked her. No one can dispute kindness regardless of motive. She died a few years ago of a bad heart. It was a surprise to everyone. Her husband continued to treat the citizens of Branchville, but without his wife pulling him to and from various events he disappeared from the social scene altogether. It wasn't until her absence that we were reminded of whom he was before he came, an outsider. The town descended, as it does for death, but he closed the door to everyone who tried to get a look inside to see how he was faring. Never mind the poor man was grieving and seeking solitude. Their judgment stuck and there it stayed.

"Northerners lack warmth," people said. "Don't try to hug one. They'll run in the other direction."

Upon seeing my predicament, the doctor is at once through the door and into the dining room. I turn on the electricity so he can see properly. Even though we are in midafternoon, the light is dark as dusk. He walks hastily through the room and places his bag beside the table settings. Retta comes with an open bottle of red wine and pours a glass for the doctor. I pat my hand on the table, and she leaves the bottle before disappearing to the kitchen. I pour a second drink for myself.

Dr. Southard unwraps the bandage, and I'm struck by how gentle he is. The object of his attention has settled him. He inspects and pries the wound. It opens to reveal the white flesh beneath. I wince and he is at once sympathetic.

"That's a nasty cut. What happened?"

"I was playing with knives."

He lifts his head at my flippant response.

"I was careless, not paying attention. That's all," I say.

That satisfies him, and he reaches for his bag.

"You need sutures. I wish I could say they won't hurt, but I've yet to meet a patient who likes being stitched up."

"That's what I have this for," I say as I raise my glass and take another drink.

"You should have some, as well," I tell him. "No doubt your day warrants a good stiff drink."

"Most of my weeks of late warrant such."

I push his glass closer and say, "Then by all means, indulge. I won't count it as a mark against your character."

He laughs and opens his leather bag to retrieve his tools.

"Retta will have a plate of food for you to eat when you are finished. You cannot go home without a full belly. I suspect you've not eaten all day."

"I haven't," he confesses and looks out the window to assess the weather. His carriage and horses are tied beneath the trees at the end of the drive.

"You'll have plenty of time to get home," I tell him. "If I am wrong you are welcome

309

to stay until it passes."

"Thank you for your kindness," he says.

"Thank you for yours."

He threads the needle easily and knots it at the end, then lays it across the china that Retta has laid out for supper. Pushing the silverware to the center of the table, he pulls back the tablecloth so he has a nice wide space to work from, and retrieves a small bottle of clear liquid and cotton from his bag. He soaks the cotton and holds my hand open along the table. I swallow a mouthful of wine.

"Are you ready?" he asks. "This is most unpleasant."

"May I call you John?"

"Of course."

"Thank you, Dr. John. I am ready."

"I apologize in advance," he says, then drenches the wound with rubbing alcohol. The sharp smell and searing pain brings tears to my eyes, and all at once I am eight years old with bloodied knees on a chair in the kitchen at our home in New York. My father cleaned my knees that day. It was then I confessed the countless brutal acts committed by other children toward me. He was shocked that anyone dared treat me poorly, and I was too young to understand the country's significant divide was further illuminated by my Southern accent. He should have known. We left for Europe shortly thereafter.

I don't flinch when John pulls the needle through my skin. It's become paper-thin in my old age so he must dig deep to secure the suture. He's kind enough not to explain himself. I know the symptoms and signs of age. They've stalked me for years. It's a relief to focus on the stab of pain as the needle works its way through flesh. I breathe through it. Physical pain is like labor. As bad as it gets, eventually it passes. You just have to get to the other side. I take another drink, and hold the glass steady in my left hand as he finishes the fourth stitch on my right. His work is clean, and his stitches smaller than I imagined they would be.

"Why, you are a tailor," I proclaim. "Have you ever sewn anything other than limbs?"

He laughs. "Limbs are enough for me."

"All the things men do in Europe, they refuse to do here. Cooking, sewing, I wonder why that is?" I ask.

"Advanced civilization, I daresay."

"Yes, we Americans are barbaric, aren't we?"

"I suppose there is barbarism everywhere, in everyone, regardless of culture."

"Do you really believe that?"

311

He raises his eyes to look at me.

"In my work you see many things you'd rather not."

He finishes and ties off the thread.

"Such as?"

"Many things," he responds.

"Retta?" I call to the kitchen.

She arrives at the door wiping her hands on her apron.

"You may serve supper."

Retta and Edna come through from the kitchen, steam rising from platters and bowls, and then our plates as Retta fills them. She's made fried fish, collard greens, black-eyed peas, and the last of the tomatoes and cucumbers of the season. Outside a lightning flash brightens the room. Edna drops the corn bread, and it scatters across the table. She apologizes, and Retta purses her lips while Edna hurries to put the corn bread back on the platter. I catch the girl's hand and say, "Five seconds equals one mile. That is the formula I was taught as a child. Count it out and you will see the storm is far away yet. There's nothing to be frightened of."

"See?" I tell the doctor after Edna flees to the kitchen. "You've plenty of time. Eat."

He spreads his hands at the bounty before him, then folds and brings them to his chest, bowing his head. I follow suit.

"We ask that You look after the sick and hurt, and we thank You, dear Lord, for Your endless bounty. In Your name's sake, we pray."

"Amen," we say together.

Thunder rumbles in the distance. Edwin and I haven't prayed at the dinner table in years. We only ever did it out of respect for his parents and the children.

"Does God watch over us?" Sarah and Molly asked when they were ten and eight years old.

They'd become fixated on Biblical miracles during that time, to the point of distraction. It became an obsession. All the children in Sunday school took to calling them Miracles to tease. Finally the teacher pulled me aside to ask if all was well at home. To put an end to it I told Sarah and Molly that God had more important things to do than to worry about each and every single person, and it was arrogant to think otherwise.

"Aren't you eating?" John asks.

"I'm not hungry. Is it good?"

"Remarkable. The best meal I've had in a long time."

He reaches for the wine as lightning flashes across the darkening sky.

"You are a religious man?"

"Not as much as I should be."

"But you pray."

"Yes, often."

"Do you think God loves monsters?"

"God loves everyone."

"Should a monster be treated as a monster or a human being?"

"I'm not sure what you mean."

The shrubbery outside the dining room scrapes the window, and the curtains blow and bellow in rippled waves. Thunder rumbles loudly again in the distance, and John gives a quick look outside. The treetops swish against one another. His horses snort and stomp the ground beneath them.

"If a human being behaves like a monster, if he does monstrous things, should he be treated as a monster or a human being?"

"The correct answer is human being, of course."

"I don't care about correct. I care about what you truly think."

He sits back, takes a deep breath, then lets it out slowly.

"I can't answer that."

"Are you happy here, John? In this town?"

His brow furrows.

"As happy as can be expected, I suppose."

"I've never fit in. I thought with enough time I could become one of them, be from here. But we will always be outsiders, you and I. Dirty Yankees. Me because of my father, and you because of yours."

A streak of lightning brightens the room again, and thunder answers in quick response, startling us both. John wipes his mouth and folds his napkin in his plate.

"Don't leave, you haven't had cobbler."

"I regret that very much, you have no idea, but I've got to go if I am to make it home before the storm strikes."

A gust of wind comes through the window so strongly the tablecloth rises at the corner and topples the saltshaker.

"Wait," I say, as John moves toward the door. "I must pay you for your services."

"The meal was payment enough. Come to my office next week so we can see how that hand is coming along," he tells me. "Keep it clean. With any luck we'll extract the stitches in two weeks' time."

Leaning into the wind he leads the horses out of the yard and is swept into the wake of coming darkness. I finish what is left of the wine knowing I'll regret tomorrow's headache, but I don't care. Lightning hits so near and the thunderclap is so strong, I wonder what tree on our property has been its victim. Shrieks emanate from the kitchen followed by Retta's quick and firm *shush*.

Pushing open the kitchen door I find Retta holding two little girls by their hands.

"Girls," I say, "how many times have I spoken to you about coming downstairs without your hair brushed?"

They stand, mouths agape, and I quickly realize my mistake. These aren't my girls. Lightning flashes so closely you can feel the crackle of electricity in the air. A mighty roar rattles the windows. The girls scream in terror, and I cup my hands to my ears for the noise. Pain shoots up my arm. The lights flicker, and we are plunged into darkness.

26

GERTRUDE

It ain't easy to bathe a dead man. Every limb is heavy. The more time passes, the heavier he gets. My brother's been dead for two hours and already he's stiffening. I ain't never seen a man naked except Alvin, and it don't seem right that I got to now, but it's my duty as his sister to see that Berns is prepared for the afterlife. Marie lies naked beside my brother. She died quick, but Berns wouldn't let me move her, so she lay cold next to him for the better part of a day and night. My own body is heavy, too. Every move I make takes all the energy I got. I can't tell if it's from my own sorrow or what I got taking root in my chest. The storm carries with it a wet, hot heat, but still a shiver goes through my bones. I watched how the sickness took them both, so I know the path before me. The fever is settling in.

I fling open all the windows and yank the

soiled sheet from under them. The force of the wind makes the stench somewhat tolerable, but does not take the smell of death away. Rain comes into the room sideways, wetting the bed frame and ticking. The pages of the Bible on the nightstand flap in the wind and hailstones clang on the tin roof. Let the heavens rage. They should. In the three days since I come here I have done no good. Useless in life and useless in death, not the sister my brother deserves. I rip the clean part of the sheet into a long strip and use it to tie up Berns's jaw so his tongue won't do like Marie's. Her tongue swoll so big after she passed I couldn't get it back in her throat. The pain on Berns's face is etched deep, even now, the sole reminder of what he endured, the one thing his body won't let loose of. The water I used to bathe Marie is gone cold, and I know it ain't right to bathe my brother with the same water as another dead person, but she is his wife and he would not mind. Marie was the only person I ever saw my brother cry for. I never witnessed that kind of love before. Likely I never will again. Berns was still with fever when I found them. He'd broke sweat, that was a good sign, but by then Marie was sick. She succumbed quick, and Berns fell into a deep mourn that he could not pull away from. He turned on his side and took her face in his hands.

"Marie," he cried. "I never had nobody love me like you."

I wanted to tell him, *I do, Berns. I love you.* But I didn't. I never said those words out loud.

I should dress them in their Sunday clothes, and Berns needs a haircut and shave. I wish I could've seen that need sooner, such an easy thing to offer, but I got to save what little strength I have for the journey ahead. I lay the fullness of the wet rag on my brother's brow until his face loosens and the last of his tension is gone.

My brother was locked in battle with Alvin on his deathbed. Before he died, Berns saw my husband and tried to warn me. He reached for me, wild-eyed.

"Alvin ain't here," I said.

But he was frantic and pointed to the empty door to show me what only he could see, and that's when I knew. Alvin took my brother as sure as I stand on this earth, then he jumped down my throat and now sits on my chest, squeezing it so tight I can't hardly breathe. I did not think what Alvin's death would undo, only what it could do. The killing of him released the fury in him. In death a spirit's force is greater. Alvin's anger never stopped. When he finishes with me, he will hunt our children and will not rest until he's taken or killed every last thing I love.

"Goodbye, sweet brother," I say. I kiss Berns on the forehead and am seized about the chest. If I don't get up and go home, I will surely die here. There's a handful of coins and a box of bullets atop the chest of drawers. I count out four pennies and pocket the rest, then empty the box of ammunition into my pockets. I place the coins on my brother and Marie's eyes, fold their hands together and cover them with one of Mama's quilts. I'll send word when I can to the Reverend.

I lift Berns's rifle from where it hangs above the hearth, and step out onto my brother's porch for the last time to walk headfirst into what I smelled coming. The black sky moves fast from the east. It's different to step into a storm here than it was in the swamp. In the swamp you're in the belly of the beast protected by the body of it, but here in the open, you face the head of the creature. There ain't nothin' between you and the power that comes bearing down.

There are evil spirits in this world, and Alvin is among them. But Berns's spirit released with a mighty roar. Berns and Marie, and Mama and Daddy — they are here with me, too. Even still I wonder if I will live to find my girls and see their faces one last time. The wind lifts and carries, whipping at my back, until I find myself at Main Street, not a soul in sight. Looks like everybody left in the middle of what they were doing to seek shelter. Open signs sit in the windows of businesses, and in the Branchville station a green-and-yellow train stands empty on the tracks as if waiting for passengers. There is a loud crack, and I turn to see two metal panels tear loose and fly off the roof of the station. I stay close to the storefronts to shield myself and am grabbed from behind by my arm. A young woman hangs on to the screen door of the general store. She is my age, maybe younger, and heavy with child.

She yells above the wind, "Come inside!"

Her fear doubles when she sees I am sick. I shake my head and wave her away. She backs up and retreats to the dark of the store, slamming shut the heavy wood door. Hailstones the size of robin eggs fall from the sky and bounce across the fields, covering the ground in a white blanket. I catch what I can in one hand and swallow the ice to ease the pain in my throat. Everything the wind touches makes noise. Even the folds of my skirt flap like I'm shaking out a rug. All around me is a choir of sound.

It is my own dread and sorrow that pushes me on. I've been without my girls for three days. I miss Mary running and jumping into my arms, wrapping her tiny body around my neck and waist. I miss my Alma's wonder at the world around her, dragging every new thing through the door to show me, and Edna, the one who loves me though I could not protect her from her own daddy's wickedness. She got the worst of him when she was small, and he locked her in the cedar chest for talking too much. She can't stand to be confined and can hardly sleep under blankets anymore. Lily, my flower, must submit to the pain of the love that grows inside her. She will understand more of me after her own child is born. No one can stop what is coming for her.

As soon as I step through the door of our home, I know they are gone. They're smart girls and know to seek help in times of trouble. To hide 'til it passes. They learned that from me because of their daddy. All those times I made them run for fear of his rage, so many times that I made a safe place for them through the cornfields, out by Sweat's Pond. They spent many a night there. That was before the swamp — the place that left us nowhere to go.

This house sits in a tunnel of wind. The floors rise and buck beneath my feet. Every wall rattles. The windows in the bedrooms are open. The girls must not have known what was coming until it was upon them. Hail spills through and balls of ice lie melting in puddles alongside my bed, spreading from one to the other to form a tiny river that disappears between the floorboards into the hidden space below where Mrs. Walker's letter and eight dollars sit. Maybe someone will find them and do the right I couldn't.

When I step away from our house and into the road toward the Coles family's plantation, I am blown sideways and struggle to stay on my feet. My chest is gripped so tight it hurts to breathe. Fat, cold rain hits like hard rocks. When I come up the back walk to the kitchen, I nearly knock, then remember to knock is to ask. I am not here to ask. I come to lay claim. The door is locked, so I knock out the glass with the butt of my rifle, reach through and turn the knob.

The kitchen is empty and dark. No sound comes from within the house. To the right is a room and in it a single bed with a white crocheted cover. Behind another door is a pantry, a room as big as where my daughters sleep, filled with rows and rows of food in jars with bright gold lids stacked neat in straight lines — enough here to last for years. Past the kitchen is the dining room where hurricane shutters are closed and locked, but in the dim light I see fine china and uneaten food on the table. My stomach turns at the sight.

Through the dining room is the finest parlor I've ever seen. A sofa covered in deep blue velvet faces two high-back chairs as fine as thrones, drenched in the same cloth. Between them on a round mahogany table sits a crystal vase filled with bright white turkey feathers, so clean you got to wonder about the bird they come from. The howl of the wind is mixed with the sound of my raggedy breath, nothing more. My girls ain't never been without sound. Even in their quiet I know where they are. I try to holler up the stairs from the foyer, they got to be hiding somewhere, but am felled by the grip on my chest. I lean to cough up the deep mucus that clogs my throat, but I cannot. I pound my chest and push my stomach to get it up and out, but only a piece comes out. The whole of it will not leave.

I rest on a velvet chair and close my eyes. My head throbs. How nice it would be to sit, to live, to eat here and to never want for nothing. I let go of Berns's gun, and it falls to the carpet, making only a muted thump. Resting my head against the side of the chair, my hair falls across my eyes. It is filled with living things. When I raise my hand to see what has come to feast, I find it covered in ants. Something bigger moves to the corner of the room. I am being watched.

"Help me," I say turning in its direction.

Then I see him, Alvin, crouched and waiting. I reach for the gun but am too sick and too slow. The cold of the steel touches my fingertips, too late — he leaps from his hiding place and is upon me. I fight best I can for I know his plan. He will take me first and then our children. I cannot save them. They are their father's prey now.

27

RETTA

Me, Miss Annie and these three children been sittin' in the dark on the dirt floor of the root cellar for the whole of the night and still there's no sign of this storm weakening. The kerosene in the lantern is getting low. Miss Annie's white face glows yellow in the light. She's in pain, I know from how she holds her mouth, rigid, but she don't complain. The shelves in the cellar hold wood boxes filled with turnips, beets and carrots. Cabbage heads hang along the wall. In this light they look human. This storm is coming off the east from the ocean. I seen enough in my lifetime to know it's got to run itself out 'til it can't go no further. Each county past us will be hurt less than the one before. By the time it gets to Odell, I pray it will be no more than an afternoon shower.

When we first come down to the cellar

Edna cried for the darkness of it so I lit the lantern to calm her, and Miss Annie said, "We are completely shielded, there is no need for tears. Nothing can hurt us here."

Mary and Alma crawled up next to her until one by one they fell into slumber with their heads in her lap. All night Miss Annie patted their backs and stroked their heads. Neither of us has slept, and we stopped talking hours ago. There ain't nothing to say. We both know what's been exposed. Now we got to sit with it through the storm.

My grandmother kept a place for runaway slaves under her cabin floor. It was dug out just big enough for three people to hide. When I was a little girl she showed me. Mama didn't like that. Wanted me only to have memories of freedom. Said I was too young to be told such terrible things.

"How she going to know how bad things can be in life if she don't got nothing to compare it to?" Grandmother asked.

Grandmother told me later she kept one colored man in that hole for almost a year 'til folks finally give up looking for him. White folks wanted him dead for a crime he didn't do, so he sat there and waited for his chance at freedom. That's a long time to live in a hole in the ground for a notion you only heard about. Finally Grandmother told him he couldn't live there no more, but by then he was too afraid to leave.

"Listen to what I tell you," Grandmother said to me. "If you reach a point in life where it feels there is only dark around you, that's 'cause there is. You got to find the light. A hole can be a haven, but you can't stay in a hole forever. What's dark must come to light. Every person needs the sun."

Edna fidgets in her sleep and wakes with a scream. Her sisters jump from their deep sleep and remember where they are. They sit upright in the dim light and stretch.

"You're all right," I tell Edna. "You're safe."

She breathes heavy like she can't catch her breath.

"My ears hurt," she says.

"Mine, too," Mary says.

"Just the pressure from the storm. We're coming to the eye," Miss Annie explains.

Alma asks, "Is this what it feels like to be a caterpillar in a cocoon?"

"I expect so," Miss Annie says.

"That'd make us butterflies," Alma says.

Mary stands and raises her hands above her head and brings them down like wings.

"My ears are gonna bust. I got to get out of here," Edna says and stands so fast she hits her head on the low ceiling above.

"We need to wait 'til the wind dies down," Miss Annie says.

"Then we can take a stretch before we settle in for the rest of what's coming," I add.

"We been in here a long time. I got to get out," she says and runs for the steps. We both try to stop her, but she is young and quick. She pushes the door above our heads, and the wind catches and flings it open. She is out in the storm before I can reach her. The wet comes in on our heads. Mary tries to come up behind me, but Miss Annie pulls her back by her dress. Alma yanks her sister from Miss Annie, who looks stricken by their betrayal.

"Stay here! I'll get her," I shout above the noise. "Ya'll got to help me with the door." Then I am up and out in the storm. It's morning. Palmetto trees bend sideways in wind that nearly knocks me over. The rain hits my body so hard it's sure to leave marks. I wrench the metal handle up from the ground and push my whole body against it. Miss Annie grasps the handle with her good hand, and with Alma's help they pull it closed. Across the fields the tobacco barn is in ruins. Boards hang and sway from the frame like wind chimes. The land is changed in the hours since we been underground.

The damage done here will take years to rebuild. Only the house remains the same.

Edna squats against the side of the house relieving her bladder. The sky flashes bright with lightning. One arm's thrown over her head, and the other hikes up her skirt. I march through the wind and mud. When I get to Edna she climbs up me like a cat trying not to drown. I wrap my arm around her waist, and we hold on to one another so we don't blow away. We scoot around the side of the house and tumble through the open kitchen door like we've been pushed from behind. There is broke glass on the floor, and the whole of the kitchen is wet with rain and tracked with mud that leads out the kitchen and into the room beyond. Somebody is here.

"Are we going to die?" Edna asks me between sobs.

"Listen to me." I give her a little shake with both hands about the shoulders. "We're coming to the center of the storm. The back half will be as bad as the front but no worse. Ain't none of us gonna die today."

Edna rights her shoulders, then wipes the tears from her face with the back of her hands, though it does no good. We are drenched to the bone. I strike a match against the box on the stove and light the lantern that hangs from the wall. The room brightens.

"Go in yonder to my room. In the closet are towels. We got to get dry. I'm gonna fetch some aspirin from the washroom for Miss Annie's hand, and get more blankets."

I follow the mud through the door, and the smell rises to meet me as I come through the dining room. Death has a smell that once you've had it in your nose, you never forget. I hold the light before me so I can see the path. I hear the wheeze and rattle of breath. I know that sound with a mightiness that takes me back many years. I lift the lantern, and light is shed to the deepest corners where I find Gertrude standing with a rifle in the corner of the parlor like a trapped animal. Her eyes are glassy with sickness. It's a wonder she can stand.

She moves her lips over and over, saying, "My girls."

"You got fever," I say. She lifts the gun she's holding at her side, cocks back the hammer and aims it at me. I lay the lantern on the coffee table, lower my hands and tell her the girls are safe. But she don't let go of her aim. Outside the wind quiets and the gray light of morning moves through the slats of the hurricane shutters, brightening the room as it travels across the floor. We will have a dangerous calm soon with no way of knowing how long it will last.

"Need my girls," she says through two rough breaths.

"Edna, come in here, honey," I yell to the other room. When Edna comes through the swinging door rubbing her head dry with a towel, I say, "Come slow, girl."

She lowers her towel and stands stock still — like a deer who's heard an unexpected sound. "Your mama's here, and she ain't feeling good."

Edna jumps and, despite what I say, runs across the room. I lay my hand out in front of me so she knows to mind. She takes heed and stops, then comes around the corner easy.

Gertrude grasps the wall with one hand to steady herself when she sees Edna.

"Mama," Edna cries and tries to run to her mother, but I catch her by the arm and pull her back.

"Don't go near her, child. You'll catch your death."

Gertrude sways and tries to speak, but her cough comes up rich and phlegmy. She is strangling on herself. The rattle in her chest is loud and harsh. In the bleached morning light, blackness rises like steam from her mouth.

She says to Edna, "Sisters."

"She wants Alma and Mary, honey," I say. "You need to go fetch your sisters."

Edna looks at me panicked. "I'm scared to go back out there."

"Listen to the wind," I tell her. "You hear how the storm is quieter? We're coming to the center. Run now and fetch your sisters while there's time. Your mama needs to see them."

Edna takes another look at her mama, then runs to do our bidding. I step toward Gertrude, and she slides along the wall, dropping the gun to her waist. The girl works for every breath she takes, and I am all at once struck by a memory from long ago. It comes clear as day, like somebody reached in and pulled it to the front of my eyes. Gertrude's mother, Lillian Caison, is before me now, wild-eyed and naked with fear.

Gertrude's chest heaves.

"Your mama's in the room with us," I say.

Gertrude looks past and around me but can't see what I can. Don't know what I know. It was winter when Lillian Caison come running up out of the woods naked, scared as could be. She was all scratched up from running through bramble. I don't know how long she'd been loose. Her mind was long broken with something none of us could see. I heard about what was happenin' to her. By then her husband was tying her to the furniture to keep her from running naked about the town. She'd done it twice before, but on this day it was me she found and ran to me with arms outstretched, screaming and crying with such fright.

"My children ain't my children no more," she cried.

I dropped what I was carrying and caught her with both arms. She held on to me shaking with fear.

"What is it?" I asked. "What's wrong?"

"Demons have gathered in their souls," she shrieked for the world to hear.

Miss Lillian was terrified of what she thought was happening to her children. It was real as the day to her. By then I had lost my own child and knew what it was to be mad with that kind of fear and pain.

The old grandfather clock in the parlor ticks from one second to the next. Loud enough that I realize the wind has nearly disappeared.

Gertrude whispers, "Mama?"

"That's right," I tell her. "Did you know your mama and me was pregnant at the same time?"

She listens.

"You're an October baby like my daughter, Esther. Pregnancy suited your mama, same as it did me. Not everybody goes easy for the whole nine months, but your mama and me was lucky that way. Oh, she couldn't wait to have you. I could tell. She rubbed her belly like she was aiming to tame you."

Gertrude's eyes fill up and spill over her face. I step closer.

"We found ourselves running into each other all the time, though we never did plan it that way. One day right about this time of year we was both tending to our shopping. Oh, it was hot and us both so big and ready to pop like milkweed in August. By that time I'd get winded after just a few steps. Did you get that way when you had your babies?"

Gertrude nods and I come closer.

"I was past my time for the baby to come and I knew if I sat down that day I'd likely not get up, so I leaned against an old stone fence so I could catch my breath. When I looked down Main Street, there was your mama opposite me, not three yards away, doing the same thing. We caught each other's eye and laughed so hard I couldn't hold my bladder. It spilled over right there on the street. We were at the mercy of our daughters even before we met them."

Gertrude opens her mouth and lets out a moan. I take another step to her, but the rush of energy that comes through the back door shakes her from the state she's in. The blackness gathers around, and she tilts her head to listen, focusing on the sound of footsteps moving through the house toward us. She stiffens and lifts the gun, taking aim at the doorway where her children will enter, and I am all at once struck with a terrible knowing of what she aims to do.

"Stop! Your mother is in this room."

Gertrude swings the gun to me, but what strength she has to stand is lost. She falls sideways against the end table and shatters Miss Annie's crystal vase that holds turkey feathers. They fly through the air. The gun falls and discharges, though I can't see where. The children scream from the dining room, and I run to catch Gertrude and lay her on the floor.

"Retta?" Miss Annie calls.

"Don't come in here."

Gertrude struggles to breathe through all that clogs her swollen throat. Seeing her so stricken makes my heart tender for what I know is happening. As surely as I am a mother without a child, Gertrude's girls are soon to be without their mother.

■ ■ ■ ■

When my daughter died I missed a thousand things about her. She was all sass. As soon as she could talk she would tell anybody what she thought about anything. She had her mind made up by the time she was two years old and didn't mind sharing it. It worried Odell how she used her tongue to say what she thought. But I told him it would serve her. She could see the wrong in a person before they could see it in themselves. She knew. I expect she could see things the way I do — maybe stronger. Had she lived she would have been a force in Shake Rag. When she was no more than four years old, I was giving her a bath in the kitchen, and she was washing her baby doll doing just like I did her.

She asked me, "Was you a baby once?"

"I sure was," I told her.

"Daddy, too?"

"That's right."

"Where's your mama?"

"She's gone to be with the Lord."

"Are you going to be with the Lord?"

"Someday, but no time soon."

"Am I going to be with the Lord?"

"Not for a long time."

"Is it nice there?"

"Nicer than anything we know."

"I want to be with the Lord."

"No, child," I said. "Don't say that."

"Why not?"

"Because I want you here with me."

"I'm here, Mama," she said patting my arm. "Don't worry. I'm right here."

When she got sick she asked me if she was going to be with the Lord. I told her no, and she said, "You don't have to lie, Mama."

Even with her dying breath I told her she was going to be fine. I didn't have the courage to tell her the truth. As mothers, don't we owe our children the truth? I ought to have had more strength, but I didn't. My girl looked at me with such fright. Maybe I could have calmed her with the idea of heaven, but I couldn't let go. In the end it was her that let go of me, and I never found her again. Lord knows I looked in every place I could think to look. I looked at the stars 'til my eyes burned when I shut them. I looked in the garden when the plants crept up from the ground, and I looked to my dreams but my sleep left me. The veil over my eyes grew dark. All the light in the world was gone.

Though I know it's wrong, I can't help myself. I tell Gertrude the same lie I told my daughter. Her eyes are wild with the knowledge of what is to befall her. She clutches her throat, and when she opens her mouth a black plume of smoke rises from within, and I smell the sulfur of death.

"Lord," I pray aloud, "I know I ain't asked for Your help since my Esther died, but I need You now. Help me with this child."

My prayer brings Edna and her sisters through the door. Miss Annie follows behind.

"Do something," Alma shouts. "Help her."

The black swirls around Gertrude, but it's Lillian Caison I see reaching wild-eyed through the blackness to me, and I remember my promise. All three of Gertrude's girls are crying. Mary and Alma grip and shake Miss Annie's skirts. They press their faces into her side. Miss Annie watches me with new eyes. I look around the room and see the tool I need scattered across the floor. Feathers. I reach and grasp the biggest my fingers can find, and strip it bare leaving a small gathering at the top, like a duster.

"What is dark must come to light," Grandmother said.

"Miss Annie, take the lantern and the girls to the cellar. Edna, you got to help me with your mother."

"I'm scared," Edna cries. "I can't do it."

"I ain't scared," Alma says.

She charges forward, but Miss Annie grabs the girl by the arm and says, "No, I'll do it."

Edna holds Alma and Mary by the hand, and Miss Annie comes to my side.

"Miss Annie, Mr. Coles will kill me if you get sick."

"I won't get sick, and Mr. Coles doesn't own me."

"Climb on top of her and hold her arms down tight. She'll thrash. You got to use all your strength. Can you do that with your bad hand?"

Miss Annie hikes up her skirts, and says "To hell with my hand," then climbs atop and straddles Gertrude. She plants her knees on Gertrude's arms and holds both shoulders down. She cries out from the pain of her wound, but she don't let go.

"Girls, go to the cellar before the storm starts back up," I holler. "We got your mama."

Edna cries, "No," but Miss Annie whirls around and says, "Do as you're told, Edna. Take care of your sisters."

Edna listens and moves with her sisters through the house without another word. When they are through the back door, stillness comes over the room like the whole world is holding its breath. I push Gertrude's head back and shove the feather down her throat, twisting to catch hold of what's there. It's thick and strong. Gertrude gags and thrashes but Miss Annie holds her with fierce determination. I feel the thing catch like the tug of a worm on a hook, but the center escapes me.

What is dark must come to light.

I push the feather further down her throat, feeling for the root. It catches and takes hold, and I hook the thing by the belly and pull. My grasp weakens, and what I've caught breaks apart. If I don't get the whole of it I'll lose her. Pushing and twisting and stabbing and pulling, I finally reach the end, but it pulls back and sucks the spine of the feather into the roiling rot, but I don't let go. With one hand on Gertrude's forehead, and the other in her mouth, I drag that feather slowly up, working my fingers up the spine 'til I can get my whole hand around the bottom of it. I yank the drudge up her throat.

"Quick, roll her to the side," I urge Miss Annie.

She turns Gertrude over and pounds on her back. Gertrude's body heaves, and I pull all of what lay inside to the surface. It comes out in a torrent of thick yellow and green

341

pus. The blackness turns to white smoke and disappears in the air. Outside the energy gathers. Windows rattle in their frame. Miss Annie holds Gertrude while I push my fist into her chest and pound three times, shouting, "Breathe," 'til she takes a sharp inhale and her chest rattles as she feebly fights for every drop of air.

The backside of the storm hits like the tail end of a bullwhip. A hurricane shutter snaps free of the parlor window, and the wind kicks in so strong hail breaks through the glass like rocks purposely flung. Outside a mighty oak is uprooted from the ground and falls sideway across the front path, taking the tree opposite down with it.

"We got to move her," I say.

"Under the stairs," Miss Annie replies, and together we pull Gertrude across the floor and through the foyer. Miss Annie unlatches the door beneath the stairwell. Her bandage is bloody. She's torn open the wound. Together, we give the door a good yank and wrench it open, ducking our heads inside and pulling Gertrude in behind us. We are shapes in the dark, the lines of our bodies blurred. We breathe together inviting Gertrude to join. Her belly rises and falls beneath my hand. She drinks each breath like water from thirst. Opening her eyes she finds the pale of Miss Annie in the dark.

"Mama," Gertrude cries thrusting her arms toward Miss Annie, but Miss Annie scoots to the back corner under the stairs.

"Mama," Gertrude cries over and over, 'til finally it's me that answers.

"I'm here, Gert. I'm right here."

IV

VI

28

ANNIE

My husband comes alone on horseback well past the midnight hour through the field down the stream of light cast by a late rising moon. A fox darts from under the rope-like roots of a fallen magnolia, spooked by the unexpected. Edwin is not unexpected to me. I've anticipated his return. He arrives without fanfare — how could there be, in light of what has happened? — but I'm surprised he is alone. He dismounts and leads the horse toward the barn but stops when he sees in full what the storm has wrought. Stooped and slow, he's become old overnight, finally joining me in the inevitable march to the grave. *Yes, we've been hit hard,* I want to tell him, *harder than you know,* but I must wait. In due time.

The view from Buck's bedroom is changed, now that the wood is gone between the main house and old slave quarters. Save the palmettos, trees have been upped by their roots and blown far from where they originally stood. Now they are laid out against harvested fields and a full moon like some strange dead crop, a gnarl of branches and trunks that suggest once living creatures killed upon some unknown battlefield.

Buck hated this room. For the entirety of his eleventh year and just past his twelfth, I woke to find my son asleep at the foot of my bed. He was too old to be in his mother's bed; that's what his father, my husband, said. "The boy's got to learn to sleep on his own."

At the start of every night, I'd open the door that separated the girls' room from Buck's and tell his sisters, "Leave this open so your brother can see, he is afraid of the dark," but every morning it was shut, each side blaming the other. I was so angry.

The windows in my son's room stand fully open despite the break in heat that has come after the storm. Tonight my breath is present in the air, and the breeze is so strong that the curtains I made, blue, marked with white sailboats, because the child loved the sea, swell to the center of the room. I've become cold-blooded. It's here I wander now, night after night, suspended in time, stranded in the doorway of the three children I lost, the three children I failed.

In the week since the storm passed Retta has come and asked for instruction on what to do with the detritus. Most of the outbuildings are torn asunder, including the slave quarters, ruined by wind or fallen trees. Only the house remains fully standing, though the chimney has fallen in on the attic, wrecking what is stored there. Water has leaked into all the bedrooms, and windows are shattered. Every day I say to Retta the same as I did the day before.

"Leave it. Don't touch a thing, even the broken glass on the floor."

I know the talk it stirs. I don't care. This house should be seen for what it is, wreckage incarnate.

It has been seven days since I last had food. Retta's worried for my health, but I am not. I've never been more clearheaded and wonder if the shift from numbness to clarity is from a lack of sustenance. If so, I should have starved myself years ago. Edwin cocks his head and points his face in the direction of the window, but doesn't look up. If he did he would see me standing and watching. I want to see his face but am not surprised when I can't. My husband is adept at hiding. I drop the curtains and walk to our marriage bed and wait.

■ ■ ■ ■

I was seventeen when I met Edwin at my debutante ball. The Hall in Charleston was far grander than any of us could have imagined. In the center of town on Meeting Street a set of steps led to majestic Greek columns. Beyond the door marble floors adorned the room that was gilded with gold fixtures and lit by gas lamps and candlelight. We were fifteen debutantes in total that year, all dressed in white with gloves and slippers. We felt like royalty and made the front page of the *Charleston Daily News,* which deemed our ball the symbol of changing times, a return to a gentler, more refined South. As soon as I came through the door I saw Edwin lined up in his tails against the wall with all the other eligible young men, and he saw me. He was first on my dance card, and throughout the night I felt his eyes on me regardless of whom I was with. I knew where he was in the room, not with my eyes, but with my body. I could feel heat from his every direction. When Edwin came courting, which wasn't often since he lived so far out of town, he was never proper. He stole kisses when Auntie was out of the room. I attributed his impetuousness to country living. There were many young men who came courting, so many that Auntie didn't know which I really liked, and I didn't let on for fear Papa would put a stop to it. By the time Edwin proposed, it was too late. Papa took the first train down to Charleston. We had a terrible row, but it was settled when he saw I wasn't going to budge. It's the only time I ever saw him cry. We were invited to Branchville to see the Coles family's plantation, the largest in the territory, with cotton fields that lined the railroad tracks and open fields as far as the eye could see. Papa begrudgingly consented, but demanded the marriage be held in Charleston. On the train ride back from Branchville, Papa said one thing and no more.

"Country life is a lonely life. Have lots of children."

I married at eighteen and had seven children by the time I reached my thirty-first year. Three are dead and gone, two stillbirths and then what happened with my sweet, sweet boy.

Edwin comes across the dining room and foyer, feet crunching on glass, and then up the steps in slow heavy rhythm. At the top he stops to catch his breath. That is when my ears tell me my husband is crying, something I've never heard or seen him do. He comes heavy-heeled into the room, and is startled to find me sitting on our bed.

"That's hardly the way a grown man cries," I say.

"What?" he asks and cocks his head as if trying to understand what I said. But he stops crying so I know he heard. That awareness is something.

"Have you grown deaf?" I ask.

"I hurried as fast as I could, Annie," he says, defensively, from the center of the room. "I'm lucky to have made it this quickly."

Does he imagine I'm angry he's been gone so long, the hurt wife fretting over her husband's long, arduous journey?

"Where are our sons?" I ask.

"The wagons couldn't get through the roads for all the felled trees. They have been kept back to help clear."

"Kept back?"

"They're in Williston."

"You left them?"

"They're fine, Mother."

He sits opposite me in the chair under the window, takes a deep breath and confesses in one long exhale, "We've lost everything, Annie. Tobacco is our ruin."

"We were in ruin long before tobacco," I

respond.

Half his face is bathed in the light of the moon, the other half cast in shadow, two sides of one face.

"What's wrong with you, Mother?" he asks. "Are you ill?"

What a very good question. There must be something seriously wrong with me to have been so blind.

"Don't call me that. I'm not your mother."

"Annie, listen to what I'm telling you. When we got to Florence, the market was flooded with growers. We camped for two days on a line that stretched through town. Half the growers came up from Wilmington in hopes of getting a better price. We didn't even get market value, Annie. We didn't get anywhere near that."

"Now what?" I ask.

"Now we consolidate our assets, leverage what we have. I don't know. Sell the Sewing Circle? We have to cover what we owe. Between the failed crop and damage to our properties we are behind, Annie, well over a hundred thousand dollars behind, and that's just this season. I'm not accounting for three years of failed cotton."

So that's his plan. The Circle. Take what's left.

"Am I supposed to feel pity for you?"

He gathers himself into composure, and we sit in silence until his confusion turns to suspicion. I do not look away. He straightens himself and turns his head from me to look around the room. My wedding rings sit on his nightstand. The glint of diamonds and sapphires is difficult to miss.

"Annie, I'm tired," he tells me, then rises and takes off his watch. He opens the night table and lays it alongside his other time-pieces, then moves his hand sideways and fingers the ring of keys. He's counting.

"You won't find the key you're looking for. I've taken it and placed it in safekeeping."

With his back to me he feigns an exasperated sigh and says, "I don't know what you're talking about."

"Oh, I think you do, Edwin. I believe you understand me perfectly."

He turns with coiled force struggling to stay controlled. The veins of his neck protrude. "Annie, you've had a fright. We've all been dealt a terrible hand, but we have to play it. We can discuss our future in the morning."

I've been dismissed.

"Spare the euphemisms, Edwin."

I stand and face him. "We've reached the end, you and I. It wasn't how I imagined, but we both deserve what's coming — all of it, you, for your disgusting proclivities, and me, for standing by you instead of our children. The good news is it will finally be over."

I leave him standing in the center of his bedroom and shut the door between us. I fall asleep just before dawn. When I awake it's late. My eyes cannot open fully in the glaring light of day. A crisp chill in the air makes the warmth of the blankets a temptation to stay beneath, but I force myself to sit up and listen to the sounds of my house. Downstairs, glass is being swept. Outside, the yard is filled with men clearing debris. They call instructions to one another across the fields. Already they've become a singular moving organism. In just a few hours' time Edwin has rallied the men in town and given them the tasks they've been begging me for the greater part of a week. What's left of the barn is being steadily disassembled. Good, I'm glad to see it go. Piles of wood are stacked in rows. Bonfires have been set near the house and around the plantation to burn the refuse. The smell of smoke lingers in the nostrils. Edna is in the yard hanging the ticking for the mattresses we use for Camp on the clothesline to dry. The pudding pot sits ready on the outside hearth — hung in preparation for Camp. Edwin has made his decision. Appearances shall be kept.

A sudden sharp breeze sends a chill down my spine. Autumn is here in force, the last gasp of life before winter turns everything dormant. Across the field my husband walks with purpose away from the slaughterhouse where another fire burns in the distance, sending black smoke into the bare blue sky. He's rid of the evidence. He stands and surveys the property, then glances at the house and raises his eyes, searching until he finds me watching him through the window. He breaks his gaze and strides away, but not before I've seen what he wears about his waist. My husband now carries a pistol.

29

RETTA

Dear Odell,
I never told you how I figured out I loved you. It's a mighty big thing to decide on love, especially when you are about to give your life to a man. I didn't have a notion about how to decide such a big thing, so I come up with two questions to ask myself. The first was, if anybody ever tried to hurt Odell how would I feel, and the second was, if somebody did hurt Odell, what would I do? The rage that answered the first question answered the second. I didn't even have time for my thoughts to think. I knew in my body I'd kill the man who hurt you. I felt I could do that. You gave me strength I didn't know I had.

I done what I promised I wouldn't, Odell. I've brought the white woman and her children into our home. Proverbs 28:27, remember, O? "He that giveth unto the poor shall not lack: but he that hideth his eyes shall have many a curse." There is no greater curse than to turn one's eyes from the grief stricken, and Gertrude's afflicted in body and spirit. Her children love her and I believe it's them that keeps her alive, but she can't see beyond the darkness. She don't know that's just the devil playing his tricks, but I do and he knows it. He'll put up a fight to hold on to what he's got, but devil be damned, I got the rage of what I understood when I figured out I loved you.

Your wife,
Oretta

Odell's grizzled face flashes before me. He's unshaven but smiling and happy to see me. His face comes right down to mine like he means to give me a kiss, but instead he whispers, "Somebody wants to show you her alphabet."

In gladness I wake and in sadness come into another day. It's just a dream, I tell myself, nothing more. I sit up in my sling to get my bearings and throw my legs to the side where they dangle above the ground where the periwinkle blossom has faded, where my baby girl is buried. If I'd known how well I could sleep outside I might have done it years ago.

It's Sunday. Sugar sees I've risen and lets go a cockle-doodle-doo.

"Too late," I tell the bird. "Where were you at dawn?"

Sugar turns his backside to me and struts to the henhouse by the stables, where I spy a little head peering around the side. Sue Ann's girl, Comfort, is watching me.

"What're you doin'?" I say. "Come over here and let me see you."

She comes around the side and skips to me.

"Why're you sleeping outside?" she asks.

"Ain't no room inside. Why're you over here spying on me?"

"I ain't spying. I'm looking."

"Your mama know you're here?"

"She's the one sent me to find out if you're comin' to Bible study today."

We've had no church sermons since Preacher and Odell left for market, just Bible study, but I ain't gone. I reach out my hand, and Comfort takes it and pulls to help me up. I rock myself back and forth 'til I can get my feet on the ground. She pulls so hard her little behind hits the ground once

I'm up and out.

"Hoo, child, you're strong," I tell her. "I mighta been stuck there all day if you didn't come along."

It takes me a minute to stand upright. Seems to take longer and longer these days to move without pain. I raise my hands up over my head and stretch.

"You gonna be at the prayer meetin'?" I ask.

"Yes, ma'am, I am."

"You gonna sing?"

"Oh, yes, ma'am."

"What you gonna sing?"

"Jesus loves me!"

"You know he does!"

"Yes, ma'am," she says. "He loves you, too."

"That's what they tell me."

She giggles behind her hand.

"Tell your mama I'll be there."

She runs out the yard and down the street to deliver the news. When she is gone I steady myself against the porch rail and close my eyes before pushing myself up the steps to live in the day. Inside Alma and Mary fold their blankets and stack them on the floor. Edna's got biscuits in the oven and coffee on the stove. There's energy in this house. Mary runs and hugs me around the legs.

"You slept late," she said.

"I sure did. Smells good, Edna."

These girls are good soldiers in their mama's army.

"Your mother up?" I ask Alma. The girl ain't been away from her mama since they got here except to steal food and hide it on a back shelf in the stable. I've not said anything yet. What can I say to a hungry child with a sick mother and winter coming?

"She's awake," Alma tells me, "but she ain't getting up."

I cross to the kitchen and pour some black pepper in my hand and hold it tight in my fist so it don't spill.

"Time for that to change," I say and Alma's eyes light up. She races ahead to the bedroom door.

"Let me do this," I tell her. "Sick people are like rattlesnakes. They don't like to be pushed or prodded."

I go into my bedroom where Gertrude lies awake on my side of the bed staring up at the ceiling wearing one of my old nightgowns. Even the blanket that covers her can't hide how skinny she is. Her hipbones jut out so far, it's a wonder they ain't broke through the skin.

"Why ain't you out of that bed?" I ask her.

She rolls over and turns away from me. I yank the cover from her with my left hand, but she catches hold and pulls it back up and under her chin, closing her eyes and pulling her knees to her chest. There's strength there. I move to the side of the bed and blow the pepper in her face. She's mad, but gets caught in a fit of sneezes. She's got to sit up to clear her head.

"It's time to get up and start working on getting you back to where you belong." I come alongside to help her stand. She pulls her arm away.

Between sneezes she spits out, "Why're you helpin' me?"

"Christian thing to do," I tell her.

She pushes herself off the bed, stands and says, "I don't need no nigger friends."

I get right up in Gertrude's face. "Don't you ever call me that again."

She don't look away, but finally says, "All right, I won't."

"Seems to me you need any friend you can get, Gertrude Pardee. Now get your tail out to that table and sit down to eat with your children. You're scaring them."

She weaves across the floor like a drunk, but I don't reach out to steady her. She's got to make her own way.

■ ■ ■ ■

When I walk out of my house there's a whole posse of turkeys in the field by the lane, eight in all. The Toms are preening. They got themselves worked up, spitting and booming trying to get the females' attention, no notion Thanksgiving is upon them. Walking down the road to Sue Ann's I am amazed all over again at how quick the good folks of Shake Rag have worked to clear the land. Trees are moved from the lane so all can pass through. Every roof and outhouse has been repaired or rebuilt, some already painted green to match the last of summertime grass. Save chimneys and outhouses blowing over, we weathered what come fairly well. Beyond us is another story all together. Telegraph poles have been moved from the road, but the lines, and all manner of debris, are so tangled in trees they hang like snakes from the branches. An automobile sits on its side in the field outside Shake Rag, and Mrs. Walker's roof is half torn off. If her heart didn't stop when it did, the hurricane most certainly would have killed her. Maybe it's a blessing she didn't have to suffer through this. I don't know. Ain't mine to see. How the other counties inward fared is my question, but they got to have done well enough for Mr. Coles to get through. If he can manage a journey at his age, then surely Odell, who is ten years younger, can too.

I hear all the women in the house from the road as I come, singing me to the porch. I'm late to join eight Sisters present and ready for the spirit. Little Comfort stands in the middle singing the song, waving her arms like she's leading a choir. Mabel and Myrtis share looks when I come through the door. It's quick but I see. I've been the subject of talk. I join the end of the song as I make my way to the empty chair next to Sue Ann and do a little dance with Comfort as I go. Sue Ann smiles as I ease myself down. No husbands are here today. Roy has to work the railroad and will be gone the better part of the week. The rest of the men are either working or too tired from working, so their wives have come to be sure they got God's ear if needed. When the song is done, Comfort goes to sit against the wall of the parlor with the rest of the children. They lift their legs one after the other as she comes through, making play out of it. Mabel nods her head to me from across the circle, and I respond in kind. Then Sue Ann asks us all to take up hands and leads us in prayer, thanking the good Lord for the day we find ourselves in, for the clear skies and good breeze, and for continued blessings on the good people of Shake Rag, particularly those in need.

"Yes, Lord," we say.

She asks special prayers for Preacher and Odell, and I squeeze her hand in gratitude. I shouldn't have stayed away so long. She says amen, looks at me and smiles. Opening her Bible, Sue Ann says, "I ain't no Preacher, Lord knows that. I'm just a woman in His service who wakes up afraid every day."

"I know that," Myrtis says.

"Afraid for my children, afraid for my husband, myself and afraid for Shake Rag."

"We're gonna be all right," I say. "We're gonna be all right."

"How you know that?" Mabel asks me.

All the Sisters get quiet. Sue Ann clears her throat but don't go on. Even the children against the wall sit still. Looks like Mabel's been put in charge; otherwise somebody would have something to say.

"I ain't the only one here knows my Bible," I say. "That's what the word tells us."

"You know the Garrets lost their boy over in Bowen to fever?" Mabel tells me. "Left behind a wife and two children."

I feel heat climb up my face. Across from me in a chair Dot Garrett is stricken by Mabel's words, like her boy's died a second time. She presses a handkerchief to her mouth.

"Oh, Dot," I say. "I'm sorry. I didn't know."

"Thank you, Retta," she whispers.

"If you answered your door you would know these things," Mabel said.

"Let it go, Mabel," Dot says. "Now she knows."

But Mabel ain't done.

"Why you close your door to me, Retta? Why am I sitting here telling you news near on two weeks after that boy was laid to rest?"

I can only shake my head. My voice has left me.

Sue Ann finally interrupts. "Psalm 46 has strengthened some of us, and I hope we will find food in that word and feed on it."

"No, Sue Ann. Let it wait," Mabel says. Every woman in the room sits upright and holds her breath.

"If I opened my door for you every time you come to me for something," I say, "my legs would give out."

"You think you're better than me," Mabel says.

The women shift in their seats, waiting for the answer.

"I don't think I'm better than you, Mabel. You're the reason we all know who to help in time of need, who's sick or needs to be fed. That's a powerful service to the women here."

Dot pats her leg but Mabel don't feel it.

"Then why you turn your back on us?"

She's got her teeth in me now and won't let loose.

"Seems to me," I tell her, "you want something more from me, Mabel. All the time you want and need something more. What is it this time?"

The children get quiet and wide-eyed at the words. Children ain't never still except in times of trouble.

"I don't want nothin' from you," she says.

The women all look to one another, but nobody meets my eye.

"Good. Anything else I need to know?" I ask the room.

They shake their heads no.

"Children," I ask, "ya'll got anything to say?"

Comfort raises her hand.

"I lost a tooth."

"Come over here so I can look."

She comes and stands in front of me and opens her mouth so I can see where a front tooth is missing, and I pull her up to sit on my lap. A child on a lap forces calm on everybody.

"We want to know how long you're going to have them white folks up in your house?" Mabel says.

"Why ya'll need to know that?"

Sue Ann clears her throat and says, "There is worry about white folks moving into Shake Rag."

Here it is. Finally. They all been wondering what I'm up to.

"This is our place, Retta," Myrtis says.

"When you lost your girl and Odell got hurt," Mabel says, "all of Shake Rag was by your side."

Dot says, "Oh, Mabel, don't."

But Mabel don't pay her no mind.

"And?" I ask.

"And seems like all you got to worry yourself with is white folks and white folk problems. You remember you're a colored woman, don't you, Retta? You remember where you belong?"

I look at each of these women 'cause I know Mabel says what all of them are thinking.

"Shake Rag ain't no pen for cattle," I say. "You think you invented suffering? Times are hard everywhere. All you got to do is step out beyond the lane and see we aren't the only ones hurting. Sorrow don't know color. Ya'll grown enough to know that."

Comfort busts into tears and says, "Why ya'll fightin?"

I rock her some. "You ever get mad at your brothers?"

She nods and I say, "That's all this is, baby, a family squabble."

I look at all the Sisters gathered 'round, and each nods in understanding. They know what I've said. All except Mabel, she won't meet my eyes.

30

GERTRUDE

My first day outside and I'm still winded from washing up at the pump, but the warmth of the sunshine is a welcome to me. My bones drink what heat there is and are warmed from the inside. Daddy would say this is potato weather, or close to it. The season's turned. You can smell earth and wood mixed together in the air. All that's missing is smoke from burning leaves.

Alma stands behind where I sit on the porch swing and brushes the tangles out of my wet hair, yanking the brush so hard it feels like the hair is coming out of my head. I'm hardheaded, but even that's got its limits. I squeeze the top of my head and tell her to brush from the bottom up. She changes direction but don't go any easier. She's trying to beat the knots out. I don't remember the last time I took a brush to my girls' heads, but Retta has. These girls are polished clean.

When Alma finishes brushing, she takes the handle of the brush and divides my hair into three sections. She's got small hands but is quick with a braid. Pulling two sides of my hair tight in each hand she lays them one over the other through the middle, pulling hard as she goes. When it's finished, she ties my hair in a knot at the bottom and drops it like a rope so it falls to the center of my spine. She pushes me between the shoulder blades with three sharp fingers and tells me to get back in the house, acting like she's the mama and I'm the child. When I don't move, she comes and stands in front of me with her fists balled up at her sides and stomps her foot.

Mary comes up from the porch steps and says, "You can't tell her what to do." She gives Alma a shove, and Alma shoves her right back so hard Mary flies backward off the porch and lands on her back. Alma jumps off the porch and is at Mary's side, sorry as can be. Mary forgives quick, always has.

"Alma," I say, "what in the world has got into you?"

She sits in the grass and scrunches up her face. "I don't want you to die."

"You think I'd be sitting up and walking

371

around if I was plannin' on dyin'? You think I'd be talking to you right now?"

"I don't know," she says.

She hangs her head and cries, worn out from worry. I hold out my arms, and she comes up the steps and to the swing with Mary following behind. I rub her back while she cries.

"She ain't dead, Alma, it's okay, she ain't dead," Mary says over and over while she pats her sister's back. Alma looks at her and laughs through the tears.

"I'm sitting right here talking to the two of you," I say. "What a scare that would be if I was dead and gone and sitting up talking like I wasn't."

They get the giggles, and we rock in the quiet of the day listening to the bobwhite call from the woods. You can't tell a child some things are worse than death. It's bad enough to carry that knowing as a grown woman.

I missed my brother's funeral. The Reverend found them. He buried them quick and then burned all the furniture in the bedroom. Weren't no visitation or ceremony — just words said over dirt. Nobody asked what I wanted or what I thought. He didn't bury Berns and Marie next to Mama and Daddy. Just set them out next to the Otts and Berrys where they don't belong. The Reverend might be new to this town, but common sense ought to tell a person not to bury kin separate. Folks will think there was strain between us, but there never was. Now the family is split apart, and I got no way to put us back together. Not even a headstone will help even if there was money for one.

A colored woman comes out of a yard from down the lane. She's the only one I've seen in the street all day. Everybody else is gone to work. She's got her daughter walking beside her. You can tell they eat good; they ain't skinny like us. The little girl's got her hair done up in cornrows. The woman keeps her eyes down until she gets in front of Retta's house, then looks up and says, "Hi do."

I give her a nod. Her little girl's got eyes for Mary. She smiles and waves. Mary jumps up off the swing and waves back. The girl holds her belly and pretends to laugh and Mary does the same. Then Mary turns in a circle and the girl gives a jump and does the same. They're showing off their dresses.

"Stop that bragging," I say.

These children got more energy than they know what to do with. They've been cooped up watching and worrying after me.

"Ya'll go earn a nickel somewhere. I know

there's work to be had after that storm. Don't take less no matter what they tell you."

Alma lifts her head. "What will you do?"

"I guess I got to sit here 'til I'm better. Can't do much else."

Alma jumps up and says, "I'll get us a dime each."

"Go on then and don't worry Edna. She's got her own work to do."

They run wild through the grassy field by the road, racing each other down the lane with their hair flying behind them. Alma's fast, but Mary's close behind. In another two years it will be a fight to the finish. I get to my feet and make my way down the porch holding the rail as I go. I feel like I'm asleep and awake at the same time; it is an odd thing, but my feet put themselves one in front of the other until I am at the edge of the yard. Retta's rooster follows at my heels. The air is as soft and mild as I ever felt. It laps at my face and I get strength from it, so I let it pull me along to the place we call home. Once I'm to the porch, I sit to rest before going to see the mess I know I'm to find inside. The view from here to the town has changed. Trees that once blocked the road from sight are gone or snapped like matchsticks near their tops where the wind was strongest. Horses and wagons and the occasional automobile drive through the crossroad of Main Street and onto places beyond. I wonder where they're going. If we had enough money, we could go, too. Ain't nothing holding us here no more.

I pull myself to my feet and make my way up the steps. The screen door has been torn away, and the wood door is swollen shut from the wet. I put my shoulder into it and shove 'til it gives. There's wasps in the kitchen, diving and burrowing together by the windowsill over the countertop. The place stinks of mildew. The rooster's followed me inside, pecking at the grub worms that crawl along the floor. The cabinets and pantry still stand but the supplies inside have gone to rot. When I open one cabinet, wasps fly out in every direction. A jar of jam has exploded, likely busted open from the pressure of the storm. Wasps cover the remnants in swarms. Flour and rice are infested with boll weevils.

The hole in the roof is at the frame line along the front of the house by the road. The wood beam lies exposed. It held steady and don't show signs of weakening, but the house around me is in ruin. Shingles and wood lie along the parlor floor. Three brown lizards run across them as I make my way through the rubble. The furniture's wet and the couch has already got mold growing. You can see the sky from where I stand in the parlor, blue with white clouds that look like cotton. The windows along the east wall toward town are broken. This part of the house needs to be cleared out and burned. There's nothing to save. The bedrooms ain't no better. I lean against the door frame of the room I slept in. I'm tired just looking at this mess. The stench of mold and mildew get caught in my throat, and I'm doubled over with a fit of coughing. The rooster pecks at my heels.

"Get off me," I say and brush him away with my foot. He backs away but don't leave my side. Queerest thing I ever did see. The board that Mrs. Walker used to cover her hiding place is swollen and upended, sitting crossways atop the other boards. I move it with my foot to peer below at Mrs. Walker's wood box, then get down on my hands and knees and lift it from the hiding place. Within is what is left of the money I took and the letter Mrs. Walker left behind. I fold the dollars and letter one on top the other and tuck them in my dress alongside my bosom, then lean against the wood rail of the bed frame and sit looking at the sky above me. A line of pelicans, thirteen in all, fly low overhead toward the east. More clouds roll behind, and I lie down on the floor next to the hole and watch them go from left to right in a lazy line. The outside breeze is a blessing to my senses.

I wake to a light rain falling on my face and the rooster crowing above me on the bed like it's morning. The day has grown and begun to fade. I've stayed past my time. Alma will be worried. I push myself from the floor and go into the girls' bedroom to look for my shotgun. The bird follows like a dog. The closet in this bedroom is intact. Everything within is salvageable. Blankets, sheets, an extra ticking for a mattress we never used sit stacked in a pile on the floor. Way back in the corner standing upright is my shotgun and, behind it, a paper bag filled with blue yarn being turned into something more. Mary's present for me? The rooster comes to peck at my heels. He flies up when I shove him away and sits on the girls' bed and crows. I reach back inside and grasp the shotgun by the barrel. An automobile pulls into the yard and stops near the kitchen door. The engine shuts off, and the gun slips from my fingers and falls sideways behind the blankets. The rooster moves up beside me and lifts his head and crows again. Outside, the automobile door slams, and a man hollers, "Hello?"

I left the back door wide open. I slide into the closet and close the door softly behind me. The gap at the bottom is big enough to put my toes through — big enough to see what or who is coming. The man's heavy footfall is at once on the porch outside. He gives three sharp knocks on the open door.

"Anybody home?"

I know that voice. The rooster pecks along the bottom of the closet door looking for me.

"St. George Sheriff's Department," the man says.

In the dark I feel something slide out from between the blankets then over and across my feet. I've wakened a snake of considerable size. It curls 'round my right foot, and I watch its tongue flick in the light from beneath the door. I killed enough snakes in cotton fields to know a copperhead when I see one. I grasp it quick by the back of the neck. Its body writhes and squeezes. I lift the heel of my shoe and place its head beneath, then push until the head is crushed and life is gone.

"Hello?" the sheriff calls again.

He walks into the parlor and stops. To listen or look, I don't know. He walks

378

through to my bedroom and kicks the floorboard that I forgot to put back in place. The box is laid open. He will know someone was here. He turns the knob of the closet door. It creaks open and shuts.

"Jiminy," he mutters, likely at the smell. "Whewee."

The shadow of him falls through the light and across the bottom of the door as he enters this room. The rooster is what saves me. Though I can't see, it's clear by the rustle of feathers and loud squawks he's gone after the sheriff.

"Shit," the man hollers.

He backs in a rush out to the parlor. There's a loud thump and everything goes quiet. The man catches his breath and finally leaves, shutting the kitchen door behind him. When I come out I find the rooster lying on the parlor floor, still breathing. He looks at me wall-eyed so I reach down and take him by the neck. With one wring he is dead and gone.

Dark has fallen by the time I make it back to Retta's house. I carry my shame in the night, gun in one hand, rooster and bag of yarn in the other, the scratch of what I stole against my bosom. Alma runs, almost knocking me over where I stand in the road. Retta comes to the porch and looks me over.

"I had to kill your rooster," I tell her. "Couldn't be helped."

"I expect he had it coming," Retta says. "Get him cleaned up. He'll be supper."

31

ANNIE

My husband wears his gun late into the evening. I've heard his explanations echo through the house and outside my window. He's stirred enough fear of post-hurricane horrors to create a small, armed militia. It's a show of force, a boy's game of soldiers. Last night he came into my room and stood for a long while watching from the foot of my bed.

"What are you trying to prove, Mother?"

I kept my eyes closed but he persisted.

"You must eat," he said. "I'm worried for you."

When I remained unresponsive he took a different tack. It was as if he was talking to himself really, speaking aloud a tale to believe.

"We're going to be fine, Mother. We will go to Camp and see if we can salvage our finances. There are ways."

Of course this is all about our finances.

"If the boys are to be taken care of in their old age I need you by my side. Do you understand?"

I wondered when he would bring the children into this.

I opened my eyes and looked at him. "No, I'm finished with Camp."

Then I turned to watch the night sky out the bedroom window — the Milky Way so clear I could seemingly reach out and touch it. My husband rocked back and forth on his feet, heel to toe, like he does when he is impatient, and finally came to stand before the window blocking my view.

"Goddammit, Annie, you're going to Camp if I have to carry you there myself."

Edwin is always so self-assured he borders on audacity, but I am no better than my husband. I believed what I wanted to believe. What I took for quiet intent and focus all these years of our marriage was, in actuality, duplicity. I simply chose to believe the wrong narrative. A person's character should be plainly seen. My papa, despite his wealth, was plain enough for the world to see. A city boy, he could fight and drink as well as the next man, but he was educated and kind. He had his idiosyncrasies. He was nervous in the country. He found the quiet impossible to gauge and slept best with noise. After I married he said, "You live in a fantasy, Annie. Don't be fooled by appearances. A quiet place can still hold chaos." None of this is what my father wanted for me.

Retta told me this morning, Edwin has decided against having the telephone repaired and has sent word to the doctor that I'm not eating. He must prove to be the concerned husband. Otherwise what will people say? *Edwin Coles's Yankee wife has lost her mind, poor man,* but my mind is quite clear. I've taken to my bed and have no intention of rising. Retta's paraded all of my favorite foods through the door, but I've no stomach for anything now. Living without food isn't as difficult as I imagined. The mind grows sharp once the headaches diminish. Grief is a mountain that rises in the throat, blocking all else.

"Miss Annie, you got to eat," Retta says. "You can't let him win."

"He isn't winning, Retta. There are no winners. He can achieve nothing without my consent."

"It would just kill your children, Miss Annie. Just kill them to see you starving yourself like this."

"No. It will release them of at least one

burden."

I wait now. Every day I wait, sitting in my bed propped against goose down pillows, a sparrow on her nest. The windows in my room give a bird's-eye view of the comings and goings of daily life. There now in the field is the largest osprey I've ever seen. He sits in plain sight where men are working, his head swiveling, owl-like, with a watchful pensive gaze. For some time he remains unseen by workers, but when one laborer draws too close, the osprey attempts to take flight, and it's then I see what the bird has been guarding. The kill in his talons is too big for him to carry. He must stay with the animal if he means to claim it for himself.

One of the Norris boys runs toward it with raised arms and the bird is forced to abandon his prey. He circles as the boy reaches the kill and holds it by the tail for the rest of the men to see. It's a raccoon already stiff with death — such an oddity. The boy swings the animal by the tail and flings it as far and high as he can. The osprey swoops in, catches it in his claws and is dragged by the weight to the tall grasses beyond the field. The men whoop with glee at the sight. They've been given a show. The sound of laughter drifts lazily through the open window in my room and is overtaken by the sound of knocking at the front door. Retta's sure footsteps click across the floor. The door is opened, and the doctor ushered inside. He waits in the foyer while Retta goes to fetch my husband.

"John," I call from my bed.

"Ann?"

"Up here."

He hesitates at the bottom of the steps, then climbs slowly toward me. He crosses the wide hallway and is all at once through my door wearing the same tattered brown suit he wore the night of his visit. I wonder at the last time he considered new clothing. I smell him. It's not a repugnant scent — to the contrary — but I know when a man forgoes his own hygiene it means one of two things: a heavy workload or poor mental state.

"Come in," I say.

I reach to the night table for the water glass there, and he comes forward in a small rush to help me.

"How are you feeling?" he asks. "How's the hand?"

I raise it for him to see. "Better."

"Shall we remove the stitches?"

"Yes, that'll be fine."

He lays his bag on the bed alongside my legs and sets to work pulling the black thread from my hand. He recognizes the repair and looks at me quizzically.

"I tore it open. Retta re-stitched it."

"You should have sent for me."

"I suspect between the sickness and hurricane you've been busy enough. Were there many injuries?"

"Could've been worse."

"I've heard you are no longer charging the poor for your services."

He grimaces, embarrassed to have his humanity on display. I've forgotten what humility looks like.

He dodges the question. "I've heard you aren't eating."

"Touché," I say.

His hands are cold to the touch, and my skin has grown into the threads, so he must tug hard to remove them. We sit in quiet as he works.

"Edwin sent for you, not me," I finally say.

"Is it true?"

"Yes."

"Why? Are you ill?"

I shake my head no, overcome by my own emotion.

"What is it then, Ann?" he asks softly.

Downstairs Edwin has come charging into the foyer.

"Where is he?"

"I don't know, sir. He was just here," Retta says.

John looks to see if I will respond, but I turn away.

"Up here, Edwin," he calls out.

My husband climbs the staircase with the same deliberation he's done for fifty-four years. When he comes through the room, he's filled with a young man's energy. His hand is outstretched and welcoming. John rises, takes Edwin's hand in his own and shakes — the respect of two men who've known each other a long time.

"Thank you for coming, Doctor."

"Of course."

"May I speak with you outside?" Edwin asks.

"If it's regarding Ann, I'd rather talk here, in front of her, if that's all right."

"Of course," Edwin replies.

This is a wrinkle in Edwin's plan.

"She won't even look at food," Edwin says. "Hasn't eaten a bite since I returned. I'm unsure of how long before that."

John sits in the chair by my side and lays his hand on the bed.

"A week, over a week? How long, Ann?"

Since our dinner is what he is asking. He's done the calculations. Both men look at me. Edwin stands quietly just beyond John in the center of the room, holding his hat. I raise my shoulders and feign ignorance.

Edwin says, "She rarely speaks, and when she does it's often nonsensical."

John ignores him and pulls the blankets back and presses on my abdomen.

"Do you know what day it is?" he asks.

"Wednesday," I tell him.

He removes his stethoscope and listens to my chest.

"That's right," he says, "and you know who I am?"

"You are our doctor."

"Do you know who he is?" John asks and looks back to my husband.

"No," I say.

Edwin says, "See what I mean?"

John places a thermometer in my mouth, then takes a small magnifying glass and looks into my eyes, holding open each lid to see if there is anything lurking within my brain. When he finishes and before he pulls away, I whisper, "I thought I knew him. I was wrong."

"What did she say?" Edwin asks.

John holds a finger up to Edwin, then reads the thermometer and looks in my ears and down my throat. When he is finished he pulls the blankets back over me and packs his bag.

"I'd like to take you to the hospital for some tests, Ann."

Edwin comes to the foot of the bed and says, "She doesn't trust hospitals. Her father died in one."

I look out the window while they discuss my fate. Retta stands beyond the clothesline inspecting Spanish moss the yard boys have brought to her. She shows them something amid the moss, unsatisfied. They drop it at her feet and run back through the fields to the woods. There will be no moss to be found in trees after such a storm. She'll have to stuff the ticking for Camp with corn husks.

"Ann," John calls, bringing me back into the room, "you won't last much longer without sustenance."

I look at them, first Edwin, then John.

"Can't you give her something to make her eat?"

"We can't force her to eat, Edwin. She has to decide that for herself."

"No hospital," I whisper.

"You understand if you don't eat, you will die?" John asks me.

He's kind, and I am sorry I didn't see just how kind much sooner. Words are pointless now, but I say them anyway, loud enough for both men to hear.

"I understand."
There's nothing more to say.

32

RETTA

"I don't remember asking for your opinion," Mr. Coles says when I tell him I fear Miss Annie ain't up to Camp this year.

"No, sir," I say to the man. "I know that, but she needs a nurse. I can't see to her and make the food for Camp if I aim to feed all them people." I know half the politicians in the state count on an invitation to eat my food. We hold the best tent in Camp for eatin', and Mr. Coles knows that as much as I do.

What's this man thinking, that Miss Annie's going to get out of that bed and sit upright in an automobile next to him for the long drive there? I am behind in my work. We got to go up and down the stairs to Miss Annie at least five times a day; whether she eats the food or not, it's got to be brought, and she needs her toilet. I can't be stopping if I aim to get everything done.

The peanuts boiling on the stove should've been done a week ago.

"Hire one, then," he says.

"You want me to do the hiring?"

"I've got more pressing things to worry about."

I want to ask, *More pressing than a sick wife who's starving herself in the bed upstairs?* But I keep my mouth shut.

"Hire a white woman," he tells me as he comes through the kitchen and grabs his hat from the peg by the back door. He runs straight into Edna, who is coming through the door like a rush of wind. He backs up to let her through, and she ducks her head and squeezes by as he slams the door behind him. Edna jumps at the noise. She's scared to death of the man. Already she's dropped a bowl and broke it in front of him. He went on about his business, but I can't trust her to serve the meals alone. She gets dropsy when she's nervous and sets Mr. Coles on edge. I can't take no chance on her getting fired before Camp. He's ready for a fight these days, and we got to be careful not to give him one.

"I stirred the pudding good," Edna says. "It's boiling. Want me to take it off the flame?"

"No, leave it. Got a couple hours yet."

"You want me to take a tray to Miss Annie while you look?"

"No, I'll take the tray. You get out there and stir 'til I tell you not to."

"Yes'm," she says. "I ain't never ate no pudding before."

"And you ain't going to anytime soon."

She sighs before going back out the door.

Miss Annie grows paler, and her face more sunken, every day from the lack of sustenance. The windows of her bedroom are open, and you can smell the pudding pot bubbling over the fire in the yard. I lay the tray on the nightstand and sit on the edge of the bed.

"I brought you some grits, just how you like 'em, Miss Annie. Extra butter and bacon."

She smiles and shakes her head no. She ain't talked since the doctor came. I fill one spoonful and hold it out to her lips, but she won't take it and I don't press. I lay the bowl back on the tray and hold the glass of milk for her while she drinks it slow. She finishes and lays her head back on the pillow, tired from the effort. She's become weaker these past two days.

"You want me to read the newspaper headlines?" I ask. She nods her head yes. The front page is all about Camp and who will be there. I read through the long list of preachers and politicians. Many names I know 'cause I fed them through the years, but one name stops me when I say it aloud, Clelia McGowan.

"Ain't that the woman Miss Molly works for?" I ask. Miss Annie furrows her brow. "You reckon if that lady is going to be there, maybe Miss Molly might come, too? Not six weeks ago you was sitting in that kitchen wishing for the girls to come to Camp. Wouldn't that be good?"

She looks down at her hands and picks at the back of them. Her nails are split, and her skin's so dry it's turning to scales.

"Don't you want to see your girls, Miss Annie?" She covers her face, and I fold the paper and leave it on the bed. There's nothing more for me to say here. Ain't my place.

I've got the tray in my hands when a shout goes up from the yard. From the window I see Edna turn in the direction of the sound. She shields her eyes from the late-afternoon sun with an upturned hand. I follow her gaze and find them against the glare like phantoms coming through the woods in a single line — horse bells jingling ahead of them. The men are back.

I drop the tray on the bureau and run for the steps. My feet can't catch up to the pounding of my heart. I go quick as I can through the house and out the back, climbing the hill of the root cellar to look out at the fields as they come into view, one after another, slow but sure. Eddie leads the way, slumped over. The strain of the journey wears on all the men. Seven wagons come before I spy Odell's, but Lonnie is the one driving. Oh, Lord.

The last of the wagons come up from the woods side by side and in rows, but Preacher and Odell are not among them. Eddie leads the wagons to what's left of the barn, but Lonnie pulls his reins to the left and toward the house. When he gets near, he jumps from his seat and walks purposeful and steadfast, only it ain't the house he's coming to, it's me. My legs get weak, and I fall to my knees.

"R-Retta," he says, squatting down next to me. "It's okay, Odell's okay."

"Where's he at then?" I ask.

He lays his arm around me and says, "Preacher m-man took sick, and Odell wouldn't l-leave him. I tried to t-talk him out of it, Retta. Eddie and me both did, but he said n-no. He m-made m-me bring you these."

He hands me a stack of letters all made out to me. I don't have to count them to know by the size of the pile there's one letter there for every day he's been gone, same as I done for him. I can't get my heart to slow.

"Where's M-Mother?" he asks.

"Honey," I tell him, "your mama's decided to lie down and die. None of us can talk sense into her."

He takes a sharp breath in and runs to the house, leaving me sitting on the grass in the middle of a workday. I pick the first letter from the pile and run my finger over the writing and along the back where it is sealed with Odell's spit. I pry open the envelope and lift out the page to read.

Oretta,
Mr. Lonnie waits while I write this so I got to be quick. Preacher is dyin' and there ain't nothing I can do but hold his hand. He told me to go home and may God forgive me, I want to. But it is a corrupt soul that leaves a friend in time of need. Neither you nor me could live with that.

When I close my eyes, it's your face I see. When I wake it's your voice I hear. O, O, O, How I love the letter O.

Ever faithful,
Odell

■ ■ ■ ■

It's dark by the time me and Edna walk home. There's a damp chill in the air. Gertrude and the girls got a fire going in Mrs. Walker's yard so big you can see it from Main Street. She's burning all the parlor furniture. Sparks fly to the sky like stars looking for a place to live. The pecan trees are lit all the way to the top branches and the flames taller than two men stacked together. Alma sits on the back steps plucking a big tom turkey. She waves when she sees us but stays steady with her work.

"How'd you catch him?" I ask.

"Rock upside the head," she answers.

Gertrude comes out of the kitchen pulling Mrs. Walker's rug behind her. Alma scoots to the edge of the step to let her mother pass. When Gertrude gets to the yard, I go and lift the back end, and together we toss it to the fire and watch it burn. Gertrude's got color in her face that is part from the fire, and part from the release of what ailed her. She's coming back to life.

"We'll sleep here tonight," Gertrude says. "We got enough to keep us warm and you been put out long enough."

"You ain't got no cause to be sleeping in

half a house on a night like this."

"I don't want to sleep here, Mama," Edna says.

"I don't care what you want. This is what we got for now. We'll make the best of it. Come Monday, I got Sewing Circle, then we'll figure this out."

"You ain't got Sewing Circle, Monday," I tell her. "The Coles family needs a nurse for Miss Annie at Camp and you're it. Same wages as Circle."

"Says who?"

"Says Lonnie and Mr. Coles. Lonnie will hold the job."

"What I gotta do?"

"You got to keep her clean and warm and see to her toilet. Feed her some if she'll let you. If you got extra time, I'll need hands in the kitchen. Next Saturday we feed a table of ten five times over for supper."

"What about my girls?"

"We'll take them instead of the yard boys. It's my kitchen, and Miss Annie allows me to dictate how it's run. They can fetch and carry and make a little money for their work. When their hands ain't busy, there's Bible school they can tend to. You'll sleep in the wagon, or under if it rains, and take your meals with me."

She turns to the girls and says, "Ya'll go

inside and get ready for bed. Let Miss Retta and me talk."

Alma goes last, holding the limp bird by the neck, and shuts the door behind them. Gertrude comes around the fire to me and stands for a bit.

"I ain't a good person," she finally says.

"Says who?" I ask.

"The Bible, for one."

I keep quiet so she can finish.

"I took what ain't mine and I'm sorry for it."

She pulls out of her apron pocket some money and an envelope, then takes my hand, presses them into my palm and folds my fingers around them.

"I found these along with a dress Mrs. Walker left for you. They were in the parlor. I don't know why you didn't see them sitting out when you found her, but I did and I took them."

All over again I see Mrs. Walker's lifeless face in my mind's eye. I hear the rush of breath in my ears.

"I spent three of the dollars on medicine. I took the dress and made clothes for my children. I stole from you, and you ain't been nothing but good to me — to us. I don't know how I'll pay you back or even if I can."

She's looking at the fire, her eyes full to the brim. I stand alongside her and turn my face to the flames to give her some privacy. The warmth feels good. There's smoke coming out of every chimney in Shake Rag. I hope Odell has a fire tonight. The tide has turned and I'm alone in the turning.

"I guess you wouldn't have took them if you didn't have need," I finally say.

I hold the money out to her. But she won't take it.

"Go on," I tell her. "You need it more than I do."

"You saved me. Why?"

"You saved yourself."

"No," she says. "You know that ain't true."

"I did what had to be done is all."

"I ain't worthy."

"Child," I say, "whatever happened to you ain't your fault."

"You don't know what I done," she says.

"I know what's been done to you. I seen it when your daddy thought he was doing right to get you married off. I seen it in the marks your husband left on you and in your worry over Mary and your girls. What speaks the truth is their love for you."

"They'd feel different if they knew what I did to their daddy."

She looks at me.

"If not him, it was gonna be you," I tell her.

"My soul is damned."

"Bull," I say. "Your soul is freed."

She takes the money when I press, and I leave her at the fire and turn toward home to shed myself of this day. The people of Shake Rag are standing in the yard and sitting up on my porch: Roy and Sue Ann, Bobo and Myrtis, Mabel and all the others, waiting on me. They stand as I come through.

"Is it true what we hear 'bout Preacher and Odell?" Roy asks.

"It is," I say. "Preacher's bad off."

They hold one another for comfort, all but Mabel who stands alone and upright by the porch steps. There's no words left for me to say.

"Preacher told us of our treasures before we understood what he meant," Mabel says. "He reminded us we all got the same thing Jesus had when He was born, God's love. Ain't that right?"

Mabel reaches for my hand, and oh, Lord, I take it and hold on tight.

"We got God's love," she says. "We are strong in His love."

"But what can we do?" Roy asks. "We got to do something."

"Go fetch Preacher and Odell," I tell them. "They're a four-day ride out, just south of Berkeley. Go get them. Bring 'em home."

Roy jumps from the porch, and the men follow to make plans. Mabel stays by my side, and when they're all gone she asks, "You need coffee?"

I nod, and she leads me by the hand to the inside of my own house.

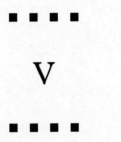

V

33

GERTRUDE

Lonnie guides the wagon down Freedom Road toward St. George where Indian Fields Campground is. October's come, and the dogwood leaves along the road have already changed, like they've been dipped in red paint. Dogwood always turns first in the fall. Won't be long 'til the sugar maples follow. The hickory trees have begun to shed their nuts, and wagon wheels crunch over them, leaving squirrels to scramble in our wake to gather their treasure. Alma and Mary hang over the backside of the wagon watching the world go by while the Missus lies covered in layers of quilts on a mattress stuffed with corn husks by the yard boys. She's been asleep since we started off from home early this morning. I've told the girls to stay quiet so as not to wake her, and they've listened.

As we get closer to Camp the world

explodes into sound. I don't know how the Missus sleeps through such racket. Folks around us call out to each other and sing. Pretty soon there's wagons everywhere we look, all headed to the same place, a stream turning into a river. A wagon rides up alongside us, the third one in an hour. Between Missus in the back and me sitting up next to her son, folks are looking for a story. Lonnie ducks his head when anybody draws near.

Alma points out a lone duck flying south. There's a mystery. Her eyes are lit with the joy of adventure, and I feel much the same. We got this one by the tail. We slow near a left turn at a wood sign with an arrow. There's no name on the sign, but no matter, everybody knows where the arrow leads. I turn to look back and check on the Missus. She's got her eyes open looking up at the sky. I whistle to Mary and Alma. They turn, and I nod to the Missus so they move to her side and rub her head like I do for them when they're sick.

Lonnie turns down an old dirt road through a thicket of woods. From the looks of it, this is an old passageway that's been cleared for our arrival. There is a forest on either side of a road so big it might be an acre wide. Ruts, shallow and deep, run through the dirt like thousands of wagons have traveled here. Beyond the woods, fields and pastureland open, and we ride until the trees disappear at our backs. There's no question the storm's touched everything and everybody, but people still smile like they're happy to be in the day. That's a wonder in itself.

Everything a person needs has to be carted out to Camp: bedding and towels, kitchen tools and food, straw for the dirt floors, kerosene lamps and torches for night. Everything. My eyes behold such sights as a cage of chickens atop a boy's head, wagons loaded with rocking chairs, a man with sausages wrapped around his shoulders like a necklace. Every time I turn my head I see something I hadn't thought of. Off to the side a bunch of girls Edna's and Lily's ages hold hands as they cut through tall grass. They got their lips to each other's ears whispering important secrets.

Some boy runs up behind them and yells, "Snake!"

The girls scream and jump away from each other, breaking hands, and the boy laughs and runs back to a passel of other boys who look like brothers, all towheaded and shirtless. I guess I'm looking around so much I ain't sat still 'cause Lonnie breaks his quiet and says, "You never been to C-Camp before?"

He's not said a word the whole way here. I see how hard it is for him to talk, but I don't mind his affliction.

"No," I say. "I've never seen so many happy people in one place either."

I feel bad for saying it once it's out of my mouth. What we carry in our wagon is a reminder that what lies ahead is not happy, it's goodbye.

"They're just p-pretending."

"They're mighty good at it."

Another wagon comes up beside us, and Lonnie grips his mouth. I turn to the man steering the horses and ask, "What're you looking at?"

His wife's eyebrows disappear under her bonnet, and the man slaps the reins and puts his horses to a trot. Nobody tries that again.

Lonnie says, "You just met the D-Drigger family and g-gave them something to ch-chew on."

"Good."

We ride on until I am compelled to ask, "How is the Circle?"

"Berlin order is complete. Got another order out of Columbia for fifty more shirts."

"That's good."

When we reach Camp I remember to keep my mouth shut so it don't catch bugs. In front of us is what Retta called tents, but they ain't tents, they're wooden dwellings, more like cabins, ninety-nine in all she told me. Each are two stories high with screened windows on every wall from floor to ceiling. They're built cheek to jowl and sit in the biggest circle I ever did see with just enough room to walk between.

Lonnie sees my awe and asks, "What do you think?"

"Retta said these were tents."

"That's wh-what we always c-called them, not sure wh-why."

"No tents like I ever saw."

Every tent's got a big green iron number nailed to the back so you know which is yours. Folks are walking and running back and forth from wagons and automobiles unloading whatever they brought with them. Downstairs men lay hay on the floors, and in the rafters above women shake out the bedcovers and hang curtains. It's like the hurricane never happened here. Like God himself put a glass bubble over the whole Camp to protect it.

All the colored help stand along the back of the tents where outdoor kitchens with wood roofs are being filled with every kind of food you can imagine. The kitchens have no walls, but the wood fire stoves are big and strong enough to heat up the whole outdoors. I feel the warmth coming off each one as we ride along the back. Negro women work at the stoves getting supper ready for tonight. Chickens run in makeshift coops along the opposite side of the road. Beyond the kitchens and across the road are outhouses with the same number as the tent that claims it. One old woman carries an armful of toilet paper across the road to her tent's privy. Further past the outhouses is the colored camp. Their children run around the field as they work to set up cook space and places to sleep. They'll sleep in or under the wagons, same as me and my girls. Horses and carriages and automobiles and people move with purpose as far as the eye can see. Already this feels like a village that has always been filled, even though everybody has only just arrived. When we grow nearer to our tent, Lonnie waves at folks and they all wave back. Everybody here knows each other.

"How long you been coming here?" I ask him.

"M-my whole life," he says.

"This place that old?"

"Older. By almost one hundred years."

"That's old," I say.

He meets my eye and smiles.

There's been a space kept for us in the back of tent fifty-six, and Lonnie guides the wagon into our spot. Edna and Retta are already at work in the kitchen. They got four pots sitting on top of the cookstove. Edna adds wood to the fire, and Retta uses her apron to pick up a lid and stir what's inside. When she sees us coming, she says something to my girl. Edna closes the oven door and looks up to wave before tending to the pots in front of her.

While Lonnie ties up the horses, Retta comes alongside and asks, "How'd she do?"

"Slept most the way," I say.

"I got her room ready," she tells Lonnie. "Your brother and Daddy are in yonder. Go get 'em and ya'll take her on in."

Me and Retta unlatch the back of the wagon, and my girls clamber down but stay close by my side to help. When Lonnie comes out of the tent with his brother and Daddy, Mr. Coles steps up and nods at me. I do the same. He spits out his chew and wipes his mouth with his handkerchief. He's got his hat pulled down low so I can't see his eyes, but he's a whole lot happier than he was this morning. When he sees Mary behind my skirts, he smiles and says,

"There's my friend, Mary."

She stares at him, and I squeeze her shoulder 'til she remembers her manners and says hello. Mr. Coles reaches in his pocket and pulls out a nickel and offers it to her, but she shakes her head no and ducks behind my legs.

"Mary, don't be like that," I say.

"I'll take it," Alma says.

He flips it in the air, and Alma snatches it with one hand. Mr. Coles laughs and ruffles her hair. Together the men pull the ticking to the end of the wagon. Eddie reaches over and picks up his mama.

"I got you, Mother," he says. She rests her head in the crook of his neck. He follows Mr. Coles and Lonnie as they carry the mattress into the tent to a room beyond.

Retta gives me and the girls each a bowl of hot grits and a biscuit with butter. We stand in a circle and eat by the cookstove. Alma giggles and Mary joins. What a thing, to be young, and laugh over nothing and everything all at the same time. Retta goes to wooden cabinets built alongside the back of the tent and says, "Ya'll come here."

She hands Alma two pieces of paper. Each says, *Return to 56.*

"Pin this to you and your sister, so everybody knows where you belong."

Alma complains that she ain't no baby, but pins the number to Mary's back and turns so I can do the same to her. Retta tells the girls, "Every child here wears their tent number. You will, too."

She tells them we all got a lot of hard work to do and no time to watch after them. They'll have duties. When they ain't working, they'll go to Bible school and learn the books within.

"Don't be running off alone with nobody, and I mean nobody," she tells them. "I'll give you a beating myself if you don't mind, you hear?"

Mary hugs Retta around the knees, and Retta says, "I'm not playing, child."

"They'll mind," I say.

She gives me a nod. "See they do." Then says to the girls, "Ya'll go take a look around while we get organized."

They run off hand in hand past the Negro camp to the woods beyond. Retta hands me a glass of milk for the Missus, and I step through the tent door and onto fresh hay that's been scattered to cover the dirt floor. It's dark and cool in the long hallway that connects the rooms on the first floor. There's a cross breeze that blows through. From the hallway I can see clear out the front and beyond. The first room to the

413

right is the Missus's room. Eddie and Lonnie are talking, so I walk past to see the rest of the tent. Steps lead to the top floor where the men will sleep. In the middle of the last room is a dining table with ten chairs. A large wooden cupboard and countertop has been built in the corner. Cabinets and drawers are open, not yet fully filled. Inside are dishes, bowls, platters and cutlery, enough for many people.

On the porch outside sit rocking chairs, and a blue hammock is drawn between two pine trees. This porch faces ninety-eight other porches where old folks sit and watch the comings and goings of the young people. Inside the tent circle is a big meadow with pine trees dotted throughout, and inside that meadow is a tabernacle with a silver tin roof and no walls. Wood benches fill the sanctuary, enough to seat more people than I ever saw in one place. Children with numbers on their backs run everywhere. Mothers and fathers stand in the open circle to talk. People run to hug each other. Every person here's got history but me. It is a sight to behold. I could stand here and watch all day long, but the milk I carry reminds me of my duty.

The bedroom door is still ajar when I come back to Mrs. Coles's room, but only

Lonnie is there. He worries over his mother's pillows so I back out and wait in the hallway 'til he's done, overhearing all he's got to say.

"I've s-spoken to Berlin's. They're h-happy with the order." He pauses but she says nothing. "They're interested in the w-w-women's wear line. I've worked out the sketches. Perhaps w-we can finalize the d-details while we're here?"

I already heard more than I should. I back away and head to the end of the hallway. Lonnie is a good son. He didn't want his mama to come to Camp. There was a fight about it in the front foyer of the main house this morning. Me and the girls could hear the yelling from where we sat waiting in the back of the wagon. By then everybody else was gone. Only we were left with the hired man Mr. Coles paid to drive. The girls and me sat along the back by the ticking already filled and ready, but when it came time to go, Lonnie said he didn't think it was good for his mother to be moved. He sputtered through his argument best he could, but Mr. Coles got mad.

"I'll decide what's best for my wife," he hollered.

Eddie tried to calm him. "Daddy, why don't we bring her on Saturday? It'll be best for everybody."

"I said no," Mr. Coles shouted. "She's coming with us."

Through the door I saw him get in Lonnie's face and yell, "Go fetch your mother."

But Lonnie wouldn't back down. He stood eye to eye with Mr. Coles and refused. Then I heard the crack of a hand on flesh, and Lonnie ran out the front door and down the steps with a red handprint on his face. Mr. Coles didn't come after him, but by and by Eddie came down the steps and out the door carrying his mother.

"You're making it worse for yourself," Eddie said to his brother as he placed the Missus on the mattress.

"Don't care," Lonnie said.

"We'll see you at Camp, Mother," Eddie said after covering her with a blanket. Mrs. Coles was asleep, or so it seemed. She's got a mighty strong will, so it's hard to say if she was pretending or not.

"Let's go," he said to Lonnie. "Daddy's waiting."

"I'll drive her m-myself," Lonnie said, taking the reins from the hired man.

"Your funeral," Eddie said and shut the back of the wagon with a thud.

When Mr. Coles passed us in the automobile, neither man looked at the other. For the first thirty minutes Lonnie didn't take his eyes off the road. I sat in the back by the end of the wagon propped up by the bundle of things we brought with us. Retta said we wouldn't need a whole lot, so I carried only some bedclothes, blankets and Mama's gun. At one stop Lonnie turned to look back at me and patted the seat beside him, so I climbed up next to him.

I'm brought back to the present when Lonnie comes up behind me and says, "Thank you for your help with m-my m-mother." I tell him he is welcome. He opens his mouth to say something more, but thinks better of it, then turns and walks out the back of the tent.

"They're all gone now," I tell the Missus as I sit next to her on the bed.

She opens her eyes. I give her the milk and she drinks it quick, spilling some down her face. I hold my apron under her chin to catch the spill. When she is done I ask her if she wants to get cleaned up and she nods her head yes. I put her in a diaper for the trip and am glad I did when I feel the wetness. She's grown too weak to walk to the toilet.

"I'll be back," I tell her, and run to the kitchen to deposit the glass and get a clean diaper.

"She talking yet?" Retta asks.

"No."

"I guess that's that."

"Guess so."

When Retta hired me as nurse, all I did for the two days before we left was sit by the Missus's side. She never said a word, like her lips were stitched together from the inside. She looked at me confused 'til I reminded her of who I was. Mr. Coles come in every once in a while to look at her. Every time he came she pretended to sleep. When he'd leave she'd look around the room 'til she found me. Then she'd relax and settle. On the day before we left, she patted the bed beside her, and I went and sat. She patted the pillow until I laid my head down. I never felt anything so soft. She stared at me like I was a question she was looking for an answer to, studied every piece of my face and moved the hair from it when it fell sideways. I guess I fell asleep after that 'cause when I woke it was late afternoon, she was asleep and both of us were covered with a blanket.

Outside there's so much hollering and laughter I feel like we are in the middle of a state fair. All this commotion is nothing new for the Missus. She's used to the big life. I push her dress up, unclasp the diaper and lift her hips to get it out from under her and drop it to the straw. I feel a presence in the doorway, but before I turn to see who is there I quick pull her dress down. The jingle of his pocket change tells me who I will find before I turn to see Mr. Coles in the doorway.

"I'll just be a minute more," I tell him.

"Go on," he says. "Don't mind me."

He aims to stand there with the door wide open while I clean his wife. I do it quick as I can, and when I am done, he unstraps his gun and hangs it on the peg by the far side of the bed, then sits to pull off his shoes. The Missus grabs my hand and holds tight. Mr. Coles strips to his undershirt, then climbs on the bed beside his wife. She rolls away from him. Mr. Coles puts both hands behind his head and says to me, "Close the door behind you."

34

RETTA

It's a dark dawn when I come out of my room off the side of the tent. I've slept in this room for Camp like my mama before me and her mama before her since I can remember. Our blood runs through this week as sure as any other person who comes here, but I never set foot — not once — on the yard and never prayed in the pews. What was, was, and what is, is. I play my part like the rest of them.

Some kitchens got their fires already lit, but I'm moving slow. There's an autumn fog that lies thick and low over the land, the ghost of summer. Watching folks move through all that white makes it seem like they're half people, spirits on the earth. Like legless folks in fog, there is a piece of me missing. No matter how much I try not to worry for Odell, I can't push him from my mind. I'm shook from my melancholy state

420

when I hear a child shout, "Chickadee, chickadee, where you gonna be?"

I know that phrase. That's the game we played — me, Odell and Esther. One of us would close our eyes and the other two would run and hide. I still hear my Esther's voice counting to ten against the fig tree — me and Odell fighting for the same hiding space. She wanted to play all the time, even in the dark. Dark never did scare that child. She'd turn and yell, "Chickadee, chickadee, where you gonna be?" then run into the black of night.

I catch sight of a Negro girl running around the backside of tent 62. Her dress flutters behind. I spin around to see who she is playin' with, but I don't see nobody. My heart comes up so fast in my throat it almost jumps from my mouth. I race six places down to the tent from ours and ask the girl at the stove, still half asleep moving through her morning chores, who the child was. She jumps like she done something wrong and says she didn't see nothin', then picks up the hot handle of the kettle with her bare hand and drops it with a bang back to the stove.

"Fetch me some water," I say, and she runs to the pitcher watchin' me the whole time.

"Where's Selma at?" I ask after I drink what she's poured.

"She ain't here yet. She's got babies to feed."

"You tell her, Oretta from tent 56 come by to ask her something."

I walk around the side of the tent to check for the girl myself, but nobody's there. *What you doing, old woman?* I ask myself. *You ain't nothin' but a damn fool.* That's one of Selma's girls. The bugle plays its wake-up call as I walk back to our tent. I lean against the wall to look out at the Negro camp. Ain't nothin' out of place, but what kind of child plays games outside in the dark of morning? Now I'm on the lookout.

All morning my heart's been skippin' beats — runnin', trying to catch up to something. I'm behind in my chores. Edna comes up from the wagon tying her apron about her waist. A boy I've seen hanging 'round the backfield since we got here crosses the road and runs up beside her, talking as he comes. He's a full head smaller, but he don't pay no mind, just flaps his jaws anyhow. Edna stops and opens her mouth to tell him something, but he don't take a breath. She looks around to see if her mama's coming, but it's me she finds. When she sees the stove ain't lit, she hightails it away so fast the boy don't have time to think.

When Edna gets the fire started I sit again, can't be helped, and by the time the men come down to do their morning business, she's got the coffee brewed and biscuits laid out in the fire to cook. I am moving some by then, but my head is so light it don't feel attached to my body. I have to stop now and again just to steady myself. I need my husband. One by one the men come from the outhouse, Eddie, Lonnie and Mr. Coles, stopping like they always do for coffee. They stand away from the stove so Edna can work. I lay out the milk and sugar. None of them talk much in the mornings. Been that way for as long as I can remember. Takes them 'til noon to work up the energy.

While they stir in the milk and sugar, Mr. Coles says to his boys, "I need you both at the supper table tonight. The mayor of Charleston and his aldermen are coming. The governor is looking to build a road from Charleston straight through to the next state, and the mayor will carry influence. We need Branchville to be a part of that road."

"Why?" Eddie asks.

"They build that road across a piece of our land, we got prime real estate for business, any kind of business. That's good money for us."

I watch them from the corner of my eye while I crack open the eggs.

"I've got to w-work l-late," Lonnie says.

"No, you'll be here alongside your brother and me. You understand?"

"The Circle m-means m-money for us, too, Father," Lonnie says.

"Get your head out of your ass, boy," Mr. Coles says. "The Sewing Circle supplements the land, not the other way around. That's seed money. Even your mother understands that."

Lonnie clamps his mouth shut and turns his back on his daddy to go sit inside with his mama. Mr. Coles shakes his head with disgust. I whip the eggs to scramble and lay the bacon fat in the skillet to melt.

"Why do you need him to come?" Eddie asks.

Mr. Coles sighs and puts his hand on Eddie's shoulder.

"Son," he says, "all I have will be yours one day. I want men of power to understand who the Coles men are. You will be dealing with them long after I'm gone."

Eddie puffs with pride. After all these years he still wants his daddy's love, still wants to believe in the man.

"He'll be here," Eddie says. "He just hates to be social."

Eddie lays down his cup and gives me a kiss on the cheek and goes inside to join his brother. Mr. Coles is headed out of the kitchen when Alma and Mary come walking hand in hand up from the wagon for their breakfast. He stops and watches as they come through the tent, still rubbing sleep from their eyes. They sit on the bench behind me while I work at the stove.

"How many for supper?" I ask Mr. Coles. "Miss Annie always tells me how many I got to cook for."

He looks at the bottom of his cup and says, "Eight." He finishes what's left of his coffee and lays it on the shelf by the door. Before he disappears inside he lays one hand on Alma's head. She looks up but by then he's gone. I give Edna the spoon, and she finishes the eggs so I can sit down.

In the four days since we got here Mr. Coles ain't told me nothin' about dinner guests. I've had to guess every night. Used to be this tent slept twelve to fifteen people, and I always knew how much to make. Now we've got so much left over, I got to repurpose it for the next day. These girls never had so much to eat in their lives. Gertrude comes up from Miss Annie's room with a full glass of milk and gives it to Alma and Mary to share.

"If she stopped taking liquids, that's that," I say.

She shakes her head and says, "Seems like somebody ought to be able to do something for her."

"Can't nobody do for her what she won't do for herself."

Edna dishes up breakfast on the plates. Mary and Alma finish the milk meant for Miss Annie and wipe their mouths on their sleeves.

"You got his pudding?" I ask Edna.

"Yes, ma'am. I got it. It's fine, too. I took a little taste this morning to make sure, and it's just as good as yesterday. How does sausage get better every day? I never had food like that before."

"I don't know what I'd do without your help, Edna," I say.

She laughs but I don't.

"I'm serious," I tell her. "You got yourself a hardworkin' girl here, Gertrude."

Gertrude smiles at her daughter, and for the second time today Edna's got nothing to say. There might be hope for this girl yet.

We got four hens need cleaned and fried by tonight. Gertrude's so fast she plucks one chicken to my half. She makes me sit while Edna and Alma work on the beans, rice and corn. Mary measures her crochet against her mother's shoulders; it's shawl length now.

"Alma," I say, "you count how many layers of corn shucks are on them cobs and tell us so we know what kind of winter we're gonna have."

"There's eight on this one, but weren't no more than four on the others."

"I guess the corn can't make up its mind what's coming."

"Guess not."

Edna pours the beans into the pot that's boiling the ham hock and onion.

Off in the distance a banjo plays "Froggie Went a-Courtin'." Some old boy's been playing that thing all day long, and now I can't get the damn song out of my head.

"God, I hate banjo playing," I tell Gertrude.

Mrs. Childress comes up from the outhouse. She waits on the roadside for a horse and wagon to pass, and I see her looking our way. Word's out about Miss Annie. Not three days ago, Mr. Coles stood out between tent kitchens talking to Mr. Childress from next door. They shared a pinch of chewing tobacco and talked about the weather. The almanac promises better this year, or so says

Mr. Coles. I don't take heed of the almanac, but Mr. Coles swears by it. Says it's the earth's bible.

Mrs. Childress came from inside to check on her husband's whereabouts.

"What's wrong with Annie?" she asked Mr. Coles.

That woman never had a problem saying what everybody else is thinking. She's quick with her tongue, which is a thing to behold 'cause her husband don't hardly ever use his. He married up. They farm the land she got as dowry, so he lets her henpeck. In the twenty years they've been coming to Camp she's gone through ten cooks. When Mrs. Childress asked after Miss Annie, Mr. Coles told her nobody knew what was wrong and that Miss Annie refused the hospital. The lie slid off his tongue like honey.

"Annie's a proud woman," he said. "She likes to do things her own way."

"Always has," Mrs. Childress said before pulling her husband away.

Since then you'd think Miss Annie had swamp sickness as much as folks been avoiding coming by. The woman's been coming here to this Camp for fifty some years, and in four days' time not a single Christian has come to sit by her side. It's a crying shame.

Mrs. Childress crosses the road, staring the whole way at the goings-on of my kitchen. She's wantin' to know how all these white girls come to work for me. She knows how I run things and don't recognize it anymore. But stopping to ask questions means she's got to see after Miss Annie, and there ain't enough curiosity in the world to make her want to talk to a dying woman. She goes through the back of her cabin without a word.

"She don't want to see nobody no how," Gertrude says like she's read my mind. "She wants to be alone."

"It don't matter what she wants at this point. Other folks got a right to say what they need before she's done on this earth."

"Maybe she don't want to hear what they got to say."

"Don't matter. Nobody come."

"Maybe nobody's got anything to say," Gertrude says.

"Oh, they got plenty to say. Only everybody's too damn scared to say it."

I cast my eyes to the road and give it a look up and down, but I don't find what I'm looking for. I expect Odell to drive up and bring me whatever I need. This year he would be bringing the shrimp in from Edisto for the Frogmore stew. His absence has thrown off my every waking moment, causing me to think on what I'm missing rather than what I have. *Chickadee, chickadee, where you gonna be?*

Come suppertime bowls and platters are filled, and the girls got their hair brushed and faces washed. They look downright respectable. I give them each a bowl of food to carry to the dining room, and we set it on the countertop of the cupboard so our guests can fill their plates themselves, then I shoo Mary and Alma out to play on the Campground. They run from the dining room to the yard where girls are skipping rope. Gertrude stays to help Edna serve.

Out on the porch Mr. Coles talks to the mayor of Charleston. He's the only man on the yard Mr. Coles has eyes for. Lonnie and Eddie been left to play host to the couple the mayor's come with. The lady is dressed so fine I know she ain't come here to stay for the week. We don't hold pretense at Camp. Work dresses and overalls are the main wardrobes here. Outside Mr. Coles has got his arms crossed while the mayor takes his turn to talk. Through the screen window Lonnie sees we're ready and elbows his brother.

"Come on in and get yourselves a plate,

folks," Eddie says.

He holds the door open, and one by one they come through.

Mr. Coles puts his hand on the mayor's shoulder to guide him inside. When the woman comes through, she says to me, "You must be Retta. Lonnie and Eddie have been singing your praises."

"Yes, ma'am."

Mr. Coles eyes the woman. He ain't happy she's talking to me, but she don't see and comes toward me with her hand out, stripping off white gloves. Nobody told this woman this ain't nothing but a weeklong picnic.

"I'm Clelia McGowan," she tells me, "and I'm so happy to meet you."

I got no choice but to take her hand in mine and say, "Yes, ma'am. I'm happy to know you, too."

Mr. Coles turns to the man with Miss Clelia, and stretches out his hand for a shake and says, "You must be Alderman McGowan. I'm pleased to meet you."

Mr. Coles don't know who he's let in his tent.

Mr. McGowan laughs and says, "No, sir, my wife's the politician, not me."

He's dressed as fine as his wife and sports a mustache that's waxed and turned up on both ends.

Mr. Coles raises an eyebrow and says to the mayor, "An alderwoman?"

"Got to keep up with the changing times, Edwin," the mayor says.

"You don't have to tell me," Mr. Coles says back. "I'm a proponent of the fairer sex in leadership positions. My wife is the proprietor of a thriving business."

He turns to Miss Clelia and takes her hand in his and brings it to his lips and says, "I'm proud to be host to history."

Her laugh is a bell.

"Why, thank you, Mr. Coles," she says. "You're too kind. I'm sorry you weren't able to meet my colleague, Belizant Moorer, our other alderwoman, but she wasn't feeling well and couldn't join us."

I sneak a look outside to see if Molly's come, but there's no sign of her. The yard empties as people head in for supper.

"How did Charleston react to two women in positions of power?" Mr. Coles asks.

Miss Clelia responds on the mayor's behalf, and the mayor don't seem to mind one bit.

"We had very mixed results, as you can imagine, but women now represent fifty percent of the voting population, so I believe we are here to stay."

"It's a wise man who goes the way of a woman," Mr. McGowan says. Mr. Coles smiles and agrees. Our guests help themselves to the food that's been laid out. The McGowans sit together at one end of the table while Mr. Coles and the mayor sit at the other with Lonnie and Eddie in between. Miss Clelia lays her plate alongside her husband but, before she sits, asks, "If you'll excuse me, may I use your facilities?"

Mr. Coles says, "Retta, show Alderwoman McGowan out back."

"Yessir," I say, and lead Miss Clelia down the hall to the back of the tent where Edna is placing two pineapple upside-down cakes in the oven to bake. I wait for Miss Clelia to return and hand her soap and a towel so she can wash her hands under the pump. Before I can reconcile whether or not I should, I open my mouth and words come out.

"Miss Molly still workin' with you?"

Miss Clelia finishes drying her hands and looks down the hall to see if anybody is coming. Why would she do such a thing unless she knows more than she's lettin' on about this family?

"Yes, she does."

"Can you tell her that her mama's real sick, and if she aims to see her again she needs to come quick and bring her sister, Sarah."

The woman holds her hand to her heart and says, "I will tell her, Retta."

"You tell her, her mama knows everything. She finally knows."

"Knows what?"

"Molly will understand."

She makes the promise. When she goes inside, a flush of heat comes over me and the world goes sideways. Edna grabs my arm, and I find my seat on the bench.

35

GERTRUDE

Mr. Coles raises his glass when I am done pouring the wine and says, "To divine providence."

Drink's not allowed at Camp, but Retta hid five bottles away for these occasions. I catch my daughter's eye, and Edna gets the pitcher from the counter to pour more sweet tea for the lady. When she is done they all raise their glasses.

"It's a miracle Camp was untouched by the storm," Mr. Coles says, "a sure sign of greater things to come. To our community and the jobs that keep it fed."

They clink their glasses and everybody drinks. Wine taste like medicine to me. I drink it only when I'm pretending it's the blood of Christ. The day has faded, so I light the candles. Got to see to eat. I help serve seconds, and Edna cleans up behind everybody. By the time dinner is over, Retta is back on her feet and has water heated for washing up. Edna clears the plates, and I bring out two skillets of cake, and cut big servings.

"Is it the Sewing Circle out toward Smoaks that your wife owns?" Miss Clelia asks of Mr. Coles.

"That's right," he says. "Do you know it?"

"I've heard some. How many women does the factory employ?" she asks.

Mr. Coles don't know the answer so he turns to his son. "Lonnie?"

Lonnie turns red like he does when he's got to talk. "Forty-seven, m-ma'am."

"Where do you distribute your goods?" she asks.

"The seed bags are bought by farmers in the surrounding c-counties, seven in total, and our new line of m-men's shirts will be distributed by Berlin's of Charleston and Chicago and Silverman's of Columbia this spring."

He gets through all that with hardly a slip of the tongue and I can tell he's as surprised as his brother and daddy are.

"That's remarkable," the mayor says.

"Lonnie and Mother expect to have over a hundred women sewing for them by this time next year," Eddie tells them.

Mr. Coles drops his knife on his plate, and

it clanks loud. He gives Eddie a hard look, and Eddie shuts his mouth.

"A hundred jobs for women!" Miss Clelia claps her hands at the notion.

Lonnie laughs and says to the mayor and Mr. McGowan, "I'm happy to give each of you a sample of our w-wares. I have some shirts in the automobile."

The mayor pats his stomach and says, "Bring me your biggest one, son. I'm going to need it after that meal."

Soon as Lonnie excuses himself from the table to go fetch the shirts, Mr. Coles turns to the mayor and says, "Ernie, what are the plans for the highway?"

The mayor clears his throat and takes a drink of coffee. Mr. Coles keeps talking.

"I don't have to tell you the benefits of Branchville, as a thoroughfare," Mr. Coles says. "What with the railroad station already a major hub, running a highway through makes good sense. We have the infrastructure and manpower. Much of my land could be put to good use for the easement."

"Your land is your legacy," the mayor says.

"There is greater legacy in joining progress."

"I'm sorry, Edwin, the governor already decided on those plans. The highway's being routed through Polk Swamp, north of

Reevesville. That deal is done."

Through Polk Swamp, just the mention of that place makes me go cold. Otto must be happy. He'll make a fortune.

Lonnie comes back and lays shirts across the table for them to choose between. The mayor picks blue and Mr. McGowan picks yellow. Maybe it's the wine, but the mayor makes Mrs. McGowan hide her eyes while he and Mr. McGowan strip down to their undershirts right there at the table to try them on. When she opens her eyes, Mrs. McGowan states they are the finest shirts she's ever seen.

"Never mind, New York and Paris," she says, "Branchville has its very own fashion designer."

Lonnie smiles and stands to check the fit on each man, but his daddy ain't smiling. Mr. Coles swallows what's left of the wine in his glass and pours himself another, glaring at Eddie who will not look his way.

I've slept in Miss Annie's room the past few nights to keep watch while the girls sleep in the wagon. Every kitchen on the backside of Camp knows their names by now, Edna's made sure of that, so folks keep an eye out for them. It's Friday, and there've been wagons coming in all morning for the weekend festivities. All day tomorrow and Sunday will be the jamboree and homecoming celebration, with three church services a day, politicians, choirs and marching bands from around the state. I didn't know this place could hold more people. It's already practically busting at the seams. Every kitchen, including ours, has increased their help by a half dozen people. The girls act like Christmas has come, and I got to say, if it weren't for the Missus, I'd feel much the same. The Missus's diaper is dry this morning, and her lips are cracked and bleeding, so I rub Vaseline on them to soothe. Mr. Coles comes to the door while I'm straightening the bedclothes. He's up and dressed in a hurry to be somewhere, so he don't come through the door.

"Mother," he says, "we'll be moving you to the bench outside tomorrow so you can join in the festivities. The governor is coming and he'll want to see you. It'll be good to get some fresh air."

She turns her head away, but he keeps right on talking like she's something to mark off a list he's made for himself. He tells me to have her ready and after he's gone, I look at the Missus and say, "You heard the man."

I fill three big kettles with water and set them on the stove to heat. Retta's done with breakfast, so the stove is mine for the taking.

Lonnie asks, like he does every morning, "What can I do before I go?"

"I got to get your mama bathed. You and your brother got time to help me with the washtub?"

He's happy to be asked and sets down his coffee to go fetch Eddie. He needs something to do for his mama. He's beside himself with worry. Since we come here he's gone to her room every morning, before driving out to the Circle, to show her drawings for a line of women's dresses. He's made four designs and has samples of deep red, green and blue rayon.

"It's a poor m-man's silk," he tells the Missus. "No reason to limit such fine m-material to m-men's ties, right, M-Mother? This m-material will be c-comfortable, affordable and b-beautiful. Berlin's has asked to see these before Christmas. If all goes according to p-plan we could have these in stores by summer. Isn't that w-wonderful?"

But no matter what he says or does, she won't respond.

"Doesn't she care?" Lonnie asked when I caught him crying in the hallway.

" 'Course she does."

He's a grown man still expecting his mama to live for him. At some point parent and child must turn each other loose. But there's history in every family, and history can make a person act in strange ways. That's plain fact.

The Missus is getting that same smell Marie and Berns got before they died, a smell that can't be hid behind talcum powder. While the water boils the brothers fill the washtub halfway with cold water and haul it to their mama's room. They both kiss and greet her, and she pats their hands, then they follow me back to the kitchen to haul the kettles of boiling water from the stove. I cover them with lids and give the men dish towels, so they don't burn themselves on the handle. One by one we pour three kettles of hot steaming water into the cold.

"Daddy's going to ask to see the books for the Circle," Eddie says to his brother.

"He c-can't have them."

"He wants to see what it's worth."

"Do you hear this, M-Mother?" Lonnie says. "He's going to try to take all we have."

He sits beside her to plead. "I need those funds. M-Mother, please, you can't let him t-take them."

But she just closes her eyes and says nothing.

"We'll let the water sit 'til it cools down," I tell them. "I can do the rest."

Lonnie stands and leaves. Eddie looks at his mother and opens his mouth to say something but changes his mind and turns to me instead. "You need anything else, you give a shout."

When they go out the door I latch it shut, look at the Missus and sigh.

"You got good boys."

She nods.

"I only got daughters. I worry for them all the time."

Her face falls but she sheds no tears, for the wells of her eyes have gone dry.

Me and the Missus got a little morning routine now. She lets me do what I can for her. She opens her mouth so I can brush her teeth. I undo the bun on top of her head and loosen the braid so I can brush out her hair. She loves when I do that. It's soft as silk and hangs to the middle of her back. I don't talk much, but the Missus don't mind. I feel like we've had whole conversations. We just don't use words.

I lay my elbow in the water and when it's just right I lift her dressing gown up and over her head careful not to let the buttons scrape her face. After I strip her naked, I carry her to the water. She is so light it pains

442

me. She knows and pats my forehead with one hand so my brow will loosen. I can't understand the decision not to eat. I've been on this side of hunger. It nags at you all day and night — a never-ending empty. I lower her slow to the water.

"That feel good?"

She lets out a little moan of pleasure, and I sink her all the way down and set her upright. She's so light the water barely laps the top.

"Hang on to the sides," I say, "so I can wash your back."

She does what I say and leans forward over her knees. I go slow and easy with the washcloth over the whole of her back and she sighs. She leans her head back while I wash her hair, rinsing it with a bowl I brung from the kitchen, holding my hand over her eyes, like I did for all my girls and still do for Mary, so the soap don't fall in. Once I'm done with the cleaning I set her up on a chair, towel her off and dust her body with powder. I worry she'll get sores from lying too long in the bed. Her backside's already showing signs of wear. She's closed her eyes, tired from the ritual. But when it comes time to get dressed she swats the clothes away.

"You hot?"

She shakes her head no.

"You don't want to get dressed?"

Again, a no. I reckon she's got a right to go out of this world the way she came in. I pull the sheet to her chin.

"You change your mind, you let me know," I say.

She's asleep by the time I hang the dress in the closet.

Across the road Retta oversees a whole hog cooking in the pit that was dug when we first got here. She's been short-tempered as a nest of hornets this morning. Alma and Mary are minding their business, cracking a bushel of pecans for pies.

"You need anything?" I yell out.

"Not right yet," she says.

"All right if I go to church?"

"Why wouldn't it be?" she asks coming back across the road.

"Ain't we the help?"

"Don't nobody out there know you're help. Go get right with yourself."

"I wanna go," Alma says.

"You get your work done," Retta tells her, "then you can go."

Folks mill about the yard and visit with one another. Quilts are laid out across the grass and young mothers lie on them with their babies. One young girl in yellow, no older than Edna, sits up on her elbows talking to friends. Her young'un pulls at her hair, and she slaps him away. He crawls off the blanket, but she pays him no mind. He's got a number attached to him, so I guess he can't get far.

I come up through the back of the tabernacle to listen. I'm told it's a privilege to preach at Camp. Every minister who's come through here is famous and from somewhere else. I read the schedule that's put up on the chalkboard outside the tabernacle every day — who's preaching and where they're from. The Reverend today is fat with a big bushy mustache and beard. He's from right here in St. George, but I never heard of him before. I guess I thought you had to be from somewhere else to get famous. I am late to the sermon and don't want to be a bother, but an old Deacon insists on taking me by the elbow and leading me to a middle row. I got no choice but to follow. The Reverend is in the middle of prayer, so I'm careful to keep my head bowed while I take my seat. A family scoots over to make room for me at the end of the aisle, and I sneak a look up once I'm seated. The morning service is as crowded as the night one. Eddie sits midway up on the same side I'm on, but I don't see Mr. Coles. When he's done praying, the Reverend wipes the sweat from his brow and talks to us like we are his own kin sitting around the kitchen table.

"I want to talk about one of my little boyhood experiences I had 'round about the age of nine or ten," he says. "My mama and daddy had some chickens. I was a mischievous boy at that age, and they had a hen that I loved to chase. I'd run her 'round the yard and every now and then I would catch her and do some bad things to her."

Everybody laughs. We remember being children.

"I didn't draw blood, I wasn't that bad." He laughs like maybe we think he was. "But she was like a little pet. I'd carry her 'round by the legs or tucked up under one arm where she couldn't get loose. But then she had some eggs in a nest she hid away from me. She sat on the nest for a while, and when she was done she had some biddies. She got up from that nest and I come to chase her 'round like I always did. She was docile before but now she had babies, but I didn't know the difference. I went 'bout my same usual way like when she was a little thing, but now that she had some young chicks, God changed the nature inside her. And when I started running after her she thought I was running after her babies.

"Ya'll know where I'm going with this?" he asks.

All across the congregation heads nod and people laugh. I do, too. Sitting between all these folks makes me feel like there's an army around me.

"There was gonna be a reckoning. She wasn't no little chicken anymore. She became a mama hen. And she thought you can do it to me, but I'm not gonna allow you to do it to my little chickens. Can I get a witness?"

Folks clap and yell out, "Yes, sir."

"That same mama hen flew up, and with her claws she scratched my face but good."

The Reverend laughs from the memory and runs a handkerchief over his wet brow. He's got stains of sweat under his arms and all along his back. He's got a lot of energy for such a fat man.

"Every now and then when the devil tries to destroy and hurt you, you got to remember — God is my protector, God is my savior. That's enough. God tells the devil, that's enough. That's enough hate. I saw you pick on her. I see how you try to rob, kill and destroy, but that's enough now. Because when I come down to fight for My loved ones, Devil, I ain't gonna show you no mercy. I see what you're doing to My

447

children. I see the sickness you try to put on them. I see the burden, the hurt and the pain you cause. But that's enough now."

He stops, then leans in like he's letting us in on a secret.

"God tells us, there is a place that you can come to. I am that place, He says. I am the refuge. I am the strength that can give you a new day."

A breeze blows through the church, and the pine trees sway and groan. The Reverend gives a nod to the back of the church, and four men with offering plates come up the center to be blessed before tithing begins. I'm sorry to be at the end of the service. I feel like I've just swallowed medicine I didn't know I needed. The Reverend holds his palms to the sky and looks out to us. He meets each eye he falls upon. And I wonder if he can see me.

"I want to pray for you. I want to help you on your journey, 'cause somebody prayed for me before I came here today. Somebody helped me, so I want to help you. I want to plant a seed in your spirit," he tells us, "so when that seed sprouts up inside you, you will grow up and out with it. Let us bow our heads."

I close my eyes and pray along with this man who speaks a simple truth.

"Lord, as we place the seed of faith inside our spirit today, we ask that You would increase its power. Increase our faith so that tiny little mustard seed that You allow to grow in our lives will remind us that You will forever be our protector and our provider. Amen."

When I raise my face, the choir stands and the old upright piano plunks out the tune "Trusting Jesus." Angelic voices carry out to the yard, and people stop what they are doing to listen — even the babies quiet. The men with offering plates turn and make their way down each side of the aisle. The plates are passed from one end to the next. One man is familiar. I can't place how I know him until he is almost upon me, and then I remember. I didn't recognize the sheriff without his uniform. When he gets to my row I take the plate from his hand and pass it to the family next to me. They place a dollar in the offering, and when it comes back to me, he holds it for just a moment in front of me, but I got no money to give. Not even a penny. I am forced to look up and shake my head to let him know to move along. He recognizes me but he's got a job to do, so he moves on to get the money the next row's got to offer. In the final verse, the Reverend makes his way to the back of the church and waits to say goodbye to each parishioner. I want to run but there ain't nowhere to go, so I stay seated and watch as the crowd leaves. Across the church the sheriff stands talking with two women. He's got his arm around one, and she keeps a hand on his belly while talking to the other. They got to be mother and daughter. You can tell by the way they stand. Though they are ages apart they are alike, separate but the same. The sheriff don't listen to what's being said. He looks around like he's lost something he can't find. When his eyes come to rest on me I know who it is he's looking for, and I do what I should have done the last time. I gather my courage and stand.

He whispers something to his woman, and she looks up at his eyes and then in my direction. When she finds me she turns back to him and nods. Whatever he's got to say, she knows of it. He stretches out his hand as he draws near and I take it and give it a shake.

"Mrs. Pardee," he says.

"Sheriff."

I don't give him a chance to go first.

"My neighbors say you come by the house to see me."

"That's right," he says. "I did."

"Here I am."

"I didn't expect to find you all the way out here," he says, smiling.

I'm taken aback at how lighthearted he sounds. His manner changes when he sees I am surprised.

"I'm sorry, this isn't a joking matter. I came to tell you that Otto and his wife died of diphtheria."

"When?"

"Just before the storm," he tells me. "Otherwise I'd have come sooner."

"What about the baby?" I ask.

"It was never born."

So that's it then. Otto's gone. He's mortal like the rest of us. Life comes and life goes, but I don't feel nothing. Sheriff scrapes the ground with the toe of his boot, and grass comes up by the roots. He's got something on his mind. I grit my teeth and wait.

"Mrs. Pardee, we've got reason to believe your husband never left St. George. We've talked to everyone. Last anybody saw was him shit-faced drunk, pardon my language, down by the river."

"That ain't no surprise."

"We have reason to believe he may have drowned. We've dragged the river, but I don't need to tell you there are gators in that water."

"That all you needed to tell me?"

He looks up at his wife who stands alone and off to the side waiting for him to come along. He turns back to me and says, "You realize your husband is entitled to all his father owned?"

I can't understand what he's saying to me, why he's still talking.

"Mrs. Pardee, if your husband is dead as we presume, as Alvin's next of kin, you and your children will inherit what was his father's."

The sound goes out of my ears and in its place is a deep ringing that stays even when I try to shake it free. Otto, who never gave us nothing in life, gives us everything in death. Before I can say more, Edna comes running across the yard hollering for me. I excuse myself and go to meet her.

"Alma's run off and Retta's fit to be tied. You better come."

In the kitchen Retta fusses at Mary who sits on the bench with her knees drawn up to her chest, crying.

"Didn't I tell you not to leave each other?" Retta yells. "Didn't I?"

Mary's crying so hard she can't hardly talk.

"What's going on?" I ask.

"I told these children to stay together,"

Retta says. "How many times I got to say it?"

"Where'd she go?" I ask Mary.

"I told her not to," Mary says, "but she wouldn't listen."

Retta lets out a sigh and turns herself in a circle like she don't know what to do next.

"Which way?"

Mary points to the woods, and though I can't speak to why, I run.

Past the edge of the wood, through the trees, between the boughs is my daughter in her blue dress standing next to Mr. Coles, who's squatted down, talking. I slow to a fast walk and calm my breath. He points to something in the trees and when Alma looks up he slides his hand under the back of her skirt. She jumps back, but he laughs and holds out a nickel like he's found it under the folds of her dress.

I shout, "Alma!" She snatches the nickel and twirls around to find me.

"Where do you think you're going?"

Mr. Coles stands and puts his hands in his pockets to adjust his manhood. I understand now why Mary didn't want his money. Now I understand. Alma comes toward me red-faced, talking fast, a nickel raised in her fist.

"There's a raffle of turkeys over in the

453

field yonder way," she tells me. "Mr. Coles said there's a big nest back here with upward of twenty eggs."

I take the nickel from her hand and yank her by the arm and give her a hard swat on the bottom. Her skirt is thick enough that I know my hand don't sting, but I make my point. Her bottom lip's out and she tries not to cry.

"Retta told you not to wander off," I tell her.

"She didn't mean any harm," Mr. Coles says. "She was just excited to see the eggs."

"I thank you for your time, Mr. Coles, but she's been told not to run off. She knows better."

"Get back to Camp," I tell Alma, and she runs for home.

"The girl has spirit and a lively mind, a sign of intelligence," he tells me, like he's the expert. "You should be glad for that."

"Yes, sir, I am glad. She's smart about some things, but ain't about others."

I hold that nickel so tight in my fist my fingernails dig into skin.

"She's a child," he says. "She'll learn."

Like Mary learned.

"She will and I aim to be the one to teach her."

When it comes to my children, what I say,

goes. I hold his coin between my fingers and hold it out for him to take.

He gives me a long hard look and says, "Keep it."

I fold the money back into my fist, and with the change jangling in his pocket, Mr. Coles turns and walks down the footpath until he disappears from view.

36

RETTA

We had the first frost of the season in the night. The ground is stone hard, and the meadow is covered in hoarfrost. I can see my own breath. Everywhere I look colored folks run from one place to the next trying to outrun the cold. Didn't none of us expect this, but if I learned one thing in all my days, it's to expect things to go wrong on a big day. That's the nature of the world. Ain't nothing against you, just is. Anymore, seems I just count up Camp problems to see which year will win the prize for most things to go wrong on a big day. This cold snap is first on my list. Let's see what's coming next.

I take two bundles from the woodpile to start the cookstove. Bobo huddles over the hog pit across the road warming his hands. He's been standing watch through the night with his collar turned up against the cold. I give him a cup of coffee to warm his bones.

His breath mixes with the steam of the hot drink.

"What time did the weather turn?" I ask.

" 'Bout three in the mornin'."

"You reckon that'll give them trouble coming home?"

"Little cold never hurt nobody. Stop your worrying, Retta. Roy'll get Odell home."

"Pull me off a taste," I tell him, and he reaches his poker down in the pit and stabs me off a good piece of meat. I take it hot from the pit onto a dish towel and blow the steam. The skin is crunchy and the meat falls to pieces as I chew.

"So tender it melts in the mouth," I say.

Bobo smiles. I tell him to pull the pig up and get him carved. If my math is right, Odell will be home tomorrow. Tomorrow, Lord willing, I see my husband again.

When I get back to the tent, Edna's got breakfast going. Alma and Mary sit on the bench wrapped together in a quilt. They watch two fat wooly worms crawl down and across their arms. These girls been stuck together since yesterday. In the dim light I can see they got color in their cheeks, and they've filled out some. Two weeks of steady food has done them good. Anybody with eyes can see the difference.

I've got a piece of smoked alligator

stripped and cubed, and the shrimp that was brought over from Edisto cleaned and peeled. I pour the lot into the Frogmore stew that simmers on the stove. Okra, tomatoes and onions float in the broth. This stew's got to cook for two hours before all the juices run together just right, then I'll add the potatoes and corn on the cob. The sun is rising through the woods behind us, and the first frost shines like glass in the light. For a minute the whole world looks make-believe. Then the sun disappears behind thick white clouds and the magic is gone.

Edna fills the breakfast plates with eggs and biscuits, then gives out a scream when she opens the ice chest. Gertrude and me jump so high you'd think a rat run over our feet. Alma and Mary give each other a quick look but keep playing like nothing's wrong.

"What is it?" Gertrude asks.

"It's gone," Edna says, then busts into tears.

"Calm down," I say and she swallows her sobs. "What's gone?"

She turns, holding open the lid.

"Somebody stole the pudding."

Sure enough it's empty. I'll be damned if pudding is going to be the thing that turns me crazy. I look at Alma and Mary, sitting so sweet and quiet, I got to wonder, but there's no time for questions.

"You two girls go to the left and ask every kitchen you come to if they got extra pudding they can spare for Oretta Bootles," I tell them, "and ya'll keep going down the row until you find some. Edna, you go next door and see if Hannah's got any left."

"Who'd take Mr. Coles's pudding?" Gertrude asks.

"Somebody who knows how much he likes it," I say. "Lord, there's going to be hell to pay."

Gertrude looks up to the rafters of the roof and takes in a sharp breath.

"Now what?"

I turn to look at what she sees, and find the third problem of our day. Sitting in the eaves of the tent kitchen looking for a crumb sits a bright red cardinal.

"Just a superstition," Gertrude says. "Don't mean nothing."

I take her hand and say, "Let's do one thing at a time. You go see if you can talk Miss Annie into putting on some clothes, otherwise she'll die from cold 'fore she dies of hunger."

After she goes I lift my dishcloth and wave it at the rafters.

The bird flies off and sits in the oak tree

459

across the road.

"Not today," I tell my Maker. "We ain't doing this today."

37

GERTRUDE

The Missus didn't sleep last night. I know
it's my fault. When I took out her nightdress
and sat on the edge of the bed to put it on,
she wouldn't let me. I held the gown in my
lap for a long time deciding what to do.

"My husband used to beat me, Missus," I
finally said. "For a long time I tried to think
what I done wrong. I figured there must
have been something to cause him to be so
mad all the time, but no matter how I put
my head to it, I couldn't figure it out. And
then he started in on my girls, and that just
wasn't right."

She watched me tell my story. Anybody
could see the wrestle in her. She worked her
fists over and over — open and closed and
open and closed. A swarm of black flies
gathered on the wall behind the bed. They
were mating one on top of the other until
they formed a tiny hill. I reached over to

461

swat them, and they separated and flew loud and slow through the room.

"I wish you could tell me what ails you, Missus," I said. "Maybe I could help you like you helped me."

But she wouldn't talk and I can't blame her. I slept at the end of her bed on a pallet and woke up every couple of hours to check on her. Each time I found her lying awake staring at the ceiling. The cold is what woke me finally. I piled blankets on top of her and crawled in beside to warm her up. I felt how cold she was; for a moment I thought she passed, but then I saw her breath coming through curls of white smoke.

"You'd be a whole lot warmer with clothes on," I said.

But she shook her head no. She's a stubborn woman — I know that. She wants to go naked into the day, she's got that right.

At breakfast this morning, after Retta told him about the pudding, Mr. Coles flung his plate against the wall and yelled, "I'm not eating this garbage." He strapped on his gun and stalked the house for an hour. When he went out for his morning constitutional we all breathed easier. I dressed Mary and Alma warm as I could, pulled on wool socks and stuffed newspaper up in their clothes, then told them to stay by the kitchen stove where it's warm.

In the yard, people run from place to place getting ready for the day's events. A bandstand has been set up beside the tabernacle so the governor can come say his words. The tabernacle and the bandstand are next to one another, one for the word of God and one for the word of man. There are campfires in front of every tent. Eddie heaps so much wood on our fire it becomes worrisome. I see the side-eye people give, but nobody says anything. They feel sorry for the man, given what's happening with the Missus. The flames rise higher and higher, and still Eddie keeps bringing more and more wood to throw on the fire.

"Eddie," I call out. "Can I ask you something?"

He drops what he's doing and comes straight to my side.

"You trying to burn down Camp?"

He laughs nervous-like and says no, but I know nothing that big is built without thought. By noon, I am ready and sitting on the bed holding the Missus's hand when all three men enter the bedroom to take her from it. I stand by the Missus like I promised.

"She ain't dressed."

"Why not?" Mr. Coles asks.

"She don't want to be."

He pushes me aside and rips the blanket away. Eddie and Lonnie turn when they see their mother naked. The Missus lies shrunken, looking at her husband with so much hate that if she weren't so weak I'd swear she was the pudding thief.

"Get some goddamn clothes on her," he yells at me.

"I tried, sir. She won't let me."

"Won't let you? She's an old woman and you can't get clothes on her? Jesus Christ, I'll do it myself."

He goes to the closet and tears a dress from the hanger. He's so mad he practically rips the buttons off trying to get the dress undone. He goes to the bed and yanks her by one arm, but she goes limp and falls sideways. Mr. Coles loses his balance and falls on top of her. He pushes himself up and tries to force the dress over her head but can't get her steady. Funny thing is, she don't cry and she don't fight. I keep looking for the sign to step in, but she don't give it. It's like she's willing him to kill her and us to be witness. Eddie bites his bottom lip but does nothing. He's frozen. Lonnie can't take it anymore and pulls at his daddy's arm, forcing him to stop.

"You're hurting her."

Mr. Coles lets go of the Missus, and she falls against the pillows. He throws the dress at her, then gets right up in Lonnie's face and says low and mean, "If you can't handle this, then get your pansy ass out of my sight. Your brother and I will see to this ourselves."

Eddie looks sideways at me, so slump-shouldered and sorrowful I take mercy.

"Don't worry, Eddie. She's doing this the way she wants."

From where he stands, Mr. Coles reaches out his arm and points a finger alongside my nose. "You concern yourself with what I want, young lady. I'm the one hired you."

"Yes, sir," is all I can say.

He's a bull in tight quarters and knows it.

"If she isn't dressed in five minutes," he says to me, "you can find yourself another job. Without my recommendation, I can promise there won't be a plantation or business in all of South Carolina that will take you on. You think about that."

He thinks his threat is the worst I've come across. I finally drop my eyes, but only for the Missus. When he leaves the room I race to cover her with a blanket. Eddie follows his daddy, but Lonnie stays. He's shaking with rage.

"Is this all a cruel joke, M-Mother? You

465

brought m-me this far, to what end? Why won't you fight him? All these years he's treated us poorly but you r-refused to see."

Miss Annie reaches out to take his hand, but he backs away.

"Whatever you're trying to prove, I'm b-begging you to stop," he tells her. "We need our mother."

After he leaves, the Missus presses the back of her hand to her mouth and shakes her head like somebody is trying to give her medicine she don't want. Her moans come from someplace I don't ever want to visit. She reaches for the dress Mr. Coles left on the bed and works to pull it over her head. When I go to help she holds her hand out to stop me, and I must wait while she fights to pull on the mantle she's tried to tear off. When she finally gets her arms and head through, she allows me to help. Tired already from her efforts, she lies back while I pull the dress over her hips and button the top around her neck.

"Gertrude," she says with a quaver in her voice, "fetch me a glass of milk."

"Yes'm," I say and run for the kitchen.

38

ANNIE

The body doesn't like to die. It fights even
when the spirit is finished. Gertrude comes
and sits beside me. She has kindness and
grit. Maybe we all have two sides. What are
mine? Cowardice and courage? I am a coin
that has lain on one side for too long. If I
mean to hasten this existence, I must turn.
Gertrude holds the glass for me as I drink.
Retta has added the brewer's yeast. It tastes
like pecans in porridge — delicious. After
every sip Gertrude wipes the drippings from
my chin.

"Go slow," she tells me when I begin to
gulp from the hunger the milk awakens,
"otherwise it'll come right back up."

I nod, take a mouthful and swallow slowly,
then wait and breathe. Her encouragement
makes me feel like a child listening to her
mother. I am pleased with the happiness
she exhibits at my effort. I don't want her

to have false hope, but that is arrogant thinking. This capable girl doesn't need my concern. When I am halfway through the glass, Retta comes bustling through the door with a small saucer of steaming grits.

"I didn't put no butter or bacon on these for fear of what that might do to your stomach, but these grits is fresh and warm just like you like 'em, Miss Annie. I put a little raw egg in there and stirred it around with some salt and pepper. You want to take a little bite?"

How can I refuse? The smell alone is enough to have me walking on two feet. The rough of the grit with the smooth of the egg is a treasure, a feast for every sense. Each component of the dish sits on my tongue in revelry. I hate to swallow for fear of losing the clarity of the sensation. The fog behind my eyes dissipates as nourishment courses through my body. As much as I want another, one bite is all I can stomach. Gertrude wipes my face with a warm cloth while Retta stands by the foot of the bed, happy to see even one bite swallowed. I take both their hands and say, "Thank you, my dears, for all your kindness."

They smile at the compliment.

"I'm ready now."

Retta opens the door. Standing on the

other side, waiting, is my husband.

RETTA

Whenever fortune would turn on a person Mama would say, without surprise, "That is a story that was bound to happen," like a person's actions was the brick and mortar of a house. She always knew a person's character. Always knew what was coming before they did, certainly before me. I got the sight, but it's Mama that had the vision. When I come from Miss Annie's room all my helpers are huddled by the cookstove warming their hands. They scatter as I come into the warmth, hurrying back to their work. Only Mary and Alma remain. I give them each a crisp piece of skin still steaming hot off the hog.

"You got any pork skin left for Sarah and me?"

I know that question as well as I know the voice asking; it's been asked of me for as long as I can remember when Sarah and Molly was growing up. I look up so fast I'm dizzy from the speed. I got to hold Mary's and Alma's heads for balance. Miss Molly and Sarah have come plain dressed in Camp clothes, alone on foot, around the backside of the kitchen. They left their riches behind, but no plainness of dress can hide the ladies

469

they've become. They were always pretty little things. They've grown downright beautiful. So many years gone but there's the ghost of youth in their faces. Molly has grown soft and plump, and Sarah is taller than I remember, but I know my girls no matter their age. I helped birth them.

Molly is upon me and in tears before I have time to think; her hardness is all but gone. It's Sarah that holds back, watching her sister and me from a distance. I reach out my hand until she finally takes it, allowing herself to be folded into our circle. Even still Sarah holds herself erect, like she's afraid of breaking. I kiss her cheek and tell her she smells like apple blossoms in springtime. Her laughter is all the release she needs, and she melts against me. If years could speak they would tell of the pain and suffering these girls know. The history is in their shaking bodies as they cry on my shoulders.

We dry our tears and I tell them, "Your daddy's taken your mama to the front yard."

Sarah takes deep breaths. When she was little, Sarah would have bouts of panic where she couldn't breathe. She'd lie on the floor 'til the feeling passed, but it got so bad the Missus had to call for the doctor to give the child something. For a year she took a pill every day. She took to hiding when a spell came on, but me and Molly knew where to look. We'd find her under the stairs rocking back and forth hitting her legs to calm her self.

"You're all right," Molly would say. "He's gone, he's gone."

Even now as grown women, Molly takes Sarah's hand, just like she used to, and says, "We'll go together."

"The governor will stop by like he always does," I tell them. "Come then."

I can do now what I couldn't do then. I remind them both of what I know to be true. "You're grown now. He can't do what you won't allow."

Sarah kisses the back of my hand and pulls herself upright. I gather them both in my arms once more before turning them loose. After they go I look to make myself useful, but anything I could do has already been done. My hands are idle on the busiest day of the year. All the help has come to know my ways almost as well as I do. The desserts are lined up on the cabinet counter, so pretty they're a shame to eat. Carolina rice simmers alongside two big pots of Frogmore stew. The hog is cut and ready for eating, the corn bread is golden and topped with butter and honey, the butter beans sit

471

steaming and ready and the sweet tea stands waiting in tall pitchers. All we got to do now is eat.

I make myself busy in the dining room, though I know counting plates and silverware is just a reason to be here. I shine each piece with my apron while I stand by Gertrude inside the screen door. Lonnie and Eddie are outside on the porch. It's through them I see Miss Annie and Mr. Coles sitting side by side on the bench we bring every year from home. Mr. Coles made that bench many years ago for Camp when Miss Annie was pregnant with Eddie. He built it for two and put rockers on the bottom so she could use it for their children. She rocked many a little one to sleep on that bench right here in this yard. Gertrude's got Miss Annie so bundled up with blankets and pillows she looks swaddled. Mr. Coles's got his arm around her shoulder, and she leans into him just like when they was first married. I watch for the girls, but don't see a sign, and I pray they did not lose courage.

GERTRUDE

I step out to the porch and stand in back of Lonnie and Eddie, so I can be of service to the Missus. I don't mind the cold like some do. I always was able to stand it better than

472

most. The shawl Mary made keeps the chill from seeping to the bone. More people have come to the yard. Seems like the whole state has come for the day. Mr. Coles looks around the side of every person he talks to. He's waiting on the governor.

A group of folks from the neighbor tents have gathered 'round to pay respects to the Missus and Mr. Coles. They gather in a half circle around the bench talking solemnly. Nobody wears their Sunday best today, though I thought they would, if only to air out the ripe of a long week with no bath. The cold has forced the practical, and folks are happier for the comfort. Men stand together in overalls and long shirts talking to each other about the coming winter, and women wrapped in shawls kneel by the Missus's side and smooth hair from her face. They fuss over her so much I'd swear the Missus was witness to her own funeral. They can't ignore what's directly in front of them. To their credit they don't try. Behind me from inside the screen door, Retta moves side to side looking for something in the yard.

Golden horns, seven in all, shine in the light as the warm-up starts on the bandstand. Their sound is so pure and strong I wonder if Gabriel himself is blowing music through them. A ripple of energy goes through the Campground, and people turn to look when a child runs across the yard yelling to his people, "The governor's here!"

ANNIE

"There we go now, Mother," my husband says when I lay my head in the crook of his neck.

"Isn't this nice?"

So many people have come to greet us on the yard I feel like the bride on the reception line. Edwin plays the doting husband well, kissing my head between visitors. His breath is hot on my forehead, a stark contrast from the cold. When we were newly married I was astounded that he never smelled poorly. I was raised with brothers, so I knew the smell of men, but Edwin was different, he was intoxicating. Even now, he smells like bark and berry. Everyone is drawn to him. He is who they want recognition from, not me. I am the means to an end, simply useful to gain advantage, nothing more. Each person that steps up to exhibit concern for me, for our family, does so in hopes of gaining or maintaining favor with my husband. What they don't see is my husband's desperate effort to maintain his good standing. If Edwin has his way, the banks will never concede that a Coles can fail. No one will.

Women I've known for years press cold hands against my cheek as if greeting a child. I yank my face away enough times that they finally become uncomfortable, and my forearm must suffice. With every handshake and every touch the level of gratitude flows ever more in our direction. Gratitude from Edwin to me because I am behaving and doing as asked, and gratitude from everyone else because Edwin is paying them heed. These two sides feed one another, he to me, they to him, until both parties are convinced what they are feeding on is real.

Polite make-believe is weary business, and there is no one better at this than Southerners. I am tired already and we've just begun. The gathered women attempt to include me in conversation, but I have no interest, so I call for Gertrude, who is at once by my side. Her entrance allows the women to excuse themselves, and once again I am grateful for this slip of a girl with the scrap of a barn cat.

"Yes, Missus?" she asks.

"Water, please, Gertrude."

There is no breeze in the trees, which is lucky, otherwise the cold would be exponential. As is, people aren't venturing far from their fires. Ours is strong enough to keep a small crowd warm. The water Gertrude brings is cool and soothing on my throat. I've come to understand one thing in all of this. Dying is easy. It's the suffering that's painful. Not the physical agony, although that comes. The cramping from hunger and thirst is significant. My body has begun to shrivel without fluids. A single sip courses through every fiber of me, filling holes that have opened in its absence. My mouth is moist again. My eyes no longer hurt to blink. One glass of water and so much progress. Still, the body wants more. A river wouldn't be enough to fill the incessant craving. There is necessity for speed in a fight. Without it you cannot survive. The body hurries to provide nutrients to dissuade the inevitability of death. Those facts don't bother me. No, it's not the physical suffering that troubles; it's the wrestling with what I leave behind and how I've left it — that's the real torture. It's by far easier to sleep. But I am awake now, revitalized from just a touch of sustenance — food and water, the miracle of life. It is difficult to fathom how the body continues despite the heart's condition, for if the broken heart ruled the physical body, I would have been dead long ago.

When the governor comes, Edwin leaves my side and goes to greet him. They shake hands and talk. His wife hasn't accompanied him; she hates these things, so I'm not surprised. We've dined with the governor and his wife, Lizzie, three times, twice in our home during the campaign and once in celebration just after their win at the governor's mansion. She and I, despite our vastly different upbringing, understand one another.

"I don't know how you continue with Camp, Annie," Lizzie once told me. "As one of twelve children from a religious family, I've had my fill."

"I don't mind the ritual," I told her. "It allows the past to live."

"If there isn't a proper bathroom and toilet, then the past can shove off." She laughed then. We both did.

Edwin contributed a large sum of money to the governor's election and made sure every plantation in the southern part of the state lined up behind him. This was, of course, before the boll weevil infestation. Once ordained, the governor inherited bad luck, poor man. The tarnish is on him now. Every decision he makes going forward will be informed by famine and need.

Our governor is a Methodist and well-loved in this Camp. There isn't a soul who doesn't watch him and Edwin speak like old friends. After all, power begets power. The governor glances in my direction as my husband talks. Edwin has told him of my condition. He takes off his hat and holds it to his chest before coming to greet me. I don't know what I'm thinking when I try to push myself up to stand. Habit? I weigh more than I thought, and for a moment the world goes topsy-turvy. Gertrude catches me and eases me back into my seat, then backs away when Edwin sits beside me and straightens the blankets.

"Darling," he says. "You mustn't overdo."

There's so much rot in his speech I am nauseous. The governor squats beside me and holds my hand.

"Ann, Lizzie told me to tell you, you're a glutton for punishment."

"She's right, Tom," I say.

Off in the distance the band strikes up a tune, "You're a Grand Old Flag." The Campground grows ever more crowded as people come from their tents to listen to music and engage in the festivities. Boys set off firecrackers in distant fields behind the tents. There is much revelry. Tom's aides, conscious of his schedule, wait close by to move him along.

"I'm sorry you aren't well," Tom says.

"That's the price you pay when you marry a monster," I say to him, clearly, directly. I want him to hear the weight of my words. Edwin tenses beside me, and Tom's face is filled with confusion.

"Excuse me?" Tom asks.

"My husband is not a good man, Tom. He's fooled an entire community for years."

"Annie," my husband says as if he is surprised by my allegations.

"That's not true, Ann," Tom says. "Edwin is a stalwart citizen, you know that."

"It's all a farce, Tom. Edwin's lost everything, his money and his family."

"She's not herself today, Governor. She's overtaxed," Edwin says.

"Ask the children what he's done," I say. "They will tell you."

"I was worried about this, but she insisted on coming to Camp," Edwin says.

I'm watching our governor. He's accustomed to politicians. Surely he can see through this nonsense.

"Did you know we had a son who killed himself? He was only twelve."

"Annie, stop it," Edwin says. He's got that edge in his voice he used with the children when they were little.

"For the longest time I couldn't under-

479

stand why a child would do such a thing, and then I discovered my husband's little secret. He likes children. He makes souvenirs of their underwear."

"Don't be ridiculous," Edwin says, but I never take my eyes off Tom. He needs to understand what I am telling him.

Tom drops his mask of puzzlement to reveal disgust. He tries to pull his hand away, but I hold on.

"I don't need a doctor, Tom," I say. "I need justice."

Alarmed, Tom turns to my husband, who sighs and hangs his head, the perfect victim.

"Illness and age have no mercy," Edwin says.

In the end the governor must settle for what he's comfortable with.

"It happens to the best of us," Tom says to my husband. He pats my arm and stands.

Men can't bear what women must. They jump to cry insanity as cause for a woman's unhappiness; the utterance of the unutterable must be dementia. It's just too much to consider otherwise. Edwin slides a hand to my shoulders and clenches my back.

"Let's get you inside to rest," he says.

Before he can turn backward to call for help, I fill my mouth with what moisture I've gathered from my morning sustenance and spit all of it in his face. Edwin stands and takes a handkerchief from his pocket to wipe his eyes and cheeks. He pulls the governor away with apologies, walking with him to the stage. I look out into the sea of eyes upon me. I used to think I was so lucky not to be them. So lucky not to have to grovel or beg for work or money; it was easier to ride above it all. Now they look at me with horror, or is it pity?

Lonnie comes beside me and asks, "Mother, what are you doing?"

"I'm telling the truth, sweetheart. I'm finally telling the truth." If it's a show they want, I shall give them one.

Around us are the families that have gathered alongside us for the better part of fifty years. We have history here, history and secrets, more than any of us are willing to admit. Amelia Childress comes forward to take control, as she always does. She is accustomed to rolling over people.

"The money is gone, Amelia," I tell her as she draws near. "We don't have to pretend to be friends any longer."

She stops, opening her mouth in surprise. I wave her away, and she goes. Lonnie reaches down and takes my hand. I search for the eyes of anyone willing to meet mine, ready to speak what I know, but they've turned away and move toward the band-stand where the governor is preparing to speak. All, that is, but one. It's Edwin's eyes I ultimately find coming toward me from across the Campground, and they are filled with fury.

"Mother," a voice cries out, and another echoes the same. "Mother!"

Edwin turns first, and what he sees hastens his stride.

I look to find the object of his discomfort pushing through the crowd like little boats moving upstream. They come holding hands just like they used to when they were small. My girls are here.

GERTRUDE

The Missus's daughters stop when they are within their mother's reach as if asking for permission to be here, but none is needed. She flings open her arms, and they fold into her like ducklings. Lonnie stands protecting the flock, and Eddie goes to intercept his father. Both men got their eyes where I got mine. It's him needs watching.

When I was ten years old a panther killed our sow but fled before he could feed. Daddy was readying to take Berns out for the hunt, and I stood at the door and begged to go. He already had his coat and hat on when he stopped to listen. I stood just like my girls stand now. There are days when I look at them and feel I am raising myself.

"This ain't like deer hunting," Daddy said. "This is a wild animal. It's dangerous."

"I can shoot, Daddy, you know I can," I told him.

He was sizing me up, seeing if I was ready. Finally he said, "Can't do no harm. Big prey is best hunted in numbers. Go fetch your mama's gun."

I back up to the porch where Retta stands holding the screen door open. I don't know if she means to come out or me to come in.

"Stay there," I say.

Edna is carrying a platter of steaming pork in from the back. "Fetch me the rifle from the wagon," I tell her.

Edna knows the signs for trouble. Knows from the sound of my voice, from the feel of things. She looks up to see what is happening in the yard.

"Run," I say. She drops the platter onto the table and hightails it down the hall.

Ain't many folks that can track a panther, but my daddy could. He knew that cat wouldn't go far, not with a fresh kill. A kill that big can feed an animal for days. No, that panther was close. Closer than we knew. Daddy said good hunters know how to go quiet and slow. You can't rile nature; otherwise you come home empty-handed. Nature gives up its own only when you can trick it into thinking you are part of it. Nature is selfish business.

We stayed together, the three of us, for the better part of the morning until we come upon a tree laid sideways in the woods. I don't know what it was about that tree, maybe there were marks, I can't recall, but it was there I was told to stay and wait. I remember that hunt like it was yesterday. Makes me itchy for a weapon.

Retta steps out and joins me on the porch. She's in a state.

"Don't be stupid," I tell her. "You ain't safe out here."

"I ain't safe nowhere, child. Look at the color of my skin."

Out in the yard the horns play their welcome, and everybody claps and yells when the governor steps up on the stage. He waves his hat to the crowd. They've all got their backs to us, facing what's important. Even the old folks have disappeared from their front porch rockers to venture out and be with their families. Retta steps off the porch and into the yard, but I grab her by the arm and hold her back.

"Just wait," I tell her through my teeth. She heeds my words.

Mr. Coles comes slowly to his clustered family. He lifts his chin, signaling Eddie to come heel behind. His son does what he's told without question, the habit of his whole life in his step. Mr. Coles sees the governor has the attention of the people. He's in the clear. Then the Missus raises her head from the fold of her daughters and finds her husband upon them. Her girls stand and turn when they feel their mother shift, but the Missus holds tight to their skirts like she's afraid they'll blow away.

"You girls got no place here," Mr. Coles says.

Retta tenses beside me, and I find myself looking over my shoulder listening and waiting for Edna's return.

Molly steps away from her sister and says, "We have every right. She's our mother."

Mr. Coles speaks quiet and calm. To the outside they look like they're talking about the weather. But this ain't no sunny day.

"For fifteen years you turned your back on your mother. That's not what daughters do. You need to turn around and go back from where you came," Mr. Coles says.

"No," the Missus cries out.

"Perhaps it's you who should go,

F-Father," Lonnie says.

Eddie touches his daddy's arm, but Mr. Coles shrugs him off and steps toward Lonnie. "Oh, you're the big man now. Is that it? Big man who can't form a coherent sentence."

I learned when I was ten years old, trapped prey is the most dangerous. Anybody knows that. If you aim to kill, you best do it quick unless you mean to cause yourself harm. I don't know what I was thinking that afternoon. It must not have been the panther 'cause I let my gun down, and when I did what was hiding in the brush was ready. When the cat leapt, it was Berns that saved me. He and Daddy never went far. They stood just to the side of me in the brush. Daddy knew the whole time that panther was there. I was the bait.

Mr. Coles reaches down with three fingers and unlatches his holster, a quick move unseen by the family, but not by me. The danger is in the detail.

Sarah says, "We've come to take Mother home with us."

"Your mother's not going anywhere."

Mr. Coles clenches his hand around the gun. Before I can stop her, Retta is past me and into the yard.

RETTA

My Odell is a wise and good man who has always stood up and done what's right. He's taught me through faith and action, and I'm better for the learning. I find the ground beneath me and do what I should have done a long time ago.

"Edwin Alistair Coles," I shout. "You leave this family be."

Edwin Alistair Coles is what his mother called him when he was in trouble. After she died nobody called him that. Nobody dared. The sky is gray all around us. A gray so big it's like we're inside the belly of the whale, like we've all been swallowed up whole. There's no color left in the world. Even the green of the trees has faded.

Miss Annie says, "Retta, don't."

She's scared. I see it in her hands, the way she twists them.

"Don't you worry for me, Miss Annie."

"Keep your mouth shut if you know what's good for you," Mr. Coles says.

"Even when you was a boy in your mother's arms you had secrets."

He starts talking over me, but I don't know what he's saying. I don't care. All the years of wait have been pent-up inside me. I am glad my husband is not here to witness my rage, for my mouth is a pump that won't

487

be shut off, and this would break his heart.

"She didn't see your evil 'cause no mother sees the bad seed in her own child. But I saw. Should have said it then. Maybe I could have stopped what you done to these children."

He is confused. I am a slave woman. He can't believe I dare speak retribution.

"You got no place here, nigger," he says. His daddy taught him those ways; that the Negro can't think for herself, that she's got to be led by the teeth and punished for wrongdoing. But the rest of what his son is, all the rest belongs only to Edwin. He's come upon a new day now, and this one ain't gonna go his way.

Mr. Coles looks back at Eddie and says, "Get her off this yard."

Eddie comes and takes my hand. "Come on, Retta," he whispers to me. "Don't do this. Please don't do this."

But I don't move, so he gives me a little pull and says, "Come inside."

"Let go, boy," I say. He wants me where it's safe, but that's a lie I told myself long enough. That's a trap. There's no such thing as safe. I can't go back. Not ever again.

"You're an evil man," I say to Mr. Coles, "and I'm tired of looking at you."

Eddie backs away when Mr. Coles lifts

the gun from his holster. It's Lonnie that grabs his father to stop him. Mr. Coles whirls and raises the gun to his own boy's head. Miss Annie and the girls scream. Lonnie falls to his knees.

Eddie runs to his brother's side and cries, "He won't do anything more, Father. Will you, Lonnie? He didn't mean anything, he'll be good."

Mr. Coles backhands Lonnie with the gun, and he falls sideways. Blood runs down his forehead and into his eyes. He knows better than to get up so he stays down. But I walk right at that miserable old cuss, shouting as I go, "You're an abomination, Edwin Alistair Coles. The curse that you placed on this family is now upon you. You belong in the hellfire."

The sun breaks through the gray, enough to set a simple ray of light in front of me, so bright it looks like God himself has reached down his hand. They'll say she was a mouthy old nigger who got her due. That's the story they will tell. Let them. Nothing I could ever do about that. I step into the light and find my peace in the center. When the shot comes I greet the darkness with gladness.

GERTRUDE

Out in the yard the governor talks and the crowd cheers. He and the band is all they can hear, but a single gunshot turns them in our direction. A ruckus comes up from the back of our tent, and when I turn it's not just my daughters I find. All the help have followed. Mary screams when she sees Retta on the ground, and Edna flies through the screen door with Mama's gun. She throws it to my outstretched hand. I thumb the lever to the side, break open the shotgun and check the shell.

"Speed and surprise is all you got for a kill," Daddy said, "but even that don't help if there ain't a bullet in the gun." I always keep a loaded gun.

Mr. Coles is a rabid old dog. His rage has him by the throat, and he can't see nothin' but vengeance. That's a misstep on his part; he ain't lookin' where he needs to. Molly and Sarah have helped the Missus to her feet and hold her between them. Eddie runs to his brother's side and helps him up. They all aim to get away, but it's the women Mr. Coles goes after. He grabs his wife by the hair and yanks her backward out of her daughters' embrace. She falls to the ground, but he don't let go, dragging her toward the tent. Lonnie tears away from his brother and charges his father. Without hesitation, Mr. Coles raises his gun for a second shot. I recognize the hate of a father for a son, but Lonnie don't stop, he runs headfirst toward his own death. That's when I step into a clear line of fire, pull the trigger and find my mark. A bullet for a nickel — that's an even exchange.

Mr. Coles grips his chest with his free hand and looks surprised or confused, can't say which, when his hand comes away wet with blood. He reaches for his handkerchief. When he brings it up and out of his pocket, change scatters — a whole pocketful of bright shiny nickels. He looks up, and it's me he finds, the dawn of a new day upon his face. The hunter is hunted.

39

In The After Retta

Lonnie carries me to the back of a waiting wagon. Bobo lays me inside, and Gertrude puts a pillow beneath my head and covers me with blankets.

"I'm gonna be fine," I want to tell them, but words don't come.

"Get her to Dr. Southard's place," Lonnie tells the driver. "Go the short way."

I am lulled to sleep by the rocking wagon. When I wake we are stopped alongside the Edisto River. Tree leaves shake against a now orange sky. There is the day. I thought it had gone. The weather's turned warm again like it sometimes does in fickle October. The breeze that floats over my skin is so sweet I could drink it. Kicking off the covers I sit up, looking for those that brought me here, but they're gone. I pull myself up and out of the wagon and step onto the riverbank to the path that is there.

I've been here before. I know this place.

Through tall, sweet grass I walk to the center of a golden meadow and wait. A deep hum comes through the wind in a song that stirs the grasses around me. The palmetto trees rattle. I can't tell if the music moves the wind or the wind makes the music. Either way it's a blessed sound. I turn in a circle looking through the woods until I see movement between the oak trees. I know what's coming and I am too jumpy to wait.

"Chickadee, chickadee, where's she gonna be?" Odell hollers.

"I'm here, Odell," I shout. "I'm right here!"

Through the Spanish moss he comes — but carries no limp, no crutch. A whole man. Shielding his eyes with one hand he comes out of the dark and into the light searching. In his arms he holds our baby girl, our daughter, our Esther.

"I'm here," I cry.

Esther turns at the sound of my voice, and flings out her arms to me, hollering, "Mama!"

GERTRUDE

Retta's people carried her home, and Mr. Coles was carried to the deathbed meant for his wife. A line of people came to bear

493

witness to the lawmen, including the governor who was held for the better part of the night. Lonnie stayed by my side until the questioning was done. He told all who would listen that I saved them. Edna and the help fed those that came and when it was over every dish was scraped clean. Mr. Coles died later that night. No one cried for his loss. Sheriff said to me, before he left, that maybe people get what they deserve. But I don't believe that's true. My mama didn't deserve to forget the family who loved her, any more than we deserved to see her suffer, any more than Retta and the Missus deserved their heartache. People get what they get.

When me and my girls returned home to Branchville two days later we found the people of Shake Rag had fixed our roof and filled our pantry with food. Our beds were made and wood was chopped and stacked for the coming winter. When the news of Odell reached us, we stood among them in their grief. He died on the road coming home to his wife. We joined the congregation at the Canaan Baptist churchyard when they laid Retta, Odell and their daughter side by side in their final resting place — their girl in the middle. Mary stood and, talking through her tears, told them her own stories of Retta and Odell and all they did for us. The congregation yelled their praise as she spoke and shared her grief as she wept. Only six years old and already the bravest girl I ever did see. After we dried our tears and filled our bellies at the church rectory, I stepped away from all I knew.

Someone has taken up residence in Berns and Marie's house. There is smoke in the chimney for the day has bite. Out on the railroad tracks a train comes through easy, slowing for the station ahead. An old man tips a blue hat to me, and quick as he came, he is gone. Deep in Polk Swamp, the quiet has begun. The milkweed bugs have flown south for winter. Cicadas, boll weevils and black flies have burrowed deep in the earth to lay their eggs and sleep. The ridge is still here, but I can't cross over, for resting in sunlight below the barren trees are too many alligators to count — a congregation.

The men will come one day soon to build their highway, turning this swamp into the fortune I will pass on to my girls. And the big mama alligator who ate my sin? She will hear the grinding of their machinery long before they arrive. She will be here, like she is now, hiding beneath the black surface, waiting, surrounded by an army of alligators.

No. None of us get what we deserve. We make the best of what we got.

In the evening as the sun drops low in the western sky I finally come to stand at the edge of a yard amid palmettos and watch my Lily clear the clothesline in back of the house she is promised to. She is swollen with child. For a moment she stands alone and quiet against the coming night sky. When she raises her head I step into the last light so she can find her mama.

ANNIE

The moon rises over the Battery, orange and fat — a harvest moon. In the bay, Fort Sumter lies dark and silent, a mere remnant of what once was. They've begun tours there, my daughters tell me. People pay money to see the cannonballs still imbedded in stone or dredged from the sea. Imagine, paying good money to see the relics of war. The tide is up, nearly covering the reeds near the old ferry landing where boats used to carry in the dead. Waves lap against the shore in rhythmic sameness. If I am still I can remember the time before it all began. How ironic. In the after, I find the before, but what good is the knowing when you can't erase the war and its aftermath? We must live in the rubble. There is a knock at my bedroom door, and I'm pulled from my memories.

"Aunt Annie," my granddaughter says. "Supper is served."

A BIT OF BACKGROUND

Growing up, I was haunted by stories of family hardships that resonated even more powerfully when I became a mother and raised a family of my own — that haunting found its way into the pages of this book. Though *Call Your Daughter Home* is a work of fiction, my great-grandmother's and grandmother's voices accompanied me so strongly as I wrote that I felt their presence in signs and wonders. I wrote on my back deck and a certain mockingbird visited me daily, following me into the house on three separate occasions over a one-month period. The bird allowed me to capture and hold it in my hands. Some mornings it stood at the back door as if waiting to gain entry. This was one of many happenings that reminded me of how connected we are to the natural world and what lies beyond.

It is a rarely talked-about fact that the South was plunged into a deep depression well before the crash on Wall Street in 1929. Cotton was the primary crop throughout the region before the boll weevil infestation decimated its economy from 1918 until the mid-1920s. Many people starved to death. My family, and so many others, suffered the one-two punch of the Great Depression that soon followed.

As a child, I traveled to Branchville, South Carolina, from Kentucky to visit my great-grandmother, Mama Lane. I boiled fresh peanuts, used the outhouse, plucked a chicken and shelled pecans from the yard for winter. Mama Lane raised five children in Branchville, living on Highway 21 (aka Freedom Road) in a small rental house that had no plumbing. A red pump by the kitchen door supplied the family with water for daily needs. My great-grandfather died when the children were young, due to an accident at the sawmill where he worked. After his death, Mama Lane farmed the children out to relatives so they would be fed until she found a job that enabled her to reunite the family.

I spent every weekend and most of my summers with her daughter, my mamaw, who worked all of her childhood picking cotton and scouring porches for a nickel. Those were, as she said, *desperate times,*

500

and she lost her teeth in her teenage years due to malnutrition. She became mother to six, grandmother to eight, and was always afraid of us children getting worms. She believed they were caused by unsanitary conditions, which may explain why she scrubbed us so hard at bath time. A remarkable low-country cook, Mamaw never used measurements, and canned and froze everything she could from her garden. Her peach cobbler recipe was relayed to me as stated in this book.

Gertrude, Retta and Annie are complete inventions of my imagination, each an amalgamation of many women I found, or know, that have endured hardship because of their circumstance or skin color. While researching this book, I stumbled upon Clelia McGowan, who plays a small cameo in these pages. Clelia is buried in the history books of Charleston, but her existence is a shining example of what opportunity, education and courage can do. After her husband died of pneumonia, Clelia was a single mother to three children. She was president of Charleston's Equal Suffrage League, and once the Nineteenth Amendment was ratified in August of 1920, the governor of South Carolina appointed McGowan to the State Board of Education, making her the first woman to be appointed to public office. In 1923, she and her colleague Belizant A. Moorer became the first women elected to the office of Alderman in the City of Charleston.

I wrestled with whether or not to use the N-word in this novel. It is a word I deeply despise, but to avoid it felt dishonest to the place and time. Historically, the N-word has been used as a tool to systematically degrade and dehumanize an entire race of people. To ignore its existence is to ignore the plight of what the African American community has endured at the hands of the white majority. I've used the word sparingly in these pages to demonstrate the low moral arc of a society unwilling to take responsibility for the pain and suffering caused to an entire population of people.

Many settings in this book exist today. Shake Rag is a small black neighborhood in Branchville. Though you won't find it on any map, ask anyone in town where it is and they will point the way. Branchville, or the Branch as it was originally called, was home to three Native American camps, and named for a branch in a trail under an old oak tree where traders came to exchange goods. That trail was so well situated that the Branchville Railroad, built in 1828, runs along those same paths.

Camp is based on Indian Fields Campground in St. George, which has been in existence at this location since 1848. This Methodist revival camp consists of an open-air tabernacle, which seats one thousand people, and ninety-nine cabins (called tents). These tents are passed down from generation to generation and surround the tabernacle in a circular shape — a symbol of shared religious experience. Camp still takes place the first week of every October, which historically marks the end of harvest season. Though electricity has been added in recent years, Camp is still quite primitive. Bathroom facilities are numbered, designated outhouses, one per tent. An unspoken competition over which tent has the best cook still exists. Pudding, made of ground-up hog lungs, is a real thing. I've tried it. Not bad.

The more I researched this story, the more in awe I became of the enduring spirit of Mama Lane and Mamaw, who, as young women with few resources, stood their ground, and survived, during a great crisis. I am humbled and inspired by the ferocity of their motherhood. Mama Lane and Mamaw are gone now, but I continue to return to Branchville and Charleston.

Mama Lane died in 1992 at the age of 92, just one week before my daughter was born. Mamaw died in 1995, eleven months after her son, my uncle Boogie, passed. Before she died she promised she would give me a sign once she got to where she was going, as proof she was all right — *likely,* she said, *through a bird.* Just before she crossed, she heard a choir singing her name. I, too, hear an unnamed voice when I travel to South Carolina. Without fail, as the plane descends over those vast estuaries, the voices come soft, but clear, whispering one word, over and over: *home.*

ACKNOWLEDGMENTS

Like any creative endeavor, many people took this journey with me. It is my honor to thank them here. To Mark Bowden, who set off a chain of synchronicity like nothing I've ever witnessed. Mark took my questions seriously and when he couldn't answer them sent me to his friend and publisher, Morgan Entrekin. I owe enormous gratitude to Morgan and his colleague Allison Malecha for reading my work and introducing me to a remarkable woman and agent, Duvall Osteen. Duvall read a series of short stories I'd written and told me those stories were novels in disguise. It was she who suggested I begin with the first story entitled "Alligator" and expand from there. Without her this book truly would not exist. To Robert Eversz, my teacher, without whom I would have stumbled in the dark for years. His support and incredible guidance during the writing of each section and draft of this book was invaluable. I hope to work with him again and again. To my editor at Park Row Books, Liz Stein, whose insights humbled me and made this book better with every draft.

I'd like to thank my friends and family in Branchville, South Carolina: Oretta and Glen Miller for their stories and many kindnesses to my family; Johnny Norris for his knowledge and service to the Branchville Railroad Museum; the congregants of Canaan Baptist Church for their generosity of spirit; and their pastor, Vernon Blanchard, whose knowledge and faith in Scripture guided me through the biblical sections and sermons of this book. I consider him my friend. Thank you to the late Myrtis Easterlin for welcoming me into her home and sharing her stories and passion for sewing despite being so sick. She was one of a kind and is missed by all who knew and loved her. Thank you to my cousins who grew up in Branchville: Juniebug (Cecil) and Barbara Berry, Ann and Ernest Walters, and Bill Barrs, with extra thanks to my cousin Marcia Jackson who was my goodwill ambassador through the stomping grounds of our grandmother and great-grandmother. She introduced me to many people, shared her stories and showed me Indian Fields

Campground. I am greatly indebted and fortunate to call her family.

I'm lucky to have a powerful coalition of women friends in my life, too many to name here, but they know who they are. I would be remiss, however, not to mention two groups: the Triangle, who kept me sane most of my life and whose nicknames are inappropriate to print here, and my GO8, who believed in me as a writer long before I knew I was one. A special note of thanks must go to GO8 member Katy Coyle, who read every single draft of this book and gave me her helpful thoughts, the mark of a true and patient friend.

I come from a long line of strong Southern women who have zero fear of hard work and opinions on everything. My mother, Pat Passmore, and her sisters, Vivian Fields and Dorothy Walker, are my guiding lights. Our fearless leader was their mother, my mamaw, Edna Alma Lane. She cussed with great regularity, and raised us like crops. I wrote this book for her and miss her every day. I'd like to thank my husband, Robert Spera, who sat with me when I cried on the couch in terror after Duvall told me to write this book. His ability with story is invaluable and his kindness unsurpassed. Rob continues to be my secret weapon. I'd like to thank our children, Rachel Alma, Nicholas Angelo and J. Aubrey, who taught me the power of a mother's love. They and their father are my everything.

ABOUT THE AUTHOR

Deb Spera was born in Louisville, Kentucky, and lives in Los Angeles. She owns her own television company, One-Two Punch Productions, and has executive produced such shows as *Criminal Minds* and *Army Wives.* Her work's been published in *Sixfold, Garden and Gun,* and *L.A. Yoga Journal. Call Your Daughter Home* is her first novel.